ELKWOOD

A MONTANA FABLE

BALTO FLICKS, INC
Author@ElkwoodsMontana.com
Post Office Box 161419
Big Sky, Montana 59716 USA

First Edition
Printed in the United States of America
Copyright ©2019 Tracie Elizabeth Pabst

Cover and Book Design by Carylee Stone, USA
Editing by Leonora Bulbeck, UK

Twinkle Toes Trout's italicized quotes
are in tribute to the indominable and magnificent,
MAE WEST.

SPECIAL THANKS

Thank you J.C., for dropping a trail of bread crumbs
throughout my life, ultimately leading me to
Big Sky, Montana … and Elkwood.

Thank you Carylee Stone and Larry Spangler
for your never-ending support and love.

Elkwood … I hope you change the lives of others
as you have changed mine.

CHAPTER 1

"Success is not defined by the wealth you acquire but by the friend you are to others."

SOME YEARS AGO, in the foggy woods of the English countryside, Elkwood Elkington III arrived into the world. He was the son of very famous parents. His father, Big Duke Elkington, was a famous pianist and jazz musician. He was known throughout the English forest as "the Big Elk with the Big Rhythm." Everyone throughout the forest knew his music, and he became very wealthy indeed. His wife was also famous in the forest world of jazz. Ella Elkington was a one-of-a-kind jazz singer with a smooth, silky voice that resonated throughout the woods whenever she performed. After she married Duke, she became the lead singer for his band, known as Big Duke Elkington and The Elkers.

When Elkwood was born, his parents hoped he would follow in their *hoofsteps* and become a talented musician. Much to their disappointment, Elkwood had no musical talent whatsoever. He had a fair singing voice but not one that would make him rich and successful. Regardless, they sent him to the finest music school in the forest, hoping he would develop some musical skills. Elkwood attended the prestigious *Ox-ford* Institute of Music, and it was quite clear Elkwood was no musical wonder. Instead of developing musically, due to the constant pampering of his parents and teachers, he became a spoiled snob.

When he was not in school, Elkwood traveled the forest, frequenting the best eateries and the finest clubs. Elkwood was a magnificent-looking elk, with big broad shoulders, and dressed in attire from the finest haberdasheries. The fur on his head, neck, and legs was a deep, rich purple, and he had a thick, luxurious mane that came to a perfect point just above his front legs. His coat transitioned into a deep tan like the color of oak bark, covering his body to his rump patch, which was even paler still. His imperial-purple mane made him feel like royalty.

Elkwood had large ears and a very handsome face, with a black nose and big brown eyes rimmed in a combination of deep tan and soft purple. His enormous antlers were his crowning glory, growing from his majestic head in a burnished tawny color fading in hue to the tips of his tines. He held them high with pride. He always wore a perfectly tied silk ascot around his massive neck. He was the envy of all the other elk, as Elkwood was commonly seen in the company of a beautiful young elk. He was handsome, rich, and well educated…with absolutely no direction in his life.

Big Duke and Ella began to worry about their son. They feared he would lead a life of emptiness and never truly amount to anything. They tried to encourage Elkwood in other directions, such as becoming a doctor, a lawyer, or perhaps a politician. Elkwood was simply not interested. He liked having fun. As his attitude continued to become more arrogant, he began to look down on other elk in the herd. Elkwood's reputation for being bigheaded and egotistical was gaining momentum. Then again, the herd he associated with was of the same ilk. They were all spoiled. Big Duke and Ella were not pleased. They had worked hard all their lives, making their own way in the forest without any help or financial assistance from their parents. They wanted Elkwood to stand on his own four hooves and become an *Elk*. His parents knew they must do something before Elkwood frittered his life away and ended up a failure.

Upon their son finishing college, Big Duke and Ella hosted a grand graduation bash for Elkwood and invited all the animals in the forest. They had discussed Elkwood's future and knew what they must do, but he had graduated, and for that they thought he should be rewarded. The extravaganza was set in a large clearing in the forest, with twinkling lights hanging from every tree surrounding the clearing. Huge logs were set up laden with every type of delicious food, and bars were set up to serve the thirsty guests. There was a large bandstand at one end of the clearing, with huge spotlights to light the stage.

It was a beautiful night, warm with a gentle breeze, and a full moon illuminated the clearing. Animals were dressed in their best finery, and everyone seemed happy and excited. There were many elk and deer, and even a few moose had traveled from Scotland. There were bears, lynx, and a select group of well-behaved wolves. Even the smaller animals were present, including foxes, hedgehogs, badgers, otters, the rare pine marten, shrews, polecats, squirrels, and rabbits. The animals danced the night away, with the smaller wildlife congregated in their own corner so they would not be accidentally stepped upon by the larger animals.

Elkwood was very happy and thrilled to be the center of attention. After all, it was his party, in his honor. Although he had not graduated with the best grades, and in fact had barely scraped by, he did not care. Everyone had gathered to celebrate him, and that suited him just fine. The truth was, everyone loved a party, whether in his honor or not. Any excuse for an extravagant social event was excuse enough to show up. But the real reason for such a large turnout for Elkwood's graduation party was that Big Duke Elkington and The Elkers would be the main event. They were the most popular jazz band in all of England, and Elkwood had no clue they were the real reason for the large turnout. Instead, he believed he was the most popular animal in the forest.

A local jazz band warmed up the partygoers before the main event. Many well-bred and beautiful young elk asked Elkwood for a dance, and he whirled them around the clearing with ease. Elkwood was actually a fairly decent dancer, and he made a fine showing as he bopped and boogied the night away.

The warm-up band finished playing their last song, and the lights dimmed. The animals were excitedly anticipating the famous jazz band they had come to see. From out of nowhere, a remarkably imposing *Elk* was illuminated by a single spotlight at the right of the stage. In a deep, rich bass voice, he announced, "Animals of the forest, we are here to celebrate the graduation of Elkwood Elkington the Third from the prestigious *Ox-ford* Institute of Music." All the animals cheered, and Elkwood bowed and smiled. "We have a special show for you tonight, so without further ado, may I present Big Duke Elkington and The Elkers!"

The clearing went wild with excitement. The single spotlight went dark, and the large *Elk* disappeared from the stage. Cracking sounds were heard as spotlights turned on, revealing Big Duke Elkington at the piano, accompanied by his orchestra, The Elkers. Big Duke opened with their finger-snapping hit

"Things Aren't the Way They Used to Be" and got the crowd of animals snapping their paws and tapping their hooves. Big Duke told the crowd how crazy cool and hip it was to snap.

Then Big Duke said in his gravelly voice, "Now, please welcome the smooth sound of my lovely wife, Ella Elkington!"

The crowd cheered wildly. The band began a jazzy tune called "Mack the Knife," and Ella sang with perfection. The animals danced while Big Duke and Ella rocked the stage. It was the performance of a lifetime, and Elkwood was very proud of his parents.

This is the best night of my life, thought Elkwood. *I am truly the best-liked elk in the forest.*

After the concert, Elkwood went backstage to thank his parents. They were pleased Elkwood had enjoyed his party. They hugged him and patted him on the neck.

The celebration lasted late into the night, and after the music ended, the animals made their way back to their dens, holes, and caves, and the night became quiet. Elkwood slowly walked home alone, enjoying the peace and the cool night air. Here and there, a few crickets could be heard chirping their songs, but after the blare of the party, the silence was welcomed.

What a grand night it had been. Everyone seemed to have had a marvelous time, and of course, it had all been in honor of him. Elkwood was elated and looked forward to his life as an *Elk* with credentials. Because he had graduated, Elkwood assumed he automatically garnered the title of *Elk*. He still did not understand that becoming an *Elk* meant he possessed the character traits of honor, integrity, fairness, empathy, humility, and the desire to work hard for one's success. Elkwood was a kind elk, but his arrogance, superior attitude, and entitled upbringing prevented him from attaining the true traits an elk must have to become an *Elk*.

As he turned to walk up the winding path to his home, he thought he saw something standing off in the woods. He stopped and peered into the darkness, trying to make out what or who was watching him. There was a light, misty fog on the edge of the woods, which shrouded the mysterious figure. As the mist momentarily lifted, Elkwood inhaled sharply, and a shiver ran down his spine. He could feel the fur on his haunches stiffen. There appeared to be a giant *Elk* standing perfectly still, staring at him. Elkwood froze, barely breathing. He squinted, trying to make out the identity of the stranger, and for a moment, he thought it was the *Elk* who had announced his parents onto the stage. Just as he began to raise his hoof in greeting, the vision disappeared. Elkwood blinked hard a few times to clear his eyes but could see nothing.

"My mind must be playing tricks on me," Elkwood said to himself. "I guess I am just tired after all the excitement. I could have sworn that was the big *Elk* from the stage." He shook his head in confusion. "Oh, silly me. What reason would that *Elk* have to follow me? Yes, it is just my imagination and the mist playing tricks on me."

Elkwood continued down the path to his home, and the night air caused chills to run through his body. He arrived home, removed his ascot, and climbed into his big bed, snuggling deep into the warmth of the covers. He drifted off to sleep, believing and dreaming his life would be grand and full of adventure and wealth. He had no clue it was about to all change, drastically.

Elkwood awoke to the beautiful voice of his mother singing a jazzy tune Elkwood had not heard before. He loved Ella's voice in the morning. But this song was sad, and she was singing about having the blues. This confused Elkwood, as his mother was always so upbeat. He fumbled out of bed, put on a fresh ascot, and headed downstairs for breakfast. He was not prepared to see both his parents waiting for him at the kitchen table.

Big Duke and Ella had made a decision about their son. After the graduation party, it was time for Elkwood to begin life on his own, without the financial support of his parents. They sat him down and explained how they believed his life was heading down a forest path of misery and worthlessness. Elkwood waited, not knowing what he had done wrong or why he was being punished. After all, he was popular, handsome, and had all the money he needed. He believed he was a great success.

Big Duke and Ella explained that they were sending Elkwood across the Big Pond to a place called Montana. Elkwood had never heard of Montana. They told him it was a beautiful place, or so they had heard, and that Montana had endless forests and mountains filled with elk. Immediately, Elkwood felt fear for the first time in his life. He was being exiled for no reason. He suddenly felt very lonely but knew there was no use arguing with his parents. He knew once they had made up their mind, their decision was final. While they would provide for his journey to Montana and would give him a small nest egg to help him start a new life, the rest was up to him. He was to leave in two days.

Seeing the shock on Elkwood's face, Ella stood up and nuzzled her son's nose. Standing behind him, she lovingly sang to him, hoping to let him know how very much she loved him. One giant tear fell from Elkwood's eye as he listened.

Elkwood went to bed that night feeling sad and alone. He had no idea where Montana was or what he would do when he arrived. When he awoke the next day, he thought he should start packing and then begin saying his goodbyes to all his friends. Then, with a force that hit him like a cold, damp English wind, he realized he did not have any real friends. This made him sadder than he had ever been before. Yes, he was very popular, but only on the surface. Deep inside he knew the other elk only liked him because of his high standing in society and family wealth. He had always been a happy elk, but after his parents' decision to send him so far away, he wondered if his life really was shallow and without meaning. Nevertheless, he would not let his insecurities show. He would hold his antlers high.

After Elkwood finished packing, he decided to go out for one last night on the forest. Elkwood donned his favorite silk ascot and headed down the path to his usual eatery and dance club, the Bear Paw. He was determined to put on a good show and let no one see the fear and apprehension he was feeling about his parents' decision to send him so far away. Elkwood knew the news had already spread about his impending departure. He decided he would go out with a bang and pretend he had not a care in the world, only a fantastically incredible adventure before him, that only he was going to take. Yes, they would all think him quite special and fortunate to be able to travel the world, seeking wonderful and exotic lands. And Montana, well, no one in the English forest had ever been to Montana. Yes, they would all surely be quite jealous of his good fortune.

Feeling better about his predicament—uh, adventure—Elkwood's steps began to lighten, and he pranced and danced as he sang a lively tune along the path to the Bear Paw. By the time he arrived at the club, he was feeling quite like his old self, happy and confident he would be the center of attention, as always.

The Bear Paw was a fine pub with a long wooden bar with flowing taps and libations of every kind. Animals were drinking and toasting and chatting and having a grand time. The Bear Paw smelled of well-oiled leather upholstery, musky fur, and the aroma of fine fodder. A local band was loudly playing jazz music, and the dance floor was lively. As Elkwood entered the dimly lit pub, his friends warmly greeted him, bought him drinks, and raised their glasses to toast his good fortune. Elkwood ordered all his favorite foods and laughed and ate and drank and bragged about his exciting adventure. He told everyone they should wish they were also traveling across the Big Pond to Montana, as it had the finest forests in the world and accepted only the best elk.

The other animals were jealous because they believed every word Elkwood spoke about his impending journey. Even though congratulations came from all, Elkwood could already feel he was being edged out of the club for the well-bred and rich. He knew their game. They would move on to the next party and the next popular animal. But he had never imagined that he would be the recipient of their snubs so quickly. His friends, he thought, were a fickle crowd. When he left, they would forget about him and focus on the next meaningless party. Even the beautiful elk that always flirted with him and wanted to be his first choice as a dance partner cooled off toward him as the evening deepened. They were all friendly and congratulatory, but he sensed they, too, were looking for the next handsome and rich elk. After all, he would soon be gone.

Elkwood worked his way over to the bandleader and whispered a request in his ear. Without any fanfare, the Bear Paw went dark and the crowd silenced. A single spotlight hit the stage, shining on Elkwood, and the band began to play a soulful tune by Big Duke and Ella Elkington. Not being a polished singer, Elkwood sang—or rather spoke—the bluesy number. He poured his heart out over his frustration about how his so-called friends really did not care about him at all. The words fell on the deaf ears of the crowd, and they had no idea what Elkwood was really singing about. He knew there would be no more invitations for him to dance. When the last chord struck, the crowd resumed their loud chatter and drinking, and the band immediately went into another jazzy tune.

The farewell celebration lasted into the wee hours of the morning. After an evening of extravagance and lies, Elkwood said his final farewells and departed. Walking home alone, with his head held high, he was determined to remain proud and arrogant. As he walked home, he pondered his life. Were his parents right about him? Was his life really useless? Had he truly not accomplished anything? He felt very confused. With each step, his troubles weighed him down, and his antlers dropped lower and lower along with his mood. Feeling frustrated and alone, he began to hum the song he had sung at the Bear Paw, then whispered the words. Yes, they couldn't care less.

By the time he walked up the steps of his parents' huge home, his shoulders were slumped over, and the burden of his magnificent rack weighed his head down, almost to the ground. He felt lost and frightened as he sang one more verse of the song on the front steps. A large elk-size tear fell from his eye. He felt utterly abandoned as he lumbered to his room, climbed into bed, and slept a restless sleep, filled with apprehension of the unknown.

The next day, he awoke to the smell of his favorite thing in the whole world: Ella's delicious chocolate chip cookies. She knew they were Elkwood's favorite treat, and she was baking a large batch to keep him fed on his journey. Loving Elkwood more than life, she knew she would miss him terribly, but this was the best way to turn her son into an *Elk*. Wanting him to always carry a bit of home with him, she wrote down the recipe for her delicious chocolate chip cookies and tucked it in the cookie sack.

Elkwood gratefully accepted the gift of cookies from his mother, hugged her, shook hooves with his father, and walked out the door of his lifelong home. As he made his way down the windy path away from his home, he heard the sweet sound of his mother's voice as she sang a sad and heart-wrenching song. He turned and looked at his home for the last time. Her voice, a voice he loved so much, would haunt him forever.

Elkwood had a long journey ahead. He decided to focus on the future instead of being sad about leaving his home. After all, he was Elkwood Elkington III, and that name held a lot of weight in the English forest.

He arrived at the dock where the ship awaited that was to take him to his new home. Many travelers, animals of all kinds, were saying goodbye to loved ones and hugging each other with tears of sadness and joy. There was an excitement emanating from the scene at the dock. There were so many there to see their loved ones off, but no one was there for Elkwood. He stood alone, observing the scene, wondering what lay ahead on his journey.

Elkwood boarded the massive ship and was led to his cabin. The air smelled of salt water and a hint of animal sweat. Thankfully, his parents had reserved a very nice cabin aboard the ship. Elkwood put his knapsack next to his bed and sat down. The bed was soft and filled with down feathers. He had never left home before and was not familiar with ship travel protocol. He realized he was famished, so he decided to leave his room in search of sustenance.

The ship's dining room was massive, with very high ceilings and large chandeliers, and it had an aroma that made his stomach growl. The tables were designated by animal type and the waiters were elk with very in-depth training. He was greeted by the *maître d' elk* and seated at a large round table. Very fine and rich-looking elk quickly filled the seats at the table. Elkwood introduced himself to his dinner companions and told them about his graduation and the party his parents had thrown for him. They all seemed rather disinterested until Elkwood mentioned that his parents were Big Duke and Ella Elkington. Immediately they all began to fall over themselves to speak with Elkwood. He told them he was traveling to Montana, where the very finest elk lived. They all seemed quite impressed. Elkwood had a marvelous evening and decided traveling across the Big Pond to Montana might not be so bad after all. After a fine meal, he bid his new friends a good night and left the room.

Elkwood went back to his cabin, exhausted from all the excitement. He lay down on his bed and tried to sleep. He was not used to the back-and-forth rolling of the ship, and he tossed and turned. Deciding it was impossible to sleep, Elkwood left his room and walked onto the large deck and up to the bow of the ship. The night was dark and clear, and a million stars were winking at him. There was soft music playing, coming from where, he was not sure. He walked across the deck and stepped up to the railing and could hear the gushing of the water as the ship cut like a knife through the big ocean.

"How exciting!" he thought.

There was such a vast, big world apart from his home that he had never experienced. Perhaps this journey was not so frightening after all. He had met some very nice elk at dinner, and they seemed to be quite taken with him. Yes, they had all wanted to know about his famous parents, but he was sure they liked him.

While he was deep in thought, a song began to play from the deck speakers that Elkwood's mother loved to sing to him. As he listened, he recalled the clear and beautiful voice of his mother and longed for home. It would be a very long time before he saw her again, which made him feel sad and alone. As the music continued, he began to tap his hooves and move to the rhythm. He loved this song, and he whirled on his hooves, jumped down to the lower deck, and began to softly tap dance. His hooves kept in time with the tune, and he felt the song was sung only for him. His mother loved him greatly, and he knew she had been sad to see him go. With a grin, he danced his soft-shoe to his mother's song about her love for him.

When it was over, he felt elated, and he bowed to his imaginary audience. As he rose from his bow, he realized there was no audience. He was alone.

That did not matter, because hearing his mother sing his favorite song had made him feel close to her. He thought he could now sleep, and slowly walked back to his cabin, disappearing into the dark.

Day after day, the ship took Elkwood further from his home. The friends he had met the first night at dinner now ignored him. Once they had realized he was not rich like his parents, they snubbed him. He was beginning to realize how cruel elk could be. It seemed if you were not rich, or had nothing to offer, you were not part of their clique.

Elkwood had a lot of time to think aboard the ship, and his thoughts turned to the new life ahead of him. He spent time walking along the deck, looking out at the ocean. It was magnificent. There was water as far as the eye could see, and it frightened Elkwood a bit. What if the ship sank? They would all surely die. The thought made Elkwood shiver. The weather had been clear and calm so far, but a storm in the middle of the ocean, with no land in sight, would be terrifying. As Elkwood continued his thoughts, he noticed clouds beginning to form in the distance. Not to worry. This was a big ship, and surely it could survive a little storm.

The next day, Elkwood awoke with a start. The ship was rolling from side to side much more than usual. He got out of bed but had a hard time standing up as the ship rocked to and fro. He left his cabin and had great difficulty navigating the hallways of the ship. He was thrown side to side, bumping against the walls, struggling to keep his balance as he made his way to the deck. As he rounded a corner in the hall, he ran right into the biggest *Elk* he had ever seen. This was no ordinary *Elk*. He towered above Elkwood and had a rack much larger than his own. His mane was thick and speckled with gray. His eyes were deep pools of wisdom, and he looked at Elkwood with an all-knowing air that unnerved him.

"Pardon me, sir," said Elkwood.

The giant *Elk* looked down at him, his nostrils spewing a warm mist that smelled of sweet loam. "You are young Elkwood, are you not?" queried the mysterious giant elk.

"Yes, I am Elkwood Elkington the Third, from England. And you are…?" asked Elkwood timidly.

"My name is not important, but my message to you is very important indeed."

Elkwood eyed the giant *Elk* with curiosity and a bit of fear. "A message? I do not understand."

The *Elk* took a long look at Elkwood, making him feel very small and uncomfortable. The heady vapor from his nostrils was overwhelming.

"Before it is too late, you must learn humility and the importance of being a true and loyal friend," began the giant *Elk*. "You have traveled down the forest path without real care for anyone. You are selfish and arrogant, and have nothing of substance to show for your life. Your parents have sent you on a great quest. You will learn many things, but the most important lesson for you to learn is that it is not what you have but who you are as an elk. Success is not defined by the wealth you acquire but by the friend you are to others. Sacrifice, Elkwood. You must learn to sacrifice your life for others. Only then will you become an *Elk*."

With that, the giant *Elk* turned and disappeared down the hallway. Elkwood tried to stand steady as the ship pitched back and forth. He was speechless. *How dare that* Elk *lecture me?* he thought. Without ever meeting Elkwood before, that rude *Elk* had had the audacity to tell him he was not a good friend and accuse him of being arrogant. *And how does he know my parents have sent me away? Who is that giant Elk?* he asked himself. He was the one who was arrogant, not Elkwood.

Furious that this stranger would assume all that he had, he hurriedly made his way to the deck. He needed some air. He was tired of everyone picking on him or acting like they cared, when he knew they did not.

As he threw open the door to the deck, he was blasted with a heavy mist of cold salt water that made him gasp for air. Elkwood was stunned by the sight before him. The ocean was exploding with mountainous waves, matched by the menacing dark clouds that shrouded the sun. Elkwood did not care and proceeded out onto the deck as the ocean splashed over the rails of the ship, making it slippery and hard to keep his balance. All he could see were huge waves smashing against the side of the ship. His hooves were skating on the water-soaked deck, but he continued forward, fueled by his anger and hurt.

Suddenly he heard a cry. Elkwood looked toward the bow and saw a tiny little elk desperately clinging to a pole coming out of the deck floor. Venturing out onto the deck had been a big mistake. Elkwood did not know what to do. If he tried to help this little elk, he could be washed over the railing. He was frozen with fear. Without thinking further, he mustered all the courage he had and took a step toward the little elk, right as a huge wave crashed against the ship. The little elk lost his grip on the pole and began to slide toward the railing. Elkwood tried to scramble after the little elk, lost his balance, and fell to his belly, his legs splayed out on all sides. He began to slide like a torpedo toward the little elk, and just as he grabbed him, they hit the railing and were tossed into the air and over the side.

The next sensation he felt was the cold, icy water as he plunged into the ocean with his front legs wrapped around the little elk. They went under into the furious waves, and terror was all he felt. The freezing water knocked the wind out of Elkwood, and he struggled to breathe. He flailed, trying to keep his head above water, and lost his grip on the little elk. The little elk disappeared into the boiling sea, then bobbed up and screamed as he, too, gasped for air. Before Elkwood could react, the little elk was again pulled under the icy water.

Elkwood heard a shout, "Elk overboard!" and saw someone standing at the railing with a large red life preserver. He desperately searched for the little elk, and when his head popped up again, Elkwood lunged and grabbed his neck with his teeth. They sank together into the frigid water, but Elkwood kicked with his powerful legs and surfaced, never losing his grip on the little elk. He would not let go! He could not let go! He saw the life preserver fly through the air toward him, and he struggled to grab the ring. The ship rolled back and forth, carrying the red ring away.

The *deck-elk* pulled the life preserver in and threw it again. Elkwood swam with all the strength he had and reached out with his hoof, stretching as far as possible, hooking the ring. He struggled against the pull of the waves, trying to get his front legs and head through the life preserver, all the while gripping the little elk as tightly as he could with his teeth. With the last of his strength, he managed a desperate and powerful lunge and slid through the ring. Others were now on the deck, and they began to pull Elkwood and the little elk out of the sea.

The life preserver was roped through a pulley, and as the rescue elk pulled and pulled, the two were raised out of the water. Elkwood hung on to the life preserver as hard as he could, fearing they would slip through again and land in the icy water. As he neared the ship, hooves reached out and grabbed him, and the pair hit the deck. They pulled the ring over his head and with great effort led the exhausted elk away from the railing and into the safety of the ship.

Elkwood was spent. He was soaked, cold to the bone, and shivering beyond control. He was laid upon a cot in a small room and quickly covered with thick blankets that warmed him instantly. His strength was drained and he was dizzy and disoriented. With nothing left, he fell into a deep sleep.

Elkwood awoke kicking at the heavy blankets, trying to free himself. As he threw them off, he realized he had had the worst nightmare of his life. He had been thrown overboard and had been in the ocean, struggling to prevent himself from drowning. He relaxed and pulled the covers over his shoulders and tried to calm his shivers. A very pretty elk came in and offered him some warm broth, which he eagerly consumed. The liquid warmed his belly almost immediately, and his shivering began to abate.

"What happened?" he asked.

"You were thrown overboard during the storm and had to be rescued," replied the elk.

"So it was not a nightmare? It really happened?" questioned Elkwood.

"Yes, but you are safe now. Just rest, and you will be as good as new in no time," said the elk.

Elkwood looked at the elk and thought she was an angel. She was the most beautiful elk he had ever seen. She was dainty in size and wore the most beautiful silky fur. Her mane framed her long, slender neck, leading to her delicate and fine-boned face. She had the kindest expression he had ever seen, aside from his mother's. He looked down, and her long, slender legs ended in the prettiest and most perfectly shaped hooves. Her eyes met Elkwood's, tying him in emotional knots, something he had never experienced. Her eyes were the deepest purple, a color reserved for royalty, and her long black lashes framed them like lace. He tried to smile at her, but exhaustion overwhelmed him again, and he fell fast asleep.

The beautiful young elk pulled the blankets over Elkwood's shoulders and touched his forehead with a soft caress. He was a handsome and very brave elk, she thought. And a very lucky elk too. She would forever be grateful to him for saving her younger brother, who had so foolishly been caught on the deck in the middle of the horrific storm. What a silly and reckless elk. She would discipline him tomorrow.

She sat for a while, watching Elkwood sleep, making sure he was not having another nightmare. Finally she sighed, took one last look at the handsome elk sleeping, and left the room.

Elkwood slept for hours and eventually awoke with a tremendous appetite. He sat up on his cot and realized he was sore all over. What a terrifying experience. He tried to stand, but his legs were wobbly. He made it to the door and slowly worked his way to the dining room. His fur was matted and disheveled, and his ascot was wrinkled and dirty, but Elkwood did not care. He could smell the seawater stench rising off his coat. He hesitated and thought better of his decision. Yes, it would be better to clean and groom himself before he entered the dining room. He headed to his cabin, took a long, hot shower, dressed in a clean ascot, and departed.

Elkwood walked into the ship's dining room through the large double doors, and the room went silent. There were animals of all varieties, with like species sitting at designated tables throughout the massive room. All the animals stood and began to cheer and clap their hooves and paws as he entered. They patted him on the shoulder as he walked by and settled him into an empty chair at an elk table. Comments of "Congratulations!" and "How brave!" came from all.

Why are they congratulating me? he wondered. He felt embarrassed and hung his head, rather ashamed he had caused such a fuss. He had stupidly gone out onto the deck in a terrible storm, been thrown overboard, and had to be rescued. He had caused a lot of trouble and put the rescue elks' lives at risk.

Then a young and very small elk came up to him and said, "Thank you, Elkwood. You saved my life."

Cheers rang throughout the room. "What? I saved your life?" he asked of the little elk.

"Yes, you did, and you are the bravest elk in the world!" Cheers rang out again.

"But I do not understand. I was thrown overboard and was saved. That is all I remember," said Elkwood, completely confused.

The young elk explained how Elkwood had attempted to save him and how, when he had lost his grip on the pole, Elkwood had grabbed him, and they both had been thrown overboard. The little elk told him he had grabbed him with his teeth while he was drowning, and held on, never letting go. He went on jabbering about how Elkwood had lunged for the life preserver, securing them both, and then had been lifted out of the water, back onto the ship.

"I do not remember anything other than hitting the cold, icy water and getting pulled out," said Elkwood, confused and amazed by the story told by the little elk.

"Why were you out on the deck in that terrible storm?" asked the little elk.

Elkwood thought for a moment and said, "I really do not remember. I think I was angry about something and was not thinking clearly. That is all I recall."

The little elk smiled and threw his tiny hooves around Elkwood's big neck and hugged him. A tear fell from Elkwood's huge eye as he held the little elk. He looked past the little elk in his arms and noticed a giant *Elk* standing alone across the room. The *Elk* nodded at Elkwood with a slight smile, turned, and disappeared. Elkwood wondered who he was, but dismissed the encounter as many elk continued to congratulate him for his brave rescue of the little elk.

Elkwood ate a delicious dinner until he could not eat another bite. Everyone continued to go on and on about his bravery and his selfless courage. He sat quietly, feeling embarrassed by all the praise and adoration. He did not feel very brave, as he still could not remember saving the little elk. All he knew was they both had nearly died, and he was humbled by the thought. Several times, he looked across the room to where the giant *Elk* had stood, but he did not return. Strangely, something seemed familiar about that mysterious *Elk*. Who was he? Perhaps others knew him. And why had he given him a nod that seemed like approval? He would look for him tomorrow and see if anyone knew him. Someone must, he thought. He was very tired and said his goodbyes, then retreated back to his cabin. After a good night's sleep, he was sure, everything would be clearer in the morning.

The next day dawned with sun streaming through the porthole of Elkwood's cabin. He had slept well and felt rejuvenated after his harrowing near-death experience. He left his cabin and headed for the deck. As he opened the door, he noticed the clouds had disappeared, the sea had calmed, and the sun was brilliant. He had been at sea for a long time and was eager to get off the ship. He wanted to avoid any more storms that might be his undoing.

As he stood at the railing of the ship, squinting in the bright sunlight, he looked to the west and could not believe his eyes. Land! Could it be? Had they finally reached their destination? He heard a loud "Land ho!" called from above, confirming what he was seeing. Land! It would be glorious to once again feel his hooves on solid ground.

Elkwood pranced and danced with excitement and began calling, "Land! Land!" Other animals came to the deck, and all were giddy to finally be near the end of their long journey. He scanned the onlookers, hoping to find the giant *Elk*. He was nowhere to be seen. Perhaps he had imagined him. After all, he had been through a very terrifying ordeal, and there was much he could not remember. Oh well, it was time to gather his things and get ready to get off the ship.

He returned to his cabin, packed his knapsack, and headed back to the deck. As the ship closed the distance to the shore, his anticipation grew. He had no idea what lay ahead in this new land, but for now, he was happy to have arrived. He saw the little elk standing across the deck, and he waved and smiled, as did the little elk. He felt wonderful realizing he had done the first truly unselfish act in his entire life. He had saved someone else, and it made him feel good.

CHAPTER 2

THE JOURNEY ACROSS the Big Pond had been long, and by the time Elkwood arrived on land, he was tired. He rested for a few days, then began his journey to Montana. He found that no one really cared much about his fancy clothing or his family's money, so he kept to himself. Elkwood traveled many days, occasionally crossing paths with other animals. He politely greeted them and moved on. He found himself thinking of his life with his parents back in the forest of England. He missed them terribly, and as much as he tried to be positive and brave, he felt dejected. What had he done to deserve such exile?

It was springtime, and the country he traveled through was beautiful. It was filled with magnificent mountains capped white with snow, streams, rivers, and huge valleys with the biggest trees he had ever seen. He had never seen mountains before and wondered how he would cross them all. They were so tall they seemed to touch the sky. The air smelled of lush pine trees, fresh green grass, rich, moist dirt, and the intoxicating fragrance of newly budding wildflowers. As he continued to put one hoof in front of the other, he began to think about what might lie ahead for him. Would he survive? Would he become a successful *Elk*? Would he make new friends? And how would he make a living? All these questions rattled around in his head as he put mile after mile behind him.

Tired from the miles of travel, Elkwood was starting to believe he would never get to Montana when suddenly he looked up and stared at an old wooden sign, half hanging on a post, that read "Welcome to Montana."

He had made it! His new home. He walked to the sign, sniffing it with quivering nostrils. With hesitation, yet also excitement, he took one step, then two, then leaped past the sign. Elkwood began to prance and dance and circle and paw the air with his front hooves.

"I am home! I am in Montana! I am a Montana *Elk*!" he shouted.

He pranced and danced with glee, frolicking around the sign, and then abruptly stopped. He looked around, and with a heavy heart, he realized he was still alone. He had no idea where to go or what to do.

He walked for a while, and the sun was beginning to set behind the immense snowcapped mountains. He sighed a huge breath that quivered his entire body, from the tip of his antlers to his tail. There was complete silence. He saw a bed of moss growing beneath a huge pine tree and decided that would be a good place to sleep for the night. He lay down atop the moss, then reached for his knapsack and pulled out one of Ella's chocolate chip cookies. He curled up as tight as he could on the moss and slowly nibbled on the cookie. He continued his thoughts of home, his parents, and all he had left behind. He would figure out where to go tomorrow. Ella Elkington was right. Each time Elkwood ate one of her delicious chocolate chip cookies, it made him think of home. As he began to doze, he could hear his mother and father singing "Dream a Little Dream of Me," a song they used to sing to him when he was a young elk. It was his favorite lullaby. Elkwood finished his cookie, curled his head around his body, and a tear fell from his big, soulful eyes. He snuggled deeper into the bed of moss and fell asleep...dreaming.

Elkwood awoke with a start. Something was on his antler. He moved this way and that way, and shook his antlers, but he could not rid himself of whatever was up there. He rolled his big eyes up, and to his surprise, there was a bird perched on his antler, and not just any bird. It was a most cheerful bird with a bright white chest, dark blue wings, and a brilliant red-feathered head appearing as if he was wearing a hat. He was a most patriotic-looking bird.

"Hello!" said the bird. "I am Theodore. What's your name?"

"My name is Elkwood Elkington the Third. Would you mind getting off my antlers?"

Theodore jumped down and rested on Elkwood's back. He shook his feathers and looked at Elkwood with curiosity.

"Why are you staring at me?" asked Elkwood.

Theodore replied, "You are clearly not from around these parts, with your accent and all. Where are you from?"

"I am from the forest in England, across the Big Pond," replied Elkwood.

"Oh my! That must be a very long way from Montana. Are you traveling alone?" asked Theodore.

"Very," said Elkwood. "Yes, very alone."

"Well, not any longer," replied Theodore. "You have met your first friend!"

Elkwood eyed Theodore suspiciously. "Why do you want to be my friend? And what kind of bird are you?"

"What strange questions," replied Theodore. "First, I am a red-headed woodpecker. And second, because you are a very fine-looking elk, and quite frankly, you look like you could use a friend. Where are you going?"

"I do not really know," answered Elkwood. "It took me a long time to find Montana, and I have traveled a very long way to become an *Elk*."

Theodore asked, "What do you mean, become an elk? You *are* an elk!"

Elkwood sadly replied, "My parents sent me here to become a successful *Elk* and to make something out of my life. I guess I have nothing to show for my life so far." Elkwood hung his head in shame.

"Now stop feeling sorry for yourself, Elkwood. You have the rest of your life ahead of you, and Montana is full of opportunity. After all, you are a very regal-looking elk and, I am sure, very smart."

"Yes, I guess I am all those things, but I do not know where to go or what to do," said Elkwood with sadness in his eyes.

"I have flown all over this land, and I know a beautiful place where the sky is big, the mountains are high, and the food is plentiful. Follow me and I will show you," said Theodore excitedly.

Elkwood stated, "But I cannot fly."

Theodore laughed in a high-pitched chirp. "Silly Elkwood! Of course you cannot fly! I will stay close and you will follow."

Elkwood asked, "Are you sure? I do not want to trouble you."

"No trouble at all Elkwood. We are friends now, so let's begin our journey," chirped Theodore.

Elkwood rose, then shook off the moss from his coat and stretched from head to hoof. Theodore flew off his back and began to fly in big circles around him.

"Stop! You are making me dizzy," pleaded Elkwood.

Theodore giggled and said, "C'mon, Elkwood, follow me to the Big Sky." And with that proclamation, they began their journey together.

Elkwood and Theodore traveled for many days, witnessing the full birth of spring. The trees were budding, and the flowers were beginning to cover the ground in shocks of white, yellow, purple, pink, and red. The beauty stunned Elkwood, and he was beginning to feel better about his future. Perhaps Montana *was* the best place for an elk.

The fast-running streams from the high mountain snowmelt quenched their thirst, and since Elkwood was quite large, he had no trouble crossing the streams or rivers. And of course, Theodore easily flew across. They met others along the trail, often stopping for a quick conversation or to share a snack. Sometimes Elkwood would offer a taste of one of Ella's chocolate chip cookies, and all who tasted them asked where they could buy such a delicious treat. Elkwood said it was not possible, for he had brought them all the way from England, and once they were gone, they were gone.

Waking early one morning, Theodore flew off before Elkwood stirred. He knew they were near the Big Sky. He flew a short route, and sure enough, there it was. He raced back, then jumped on Elkwood and feverishly flapped his wings in glee.

"We are *here*, Elkwood! We are *here!*"

Elkwood moved his nose to knock Theodore off him so he could continue sleeping, but the bird was relentless. He kept calling, "We are here! We are here! Wake up Elkwood!"

Finally Elkwood said "Here? Where?" with a big yawn.

"The Big Sky, Elkwood. We have found the Big Sky. Get up and follow me. *Hurry!*"

Elkwood rose, shook off the ground from his fur, stretched, and trotted after Theodore.

"Hurry up, Elkwood," chirped the excited woodpecker.

Suddenly, as they stepped from the forest into a huge meadow filled with wildflowers of every color, before them stood the most beautiful sight Elkwood had ever seen: the most magnificent mountain in the world, covered in white from the winter snow. It stood taller than he thought possible. Before him rose a giant, solitary mountain.

"I have seen pictures in books of pyramids in Egypt. That must be a pyramid. Who built it?" asked Elkwood.

"Silly Elkwood! It's a lone peak in the middle of the Big Sky. I knew we would find this place. I think it is *the* very *best* place."

Elkwood stood in wonder and awe, staring at the magnificent mountain. More mountains were in view, but none like the lone peak before him.

"Theodore, does it have a name?"

"I don't think so," replied Theodore.

"I will name it, then. The Lone Peak, that is what we will call my mountain," declared Elkwood as he puffed out his chest in pride.

"Excellent," replied Theodore. "A very great name, my friend."

The two continued to explore the Big Sky, and as they walked, Elkwood told Theodore all about his life in England, his very famous parents, and his journey across the Big Pond to find Montana. Theodore was mesmerized by the incredible story and listened intently as the adventure unfolded.

They found themselves hiking on the lower trails of the Lone Peak. Then suddenly Elkwood saw the most amazing sight. A small waterfall was coming down the mountain, and it appeared to be teeming with chocolate chips.

"Look, Theodore, there are chocolate chips in the waterfall. It is a chocolate chip waterfall!" he shouted. "I have found a chocolate chip waterfall. Wait, that is the answer. I will make chocolate chip cookies and sell them to all the animals in the forest. They will love to eat them and will buy them every day. *That* is how I will make my living. I will call my store the Eat Me Cookie Company, Theodore. After all, what else would a cookie say?" Elkwood was out of breath with excitement.

"Genius, my friend! Simply genius!" chirped Theodore.

"And I will name the cookie the Big Elk cookie, as it is my cookie and should be named after me," pronounced Elkwood.

"Magnificent, my friend," agreed Theodore. "You will be rich beyond your wildest dreams. Bravo!"

"Do you really think so?" asked Elkwood. "Do you think the animals will buy Big Elk cookies?"

"Of course they will. Everyone in the forest loves chocolate chip cookies. You will be a huge success!" chirped Theodore.

"I am very excited," admitted Elkwood. "We must find a place for me to live, and also a place for my store. But first let's gather lots of chocolate chips from the waterfall so I can make my first batch of Big Elk cookies."

Elkwood gently pulled chip after chip from the waterfall and placed them in his knapsack. Theodore, with lightning speed, pecked chips off the waterfall with his beak and dropped them in the knapsack.

"There, now I have enough to open my store," said Elkwood triumphantly. Suddenly Elkwood stopped in his tracks and said, "Theodore, I cannot open a cookie store. I don't know how to make the cookies. What will I do?"

Theodore tried to comfort his friend, but words were of no consolation.

"Let's try and find a place for you to live, and we will figure out the rest later. For now, that is all we can do," expressed Theodore.

Just when Elkwood had thought things were looking bright and happy, his hope for happiness was instantly dashed. Without the recipe, he had no idea how to make his mother's chocolate chip cookies. He hung his head in shame and sorrow, his shoulders slumped. Theodore saw the immense sadness on Elkwood's face and knew of no way to make his new friend feel better. The best he could do was to stay by his side. Surely things would improve and Elkwood would be happy again.

Dejected, Elkwood and Theodore began searching for living quarters for Elkwood. They meandered to the base of the Lone Peak, and the land opened up into a big valley. Elkwood and Theodore stopped and stood in amazement. It was beautiful and a perfect place to live. There was a small stream that cascaded down from the mountain and formed a lake in the middle of the valley. Majestic, snowcapped mountains surrounded them. It was breathtaking. Not far from the base of the Lone Peak, they came upon two gigantic old trees, near a small clearing, that were hollowed out. Someone must have made the trees their home long ago, but they were now vacant. Elkwood decided at least one of the trees would be perfect for his home. Each of the trees even had windows carved on either side of the door to let the light shine inside.

He opened the door to the smaller tree, and it was a mess. Dirt and cobwebs were everywhere. It was time to clean, and the two began, working tirelessly. Elkwood started by sweeping the floors with an old broom he found inside the tree. He swung the broom in big arcs over his head to rid his new home of cobwebs. As they readied the tree home, the hard work made him forget about his troubles.

Theodore flew away, then came back with big leaves strapped to his wings and began fluttering against the windowpanes to wipe them clean. He shined them until they sparkled, and Elkwood smiled at the clever bird. There were even flower boxes below each window, filled with crumbled, dead flowers. Theodore dug up the dead blooms with his beak and flew away again, returning with a *beakful* of beautiful red Indian paintbrush, purple willowherb, and white Alp lily wildflowers. He filled each flower box with the beautiful flowers and proudly surveyed his handiwork. Elkwood dragged sheets of fresh moss into the tree house and placed them in the corner for his bed. After several hours, it was looking quite livable, and the two smiled with satisfaction.

"I almost forgot." Theodore flew away with a flutter. He returned shortly with more wildflowers in his beak and placed them in an old vase sitting on a shelf. "There," he chirped happily. "Now this looks like a home."

"How beautiful," exclaimed Elkwood. "Thank you, Theodore. They are simply perfect."

The joy was short-lived. Elkwood was tired and hungry, and his depression resurfaced, remembering he did not know how to make his mother's precious chocolate chip cookies. Theodore saw the pain in his friend's eyes but had no words of comfort. Silently they wandered down to the nearby stream, with Theodore, as was his custom at times, perched upon Elkwood's massive antlers. As Elkwood lowered his head to the water, they both took a long, cool drink to satisfy their thirst.

"Would you like to share the last of my mother's cookies with me, Theodore? They are awfully good," offered Elkwood, feeling very sad they were about to eat the last of Ella's cookies.

"I would be honored. Thank you," said Theodore quietly.

Elkwood reached into the bottom of the cookie bag to retrieve the very last cookie. Ella's chocolate chip cookies had provided him with sustenance for a long time, and each cookie had made him think of home. How he missed his mother and father. As he grabbed the last cookie with his hoof, he felt something wrinkly at the bottom of the bag. It was a folded-up piece of parchment. He slowly pulled it out of the bag and sat perfectly still, holding the folded note.

He looked at Theodore, and Theodore asked, "What is it? Open it, please!"

Elkwood slowly unwrapped the folded parchment and recognized his mother's *hoofwriting.*

Dearest Elkwood,

By the time you find this note, I hope you will have made it safely to Montana. It is only the beginning for you. You will never know how difficult it was for your father and me to send you so far away, but we believe it was the best thing for you. We know you will find your way, learn about becoming an Elk, and be very successful. We know you will make us proud. I could not send you so far without ensuring you would always have a little bit of home. On the back of this letter is my recipe for chocolate chip cookies. Do not share the recipe with anyone, as it has been in our herd for generations. Every time you eat a cookie, let it remind you of how very much we love you.

Mother.

Elkwood could hardly believe what he was reading. He looked at Theodore, who was tilted forward on his tail in anticipation, and slowly turned over the letter. There it was. His mother's recipe. He was saved!

He jumped up and began to prance and dance in circles, singing and laughing and pawing the air with his hooves. Theodore was flying and swooping in big circles, chirping and singing along with glee for his friend's good fortune.

"I am going to be a famous *Elk*," shouted Elkwood, "with the most delicious cookies in the forest. Yippee!"

The two friends danced and pranced and flew and swooped until they were exhausted. Munching on the last of Ella's cookies, with Theodore riding on Elkwood's antlers, they walked together back to Elkwood's new home.

As they approached the door, Theodore said, "See ya tomorrow, and… congratulations!"

Elkwood asked, "Where are you going? Please…come inside."

Theodore flew off Elkwood's antlers and stood outside the door as Elkwood entered the treehouse.

"Please come in, little friend." Elkwood swept his hoof, extending the bird an invitation.

Hesitantly Theodore hopped into Elkwood's home. Upon a shelf on the tree wall rested a beautiful and perfectly shaped nest.

"For you, my dear little friend." Elkwood nodded toward the nest.

Choked with emotion, Theodore hopped onto his nest and, with a tear falling from his eye, said, "Thank you, Elkwood. This is the finest nest I have ever set my feathers upon."

Elkwood replied, "I could not have come this far without you. It is my way of saying thank you."

In silence, the two curled up in their beds, Elkwood in his bed of soft moss, and Theodore in his soft nest. As Elkwood drifted off to sleep, he recalled the voice of the giant *Elk* from the ship, saying, "Before it is too late, you must learn humility and the importance of being a true and loyal friend." He realized that he had made a true friend. He was happier than he had ever been.

Morning broke with rays of sun filtering through the sparkling windows of Elkwood's new home. Elkwood lay sound asleep, curled up on his soft bed of moss. Theodore had already been out enjoying the magnificent day, flying around the forest, chirping "Good morning!" to all the forest animals. He swooped back through the windows of Elkwood's tree home and landed right in front of Elkwood's big black nose. Elkwood was breathing heavily, and Theodore could not resist a little teasing. He lightly tickled Elkwood's nose with the tip of his wing feathers. Elkwood wrinkled his nose but continued to sleep soundly. Theodore tickled again, and again, with no luck waking the slumbering elk. He decided drastic measures were in order, so he put the tip of his feathered wing in Elkwood's large nostril and wiggled it around. Elkwood snorted hard, and the force blew Theodore off his tiny feet. He landed on his back with a soft thump and a giggle.

"You are a pesky bird," yawned Elkwood.

"And you have a big, snorty nose, my friend," chirped Theodore. They both laughed. "Now get up, Elkwood. We have to get the other tree ready so you can open your store."

Elkwood squinted against the bright sunlight hitting him directly in the eyes. "Maybe I should move his bed to the other side," mumbled Elkwood.

"Elkwood!" the bird chirped loudly.

"All right, Theodore, all right, I am getting up." Under his breath, he murmured, "Pesky bird," and winked at Theodore.

There was much to be done to get the Eat Me Cookie Company open for business. The nearby tree, which was larger than Elkwood's home, was the ideal place for his store. Elkwood and Theodore worked for hours, tirelessly cleaning the store and moving in supplies. They fashioned an oven of rocks and clay, which would be heated by wood gathered in the forest. Then they collected all the ingredients needed to make the cookies. Theodore pecked a window into the tree door, and the sound of his rapid pecking echoed through the forest. He added a shelf to serve the cookies and made bowls, ladles, and spatulas from old driftwood he found along the river. He carved and pecked the wood with his beak until the bowls took shape, dusting out shavings with his tail. It was amazing how fast Theodore could work. After all, he *was* a woodpecker. Finally it appeared everything was ready to go.

Then Elkwood stopped dead in his tracks. "Theodore, I don't have a sign for my store. No one will know it is here. What will I do?"

Theodore flew away without a word and left Elkwood standing alone and confused. *Why has my friend left me in my time of need?* he wondered. He stood, antlers lowered, feeling sad. He did not know how to make a sign, and without one, the store could not open.

After a short time, he heard fluttering and looked up to see Theodore flying toward him with considerable effort, carrying something in his beak. He flew straight at the tree, stopped just above the door, and flipped his beak to deposit his surprise. He had made a sign from an old piece of driftwood, which read "The Eat Me Cookie Company."

Elkwood could only stare in amazement. With tears welling up in his big brown eyes, he said, "Theodore, that is the most beautiful sign I have ever seen. I cannot believe you made that for me."

"Of course," said Theodore. "That is what friends do. They help each other."

Elkwood thought about what his friend had said. Having a true friend was much more than he had ever understood. "Thank you, Theodore. You are a very talented woodpecker. I think there is nothing left to do but open the Eat Me Cookie Company and sell lots of cookies."

And so the Eat Me Cookie Company opened for business. Animals from all over the Big Sky lined up daily to buy Big Elk cookies. There were deer, rabbits, mice, raccoons, squirrels, skunks, porcupines, bears, river otters, elk, moose, foxes, and even an occasional bald eagle, all lined up to buy a Big Elk cookie. The reclusive wolves and mountain lions made an appearance, and a few bison showed up as well, having smelled the irresistible aroma wafting through the forest. A family of bighorn sheep wandered by and joined the line to buy a cookie. The animals of the forest agreed to lay aside their natural predatory instincts and declare a "truce" so that they all may enjoy a delicious Big Elk cookie.

Theodore threw open the window to the Eat Me Cookie Company and gasped in surprise when he saw the huge line of animals waiting for the store to open. "Elkwood, come look! There are so many customers. All the animals of the Big Sky have shown up for our grand opening. Oh my! Will we have enough Big Elks for everyone?" he asked with nervous excitement.

Elkwood leaned forward to peer out the window and saw the massive crowd lined up outside the store. "No time to fret, Theodore. We have to keep making Big Elks." Calmly he shoved another tray of cookies into the oven.

Elkwood pulled the hot cookies from the oven, quickly wrapped each one in a leaf bag, and stacked them one by one. Theodore would flit over to the stack, grab a *beakful* of bags, and fly them to the window. Pine cones were the currency of the forest, and as the customers dropped their pine cones on the window shelf, Theodore handed them a bagged cookie, then swept the pine cones into a basket with his tail. And so the day progressed, until the line had thinned and the cookies disappeared.

Theodore and Elkwood were exhausted, yet also exhilarated, when the last happy customer grabbed a leaf-wrapped Big Elk and departed. They closed the window of the Eat Me Cookie Company, and Elkwood exclaimed, "What a grand success! The animals of the Big Sky could not buy my Big Elks fast enough. The Eat Me Cookie Company is a smashing success, Theodore." Elkwood reached toward Theodore with his long neck and licked the bird with his huge tongue.

Sputtering from the tongue bath with a giggle, Theodore shook his entire body and fluffed his feathers. "Congratulations, my friend! You did it!" The woodpecker began to fly and swoop and chirp with glee around the store. Elkwood, caught up in the moment, began to prance and dance and spin and twirl in celebration with his feathered friend.

Dizzied by the explosion of dance, Elkwood fell to the floor, happily exhausted, and Theodore flew over to him and perched on his nose. Elkwood stood up and tried to focus on the bird on the end of his nose, his head already spinning.

"Theodore, hold still. I see two of you," moaned Elkwood, with his eyes crossed.

Losing his balance again, Elkwood tried to brace himself with his hoof, but the spinning and eye-crossing was too much. His hoof slipped out from under him, and Theodore flew off his nose just as Elkwood's hoof caught a large bowl of flour. The bowl flipped into the air, and as Elkwood landed on his rump with a loud thump, the flour covered them both. The two looked at each other and burst into uncontrollable laughter.

"Thank you, my friend, for all your help," laughed Elkwood as he shook off the flour. "I could not have done this without you. Once again you have proven to be a true and loyal friend."

Theodore jumped onto Elkwood's nose again and said, "Close your eyes."

Elkwood closed his eyes as the woodpecker gently swept some flour off his face with his wings. Then, in a moment of emotion, Theodore wrapped his wings around Elkwood's face in a hug, causing a huge tear to fall from Elkwood's long lashes. Of course, the tear turned to paste as it mixed with the leftover flour. The two giggled together as Theodore rubbed the paste off Elkwood's face.

"We had better clean up this mess and make more Big Elk cookie dough for tomorrow," said Elkwood as he struggled to get up, shaking the last of the flour off his massive body. "I believe tomorrow will be even busier than today."

Theodore smiled with pride at what the two had accomplished. Then he busied himself getting ready for tomorrow.

The tantalizing aroma wafted through the forest, bringing more and more animals each day to the Eat Me Cookie Company to buy the best cookies they had ever tasted. Each week, Elkwood would close the store for two days so that he could restock it with supplies, and rest. On his days off, Elkwood and Theodore would hike through the woods and talk about how successful Elkwood had become. Elkwood never asked about Theodore's life, and honestly, there was not much to tell. Theodore had always had a good life and was friendly to all. He had mostly spent his days foraging for food and eating. Meeting Elkwood was the most exciting thing that had ever happened to him. So even though Elkwood was self-centered and arrogant, Theodore did not mind. He liked Elkwood and looked forward to each day, and every new adventure that came their way. No, he would not trade his friendship with Elkwood for anything. Elkwood needed him, and he was not the kind of woodpecker who would ever let go of a friend.

CHAPTER 3

There are four enemies that threaten the life of a trout. Large birds, bears, river otters, and man. The cleverest, of course, is man. They fish in the rivers using a technique called "fly fishing," with bait that mimics what trout love best... bugs. From nymphs to emergers and dry flies, a fly fisherman carries all in his arsenal to catch trout. From the trout's perspective, they are tricked into believing they are biting on a tasty morsel, when in fact a deadly hook is hidden within the deceptive bug.

EARLY SUMMER IN THE BIG SKY is a time for rejoicing on the river. The ice and snow have melted, the runoff has calmed, and the river is crystal clear. Trout frolic everywhere with the coming of the hatches—millions of bugs fly over the water. Sunshine is abundant, and the river trout rejoice in the warmth and feeding frenzy. It is also prime time for fly fishermen to catch a prize trout. If the fisherman is smart, he will bait his line with a fly that looks just like the bugs hatching along the river. To a young, inexperienced, and hungry trout, any bug is irresistible.

The girl parked her truck at her favorite fishing spot and opened the door. Out jumped two very excited Alaskan huskies. Balto and Chaser were very familiar with this spot and knew they were in for a glorious day of fishing.

The forest along the river was lush with willows, huge pine trees, and fresh green grasses. Wildflowers were everywhere, madly covering the ground with color. The dogs ran excitedly along the trail, sniffing all the new scents of the budding season. If they were lucky, they might even find the prize carcass of an elk or moose that had perished during the previous winter. What a treat to gnaw on the bones.

As the girl meandered the trail alongside the river, she marveled at the beauty of early summer in Montana. Everything was so green, and the river was glistening in the bright sunlight as it ran its course. The earth smelled of rich loam, and she could feel the moisture rising from the ground like a sauna, drawn out by the warm sun. The river was dark blue and crystal clear, painted with bands of gold and green reflected from the sun and foliage on the opposite riverbank. Huge rock cliffs bordered that side of the river, towering toward the brilliant blue sky. If the girl was lucky, she might see a majestic bald eagle perched atop the cliffs. She marveled at the beauty of her peaceful environment. Fly-fishing was a relaxing sport and a fun time for her and the dogs. Catching a trout was the purpose and always exciting, but the beauty and tranquility of the river was what drew the girl to fish.

Sighting her favorite fishing spot ahead, she moved off the trail, down the embankment of the river, and into the water. She could feel the cool water surround her legs, and the dogs followed her in, enjoying the refreshing feel of the water as it wet their coats and cooled them off. Balto and Chaser knew the drill. They would patiently stand by her side in the river while she cast her line in hopes of landing a big trout. Although she was determined, the girl did not always catch a trout, so the dogs often ventured off to explore the forest or took a nap along the riverbank, always alert for the shout of success. "I got one!" she would cry, and the dogs would run into the river to play with the trout.

The day was perfect, and Twinkle Toes Trout was swimming with abandon and leaping into the air, catching her fill of delicious bugs hovering above the water on the river. She was a young trout and just beginning to show her brilliant colors. Her body was bright, hot pink contrasted by dazzling lime-green fins. A stripe of perfectly placed lime-green spots ran down the length of her body on both sides. Her face was beautifully speckled, and her full, perfectly shaped lips were yellow like the sun. Her mother had told her she was the most beautiful trout in the river, but Twinkle Toes paid the compliment no heed. She was having too much fun swimming and leaping through the air each day. The more she leaped and snacked on bugs, the more she discovered her ability to *dance* on the river. She did flips and spins and dives that no other young trout could maneuver. Her mother had nicknamed her "Twinkle Toes" because of her amazing talent. The name had stuck, and all the trout in the river marveled at her acrobatic skills. Even though all were impressed, the other trout in the river shunned her. They were jealous. She was far too pretty and talented to be part of their school. Although Twinkle Toes did not understand why the other fish did not like her, she did not mind. She was truly a happy trout without a care in the world.

Now old enough to begin traveling the river without the protection of her mother, Twinkle Toes reveled in exploring the waters and dancing with delight. Each day, she became stronger and more skilled with her leaps and dance technique. She loved rising from the water and dancing along the ripples on her tail fin. Life in the river was joyous, and Twinkle Toes loved exploring and swimming the river at leisure. As a young trout, her mother had told her over and over to be wary of the dangers on the river. She warned of preying birds, bears, and the ever-playful but deadly river otters. But mostly she warned her offspring of man. She tried to educate Twinkle Toes in the art of telling the difference between a real bug and the fake bugs used by man. She was an adept student and listened closely to all her mother tried to teach, but on a glorious summer day, with the sun's rays dancing on the water, she could not help but dance too.

Each morning, her mother would sigh as Twinkle Toes swam away, calling, "Be careful, my love. Beware of danger." She wondered if the day would come when Twinkle Toes would not return, and it saddened her heart. She had never borne such a magnificently beautiful trout, and her tail fin quivered, fearing what might become of her cavalier little youngster.

Twinkle Toes swam to her favorite stretch of river on this fine day. She happily greeted other trout as she swam by and leaped out of the water, grabbing a bug here and there. Life was grand, and today would be exhilarating. Her favorite spot in the river had several stretches of calm water along the shore, with towering rock cliffs above. She fancied she could leap with all her strength and land on the top of the cliffs. With each leap, she would fly higher and higher, but the cliffs were out of reach. *Who cares?* she thought. It was just fun to try.

As the girl began casting her line across the river, she spotted a colorful trout rising magnificently out of the water. What a show it was putting on! The girl knew the trout was feeding, and thought it was a perfect chance to catch herself a fish, although often, when the girl saw fish leaping and jumping, she wondered if that was for their own enjoyment. This trout certainly appeared to be having a marvelous time, and the girl thought it must feel wonderful to be able to leap out of the water. As she moved into position to cast her line near the lively trout, Balto saw it leap out of the water, while Chaser sensed the movement. On high alert, they both froze at the riverbank.

Chaser was a very tall, long-legged, slender black-and-white sled dog… who, as it happens, was completely blind. He had large black spots dotting the white fur on his back, which made him look like a dog in a cow suit. Along his legs and shoulders, he was white and speckled with small black dots, like a leopard. He had a long neck and a powerful head with very large ears. His face was beautiful, with traditional husky markings, and he had large white "dashes" over his eyes, like eyebrows. Legend has it that dogs with dashes look like they have four eyes, and when sleeping, predators think they are still awake. Thus, they stay away.

The girl had adopted Chaser when he was one year old, and within six months, Chaser had begun to lose his sight. After taking him to a specialist, it was discovered he had a hereditary disease that caused his retina to detach, thus causing blindness. The girl had been heartbroken, but Chaser proved there was no need. He ran free each day, navigating the world with ease. He could climb ten-thousand-foot peaks, ski in the back country, hunt voles with expertise, swim mighty rivers, and of course, he loved to fish. His senses were acute and he rarely made a mistake. His highly developed skills gave him great confidence and courage, and his whiskers served as a sort of radar, alerting him to objects in his path. He would swerve and veer just as well as a sighted dog. The girl loved him all the more for his bravery in the face of such a great obstacle. Despite his blindness, Chaser knew the animated fish was still leaping out of the water, keenly aware of the splashes.

Balto was a few years older than Chaser and had fished many times with the girl. He was a beautiful pup with a full mane of thick fur. He was the color of cream with black and tan markings and had the biggest ears. His face had multicolored bandit circles around his huge, soulful eyes, and a very black nose. Although Balto loved to fish, his most favorite thing in the whole world was to run. He had the graceful gait of a thoroughbred and ran for the sheer pleasure of running. He loved to explore, and going fishing gave him the perfect opportunity to hunt in the forest while the girl fished. He loved her excitement when she caught a trout, and could not wait to try and take a tasty bite. Balto had actually never eaten a fish, for trout was not to his liking. He just liked to give the fish a little kiss on the lips. He could see the terror in the caught trout's eyes, and it made him laugh, for he knew the girl would release the catch back into the river. The girl loved Balto and admired his speed and grace. He was her first dog. Thus, he was very special to her.

The girl began casting her line in the direction of the dancing trout. What a prize to catch this magnificent acrobat! This particular trout was beautiful, with colors unlike any trout she had ever seen. The girl always released every trout she caught back into the river. She just could not bear to kill such a beautiful creature, and certainly could not imagine cooking and eating her catch. Catching a trout was very exciting, so she gracefully and deliberately cast and cast, hoping to attract the trout with her fly.

Diving deep with each leap, Twinkle Toes was thoroughly enjoying herself, and oblivious to the girl fishing in the river. Yes, she was hungry, and with each leap, she grabbed a bug. But for the young trout, the sheer joy of river dancing was what excited her most, and today was too good to be true. As she leaped into the air and splashed back into the river, the ears of the girl's dogs perked up. She dove deep into the cool water and spun around for another leap. As she raced for the surface, she spotted a bug sitting on top of the water…an easy catch. With one great swish of her tail fin and a grin on her lips, she opened her mouth and snatched the bug from the surface. As she whirled to dive, she felt a shattering pain in her mouth. A hook! She had been hooked! All her mother's teachings ran though her mind in an instant, and she panicked.

Twinkle Toes dove into the depths of the river as the girl cried, "I got one!" Balto and Chaser ran to her side in the river, jumping with excitement, for they knew she had caught a fish. Twinkle Toes was terrified. She felt the hook tugging at her mouth as the girl reeled her in closer and closer. The line would slacken, and Twinkle Toes would swim for the bottom, only to again be dragged closer to the girl. She fought and leaped into the air, trying to free herself, but the pain of the hook piercing her perfectly shaped lips deterred her. She would not give up. She must free herself of the hook, but the more she struggled, the closer she was reeled in by the girl. Feeling all hope was lost, she succumbed to the fear, panic, and pain.

Suddenly Twinkle Toes felt a vise grip close around her body as the girl grabbed her and lifted her from the river. She immediately began to gasp for oxygen, and writhed and wriggled to free herself. Then the most horrific event of her life took place.

The girl, holding the trout with a tight grip, leaned over and placed Twinkle Toes right in front of the most terrifying animals she had ever seen. Wolves! She had seen them drinking on the riverbanks many times. They were huge, and the girl appeared to want to feed her to her wolves. As she came closer to the terrifying beasts, she screamed as the big black-and-white one reached out his nose and licked her face. Ick! She was being licked by a wolf. The big black-and-white wolf came at her again for another taste, and she lunged at him and bit him on the nose. The wolf yelped and the girl giggled. Then the girl held her in front of the other beast, and Twinkle Toes knew this would be the end. This wolf would surely eat her. As the smaller wolf lunged, with one last rush of strength, she flipped her body and flew out of the girl's hands into the water.

The girl shrieked in surprise as the trout leaped from her grasp. Twinkle Toes tried to swim away, but there appeared to be a forest of long wolf legs surrounding her, and the pain of the hook tugged on her lip. She was not free, and she was sure they would stomp her to death. She must escape, but the more she tried, the more the wolves danced, blocking her from fleeing. The girl struggled to grab the fish as the excited dogs frolicked in the water. Twinkle Toes frantically swam in and out of their gigantic legs. The pain she felt from the hook was secondary to the fear and desperation overwhelming her. Finally, when the terrified trout thought all was lost, the girl grabbed her tightly once again and pulled her from the chaos.

"What a beautiful trout you are, and such a fighter," cried the girl.

Twinkle Toes gasped for oxygen as the girl grasped the hook and gently removed it from her lip.

"I have never seen such a magnificent trout." The girl kissed Twinkle Toes right on her beautiful yellow lips. "Swim, little trout." Carefully the girl placed the terrified fish in the water, facing it upstream, giving the young trout the best chance to recover from being caught.

Twinkle Toes took a giant breath as the oxygen in the water revived her. With renewed strength, she flipped her tail fin and darted from the girl's grasp and away from the terrifying wolves. She frantically swam as fast as she could across the river, grateful for her freedom. Not being able to help herself, she dove once again, only to resurface in one final acrobatic leap into the air, letting her attackers know she had triumphed. The girl laughed, and the dogs perked their ears before trotting to the shore for a nap. The girl decided Twinkle Toes was the best trout she had ever caught, and with that thought in her mind, she waded to the bank of the river, called her dogs, and made her way back to her truck. Feeling good about her catch, the girl smiled, knowing she had saved the trout.

Twinkle Toes, however, was not smiling. She was quivering from nose to tail fin and still could not believe she had survived. Her lip, pierced by the hook, was throbbing, and she tasted blood from the wound. This was a lesson she would not forget, and she vowed to *never* be hooked again. But how? Where would she go? She had to live in the river, but nowhere seemed safe. As she cautiously swam, she recalled the tale she had heard about the legendary beaver dam. She had never seen it herself, but the avowed legend was that any trout who could make the leap over the dam would be safe forever. She decided this would be her mission and returned home to tell her mother of her decision.

Exhausted, Twinkle Toes swam home. Upon her daughter's arrival, her mother took one look at her swollen and cut lip and knew what had happened. She had been caught by a hook. Twinkle Toes told her mother of the terrifying experience. Not only had she gotten hooked, but wolves had tried to eat her. Her mother was horrified and scolded her for not being more careful. Twinkle Toes, feeling shame for the first time in her life, told her mother she would never be caught again. She recalled the legend of the beaver dam and resolved to find it and live there in safety. Her mother, doubtful, said even if it truly did exist, making the jump over the dam would be suicide. Twinkle Toes considered the warning, but fear motivated her to pursue her quest.

She spent the night with her mother, snuggled next to her for comfort. Sadly, she knew she would never swim with her mother again. Twinkle Toes had made her decision, and tomorrow she would search for the beaver dam. Whatever happened, it would be better than being hooked again and attacked by wolves.

The next day dawned, and Twinkle Toes wrapped her lime-colored fins around her mother in one last hug goodbye. Her mother, with tears falling from her eyes, gave Twinkle Toes a small sack.

"What is this, Mother?" asked the little trout.

"I know how you love my river sugar cookies, and they are the only thing I have to give you for your journey. There are enough cookies to last you several days. The recipe is written on a piece of river grass in the sack, so keep it with you always. It will make you think of home. Be careful, Twinkle Toes, and know I love you," said her mother.

She took one last look at her mother and the home she had always known, grabbed the sack of sugar cookies with her fin, and, with a swish of her tail fin, swam away. She was determined to find that beaver dam and be safe forever.

Not wanting to get caught again, Twinkle Toes swam only at night. During the daylight, she never fed, fearing man and his hidden hooks. She would find a safe spot under a rock and rest. She asked all she met if they knew of the beaver dam. The other trout had heard of the legend, but none knew of the dam's location. They all thought she was foolish in her quest and regarded her with jealousy and disdain. Secretly the other trout wished they were as beautiful and talented as Twinkle Toes and envied her courage to find a safe home. After all, most of them either knew a trout who had been hooked or had personally experienced the terror.

Twinkle Toes had traveled a great distance, and although her hope was dwindling, she continued on her quest, against the advice of every trout she encountered. Her goal was so great and her focus so intense, she paid no attention to the sneers and whispers coming from the other trout. Twinkle Toes was a kind and friendly trout, and it never occurred to her the others were envious of her beauty and talents. Even if it had, it would not have deterred her from her goal.

Alone and tired, Twinkle Toes searched and searched for the beaver dam. "What if it doesn't really exist?" she fretted. "Oh, it must. It has to, or my mission will have been in vain."

She contemplated life in the river without safety, and her fear of being hooked continued to haunt her. Her lip, still somewhat swollen, was a constant reminder of the danger she faced living in the river. Lost in thought, she did not see the obstacle in front of her, and her nose smashed into a pile of logs.

"Ouch!" she cried. Reversing direction, she swam to the surface of the water.

With her head ever so slightly above the water, she looked around and saw she was at a fork in the river. One side flowed through downstream, but the other side had a massive tower of logs, mud, and willow sticks built so high she could not see over the top.

"*This must be it!*" she cried. "The beaver dam! It does exist! *I have found the beaver dam!*"

Suddenly she froze, motionless in the water. Hundreds of fish bones were strewn all over the front and sides of the dam. She shuddered in fear, and the sight made her feel ill. The legend told of the many trout who had tried to jump the dam to reach safety, but none were known to have succeeded.

"These must be the skeletons of all the fish who have tried and failed to reach the other side," she realized.

The horrific sight terrified her, and her dream of finding a safe place to live seemed hopeless. Pausing, she looked at the mass graveyard of fish bones and began to assess the situation.

"I can leap higher than any other trout in the river," she exclaimed. "Surely I can leap to the other side."

Before fear could dissuade her from her mission, she turned and dove into the river. She scanned the riverbed, looking for a deep hole, as the water was shallow on the front side of the dam. She thought if she could dive deeply enough, she could gain a lot of speed and easily leap out of the water and over the dam.

There it was, a hole in the riverbed! She swerved and dove into the hole, and as the bottom approached, she made a sharp U-turn and headed for the surface with great speed. With an enormous swish of her tail fin and powerful flap of her fins, she exploded from the river and flew toward the dam. The jump was huge, but not huge enough.

Her body smashed into the maze of sticks and bones, and Twinkle Toes screamed as she plummeted back into the river. She surfaced, coughing and spitting from the pain of the impact. She had come too far to give up now, and her leap was close. She knew she could make it, and she had to keep trying.

She dove to the bottom of the hole again and burst through the surface of the water with another great leap. Again she hit the graveyard wall and fell into the water, bouncing off bones, logs, and sticks. Pain screamed from every scale on her body, but she would not give up. She had come too far to be defeated. Gasping in pain from the impact of her failed leaps, she slowly flapped her fins in the water as she looked up at the carcass-ridden dam.

"If I cannot jump this dam, no trout can!" cried Twinkle Toes.

With her body throbbing from her failed attempts, she paused to survey her situation. Perhaps she did not have enough speed coming out of the hole. She swam as fast as she could from the bottom of the hole, to no avail. She looked around and noticed the river below the dam was shallow but had many large rocks strewn haphazardly throughout its course.

Maybe I'm going about this all wrong, she thought. *Maybe a longer swim to build up more speed would do the trick. The other trout must have tried to use the same hole to build up speed, and look what happened to them.*

She shuddered, looking at the wall of death before her. It was the only option left, as another crash against the dam would ensure she would end up with the rest of the fish bones. She slowly swam downriver, noting the positioning of the river rocks in the shallow water, and plotted her path. The current was not strong, but she knew she would be swimming upstream, against the flow of the water. She would have to take the force of the current into consideration for the length of her run. She had one last chance to make it over the dam. If she missed, it would end in disaster. At the speed she would be swimming, a crash into the dam would result in instant death.

Some distance from the dam, Twinkle Toes stopped and turned back toward the dam. This was her final chance. There was no other way. She would have to swim with all the speed she could muster and, at the very last moment, leap into the air and over the dam. Her arc had to be perfect. If she took off too soon, she might not make the distance. Her timing had to be perfect. If she took off too late, she would leap directly into the wall of the dam. With one last look at her path and the height of the methodically built structure, knowing this was her only chance at a safe and happy life, she dove under the water and began to swim toward her destiny.

Twinkle Toes swished her tail fin side to side with all her strength, her side fins whirring in a constant spin. She zigged and zagged, dodging the river rocks obstructing her path. Faster and faster she swam as she neared the dam, torpedoing past the rocks, cutting a perfect path toward the dam. Everything around her became a blur as she focused solely on the jump.

Suddenly her nose broke through the surface, and with one final massive swish of her tail fin, she flew through the air in an enormous leap. She flapped her side fins to give her flight as she catapulted through the air. With a leap so gigantic, Twinkle Toes appeared to hang in midair as she approached the top of the dam. There was no turning back. With one last swish of her tail fin, Twinkle Toes soared over the top of the dam and slammed into the water with a massive *splash*. The impact was so forceful it would have broken all the bones of a normal trout. Twinkle Toes sank to the bottom of the pond, feeling the excruciating pain that ran through her body. She slowly moved her tail fin, her side fins…and then wriggled her body. She was alive!

She gently flipped her tail fin and headed for the surface. As her face popped out of the water, she was stunned by the vision before her. She was in a large pond with calm water and a gentle bank incline on two sides. There was a beautiful waterfall at the opposite end of the dam, filling the pond with fresh water from the mountain runoff. The pond was surrounded on one side by massive pine trees, and on the other, there was a large clearing of grass and wildflowers. She had made it! She had jumped over the beaver dam!

She had begun to twirl in delight when, without warning, there was a loud slap on the water. She froze. Slowly she turned and scanned the pond but saw nothing. With her back to the forest, she heard soft giggling and then what sounded like applause. She spun around and saw five beavers sitting on the riverbank, slapping their tails on the ground and clapping their hand like paws.

"Bravo! Bravo!" they shouted. "Magnificent!" they cried.

"You are the first trout to have leaped over our dam," said the largest beaver. "Many have tried and, sadly, met their death, but you have succeeded where all others have failed. Bravo!" And they all cheered.

Twinkle Toes stared at the beavers. They appeared to be a family, with two very large parents and three smaller kits. She had never actually seen a beaver up close before, and she thought they were very odd-looking creatures. They had small ears, beady little eyes, large paddle tails, and huge orange front teeth. Hearing them speak, she had to stop herself from giggling. When the beaver pronounced a word with an "s" sound, it came out with a whistle due to their comical oversize teeth.

The five beavers slid into the water and approached Twinkle Toes, but she feared them. She had not thought about what it would be like to live among them, only that she needed a safe place to live. She worried they would kill her and then eat her.

The beavers, sensing her fear, stopped, and the largest said, with a very obvious whistling lisp, "Please do not fear us, little trout. We will not harm you. You are the first trout to grace our pond, and we invite you to live happily and safely with us." And they all cheered again, clapping their front paws and pounding their tails on the surface of the water.

She fought hard not to giggle with every whistle. "Thank you very much, beavers. I am Twinkle Toes Trout, and I have come a very long way in order to avoid being hooked by man and attacked by wolves. Oh my! I have had such a journey. Am I really safe?"

"Yes, my dear," said the mother beaver. "You have impressed us greatly, not only with your amazing leaping skill but also with your beauty. We would be happy and proud to share our pond with you and will offer you our protection. If ever there is danger about, we will slap our tails on the water to warn you to dive."

Twinkle Toes could no longer hold in her laughter. The whistling *s*'s were just so distracting. Not wanting to be rude or offend the beavers, she composed herself and asked, "But how will I ever leave this pond? I don't think I can make that jump again."

The large father beaver replied, "If you ever have need to leave the pond, wait until you grow into a full-size trout. You will then be much stronger, and now that you know the secret technique required, you can easily make the leap whenever you want to explore the river. But know that once you leave the pond, we cannot protect you. So be wise, Twinkle Toes, and only leave the pond at night, when danger is not present."

"That is very good advice and I will take heed. May I show you my gratitude with a little dance? It is what I do best," she humbly offered.

"Oh my!" they all exclaimed. "Yes, please dance for us!"

Their unison whistling was too much. Giggling, Twinkle Toes dove to the bottom of the pond and broke through the surface in a magnificent flip with a double twist, splashing back into the water. Loud applause erupted from the beavers. She surfaced and rose up on her tail fin, then began to sing in a beautiful and haunting voice, all the while swishing back and forth through the pond.

They grinned and applauded her performance. "Bravo again, little trout, and welcome to our pond."

Twinkle Toes finished singing and told the beavers she was very tired and needed to rest after her long journey. As they nodded in understanding, she said, "Thank you, my friends, for allowing me to share your pond. After what I have been through, I already feel safer." She then waved her fin and disappeared under the water. The beavers grinned and wandered off into the forest to gather some willow branches for dinner.

Twinkle Toes swam to the bottom of the beaver pond and found a small den that would be perfect for her private home. She gathered some river grass with her fins and wrapped it around herself like a blanket to keep her warm. As she nibbled on the last of her mother's sugar cookies, she thought about her adventure and her new friends. Exhausted, she fell fast asleep.

The next day, Twinkle Toes awoke with a start. She was disoriented. "Where am I?" she asked herself. Her memory snapped into place, and she realized she was safe in her new home in the beaver pond. She lazily stretched her fins and slowly swam to the surface. It was a wonderful day and the sun was shining brightly. She thought it was a perfect day to sun herself on the pond bank, as she knew she would be safe with the beavers nearby. With a slight flip of her tail fin, she flopped onto the bank. She stretched again in the warm sun and smiled at her newfound home and happy life. Rolling over toward the pond, she put her fin under her head to rest. Closing her eyes, she began to hum. She was delirious with joy. A short while later, she opened her eyes and looked down at the pond. She was bewildered by the vision she saw in the smooth water.

"I thought I was the only trout in this pond! Who are you?" she asked the vision.

There was no response. She tightly closed her eyes, as if to block out the apparition. Then ever so slowly she reopened her eyes and peered into the water again. Her doppelgänger appeared before her, yet again. The realization suddenly hit her: she was seeing *her* reflection in the water. She had never seen herself before and could not stop staring. She was beautiful.

Stunned by her beauty, Twinkle Toes could not take her eyes off the image she reflected on the clear water. She was not just pretty, or even beautiful, she was magnificent! She turned this way and that, looking at every part of herself in the reflection. She had never seen another trout in the river with such vibrantly colored scales and so many perfectly placed spots. She smiled and hugged herself with her fins out of pure joy. Then she gasped in horror.

"*My lips!*" she cried. "My beautiful lips are scarred from that nasty hook."

She stared into the water and began to softly cry. Her lower lip had a small scar that she had not realized was there.

"Oh, how the other trout must have thought me ugly and deformed," she wailed.

The truth was, the scar was so small that no other trout had even noticed it was there. But having just discovered her beauty, Twinkle Toes was devastated by the small flaw. She looked at her reflection again and gasped, putting her fin over her mouth to hide her defect.

"Oh, this is just horrible," she moaned. "I'm so amazingly beautiful, but my lip is gruesome and ugly. What will I do with the rest of my life if I am flawed and hideous looking?"

So taken by her beauty at first sight, Twinkle Toes saw her flaw as an insurmountable obstacle to her happiness. She hid her face in shame as she cried on the bank of the pond.

One of the beaver kits heard Twinkle Toes crying and swam up to ask her what was wrong.

"Why are you crying, Twinkle Toes? I thought you were so happy to be safe in our pond," whistled the kit.

"Oh, you wouldn't understand," whimpered the trout.

"I can't help you if you won't tell me what's wrong," pressed the kit.

"It's the scar on my lip. I'm so beautiful, but the scar makes me so ugly." Embarrassed by the flaw, Twinkle Toes moved her fin slightly to show the kit her scar.

"That? That's why you are so upset? Why, it's barely noticeable. You are far too beautiful to let a tiny scar get you so upset," consoled the kit.

"You don't understand. I just saw my reflection in the water for the first time. I never knew I was so beautiful. That dastardly hook has ruined my lips," stammered Twinkle Toes. "Now I must hide my face in shame." She continued to cry, again covering her face with her fin.

"I have just the thing." The kit dove, disappearing beneath the surface of the pond.

Moments later the kit resurfaced in front of the weeping trout. "Here, rub this on your lips and it'll hide your scar," announced the kit, quite proud of himself for finding a solution.

Twinkle Toes looked at the kit from behind her fin and saw he had something orange and thick in his paw. "What is that?" she asked.

"It's clay from the riverbanks. We use it to seal up the holes in our dam. It will hide your scar. Put a little on your lips and see," exclaimed the excited kit.

Hesitantly Twinkle Toes reached out with her fin and took a dab of the clay from the kit's paw. She leaned over and, looking at herself in the pond, smoothed the orange clay over her lips. The result was astonishing. The orange over her yellow lips turned her lips a brilliant red and hid her scar. In fact, her lips were now more beautiful than ever, and she smiled in satisfaction.

"Oh, you are a genius, *suga!*" She stared at herself in the pond. "I am more magnificent than ever. You must bring me some clay every day, *suga*, so I can be beautiful all the time," she exclaimed.

"Okay," agreed the beaver, "but why did you call me, *suga*? That's not my name," stated the kit. The beaver's whistle, emphasizing *suga*, made Twinkle Toes giggle.

"Because you made me beautiful again, and because I love the sugar cookies that my mom made for me, and…I don't know…just because." She giggled again.

The kit noticed something was very different and strange about this trout. She was beautiful indeed, scar or no scar, but now she was talking in a fancy way, sort of drooling her words from those red lips. And calling him *suga*? How embarrassing.

"Well, I have to go now, but I will keep you supplied with clay each day for your lips. They do look very red and pretty, and your scar doesn't even show."

The kit noticed Twinkle Toes wasn't at all paying attention and hadn't heard a word he had said. She was so immersed in her vision in the pond that she was deaf to his words of praise. With a flip of his tail, he dove into the pond and swam away to join the other kits in the forest for some play. She was a strange trout, he thought as he swam away, but he liked her. How could he not like something so beautiful?

Now that her lips had been repaired and her beauty had been restored to perfection, Twinkle Toes was on cloud nine. While she stared at her reflection in the beaver pond, her narcissism blossomed. Her persona became consumed with an irrational love of her own beauty. She had decided her home, her beauty, and her amazing talent was all she needed. Not being able to take her eyes off her reflection, she began to softly sing, the words revealing her brazen self-love. She was beautiful, talented, and very amusing, and it was difficult not to adore her. As she sang herself a love song, Twinkle Toes slid into the pond and danced slowly, enjoying every moment of her newfound life, completely in love with herself.

As Twinkle Toes finished her love song, she flipped onto the pond bank, hugged herself, and cooed "'*Anything worth doing is worth doing slowly*'" while she continued to admire her reflection.

CHAPTER 4

TWINKLE TOES spent her days on the banks of the pond, sunning herself and staring at her magnificent vision in the water. With one fin almost always in the water, she frequently splashed herself to wet her gills and scales. Now and again, the beaver family would pop by to say hello, but their new neighbor was far more interested in looking at herself than conversing with them. That was just fine with them, for they kept quite busy managing the dam, foraging for food, and playing. Summer was also their time to begin cutting wood to build their lodge in the fall, which would serve to protect them during the winter. They traveled daily into the woods to cut down small trees with their powerful teeth. Then, one by one, they dragged the logs back to their pond.

On particularly warm days, the busy beavers would take a break and slide into the pond to cool off. Twinkle Toes, sensing an audience, would dive deep and then rise out the water in a magnificent, soaring leap. The beavers loved watching her perform and would clap their paws and slap their tails in appreciation. The beautiful trout's dancing feats were awe-inspiring, and the bigger she grew, the higher she leaped. She would dance on her tail fin across the pond to the delight of the beavers and perform spectacular jumps, twists, and flips. Sometimes the beavers could not bear to simply watch, so they would slide into the pond and swim around Twinkle Toes, slapping their tails in play. They wanted to be part of her show, and she enjoyed having backup.

Occasionally, while they were out gathering wood, they would hear her singing in a slow and sultry voice. They all agreed she was indeed a superbly talented trout, and they enjoyed having her live in their pond, even if she did seem rather self-absorbed.

Twinkle Toes had undeniably changed. Now that her beauty was completely restored, she was more enraptured by herself than ever. She spent most of her days looking at her reflection in the pond, bewitched by her own beauty. But she was not stupid. She discovered she could use the reflection in the pond to alert her of any threat that might approach, but her own conceit kept her attention focused upon herself. She tried her hardest to pay attention to this added safety feature, but she was not as diligent as was necessary to keep her safe. Surely there would come a time when an enemy might sneak up on her when the beavers were not around to sound their warning…an enemy that might cause her harm. But she was so taken by her own beauty that her guard was lax. Nevertheless, the danger was *very* real.

Twinkle Toes had also adopted an entirely new way of speaking. It was as if she had morphed into another trout. She spoke in a slow and sultry fashion, and words drooled off her lips. Her conceit had taken over her entire being. She fancied herself completely irresistible, and her voice, speech, and mannerisms matched her movie star aura. To cap off her chameleonlike change, she thought it quite grand to call everyone *suga*. Twinkle Toes was not cruel or mean to anyone. And she was most appreciative of the beavers for sharing their pond with her. But once she realized how beautiful she truly was, something just changed. She would never be the naive, innocent, sweet little trout she had always been. Life had taught her a harsh lesson, and she was determined not to repeat the mistakes of her past. However, it was her future mistakes that should have worried Twinkle Toes.

On a beautiful sunny day, Twinkle Toes was lounging along the bank of the pond, lazily splashing herself with one fin in the water, when she noticed something floating nearby. Perhaps it had come over the waterfall. She flipped her tail fin and slid into the water to investigate. There was a clear vessel bobbing along the water, and as she approached it, she had an idea. What a perfect container to put a drink in while she sunned herself. She loved the slime that grew under the banks of the pond. She often hovered along the edge and sipped at the slimy goo, so having a cup would be just perfect. She could mix the slime with water and drink it while she was sunning. She pushed the cup to the edge of the pond with her nose and scooped up the slime and water.

Then she grabbed the cup with both of her side fins, and with one swish of her tail fin, she rose up and set the cup on the bank.

"Oh, this will be wonderful," she exclaimed. "Now I can relax in the sun and drink my favorite drink while I spend more time looking at myself."

While she leaned over the bank, admiring her beauty, a fat, juicy bug landed on the water. It looked very tasty, but she was so enjoying looking at herself that she did not want to trouble with the bug. She was hungry though, and that gave her an idea. She slid back into the water and swam over to the dam. Grabbing a small twig with her teeth, she tugged until it dislodged from the tangle of twigs and branches. She chewed one end of the stick until it formed a sharp point. Holding the stick tightly between her teeth, she swam just below the surface of the water, and when a bug landed, she would lunge at it and impale it with her sword. She continued until the stick was stacked with bugs. Flipping herself back onto the bank, with her snack stick between her teeth, she dropped it into her delicious cocktail of pond slime.

"Perfect!" she exclaimed, and resumed staring at herself in the pond, drinking, and nibbling on the tasty bugs when the desire arose.

The more Twinkle Toes stared at her reflection in the water, the more she became oblivious to the dangers of the forest. Suddenly she heard a loud slap on the water, and instinctively she flipped into the pond. The beavers were nowhere to be seen. They had sounded the alarm for danger and quickly disappeared. Not knowing what danger might be imminent, but always curious, Twinkle Toes surfaced just enough to see what threat might be lurking nearby. Looking down at her, from the clearing next to the pond, was a gigantic wolf... the biggest she had ever seen. Twinkle Toes had seen wolves before—in fact, two had tried to eat her—but never one as big and majestic as *this* wolf.

Wolfrik von Spice was massive, with long legs and a body that was lean and muscular. His fur was exquisite. The fur on the wolf's face was a creamy-almond color, framed by dramatic markings of rich blues and nutmeg. Traveling down his long neck, his fur thickened, creating a luxurious mane with deep shades of blue blended with nutmeg hues and hints of almond, merging into a point at the bottom of his powerful chest. The same colors marked his powerful body, and his long legs and belly were paler, melding the colors of almond and nutmeg. The fur undercoat of his muscular body was layered with the same palette, only paler and softer. His tail was long and full, fading from dark to light blue, with tufts of nutmeg and a cream tip at the end. The wolf had large, furry ears that were trimmed in dark blue. His one eye was a deep golden amber with a jet-black pupil, and over the other, he wore a black eye patch. A cream silk scarf was draped around his neck, adding to the magnificence of the dashing wolf.

He was the most handsome and fearsome animal Twinkle Toes had ever seen, and she stared in disbelief. The wolf saw the shock and fear on her face, and he clicked his back paws together, bowed his nose to the ground, and grinned, showing his very white and very large teeth. Not to be outdone by this superb specimen in front of her, she dove deep into the pond, reversed direction, and gaining speed, she burst through the glass surface in an enormous leap. In midair she spun three times and performed two and a half flips before cleanly nose-diving back into the pond. She surfaced, and still feeling the need to prove her superiority over this impressive wolf, she rose onto her tail fin, dancing and spinning around the pond. She slipped back into the water and surfaced with a very flirtatious smile across her beautiful red lips.

The wolf bowed again and, with a heavy German accent, said, "Well done, little trout! That was quite *zee* performance."

Twinkle Toes smiled again and, in her most sensual voice, replied, "'*I'm a "trout" of very few words…but lots of action.*'"

The wolf frowned at the arrogance of the little trout. "You know, I could eat you if I so desired," said the wolf with a mischievous grin on his face.

"But you won't, will you, *suga?*" she answered with an air of confidence and challenge in her voice.

"And why would you think I will not eat you, little trout?" asked the wolf with a devilish grin as he teasingly licked his lips.

"Because I have been through far too much to be eaten by you, and really, *suga*, am I not far too beautiful to eat?" She winked at the massive wolf.

"You are correct, little trout. I shall not eat you, because you are indeed quite beautiful."

Twinkle Toes smiled her most alluring smile, and the wolf once again bowed his nose to the ground.

"My name is Wolfrik von Spice and I am from Germany. And you are…?" he asked.

"I'm named Twinkle Toes Trout and I'm the best dancer in the river. I was caught by a fisherman's hook, and then she tried to feed me to her wolves. I searched a very long time for a safe place to live, and I'm the only trout to have ever made the leap over the dam into this pond. The beavers protect me by alerting me when danger is afoot," she stated with great pride.

"I fear, Twinkle Toes, that because you are so mesmerized by your own reflection, you will someday meet a most terrible end. I could have easily sneaked up on you, as I was watching you for quite some time from *zee* forest. But you have captured my heart with *zee* tale of your harrowing journey and with your beauty and talent, and for that I will do my best to always protect you as well."

In a great effort to appear humble, Twinkle Toes grinned and responded, "'*I never loved another the way I love myself,*' *suga*," and she twirled in the water, hugging herself with her fins.

Wolfrik von Spice was not quite sure how to respond to this narcissistic little trout, but before he had the chance, she continued. "You are a most powerful wolf, and I've no doubt you can protect me. But, *suga*, why do you wear *zee* eye patch?" she inquired, teasingly winking at the wolf. "And why are you called Wolfrik von Spice?"

Liking Twinkle Toes, and admiring her for her bravery and her humor, Wolfrik von Spice decided to confide in the little trout and share his horrific memories with her. Sensing he was uncomfortable about his eye patch, she dove to the bottom of the pond and grabbed a piece of river grass. She tied it around her head so it covered one eye, just like his eye patch. She then flipped onto the bank and leaned on her fin, then with great effort gave Wolfrik her full attention.

When he looked down and saw what she had done, he heartily laughed. She had certainly caught him by surprise. Wolfrik was not prone to laughter, for he was a most serious wolf, but it felt good to feel the emotion as he warmed to the little trout. Twinkle Toes's display of compassion was uncharacteristic for her, but she had never met such an alluring animal, and she could not help but give him her full attention. Perhaps beneath all her arrogance and vanity, she indeed had a kind heart. Wolfrik did not have any friends, for he traveled and lived alone, and he trusted absolutely no one. The one and only time he had, had ended in disaster and death for his beloved family.

Wolfrik began to tell Twinkle Toes of his life growing up in Germany. His parents were very powerful wolves in the forest and were respected by all. His father was the alpha of their pack and had chosen his mother for her own bravery and, of course, her beauty. She had the same soft-blue, almond, and contrasting dark blue markings that adorned Wolfrik. He had two brothers and two sisters, but he was the standout of the litter. His mother noticed, the moment he was born, that he was different, and she instinctively knew he would grow up to be a great and most powerful leader of all the wolves. As a pup, Wolfrik played with his siblings and wrestled with them constantly, but knowing he was bigger and stronger, he never took advantage of them and never played too roughly. Whenever the other pups in the pack tried to bully his brothers or sisters, he protected them without hesitation. His mother knew this was a sign he would be a strong and fair leader.

Wolfrik and his siblings were taught never to stray too far from their den, for danger might be lurking close by. One typical spring day, while their mother was cleaning their den and the alpha was out hunting, Wolfrik heard what he thought was a low growl coming from a large, nearby bush. His siblings were so focused on their wrestling match, they did not hear the sound.

Wolfrik cautiously stalked the bush, ready to attack anything that might threaten him or his pack. Thinking the noise was probably another pack pup teasing them, he crawled toward the bush, low on his belly, and with a playful pounce, he flew through the air and landed on the bush. He heard a cry as he landed right on top of another wolf pup. The pup was terrified and tried to claw and scratch at Wolfrik to defend himself. Wolfrik, not recognizing the pup, used his superior weight to pin the pup on his back and, with a ferocious growl, held him firmly underneath him. To his surprise, the pup began to whimper and scream, and Wolfrik could see the fear in his eyes. He stared down at his catch and eased his hold as the pup squirmed to free himself.

"Who are you, and why have you intruded upon our territory?" demanded Wolfrik, trying to act tough in order to intimidate the smaller pup.

The pup sputtered and whined and stuttered as he tried to get out his words. "Let me go! Please, let me go! I'm alone and lost, and my pack is gone. Please let me go!"

Wolfrik softened his grip further as tears welled up in the little wolf's eyes. "Wolves outside our pack are not welcome here," he stated firmly.

The small pup began to shake, and Wolfrik could see he was truly frightened. "Why have you trespassed into our territory?" he asked again.

"Because I did not know what else to do to survive. I am tired and hungry, and have nowhere else to go," he said fearfully, his stuttering worsening. "I was hoping to find a kind pack to take me in and make me part of their family," he whimpered softly.

Wolfrik could barely make out his words. "Do not be absurd. Don't you know outsiders are killed when they cross into our territory?"

By now the pup was clearly distraught, and Wolfrik began to take pity on him. He was a handsome little wolf, and Wolfrik could not help but notice he was alarmingly thin and filthy.

"How long have you been wandering by yourself?" he asked.

"I do not really know, but it seems like a long time. I have been mostly hiding so I would not be eaten. You and *zee* others looked like you were having so much fun; I thought, just maybe, you would let me join you. Perhaps I could meet your alpha, and he will take me into his pack," said the little wolf, sniffling and stuttering.

"He would never allow it!" cried Wolfrik. "He will kill you *zee* moment he lays eyes on you."

"Oh, please, help me. If you ask him, maybe he would let me join his pack. I am alone and can do none of you harm, and you are all bigger and stronger than me. Please, would you at least try? It's *zee* only chance I have. Otherwise, I will starve or be killed. I have nothing left to lose," said the lone pup desperately.

Wolfrik took a long look at this rogue wolf pup and knew that without his help, this pup would surely die. Although that was certainly the way of the wild, his sense of fair play told him he should intercede on the pup's behalf with his father. Perhaps the alpha would allow him to join their pack and become a brother. The stronger his pack became, the better chance they would all have to successfully hunt and survive.

"I am Wolfrik von Spice, of *zee* pack von Spice. I will take you to my father and ask if you can join our pack. And stop your stuttering. My father will not be impressed by a stuttering outsider. What is your name?" he asked.

The young wolf sputtered in fear, "*Zee* alpha is your father?"

"Yes, my father is *zee* alpha of our pack. I am next in line to be alpha. What is your name, young pup?" asked Wolfrik, becoming impatient with all the outsider's questions.

"I am called Bardawulf. My mother said it means 'ax wolf' and that someday I would grow up to be a strong and great leader. I am sorry. I only stutter when I am scared. I think she must have given me *zee* wrong name." Bardawulf began to whimper again.

"Stop your whimpering!" demanded Wolfrik. "My father will not tolerate a whiny pup, so act like *zee* name you have been given, and be strong. That will impress him."

Bardawulf stood up, legs shaking, and Wolfrik noticed he was bigger than he had originally thought. Not as big as he, but clearly this pup would grow into a strong and powerful wolf. He hoped his father would be pleased and view him as an asset to the pack.

"Follow me, Bardawulf. We will go meet my father." As he turned, he teasingly growled at his siblings and led them all back to their den.

The alpha had not yet returned from his hunt, and Wolfrik's mother was busily sweeping out their den. When she saw her pups approaching, she went to greet them, then froze when she saw the intruder trailing at the back of the pack. As she crouched back on her haunches, her ears went flat against her head, and she snarled in disapproval.

Just as she was about to leap and kill the stranger, Wolfrik cried out, "Mother, wait! This is Bardawulf and he is alone. He has lost his pack and is hungry and would like to join our pack to live and hunt with us. Please, Mother, he has nowhere else to go and will not survive long without our safety." Wolfrik pleaded with his mother not to kill Bardawulf.

The large she-wolf crept around her pups and positioned herself between them and the intruder. In a low growl, she asked, "Why have you come here, and what do you want?"

Bardawulf looked up at the very protective she-wolf standing between him and her pups, and hesitantly responded with just enough of a stutter to evoke sympathy from her. "I am alone without a pack and am not big enough or old enough to survive on my own. I know it is not *zee* way of *zee* wolf, but please, may I join your pack? Wolfrik said you would help me." The sly wolf lowered himself to the ground in his most submissive posture.

The she-wolf had a kind heart, and this little pup was certainly brave to have come into another pack's territory. Perhaps he would grow to be a good and strong hunter and help provide for the pack von Spice. Her stance softened and her ears perked up slightly. The glow in her eyes told Bardawulf he had won her over. Maybe. He knew one thing for sure: he could not trust anyone, and never would. But he needed the companionship and protection of a pack, and this was his only chance. If they refused him, he would be killed. Even that big brute Wolfrik could easily kill him, for he was not as old and not nearly as big…yet.

Taking a risk, Bardawulf slowly and humbly crawled on his belly to the she-wolf and submissively licked her paws. The she-wolf looked down and her heart melted. "I cannot make *zee* final decision. We will have to wait until our alpha returns. His decision will be final." And with that, she turned and disappeared inside the den.

Bardawulf felt a great sense of relief sweep over him, knowing he had played his hand well…so far. The best he could hope for was that Wolfrik and his mother would plead his case and beg the alpha of the pack to allow him to live. The she-wolf continued her chores in the den but kept a watchful eye on Bardawulf. He was a scrawny wolf pup, she thought, but with some food and time, she knew he would grow into a formidable wolf. She admired his bravery but also believed his humility was genuine. Time would eventually prove that her instincts about Bardawulf could not have been more wrong.

The tired and hungry pup sat off by himself near the entrance to the den. He had the saddest and most forlorn look on his face the she-wolf had ever seen. He was so thin, and his ribs protruded through his mangy fur. She knew he must be starving, and there was no telling when the alpha would return with food. She decided to make the pack's favorite wolf treat in the world.

The German pack von Spice had been in the territory for many generations, and the spice cookie recipe had been handed down from she-wolf to she-wolf. It was a coveted recipe and had never been shared with another pack. Wolfrik von Spice loved his mother's spice cookies, and he was always first in line when she baked.

Oh, how she loved Wolfrik. He was her pride and joy, and the most magnificent pup she had ever seen. He was big for his age and strong, and he had a brave heart. Further, he was kind and patient with his siblings. She knew he would someday take over the pack von Spice. Thus, she had named him Wolfrik, which meant "wolf ruler."

The she-wolf hoped her cookies would perk up the sad little Bardawulf. The aroma of the spice cookies began to drift through the air, and Bardawulf did indeed perk up. He had not eaten for days and was so hungry that the smell wafting past his nose caused his stomach to growl and his mouth to water. Curious, Bardawulf crept closer to the den to take a peek inside. He saw the she-wolf scooping cookies onto a flat piece of wood. With his hunger getting the better of him, he took another step closer before realizing he must show some respect for the hierarchy of the pack. If he was to be accepted, he had to remember his place. Wolfrik was older and bigger than he, so he stepped back and waited.

Wolfrik was rolling around in front of the den, playing with his siblings, when he caught the scent of his mother's spice cookies. That was a smell he knew well, and when he saw his mother exit the den with a plateful, he disentangled himself from his siblings and scampered over to be the first in line for a cookie. The she-wolf presented the cookies to her son, and he grabbed a handful with his large paw. As he was about to gobble a giant one, he saw Bardawulf out of the corner of his eye. He trotted over to the little wolf pup and handed him two very large spice cookies. Bardawulf gratefully accepted the offering and immediately gobbled them up. Wolfrik sat down next to him and quietly ate his cookies, offering another to his new friend.

"Thank you, Wolfrik," the pup said. "These are *zee* best cookies I have ever eaten." The she-wolf smiled as she watched the two pups devour her delicious cookies. She hoped the alpha would allow Bardawulf to join the pack von Spice.

Bardawulf was exhausted by the adventures of the day, and with a tummy full of spice cookies, he curled up and fell asleep next to the entrance of the den. It was almost dusk when the alpha returned from a long day of hunting, carrying the carcass of a deer to feed his family. As he entered the clearing and dropped his kill on the ground, he detected an unfamiliar smell. He noticed his pups sleeping across the clearing, and his eyes traveled toward the unknown scent. Focusing on the intruder, he growled and gathered his haunches in readiness to attack and kill to protect his pack.

Just as he was about to spring, Wolfrik cried out, "No, Father! Please, do not kill Bardawulf!"

The she-wolf ran out of the den, and she, too, cried, "Wait! Do not kill *zee* wolf pup. He has bravely come to us for protection and has asked to join our pack."

The alpha turned and growled at the she-wolf, then took a step toward Wolfrik and cuffed him with his front paw. Wolfrik tumbled from the force of his father's swipe.

"Who is this mongrel, and why is he still alive? Have I not taught all of you *zee* dangers of allowing an intruder into our midst?" The alpha growled ferociously at all of them.

"Please, Father," pleaded Wolfrik. "This is Bardawulf. I found him in *zee* woods today, and he is all alone and his entire family was murdered. He would like to become part of our pack and help to hunt and provide for us. Please, Father, let him stay."

Bardawulf had confided to Wolfrik that another wolf pack had surprised his pack in a raid and killed his entire family. He had been able to hide and narrowly escaped death. What he had not told Wolfrik was that now he was filled with hatred.

"Silence!" growled the leader. "Approach!" he commanded as he glared at the wolf pup.

Bardawulf was no fool, and he knew his time had come. He would either be allowed to join the pack, a rare occurrence, or he would be killed instantly. He looked at the leader and knew crying and begging would not impress this powerful wolf. He stood up and slowly but proudly walked over to the leader. There was no denying he was terrified, for the moment of truth was before him. But he refused to show fear in the face of this pack leader. Wolfrik looked at the scene before him and could not believe the whimpering pup he had recused was now standing before his father with his head held high, refusing to back down. In that moment, Wolfrik felt a newfound respect and kinship toward Bardawulf and hoped he would become his brother.

Bardawulf held his ground, and with a show of respect, neither did he look into the eyes of the alpha of pack von Spice, nor did he hang his head in submission. The leader towered over the young wolf pup that stood before him. Bardawulf could smell the pungent odor on the leader's body of the kill that he had brought home to the pack. It made his stomach growl. The alpha's great fangs were bared, and Bardawulf could smell the heady scent of blood. In an instant, he could be killed. But he had come this far and would not back down.

Time stood agonizingly still as the alpha sized up this filthy cur daring to ask for acceptance into his pack. His yellow eyes glared at Bardawulf like lasers, but Bardawulf did not tremble or back down. He held his stance, continuing to look at the ground. After what seemed like an eternity of silence, except for the raspy breaths coming from the alpha, he finally spoke.

"Who are you, and why have you dared to cross into our territory?" he demanded with a threatening growl.

Without looking into the eyes of the leader, Bardawulf quietly replied, "I am Bardawulf, and my pack was killed by an enemy pack. I was *zee* only survivor. My only hope is to join *zee* pack von Spice. I ask that you take me under your protection in trade for my loyalty and my willingness to become a strong and skilled hunter."

The silence was deafening. Neither the alpha nor the young pup moved a muscle. Fear and tension hung oppressively thick in the air. Bardawulf was barely breathing, and even though he acted brave, his terror of this great wolf was very real.

"Go! Help *zee* others with my kill." The alpha smacked the motionless pup with his giant paw, throwing him several feet to the side.

The she-wolf looked at her mate and smiled her approval. The alpha turned and silently stalked off into the night.

"What just happened?" mumbled Bardawulf as he picked himself up from his tumble and shook off the dirt.

"Father has accepted you into our pack," howled Wolfrik. "You are now my brother. You are Bardawulf von Spice." Wolfrik pounced on Bardawulf, and the two rolled and wrestled in a ball of fur.

"Come on, you two. Let us enjoy *zee* meal your father has provided for us." The she-wolf grabbed each pup by the scruff of the neck and pulled them apart.

The family eagerly ate the alpha's kill, and Bardawulf in particular gorged until he could not eat another bite. When the feast was over, Bardawulf thanked the she-wolf and said he wanted to be alone for a while. The rest of the pack snuggled together to sleep while Wolfrik watched his new brother walk into the dark forest. He wondered where he was going. Not long after, just as Wolfrik was about to fall asleep, he heard a long, high-pitched howl pierce the quiet of the still night. Wolfrik knew it was his brother celebrating being welcomed into the pack von Spice.

Wolfrik was wrong. The howl was not in celebration but emanated from an unbearable pain. Bardawulf stood at the top of a huge rock formation above his new pack's den. He was relieved he had been accepted by the alpha of the pack von Spice, but he would never forget the horror of seeing his own pack brutally murdered. The pain ate at him and gnawed at him until he thought he would explode with anger and hatred. He had never been a particularly well-behaved pup, but now his rage seethed within him. Any pack, even this pack, could turn on him. They could kill him at any time.

He pointed his nose toward the thin sliver of moon and howled in a high-pitched and ragged voice that was filled with deep sorrow. Tears streamed down his face as he howled and howled until his throat ached. He had been forced to beg for his life from the pack von Spice, and his humiliation disgusted him. Never again would he beg or be submissive to another wolf. Never again would he be in a position of weakness. And never would he trust or love another and risk being so unbearably hurt again.

As the seasons passed, both Wolfrik and Bardawulf grew into fine and power-ful wolves. They hunted side by side and astonished their parents with the success of their numerous kills. The pack thrived, and the alpha and she-wolf were pleased. Although Bardawulf was happy, he never let his true self show through. After witnessing his parents and siblings die at the hands of a marauding, bloodthirsty pack of wolves, he had a vengeance and hate inside him that longed for release. There had been no reason for the attack, and the nightmares he had of his family being ripped to shreds and eaten by the evil pack haunted him nightly. He had been randomly kicked aside during the fray and had hidden under a bush, undetected by the murderers. He did not share the blood of his new pack. Thus, he knew he could never trust any of them. But deep inside he desired to be important to the pack, and believed he brought the pack great value. Wolfrik had been a true and loyal brother and had defended him against their enemies many times. But still, he felt a dis-tance between them, one that Wolfrik would never understand. Wolfrik, on the other hand, could not have been prouder of the pup he had helped bring into the pack von Spice many seasons ago, for he truly thought of Bardawulf as his brother. And he trusted him with his life.

When the day came for the alpha to gather the pack von Spice and make an announcement, the pack knew what was coming. The alpha and she-wolf were getting older and no longer had the speed and strength to lead the pack von Spice. It was time to choose a new alpha. Ever since his pack had been killed, Bardawulf had longed to lead his own pack, vowing he would never allow his true blood pack to be killed. He had proven himself to this pack and believed he deserved to be their alpha. Wolfrik had no idea what was running through the mind of his brother. When the pack von Spice gathered and the alpha announced Wolfrik as the new leader, Bardawulf seethed with anger and jealousy. The choice confirmed to him that he had never truly been ac-cepted, because he was not blood. He vowed that someday he would be the alpha…no matter the cost.

As the new alpha of the pack, Wolfrik had the right to choose a mate. He had taken a special liking to a she-wolf named Adalwulf, which meant "noble wolf." She was known as Ada and was very beautiful. Unbeknownst to Wolfrik, his brother Bardawulf had eyes for Ada as well. When Bardawulf learned of his choice, he was furious. Not only had Wolfrik been chosen as the alpha, but he had now stolen his choice for a mate. This was too much, and he would have his revenge.

Wolfrik and Ada lived happily together as mates, and in the spring, Ada bore her first litter of pups. Wolfrik felt an immense sense of pride as he saw his four offspring for the first time. There were two females and two males, and he knew at first glance that they would all grow up to be strong and powerful wolves. Bardawulf was beside himself, for he was still alone. Over time, he had become quite sulky and unpleasant to be around, making it difficult for him to find a mate. It was not fair that Wolfrik had everything and he had nothing. Irrationally he decided it was time to act. He vowed to take away everything his so-called brother held dear.

At this point in his story, Twinkle Toes could see that Wolfrik was visibly upset. At the same time, she was so enthralled and excited by the wolf's tale that she had become rather overzealous in her efforts to keep herself wet. By the time she realized what had happened, she was surrounded by a puddle of water and Wolfrik was dripping wet.

"Oh my, *suga*! I was so caught up in your story, I guess I over splashed myself," she said with a sheepish grin. Wolfrik nodded with a forced grin. "You will forgive me, won't you, *suga*?" she said quite demurely. The wolf nodded. "Please, go on. I am hanging on your every word, *suga*. What happened next?"

Wolfrik shook the water from his fur and continued his tale. He told Twinkle Toes that Bardawulf was not the brother he had thought him to be.

Wolfrik left for a hunting trip, and Bardawulf stayed behind to protect the she-wolves and pups of the pack von Spice. Rarely did Bardawulf miss a hunt, but he insisted. Lying, he claimed he had seen an enemy pack recently near their territory. He would stay and keep the pack safe. Wolfrik knew how his family had been killed, so he allowed Bardawulf to stay behind, believing he would protect the pack with his life.

Bardawulf was out of his mind with hatred and rage. It did not matter to him that the pack von Spice had taken him in and embraced him as a member of the pack. It did not matter to him that Wolfrik considered him his brother and truly loved him and trusted him. Watching his family being killed had short-circuited Bardawulf's sense of rational behavior. All he could see was what he had lost and that he had been left out: left out of becoming alpha, left out of taking Ada for his mate, and left out of being a real part of the pack. He had become a demon-possessed wolf, and revenge was his only cure.

Ada was off in a nearby meadow, frolicking with her four pups, when Bardawulf picked up their scent. He tracked them to the meadow and crouched low to watch. He knew what he had to do, and blinded by rage, he stalked Wolfrik's family. Within striking distance, Bardawulf charged. Ada stood her ground, unable to defend her pups against this larger and much more powerful wolf, yet unwilling to cower before him. One by one, Bardawulf effortlessly killed Wolfrik and Ada's precious offspring.

After he had killed the last pup, Bardawulf turned to face Ada, bright red blood dripping from his fangs. Ada lowered her head, and with bared teeth and tears streaming down her face, she growled at her attacker. "Why would you betray your brother? Why? He loves you and trusts you," she screamed.

"I am surprised you would ask such a stupid question. I deserve to be *zee* alpha, and I deserve to mate with you, Ada." His face softened for a moment. "I loved you *zee* first time I saw you frolicking in *zee* meadow. But everything always goes to Wolfrik," he hissed, anger and hatred returning to his voice. "I lost my pack, my family. I watched them being torn to shreds by an enemy pack, and there was nothing I could do to help them. I relive that horror every single day. I have earned my rightful place in this pack, but it is always, always Wolfrik." The pain in Bardawulf's voice was horrific, and his face was twisted in anger and hate.

"Wolfrik took you in and protected you. He made you his brother. You hunted and fought alongside him. *How could you do this to him?*" shrieked Ada. "You were part of our pack, Bardawulf. You were! Blood did not matter. We loved you!"

Bardawulf stood breathlessly still, frozen in confusion. Had he made a mistake? Did this pack he had run with for so long really love him? Was Ada just not meant to be his? Did Wolfrik truly think of him as his brother?

Uncertainty tortured his mind, and Bardawulf felt dizzy and sick. He had just murdered all of Wolfrik's pups. And now no reason seemed good enough. But there was no turning back. Wolfrik would kill him for what he had done, so he had to finish this. If he was to survive and be happy, he had to kill Ada, and then Wolfrik. Insanity took over, and he became even more crazed with anger. Nothing made sense.

"I have murdered Wolfrik's offspring, and after I kill you, I will wait for him to return, and I will kill him too. I will finally take my rightful position in *zee* pack von Spice. I will be *zee* alpha," he howled.

"You will never be *zee* alpha," Ada screamed, as hot, painful tears streaked down her beautiful face. "You are no longer a von Spice. Wolfrik will kill you and he will still be *zee* alpha. You can never take that away from him. Never!"

All reason lost, with one terrorizing leap, Bardawulf flew through the air, fangs bared, and knocked Ada to the ground, sinking his fangs deep into her neck. She died instantly. With blood dripping from his face, he howled a scream fraught with unbearable pain, unlike anything ever heard from a wolf. It was finished.

Bardawulf skulked off to wait for Wolfrik's return, with fear, anger, and rage driving him to continue his mission. He would make the pack his own. As he approached the pack's den, Bardawulf veered off and hid in the bushes, anxiously anticipating the fight that he knew would be to the death.

Wolfrik returned from the hunt later that day with his kill in tow. It would feed his family well. He approached the large meadow near his den and caught the scent of something sickening. Death. He knew the scent all too well. He froze, dropping his kill, and every hair on his back rose in alarm. He crouched low to the ground and slowly crept into the meadow, tracking the vile scent. Suddenly Wolfrik caught his breath and began to wheeze in distress at the sight before him. Ada and all of his pups lay slaughtered in the tall grass of the meadow. He could not breathe as he struggled to gain his composure. Except for the gash on each of their necks, their bodies were not harmed.

Wolfrik could not understand the sheer horror he was witnessing. Anyone who had killed his family would have killed them for their meat or their fur. Never was a wolf left intact to rot. Searing tears fell from his golden eyes, and his breath came in sharp, painful gasps. He approached his lifeless pups. One by one, he picked them up and carried their limp bodies to their mother, laying each beside her. He then gently lay down beside Ada and the pups for the last time. He buried his nose into the thick mantle around Ada's neck and deeply inhaled the light scent of spice emanating from her fur.

Eyes blurred with tears, Wolfrik lifted his head and scanned the area, noticing large prints in the dirt. Slowly he rose to his feet and sniffed the prints, instantly knowing who had killed his family. With a rush of rage and fury, his chest swelled, and as his nose pointed toward the sky, he released a howl of desperate heartache and agony. He kept howling until he collapsed once again alongside his family, exhausted from the trauma of his loss.

Wolfrik knew he could not leave his beloved family out in the open, for they would be eaten by other predators. He clawed and dug ferociously at the ground, his grief and loss fueling his strength. Deeper and deeper he burrowed into the dirt in order to make a grave for his beloved family. When he was spent from his digging, he walked over to Ada, then gently pulled her over to the grave and pushed her into place. One by one, he carefully picked up each pup in his teeth and laid them again by her side. His massive chest heaved with sobs of grief. Tears streamed down his face as he took one last look at the family he loved so intensely. He bent over and pushed dirt into the grave with his nose. He pushed pile after pile of dirt on top of the lifeless piles of fur. When the grave was completely covered, he turned and walked away, his life now shattered.

Wolfrik loped through the meadow and into the forest. With each stride, his head cleared as he focused on the task ahead. He would find and kill Bardawulf. No other wolf had prints the size of Bardawulf's, and his scent was unmistakable. He did not need a plan. All he needed was his fury and rage and the strength to complete what he knew must be done. As he neared the pack von Spice's den, he did not need to stalk his prey. No, he could smell him and knew immediately where the coward lurked. He wanted Bardawulf to see him coming, so he boldly entered the clearing and stood, challenging his murderous enemy.

"Why did you kill my family?" Wolfrik shouted as he strode to within a few feet of his brother.

"Because you have everything and I have nothing," hissed Bardawulf. "I deserve to be alpha, and Ada should have been mine. I will no longer be subject to your rule of this pack or of me. It is mine now." Slowly he leaned on his back haunches, ears pinned back, ready to attack. His eyes burned with hatred, and his lips were tightly curled back, revealing huge, sharp fangs dripping with saliva. Dried blood from the murder of Wolfrik's family still stained his face. He now hated himself for the killings, but not nearly as much as he hated Wolfrik.

"My father brought you into this pack. We have hunted together and provided for our family together," growled Wolfrik, barely able to contain his disgust for the shameless monster before him. "I have called you brother, Bardawulf, yet you killed my family and now wish to kill me."

Wolfrik could see the slight twitch of Bardawulf's tail, and he knew he was about to strike. The rest of the pack von Spice cowered at the edge of the clearing, fearing what was about to happen but not daring to interfere. They knew this would be a fight to the death, a fight that must take place with no interference from the pack.

Bardawulf glared at Wolfrik, and although it was true, they had hunted many times together, there was no turning back. He had killed Wolfrik's family and now he must kill him. It was the only way he would survive and lead his own pack. There was no other option.

Wolfrik was stunned by the rabid hatred he saw in his brother's eyes, and knew he would never understand what had led him to such a drastic and horrific course of action. Suddenly, before another thought or emotion could wage battle in Wolfrik's mind, Bardawulf took two huge leaps and slammed into Wolfrik. The force knocked Wolfrik onto his side, but he scrambled quickly to his feet, ready for the next assault. Bardawulf came at him again, and Wolfrik met the attack with a force so great it threw Bardawulf off his feet, and he skidded into the dirt. The screams and growls that rang through the air in the next terrifying minutes were savage. Bardawulf dragged himself to his feet, and with all the strength left in his body, he lunged at Wolfrik and, in doing so, slashed Wolfrik across the face with his sharp claws, drawing blood. It wasn't enough. That was the last opportunity Bardawulf had for revenge. Wolfrik, his muscles taut, leaped through the air and landed atop his foe, knocking him to the ground. With one final strike, like that of a serpent, he sank his fangs into the neck of Bardawulf, killing him instantly. Bardawulf's limp body lay motionless on the ground.

Wolfrik stood over his brother's limp, motionless body with blood dripping from his face. He could no longer see out of his left eye. He sensed the presence of his pack nearby, but they remained silent. With one great lunge of his head toward the sky, Wolfrik let out a howl full of raw, untempered emotion and pain. It was a cry of triumph and a cry of sorrow rolled into one long, agonizing release.

The pack von Spice waited, not knowing what to do next. Wolfrik was injured and would never survive as the alpha. An injured wolf should be cast from the pack to live alone. It was simply the way of the wolf. But after what they had witnessed, no one in the pack had the courage to challenge their alpha.

Wolfrik stood panting, the blood from his wounded eye dripping down his face. "My brother has killed my family and betrayed our pack," he began in a strained, hoarse voice. "It was my duty as your leader to kill Bardawulf. Let *zee* name of Bardawulf never be spoken again," he declared. "I am injured and thus must step down as your leader. You"—he pointed to a very large and strong young wolf—"you will be *zee* new alpha of *zee* pack von Spice."

The new alpha stood and bowed in respect for the battle-torn leader of the pack von Spice. Wolfrik nodded regally and said, "I will leave and live my life in exile, but remember this, all of you: *zee* pack von Spice will, and must, survive. Never again take in an outsider, no matter what their pain or circumstance may be. Never. Our strength lies in the blood of *zee* pack. That is *zee* only thing that can be trusted. You must never let go of *zee* strength of *zee* pack."

Wolfrik took one last look at Bardawulf lying dead before him and slowly turned and walked into the woods. His head hung low in sorrow over what had unfolded. It was a day he would never forget. Blood continued to slowly drip from his injured eye, but the physical pain was nothing compared to the emotional pain he was suffering. Not only had he lost his precious mate and his pups, he had lost his one true friend and brother. He had loved Bardawulf and trusted him, and although wolf law dictated he be killed, it had been no easy battle for him. He had truly seen Bardawulf as his brother, and blood had not mattered. He was heartbroken by the magnitude of his losses.

Immersed in grief, he looked up with a start as his father and mother stepped out in front of him. They had witnessed the entire ordeal and were waiting for him.

"Father. Mother. Why are you here? I am in exile, and you should not be seen with me," he pleaded.

His father, older now but still quite an imposing wolf, took a step toward his son and said, "Wolfrik, I am sorry for all that you have lost. You have honored *zee* pack von Spice by killing *zee* one whose name will forever be unspoken. I have seen how you counted him as your brother, but I have also seen *zee* jealousy and rage he carried in his heart. This was inevitable. Leave you must, but never live in regret for what has happened, for it will eat you alive. Move forward, my son. Find a new mate and start a new pack. You have *zee* royal blood of *zee* pack von Spice running through your veins. You are a strong and skilled hunter, *zee* best I have ever seen, even better than I was in my younger days, my son. Go, forget your past. Live and be proud. Always remember *zee* strength of your pack." The elder wolf lowered his head in recognition of his son, and with a final look filled with love, respect, and heartbreak, he turned and walked slowly into the forest.

Wolfrik watched as he disappeared into the dense thicket, knowing he would never again see his father. Wolfrik's mother remained. Stepping toward her son, she gently rubbed her nose along the side of his face. Comforted by her touch, Wolfrik dropped his head, and she tenderly licked the blood from his wound.

"I cannot see with this eye, Mother," moaned Wolfrik, now feeling the physical pain from his wound.

The she-wolf continued to lick her son's face until the pain subsided. The scratches from the battle had damaged Wolfrik's left eye, and although the scratches would heal, the eye never would. He would be blind in one eye. Having recognized the severity of her son's injury during the fight, she had quickly fashioned an eye patch out of a piece of hide and now gently placed it over Wolfrik's eye, tying the laces behind his head.

"There," she exclaimed. "You look even more handsome than ever and very mysterious and dashing, my son."

She handed her son a piece of parchment and said, "Here is *zee* recipe for *zee* von Spice cookies. It has been in our pack for generations, so keep it with you always. It will always remind you of *zee* greatness of *zee* pack von Spice."

The she-wolf stepped back from her son, and with a single tear falling from her eye, she bowed low, touching her nose to the ground.

Wolfrik moved closer to her and nuzzled her along her neck, then whispered, "Thank you, Mother. I shall miss you a great deal. Father too; tell him for me. I love you both so much." And with that, he turned and loped into the depths of the forest.

"I never saw a wolf from my pack again," said Wolfrik.

Twinkle Toes was so completely spellbound by Wolfrik's story, she had not realized the sun was setting and it was getting late.

"My eye was badly damaged in *zee* battle. Thus, I wear an eye patch to hide *zee* wound." Twinkle Toes hung on his every word. "I became an operative in Germany, helping out *zee* other animals when they were threatened or in need of assistance, but eventually, I decided I *must* leave my home country. I needed a fresh start. I needed to find a place where I could be happy and forget about all that had happened. I had heard about *zee* majesty of Montana, so I decided to journey here to begin again. You now know my story, one I have not told to another living creature."

Twinkle Toes's heart ached for the magnificent wolf, and she felt like it had shattered into a million pieces. Since she had arrived at the beaver pond, she had not felt any real emotion for anyone.

Oh well, she thought. *He is a very handsome and strong wolf with a captivating yet devastating story. It would serve me well to keep this wolf as a friend, for I might be in need of a spy, and his protection will certainly come in handy.*

She then dismissed any real feelings she may have had toward the wolf. But she could not help but feel compassion for him…*that* she could not deny.

Gently stroking Wolfrik's leg with her fin as he sat in silence, she cooed, "*Suga,* that's the most exciting story I have ever heard. And you are the finest-looking wolf I have ever set eyes on, and fantastically brave too. I would be quite pleased if you would protect me from the dangers that lurk near my pond, and I would absolutely adore going on secret missions with you, *suga.* How exciting and dangerously fun. But, oh, how will I ever leave the pond?" Twinkle Toes flipped her tail fin and slid into the water with a very large pout on her luscious red lips.

"I am flattered by your offer, little trout, but I am a loner and trust no one," stated the very serious wolf.

"Oh, *suga, 'too much of a good thing can be wonderful!'* And I am certainly the best thing you have found in a long while," she giggled with delight.

She began to dance on her tail fin and spin with abandon. Then Twinkle Toes stopped, balancing on her tail fin, and looked right into Wolfrik's soulful golden eye, and with a sly grin on her face, she disappeared. It was as if the water had dropped out from underneath her. Seconds later she burst through the surface and leaped into the air, spinning and flipping in one of her most spectacular displays, then dove cleanly back into the pond. She popped up through the surface and was delighted by what she had seen on the edge of the clearing at the height of her jump.

"What is that thing over there?" she asked as she pointed to the contraption with her fin.

Wolfrik trotted over to his motorcycle, straddled the saddle, and started it with a loud *vroom,* then spun around and drove over to the pond. It was a shiny silver bike with a sidecar attached to the right side.

"Oh, *suga!* It *is* magnificent!" cried Twinkle Toes. "You will take me for a ride, won't you, *suga?*" She fluttered her fins and smiled her most alluring smile.

Wolfrik considered her request, and although he thought it quite impractical to take a trout for a ride, he knew he could not resist her. He hopped off the bike, released the sidecar, and carried it to the pond, then proceeded to fill it with water.

"How clever you are, *suga*," marveled Twinkle Toes, for she knew exactly what the wolf had in mind.

Reattaching the water-filled sidecar, Wolfrik spun around and situated the bike alongside the pond. With a flip of her tail fin, Twinkle Toes flew through the air and landed with a *splash* in the sidecar. Wolfrik pulled a cream leather pilot's cap over his head, with holes for his ears, of course, then strapped on his silver-blue goggles and started the bike with another loud *vroom*. He tossed Twinkle Toes a smaller pair of goggles that were just like his, and she strapped them on. Tingling with excitement, Twinkle Toes nodded her readiness, and off they sped through the forest.

No trout had ever experienced such a marvelously wild ride, driven by a dashing and deliciously mysterious wolf. Twinkle Toes was having the time of her life, swaying with the motion of the motorcycle as it careened along the trail. She held on to the edges of the sidecar as the wind rushed past her gills. Wolfrik was greatly amused by the little trout.

She is certainly very brave, thought Wolfrik as he swerved around a tight curve. Water splashed out of the sidecar, and Twinkle Toes laughed, holding on for dear life. As they rounded the next curve, he slowed and said, "I think that is enough for one day, my little trout. I will take you back to your pond now."

"Oh no, *suga*! I am having such a grand time. Don't you have a secret mission we can go on or something dangerous to do?" she asked, eager to keep the moment alive.

Just as Wolfrik was about to respond, a huge and very ugly coyote jumped out in front of the motorcycle, blocking their path. Wolfrik screeched to a halt, almost flinging Twinkle Toes from the sidecar, water splashing everywhere.

"If you want to live, Puck, get out of our way, *now!*" growled Wolfrik.

Twinkle Toes let out a little scream as several more coyotes skulked out of the forest, blocking their path.

"We mean you no harm, Wolfrik," said the clever coyote. "We just want to see what you have there in your sidecar. Is that a fat, juicy trout?" He licked his lips, exposing his yellow fangs.

"You are the most hideous and vile vermin I have ever seen. Be gone! Or my friend, who is much bigger and stronger than you, will eat you!" challenged Twinkle Toes.

The filthy beast laughed a hissing laugh and took a few steps toward the sidecar.

"Not another step closer, Puck," warned Wolfrik, who was now standing up over his motorcycle, ready to attack.

"Calm down, calm down. I mean this mouthy little trout no harm. You're certainly full of yourself, aren't you, little trout?" taunted Puck.

With an air of complete disinterest, Twinkle Toes replied, "'*I used to be Snow White...but I drifted.*'"

Wolfrik grinned slightly, and Puck hissed in contempt at the smart-aleck little trout. "You talk big, little trout, with your big bad wolf protecting you. I bet you will not be so smart when I catch you in your pond and *eat* you," he snarled, again baring his repulsive yellow fangs.

"*Enough!*" roared Wolfrik. "Leave now, Puck, and don't bother either of us with your threats again. Mark my words and hear me well. I will kill you and destroy your pack of filthy dogs if you ever try to hurt Twinkle Toes. Now *go!*"

Puck glared at Wolfrik and Twinkle Toes, and hissed, "This isn't over," and ran into the forest, followed by his ragtag pack of filthy dogs.

"How exhilarating!" cried Twinkle Toes. "And, *suga*, you were magnificent and so very valiant defending me against that mangy cur. You are my hero." The flirtatious trout fluttered her fins and spun in a circle in the sidecar.

To Wolfrik, this was no matter to celebrate. Puck was dangerous. He had met him upon arriving in Montana. He knew he could defeat Puck and was pretty sure Puck was not stupid enough to wage a battle with him. But Twinkle Toes was easy prey for the likes of Puck. He would have to regularly spy on Puck and keep an eye on the beaver pond to make sure the beautiful trout did not become a snack for the evil coyote.

Knowing it was useless to calm down this passionate little trout, he started the motorcycle and sped off. Wolfrik was a daredevil and loved driving at breakneck speeds through the forest, much to the delight of his partner in crime. When they arrived at the beaver pond, it was dusk, and the stars were beginning to dot the sky. Wolfrik pulled alongside the pond, and Twinkle Toes flipped her fins and leaped into the water.

"I had a marvelous time, *suga*! Don't forget to '*come up and see me sometime,*'" she said with a twinkle in her eye.

The wolf, continually amused by the extraordinary trout, responded, "I will never forget you, Twinkle Toes."

"'*No one ever does…*'" And she dove into the pond and disappeared into the dark water.

CHAPTER 5

THE DAYS OF SUMMER blurred together while Twinkle Toes thrived in the beaver pond. As much as she adored the exciting Wolfrik, she was curious about what was happening in the river. And as much as she adored the admiration of the beavers, she wanted more. It was time for her to explore the world outside the pond. She had become a large and strong trout, and her leaping skills were unmatched. Making the leap back into the beaver pond would not be an issue…she hoped. With danger always lurking during the day, Twinkle Toes knew she would have to do her exploring at night. She decided tonight would be the night. The skies were clear and there would be no moon. It was a perfect night to go out undetected. She rested, anticipating her night of adventure.

When the sun dipped deep behind the mountains and the stars began to appear, Twinkle Toes readied for her adventure. She knew the leap out of the pond would be easy, but she had to land in the deep river hole in order to avoid smashing into the river rocks in the shallow parts of the river. Having made a mental note of exactly where the hole was, she swam to the edge of the pond at the dam. It would not take a great leap, just enough to roll over the top of the dam. But hitting the hole could be tricky.

She thought about that for a moment, and with the last of the evening light barely highlighting the dam, she had an idea. She would gingerly jump onto the top of the dam instead of leaping over it, then find her mark and dive into the hole. The light was leaving quickly, so without another thought, she flipped her tail fin and landed on the top of the upper sticks of the dam. Righting herself, she balanced on her tail fin and looked down, spotting the deep darkness of the hole. With another small flip of her tail fin, she arched into the air with a deep dive down to the river. Her nose broke through the water, and she plunged straight down into the hole, veering at the bottom and coming back up to the top.

"I did it! And it was easy! Now, where to go, and what to do?" she wondered.

She began to slowly swim along the shallows of the river, enjoying the freedom of the endless water. She noticed a few schools of trout heading upriver in the same direction, and decided to follow, keeping at a distance so as not to be noticed. She was unfamiliar with this new part of the river and wanted to make sure it was safe.

As she cautiously swam close to the riverbank, more trout joined the schools, all heading in the same direction. She swam slowly as she watched the increasing numbers of trout, all swimming somewhere…but where? Then, all at once, throngs of trout seemed to just disappear. Alarmed, Twinkle Toes approached slowly, with a mixture of fear and excitement.

She heard music coming from a short distance away. As she approached, she saw a large boulder close to the riverbank. Below the boulder, the water was very deep and moved in a circular, upstream motion. Twinkle Toes knew that getting caught in an eddy was like being caught in a whirlpool. The circling current would suck a trout down to the bottom of the river.

Like a bolt of lightning striking in the sky, the eddy whirlpool magically lit up in a spectrum of colors, and the music changed, becoming lively, rhythmic, and very loud. Fish were spilling over the edge of the whirlpool, diving deep into the hole of lights. She trod water in the current alongside the eddy and was entranced by what she saw through the clear water. Allowing herself to be pulled in a little closer, she was amazed to see trout of all sizes and colors dancing along the bottom of the river to the beat of the music. Around and around they went, spinning and reeling with joyful abandon. There was actually a dance club at the bottom of the river. Twinkle Toes was so excited she could barely contain herself.

Without another thought, she flipped her tail fin and dove into the whirl-pool, straight down to the club. She saw a large, brightly lit sign that read "Nymph Disco," and she giggled. Lights of all colors were flashing and strobing everywhere, and the river bottom was alive with dancing fish. New to the Nymph Disco, and not knowing anyone, Twinkle Toes kept a low profile, surveying everything that was happening. There were smoothly flattened rocks positioned throughout the disco, with beautiful trout dancing atop the platforms. Above the pandemonium was the DJ booth, positioned on a rock shelf. The very famous disc jockey, DJ Trout, wearing large headphones over his gills, was spinning music for the dancers. Beautiful trout with fishnet stockings covering their bodies carried trays of drinks and nymph hors d'oeuvres.

Twinkle Toes was in awe at the scene before her. She had no idea what she had been missing. One of the trout dancing on a rock platform jumped off to take a break, and without thinking, she flipped her fin and took her place. Uninhibited, she danced and spun on her tail fin, and her moves were so spectacular the crowd began to take notice. DJ Trout also took notice and abruptly stopped the music.

"Hey, all you trout! Are you having fun tonight?" shouted DJ Trout. The crowd cheered in delight. "Looks like we have a new dancer on the rock tonight! How 'bout we see what she's got?" The throng of trout cheered wildly.

Twinkle Toes could not believe what was happening. She was going to be the main act at the Nymph Disco!

"Let's all pump our fins for…"

Twinkle Toes mouthed her name, "Twinkle Toes Trout!"

A new song blared, and Twinkle Toes began to spin and dance and flip her fins to the driving beat, dancing like she had never danced before. The more everyone cheered, the wilder she danced. The Nymph Disco rocked as the trout jumped, with their fins pumping in time to the music. Twinkle Toes put on a show like no other. Lights flashed across her, showing off her magnificent hot-pink and lime-green scales, and her red lips smiled as she danced with total abandon. Everyone was wondering who this beautiful and magnificent dancing trout was and why they had never seen her before.

When the song ended, the crowd cheered wildly for the new Nymph Disco star. Twinkle Toes gracefully and slowly bowed and acknowledged her own greatness. She saw DJ Trout waving for her to come up, so she leaped off the platform and swam to his booth. A new song began playing, and the disco erupted with increasing numbers of jubilant, dancing trout.

"You were wonderful tonight!" raved DJ Trout.

"*'I'm always wonderful at night,' suga*," replied Twinkle Toes as she put one fin on her hip and the other in the air.

"Where did you come from, T.T.?" asked DJ Trout.

"*Suga, 'it doesn't matter where I came from, it's where I'm going that counts.'*" And she rocked her hips in time to the music.

"Oooooh, you are one fine-looking trout, T.T. And that is some serious attitude you've got, girl," said DJ Trout, grinning as he admired Twinkle Toes from head to tail.

"I always say, '*Look your best. Who said love is blind?*'" And she continued to move to the beat of the music.

DJ Trout was the best vinyl spinner in the river. He had dark emerald-green scales with deep-purple spots down each side of his body. He wore black wraparound sunglasses and wore his headphones either over his gills or loose around his neck.

"*Suga*, where did you get those sunglasses? You wouldn't happen to have another pair, would you?" And she gave him her most flirtatious smile.

"Sure do, T.T. Have some shades right here I think will do you just fine." And he handed her a pair of black butterfly-shaped sunglasses.

"For me? You do know how to make a girl happy," she drooled as she took the sunglasses with her fin and flipped them onto her face.

"Those look real fine on you, T.T. ... like a movie star; you look just like a movie star." DJ Trout gave Twinkle Toes a little bow. "Hey, T.T., can you sing as well as you can dance?"

"Sure, I can sing, *suga*." And she flipped through the songs with her fins, grabbing one and tossing it to DJ Trout. "Spin that for me, will you, *suga*?" And Twinkle Toes swam out of the booth and over to the main rock platform.

The lights dimmed in the disco, and as the upbeat boogie song "Treat Him Right" started to play, a single spotlight illuminated the star attraction. Immediately the myriad trout began to boogie and jive to the nostalgic tune. Twinkle Toes looked dazzling with her scales sparkling in the bright lights as she sensually swayed to the introduction of the song. She leaned to one side and tapped her tail fin back and forth to the beat of the music. The crowd went crazy as they were swing dancing and bebopping to the lively tune. Twinkle Toes had a way of oozing the words out of her mouth as she sang that made her all the more alluring and appealing, and her new sunglasses completed her magnificent appearance.

When the song was over, she bowed and, with a wave of her fin to DJ Trout, swam straight up to the surface, spinning as she rose. Illuminated by a spotlight, her spin was so fast she looked like a pink torpedo heading for the surface. The sky was pitch-black with a dizzying number of stars, many shooting across the sky like a background of fireworks. As she broke through the surface, she leaped into a magnificent triple flip, triple twist, then cleanly dove back into the water and disappeared into the night. From the Nymph Disco, at the bottom of the river, her exit was dazzling. Cheers and screams of approval could be heard throughout the club following Twinkle Toes's final jump. The Nymph Disco patrons were stunned. They had never seen anything like the fabulous Twinkle Toes Trout…ever.

A star was born, and Twinkle Toes was filled with joy beyond anything she had ever experienced. Her unplanned debut at the Nymph Disco was a spectacular hit, and she had been the center of attention, which suited her just fine. Ideas were flooding through her mind for all the different feats she could unveil in future performances, and at that moment, she made a decision.

"I will perform at the Nymph Disco every night. It was the most fun I have ever had. They all loved me, but not quite as much as I love myself." She hugged herself with her fins, smiling from gill to gill.

Approaching the dam, she slowed to make sure she would make a safe jump. It was dark out, and the dam was barely visible, only slightly illuminated by the countless stars in the sky. She started her approach, swimming faster and faster, dodging rocks and obstacles, and at the perfect moment, with a great flip of her tail fin, she leaped out of the water, into the air, up and over the dam, splashing down on the other side, safely back in her pond.

"How easy that was compared to my first attempt, and how wonderful I feel," she said as she hugged herself again. "'*I never said it would be easy. I only said it would be worth it,*'" she giggled. "The only thing missing from this night is a moon bright enough for me to see my beautiful reflection in the pond." In true character, her full red lips mimicked a childish moue.

"Why are you pouting, Twinkle Toes?" asked the kit, surprising her.

"Oh, I had the most marvelous evening, but now I can't see my beauty in the pond, because the evening is so dark. I have a lot of energy, and I'm not quite ready to go to sleep," replied the pouting trout.

"We saw your performance tonight at the Nymph Disco. You really were very wonderful," congratulated the kit.

"You were there?" asked Twinkle Toes.

"Of course! We often go to the disco to listen to the music and watch the dancing trout. We sit on the edge of the river, and when the Nymph Disco lights flash on, everything on the river bottom is visible through the crystal-clear water."

"Why didn't you tell me about the Nymph Disco? Why would you keep such a secret from me, *suga?*" asked the pouting trout.

"We didn't exactly keep it a secret. We just thought, when you were ready to explore the river, you would. And you were bound to find the Nymph Disco… everyone does. And now you are big enough and strong enough to easily make the leap back into our pond, so it all worked out. Since you are not ready for sleep, why don't you sing us a little song?" The kit whistled several times through his teeth, causing Twinkle Toes to giggle.

Instantly the rest of the beavers' heads popped up in the dimly lit pond, followed by another giggle from the startled trout. They all crawled onto the pond bank and lined up side by side, ready for the show.

Twinkle Toes looked at the kit with a scolding gaze but said, "Oh, all right, *suga.* Just one song, then I must get my beauty rest." She winked at the kit.

As she was about to begin her performance, Wolfrik stepped out of the shadows of the forest.

He loped over to the pond and said, "*Guten Abend*—good evening, Twinkle Toes. That was quite *zee* performance you gave this evening." He bowed to the trout.

"Well, good evening, *suga.* I had no idea I had so many fans. You're just in time for a little lullaby before I say good night." She removed her new sunglasses and fluttered her lashes flirtatiously at Wolfrik.

Wolfrik looked fondly at the little trout. She had no idea how often he was in the shadows, watching her…protecting her. He had seen her leap over the dam into the river and then followed her along the riverbank to the Nymph Disco. Trained as an operative, he knew the importance of learning the habits of those he protected so that he might anticipate unexpected dangers. He was pleased Twinkle Toes chose to explore the river at night, because the danger was lessened. The Nymph Disco held no real peril, unless one of the trout decided to become unruly. From what he had heard, that rarely happened.

With both ears on alert, Wolfrik sat down next to the pond bank, across from the beavers. The stars, shining brilliantly in the sky, were mirrored on the pond like a million tiny diamonds, setting the stage for a slow but jazzy rendition of "I'm in the Mood for Love."

Twinkle Toes gracefully swayed through the water on her tail fin as she sang the opening line, followed by the beavers swaying side to side, singing backup. Twinkle Toes looked adoringly at the massive wolf. Wolfrik had to admit, she was very talented, and the beavers were quite melodic as well.

When the song was finished, Twinkle Toes took her bows, the beavers clapped their paws and grinned, and Wolfrik stood and acknowledged her talent with a low bow, touching his nose to the ground in the highest form of admiration he could offer her.

"Good night, Twinkle Toes," said the beavers in unison, and they slid into the pond and vanished.

Twinkle Toes smiled at Wolfrik and said, "What a wonderful evening I have had," and she hugged herself. "I believe I am rather sleepy. '*Too much of a good thing can be taxing.*'" With a sultry wink and an adoring grin, she disappeared into the depths of the diamond-studded, inked surface. Wolfrik turned and loped into the forest, well pleased with the events of the night.

CHAPTER 6

THE MORNING WAS GLORIOUS, and the sun filtered through the trees, warming Elkwood. As he walked alongside a stream, he was thinking about how successful he had become. The stream was fed by mountain snowpack and, at times, rushed over rocks and created small waterfalls. It was very serene and his mood was relaxed. As he strolled, the terrain dropped, and he noticed a slightly larger waterfall cascading into a pool of water. Elkwood wondered what was causing the water to pool as it was, and he found the answer rather quickly. He noticed a beaver dam had been built on the other side of the pond. The structure allowed small amounts of water to trickle through, continuing its flow below the dam and into the river. Elkwood heard the sound of splashing, and he thought it might be beavers playing, so he quietly approached the pond, hoping to sneak up on them. Instead, lying on the bank was the oddest thing Elkwood had ever seen.

Lazily sunning on the bank of the pond was a beautifully unusual trout wearing black butterfly-shaped sunglasses. She was hot pink with brilliant lime-green fins and lime-green spots running the length of her body. She had perfectly shaped bright red lips that made her look like a starlet from the golden era of film. She kept one fin in the water, frequently splashing herself, and the other fin was wrapped around a tall green drink, which she was sipping. There was a thin stir stick in her slime cocktail, stacked with impaled bugs. In an amazing rhythm, the trout splashed, sipped, and snacked as she leaned over, looking into the water, admiring her reflection. Elkwood smiled with amusement.

The beavers sounded their danger alert with a loud *thwack* of their tails on the water. Elkwood's arrival had been announced. Clearing his throat, Elkwood said in his formal British lilt, "Good morning, trout!"

The trout, completely aware of his presence, quickly rolled sideways and splashed into the pool to protect herself from the intruder. Elkwood snickered, and the trout looked at him with disdain.

"Forgive me. I did not mean to startle you, but I could not help but stare."

The trout oozed charm and said, "'*It's better to be looked over than overlooked,*' *suga.*"

"Allow me to introduce myself. I am Elkwood Elkington the Third, from the forest of England, across the Big Pond," he eloquently stated.

"Oh my, *suga*! You're a long way from home," she exclaimed. "And you didn't startle me. I saw you in the water."

"No," replied Elkwood, "my name is Elkwood."

"Oh, I got that, *suga*. I call everyone *suga*. I'm Twinkle Toes Trout, and I'm the best dancer in the river, and the most beautiful of all the trout," she said quite matter-of-factly.

"You are indeed quite beautiful," praised Elkwood.

"And you, Elkwood, are a most regal-looking elk. I *adore* how marvelously well you wear purple, *suga*," she said, fully admiring the impressive elk standing before her.

Elkwood was very curious about this delightful little creature. He had never met a trout before. Elkwood sat down and listened to Twinkle Toes telling him about her life. She told him she was the smartest trout in the river. She described the terrifying day she had been caught by a fisherman and licked by vicious wolves. She exclaimed how she loved to dance and party all night at the Nymph Disco at the bottom of the river. She told him it was a famous club and she had been going there longer than any other fish. With a sigh, she told Elkwood that she had noticed many trout had been failing to show up night after night.

Elkwood asked, "What happened to all the other trout?"

"They've been caught by the fishermen's hooks in the river," replied Twinkle Toes.

Elkwood was horrified by the thought that someone might hook this beautiful, brightly colored trout. She bragged that she had not been caught, because she partied all night at the Nymph Disco and sunned and napped all day at the pond.

"When they're fishing in the river, I remain here at the pond, out of their reach. Fishermen prefer to fish in the faster water," she said with authority.

"But don't any animals try to eat you while you sun yourself and nap?" Elkwood asked.

"Oh no, *suga*. I'm loved by all the animals in the forest. They're not interested in eating me. And the beavers alert me of danger with a big slap of their tails." With perfect timing, the family of beavers surfaced, waved their tails, and dove under the water.

She amused Elkwood with her stories of dancing through the water and leaping in the air and how all the other fish were very jealous of her because she was so talented. She told him over and over she was the most beautiful fish in the river, with the brightest colors and the best-looking tail fin. The two talked for a long time, and Elkwood learned about life in both the river and the pond. He tried to tell Twinkle Toes about his life, but she seemed more interested in talking about herself. She did not seem at all interested in his exile from England or his long journey or the simple fact that he was in a strange country, trying to make his way. Although he concluded she was a very narcissistic trout, he decided he liked Twinkle Toes because she was so very interesting and full of life. *Sometimes one just has to overlook a negative trait in another*, mused Elkwood.

As the morning turned into midday, Elkwood's stomach began to rumble in hunger. He reached into his knapsack and pulled out a Big Elk cookie. He took a bite, and Twinkle Toes eyed him with curiosity.

"Forgive me," Elkwood exclaimed. "May I offer you a Big Elk chocolate chip cookie?"

She replied, "Oh, *suga*, although I'm sure they are delicious, I quite prefer the *suga* cookie. Do you have a *suga* cookie?"

"No," Elkwood replied. "I only have Big Elk cookies. I have a store, and all I sell is Big Elks. They are very popular, and all the animals love them."

"Oh my, *suga*," she cooed. "That's all you have? Well, everyone knows the *suga* cookie is the most delicious."

Elkwood took a long breath and said, "I beg to differ, Ms. Twinkle Toes. The Big Elk is the finest cookie in the forest. Everyone loves chocolate chip cookies the best."

She replied, "Really, *suga*, you only sell chocolate chip cookies? Well, that will just not do. You must have *suga* cookies too. You just have to sell the most sinfully delicious cookie of all."

Elkwood was beside himself. How dare this trout say sugar cookies were better than his Big Elks? He stomped his hooves and said, "How would you know which cookie tastes the best? You have never eaten a Big Elk."

Twinkle Toes replied, "Well, *suga*, '*I'll try anything once, twice if I like it, three times to make sure.*'"

Elkwood thought about that for a moment, then reached into his knapsack and pulled out a Big Elk. She took it with her fin and slowly brought it to her lips and nibbled. She flipped her other fin in the water and acted quite disinterested. She tried the cookie a second time, and a look of pleasure washed over her face. She took a third bite and said, "*Suga*, this is a very tasty cookie, but why would you want to sell just one kind of cookie when two would be far better?"

Elkwood had never considered offering more cookies, because the Big Elk was so very successful. After all, it was his cookie. But he had to admit, she did make sense. He could offer more variety, and his sales would increase, and he would become wealthier. He told Twinkle Toes how he had founded the Eat Me Cookie Company. She seemed intrigued, but Elkwood suspected she would only join the company if it appeared to be her idea. He thought maybe he had met his match in the arena of believing he had the best cookie.

He cleverly baited her by asking, "If your sugar cookie is as sinfully delicious as you say, then will you give me the recipe so I can offer it at the Eat Me Cookie Company?"

She replied, "'*I generally avoid temptation, unless I can't resist it.*' *Suga*, you have a deal."

"Splendid," replied Elkwood. "I will call your cookie the Big Trout—that is, if it is as delicious as you claim."

Twinkle Toes liked the idea, and with a slight pout, she nodded her approval. "Oh, *suga*, it will be. You might as well start adding up the profits." She did not like that this elk seemed to think his cookie was superior to her cookie.

Elkwood raised his eyebrow at the smug little trout. She was indeed quite delightfully full of herself. He reached out his large hoof to the trout to nudge her fin in a shake and accidentally pushed her into the water.

She came up smiling, and seeing an opportunity to take center stage, she said, "I like you, *suga*. How would you like to see a little dance?" And with that, she dove into the water, U-turned gathering speed, and flew up in the air in a magnificent leap. She dove back into the water and again broke through the surface, soaring into the air with a double-twisting flip, and cleanly dove into the pond.

She surfaced and slid back onto the shore, resuming her position of sipping her pond slime cocktail, nibbling bugs off her stir stick, and admiring her vision in the crystal-clear water.

Elkwood was awestruck by the performance of the trout. Never had he seen such beauty and grace of motion. "Bravo, Twinkle Toes! You are indeed a grand dancer." She nodded her gratitude while simultaneously completely immersed in her own beauty.

Suddenly they heard a horrible growl coming from the forest, and out leaped a huge coyote with fangs bared, dripping with saliva. He sprinted to the river's edge, and just as he was about to grab Twinkle Toes with his fangs, Elkwood lunged forward and kicked the coyote with his powerful hooves. The coyote yelped and flew sideways, rolling several times, but quickly got back to his feet. He held his stance, eyes glaring, and growled ferociously.

"You have just stolen my lunch, friend," he growled.

"You are no friend of mine, sir, and Twinkle Toes is not your lunch," warned Elkwood.

Twinkle Toes slowly slid back into the river, ready to dive should the coyote attack again.

"Maybe not today," replied the coyote, "but someday...very soon."

"Be gone, you ugly coyote!" shouted Elkwood. "And do not come near here again."

"Oh, I'll be back," sneered the coyote. "You won't know when and you won't see me coming, but I'll be back. You have not seen the last of me."

Elkwood charged at the coyote with great force and speed, catching him by surprise, and brought a hoof down on his shoulder. The coyote yowled, spun around, and ran to the forest edge. He turned and glared at Elkwood.

"You have made an enemy of me today...Beware," he snarled, and ran off into the forest.

Elkwood stood his ground even though a slight shiver ran through his strong body. He turned to make sure Twinkle Toes was safe. She was lounging on the pond bank again, sipping her drink and eating a bug off her stir stick as if nothing had transpired.

"Were you not frightened? I thought all the animals loved you and would refrain from eating you," questioned Elkwood.

"No one will eat me when I have a big strong *elk* like you to protect me. Thanks, *suga*," she cooed.

"Who was that vile coyote? Do you know him?" asked Elkwood.

"Oh, that's Puck. He's been trying to eat me for some time. He and his nasty pack are my only enemies. And now he's your enemy. Watch out for him, *suga*. He has others that follow him."

Elkwood considered the warning, knowing how dangerous a pack of evil coyotes could be, especially to a lone animal. "But how have you protected yourself from him? Without me, he surely would have eaten you," wondered Elkwood.

"I knew he was there all along. I saw his reflection in the water. *Suga*, Puck's mother '*should have thrown him away and kept the stork*,'" she laughed. Elkwood laughed too, but he feared they had not seen the last of Puck.

It was time for Elkwood to leave, and Twinkle Toes gave him her sugar cookie recipe and told him it was a very prized recipe and must be kept secret. He vowed to protect her sacred family recipe.

"Please be careful, Twinkle Toes. You will soon be part of the Eat Me Cookie Company, and you will become rich and famous."

She lazily dipped her fin into the water and said with a grin, "I'm already famous, *suga*. '*Why don't ya come up and see me sometime? I'm home every evening*,'" she cooed with a wink and a grin. With that, she slid into the water and disappeared.

Elkwood headed home, thinking about his encounter with Twinkle Toes Trout. She was very beautiful and was certainly not shy about her attributes. He had noticed that she constantly looked at her reflection in the water, and wondered how she could be so in love with herself. Yet he still found her delightfully amusing. And she *was* a grand dancer who could sing a nice tune as well. So far she had succeeded in avoiding getting hooked, but he wondered how wise it was to leave her so vulnerable by the side of the pond. What if she dozed off and Puck got the drop on her? It seemed to him her plan was not foolproof and someday she would pay for her vanity.

But for today he had saved her, and he was excited to get back and make a batch of Big Trout cookies. Of course, they would not be as delicious as the Big Elks, but having another cookie to sell would increase his sales and make his customers happy. He would begin selling them as soon as the store opened the next day. That is … *if* they were tasty.

The subtle aroma of Big Trout cookies baking in the oven wafted from the Eat Me Cookie Company. Elkwood could not wait to taste the new addition. Once they cooled, he picked one up with his hooves and took a bite. Then he took another bite, and another…The Big Trout was delicious.

"I am a genius and a very smart *business-elk*. I now have two delicious cookies to sell to the animals of the Big Sky. I will be rich beyond my wildest dreams, and everyone will envy my success and wish they also had a cookie company."

Theodore flew into the shop, curious about the new aroma.

"Theodore, try my new cookie, the Big Trout. It is amazing!"

Theodore nibbled at the Big Trout and agreed it was truly yummy. He then asked, "Where did you get the recipe, Elkwood?"

Elkwood told Theodore about his encounter with Twinkle Toes, who was both beautiful and amusing. He told him about how Puck the coyote had tried to eat her and how he had saved her life.

"I am a hero," he pronounced.

Theodore was most impressed with his story, but something about his friend had changed. Elkwood was becoming more arrogant. All he talked about was himself, and never once did he ask about him. After all the help Theodore had given his friend, he now felt second to that silly trout. Still, he knew the meaning of friendship, and he would not desert Elkwood. And it would be only fair that he should reserve judgment about Twinkle Toes Trout until he had been introduced to her.

He helped Elkwood make cookies for the day and was ready with a cheery chirp when the store opened. As the animals of the forest lined up outside the Eat Me Cookie Company, a new aroma was in the air. The crowd was chattering with anticipation. Elkwood opened the window, and Theodore began to sell cookies. Everyone wanted to try the new Big Trout.

The reviews were in, and the Big Trout cookie was a grand success. Not only did the animals buy Big Elks, but many also bought Big Trouts. They were hooked. His cookies were the best in the world. As soon as they closed for the day, Elkwood would tell Twinkle Toes about their success. After all, she was now his partner.

Elkwood finally closed up shop after the busiest day ever at the Eat Me Cookie Company. He asked Theodore if he would like to come with him and meet Twinkle Toes, but Theodore said he had other pressing business. Truth be told, Theodore had had enough of Elkwood and his arrogance for one day. Elkwood bid him farewell and pranced off to visit Twinkle Toes.

As he entered the clearing at the pond, he stopped dead in his tracks. A very large wolf was standing next to Twinkle Toes. Being her hero, he leaped into action to confront the wolf.

Twinkle Toes saw him coming and called out, "Hello, *suga*. Come meet my very dashing…friend."

Elkwood skidded to a stop with surprise on his face. "Your friend? I thought he was going to eat you!"

Twinkle Toes giggled. "'*Every "animal" I meet wants to protect me. I can't figure out what from*,'" she said dryly. "Elkwood, this is my dearest friend, Wolfrik von Spice, from Germany. Say hello to Elkwood Elkington the Third, from England…my hero," she giggled.

Elkwood felt slightly embarrassed but held his head high.

Wolfrik von Spice clicked his back paws together and said, "*Guten Abend*, Elkwood."

Elkwood eyed Wolfrik suspiciously and extended his hoof to the wolf's paw. "*What* did you say?" he asked.

"I said, 'Good evening, Elkwood.'"

Elkwood noticed that Wolfrik had a habit of speaking very fast and abruptly, with a thick German accent. He was quite large and beautifully colored, and Elkwood was curious about the black eye patch he wore on his left eye. He sniffed the air and detected a faint tang of spice emanating from the wolf. Elkwood had never seen a more handsome and dashing wolf. Wolfrik von Spice had a sophisticated air about him, but the look he had in his eye seemed distant and not particularly friendly.

Wolfrik was a loner. In Germany, he had been hired by animals of the forest to solve crimes and mysteries. He was a daredevil and loved taking risks. This was simply part of his nature. Friendship was unfamiliar to him, yet he *did* like Twinkle Toes. He thought her cavalier lifestyle was very dangerous, and he found he wanted to protect her and keep her safe. He did not trust easily, and his instincts never let him down…except for once. An event he preferred not to discuss again. Thus, he eyed Elkwood with distrust.

Distracted by the wolf, Elkwood suddenly remembered why he had come to visit Twinkle Toes. "Our cookies are a huge success," he blurted out. "All the animals loved the Big Trout cookie, and I sold more cookies than ever before."

"Well, of course, *suga*. I told you they were *sinfully* delicious. Wolfrik has come to take me for an evening ride, so why don't we go see your cookie company?" she suggested.

"*Jawohl*," said Wolfrik.

Elkwood gave Wolfrik a confused look and was wondering how Twinkle Toes could leave the pond when he noticed a strange-looking contraption parked in the clearing. He had seen motorcycles before but never one with a sidecar, and certainly not one filled with water. It was a beautiful, shiny silver and looked very fast.

Wolfrik trotted over to his motorcycle, pulled on his leather pilot's cap, with holes for his ears, of course, strapped on his silver-blue goggles, and started the bike with a loud *vroom*. He drove over to Twinkle Toes, and with a great flip of her tail fin, she leaped into the sidecar with a giant *splash*. Stunned and amazed, Elkwood now understood why the sidecar was filled with water. He snickered at the clever mode of travel Wolfrik had developed for the adventurous trout. Wolfrik tossed Twinkle Toes a tiny pair of lime-green goggles, which she adeptly caught with her fins and promptly pulled over her eyes. With another loud *vroom*, Wolfrik zoomed out of the clearing.

Wolfrik drove through the woods at breakneck speed, screeching around curves and barely missing trees along the way. Twinkle Toes was hanging on with her fins, swaying back and forth to the rhythm of the ride, water splashing everywhere. She was clearly enjoying the excitement of the escapade.

Elkwood feared she would fly out of the sidecar with each erratic swerve. He thought it was the strangest sight he had ever seen, and he smiled in amusement. Even odder was the pairing of a wolf and a trout. But then again, everything about this unusual trout struck him as a bit odd. Clearly Twinkle Toes had a magical personality that was spellbinding to all. Otherwise, she would make a wonderful snack for a wolf. He shuddered to think of such a horrible outcome. He galloped alongside the pair, dodging obstacles as they traveled to the Eat Me Cookie Company. He was an agile elk but found it difficult to keep up with the wolf's wild and fast driving.

As they came to the clearing in front of Elkwood's fine establishment, Wolfrik circled once in front of the store, then came to a screeching halt as water splashed out of the sidecar.

"Marvelous ride," Twinkle Toes exclaimed. "Oooh, you are so fearless and intoxicating," she said as she looked adoringly at Wolfrik.

As she removed her goggles, Twinkle Toes rose up on her tail fin and looked very intently at the sign posted on the front of the tree that was home to the Eat Me Cookie Company. "Oooh," she cooed. "Lovely store, *suga*."

"Would you like to come inside and look around?" asked Elkwood.

"She cannot," said Wolfrik. "There is no water."

Elkwood thought about that and quickly went inside his store. Wolfrik and Twinkle Toes could hear him rummaging around. Elkwood came out of the store carrying a deep bowl and trotted up to the sidecar. With one big scoop of water *and* trout, he lifted Twinkle Toes out of the sidecar. She giggled in delight.

"This will have to do for now. Let me escort you inside and give you a tour."

Elkwood carried the trout while she oohed and aahed at all he had done to design the store. Elkwood extended an invitation to Wolfrik. "Come and take a look...please."

Wolfrik entered the store and looked around with an approving nod. Just then Theodore fluttered in and perched on a shelf.

"Hello, Theodore," exclaimed Elkwood. "Please meet my new friends. This is Twinkle Toes Trout, creator of the Big Trout cookie, and her friend Wolfrik von Spice, from Germany."

"Pleased to meet you," chirped Theodore.

Wolfrik clicked his back paws together and gracefully bowed his head toward Theodore.

"Your Big Trout cookies are delicious," Theodore said to Twinkle Toes. "They have increased sales tremendously."

"Of course, *suga*. They are the most delicious in the forest." She knowingly winked at Theodore.

Elkwood stiffened a bit, as he did not appreciate her humor or her declaration. He knew his Big Elks were the best cookie but decided not to argue... for now.

"And which cookie do *you* prefer, Wolfrik?" Theodore asked.

"I have no opinion, as I have not tasted *zee* cookies."

"Well, you must," replied Elkwood, and he grabbed one of each off a nearby tray.

Wolfrik took a bite of each cookie and stood expressionless.

"Well, which one is the best?" asked Elkwood.

"Neither. It is *zee* spice cookie that is *zee* best cookie," said Wolfrik, very matter-of-factly.

"The spice cookie?" they all exclaimed in unison.

"There *is* no spice cookie," said Elkwood.

"*Suga*, have you been holding out on me?" asked Twinkle Toes, looking lovingly at Wolfrik.

"*Jawohl*, my little trout. I have been eating *zee* spice cookies since I was a pup in Germany. They are *zee* best."

"Care to make a batch?" challenged Elkwood.

"Oh, yes, that's a fine idea," chirped Theodore. "Then we will have three delicious cookies to sell."

Wolfrik trotted outside and grabbed a few ingredients from his motorcycle, then returned to the store. He began mixing various ingredients in a large bowl, adding a pinch here and a dash there. He formed the dough into round balls, patted them down with his giant paws, leaving his signature *wolfprint* on each cookie, and shoved the tray into the oven. The aroma began to fill the store as the cookies turned golden brown. The scent was intoxicating and beyond description. It reminded Elkwood of the faint spiciness he detected coming from Wolfrik.

Once cooled, Wolfrik very formally offered a cookie to each of his friends, clicking his paws and bowing with each cookie. Theodore, Elkwood, and Twinkle Toes each took a taste, and none could speak.

Finally Elkwood said, "May I have another, Wolfrik?"

"*Jawohl*," said Wolfrik, and he offered him another.

"This cookie is very good and will be known as the Big Wolf cookie," declared Elkwood. "That is, of course, if you are interested in becoming a partner in the Eat Me Cookie Company, Wolfrik."

Wolfrik von Spice was not a joiner, but he stood contemplating the offer. "*Jawohl*," said Wolfrik, without emotion.

"A marvelous idea, *suga*," cooed Twinkle Toes.

"We are becoming bigger and better all the time," bragged Elkwood. "Our cookie herd is growing, and we shall be known as the Eat Me Animal Herd. All the forest will buy our delicious cookies, and we will become rich beyond our wildest dreams."

Theodore sat quietly on his perch. Once again he had been overlooked and felt very sad that he did not have a cookie to contribute. But it was not in his nature to complain, so he kept silent. Instead he congratulated the Eat Me Animal Herd and unselfishly offered his services at the store. Someday maybe he, too, would have his very own cookie.

They all chatted for a while, eating the mouthwatering cookies while discussing how rich they would become...except for Wolfrik. He sat in silence, taking in the experience. Secretly he was pleased to become part of the Eat Me Animal Herd, but his mistrusting nature made him hold back his emotions. He had trusted before, long ago, and had paid a very high price. Yet something in his heart told him he was safe, that these would be his friends for life. He admired Twinkle Toes for her light spirit and desire to experience adventures. Although she was very vain and narcissistic, she was truly a delight. And she clearly had a crush on him. He knew that would never do, but it warmed his heart toward the little trout. She was indeed the most beautiful and talented trout he had ever seen, yet he worried her selfish nature would be her undoing.

Theodore was a cheery woodpecker and seemed to always want to help his friends. He seemed harmless, and Wolfrik believed he might be trustworthy as well. Regardless, Theodore could be a snack with just one quick bite, so he was assuredly not a threat to Wolfrik.

Elkwood, on the other hand, was arrogant, always wanting to be the best. He was also quite big and very powerful. Even though Elkwood was a bit of a dandy, Wolfrik knew that he might not fare well in a battle against the large elk. Wolfrik was also immensely powerful and had always triumphed in battle... except for once. Although he was a superior wolf, he had been forced to learn humility from his experiences. Believing one could not be defeated was a grave mistake. That type of arrogance only led to disaster or even death. He saw this trait in Elkwood. He was naive about the dangers of the forest and had obviously led a very privileged and pampered life. Although he seemed quite friendly and generous, Wolfrik was not convinced Elkwood would *buck up* if things became dangerous. From Wolfrik's vast experiences, that type of elk would never have his back, although, he thought, Elkwood *had* rushed in to save the little trout when he feared Wolfrik would eat her. And Twinkle Toes *had* told him all about how Elkwood had charged in to save her from Puck. He knew Puck and was quite aware of the crafty and malicious nature of the evil coyote. Maybe there was hope for Elkwood. Perhaps he could become a good and loyal *Elk*. Wolfrik would watch him but would not give his trust away easily. Once betrayed...

As the evening waned, the stars began to appear, and Twinkle Toes said to Elkwood, "*Suga*, I must return to the river. I never miss a party at the Nymph Disco, and I don't want to keep my fans waiting."

Elkwood wished he could see his friend dance at the disco, but in the dark of night, he did not believe viewing her dance would be possible. He picked her up in her bowl and poured her into Wolfrik's sidecar. Wolfrik hopped on his motorcycle, and as they donned their goggles, he started it with a big *vroom*. With one paw and one fin raised in farewell, they sped off into the night.

Elkwood and Theodore were exhausted from the day, so they retired to their home, snuggling into their beds. Elkwood said, "Sleep well, my friend. Tomorrow is going to be a very big day now that we have the Big Wolf cookie to debut."

Theodore agreed, and as they both fell fast asleep in their warm, cozy beds, Elkwood dreamed he heard the voice of the giant *Elk* repeat, "Success is not defined by the wealth you acquire but by the friend you are to others."

The day dawned with a new tantalizing aroma in the forest. Animals came from miles around to buy Eat Me cookies. They all raved about the new Big Wolf cookie, and Elkwood was very proud.

Wolfrik had risen early that morning and returned to the Eat Me Cookie Company. He parked his motorcycle some distance away and crept to the forest's edge to watch the scene. He saw Elkwood and Theodore busily making, wrapping, and selling Eat Me cookies. He heard grand praise for the newest cookie, *his* cookie. He was pleased. He admired Elkwood for his business savvy, as surely he had become a very successful elk. His character as a friend? Only time would tell.

Wolfrik von Spice suddenly detected a new scent. Using his acutely refined skills, he sniffed the air with his powerful nose. The foul scent led him to direct his eye across the clearing, where he spotted Puck hiding behind some dense brush. The odor made his nose wrinkle. Yes, he knew Puck. They had had several run-ins. Puck was clever and devious, and Wolfrik knew he was eyeing the Eat Me Cookie Company and, in particular, Elkwood. After the incident with Twinkle Toes, Wolfrik knew Puck would stalk Elkwood and wait for the perfect time to attack. Although a coyote attacking an elk was quite foolhardy, Puck was just crazy enough to try. Then again, Puck, accompanied by his band of ugly, flea-bitten beasts, could do serious harm to an elk.

Wolfrik watched his enemy and saw his bared fangs glistening with drool. His yellow, bloodshot eyes bugged out of his head, shooting daggers of hatred toward his prey. Puck was crazy and vicious, but he was not stupid. He would never attack with so many animals visiting the cookie store. Wolfrik watched and wondered what Puck was planning. Rather than confront him and frighten all the other animals, he decided to simply observe. Puck slowly ran his tongue around his lips as if anticipating a delicious meal, then turned and skulked back into the forest, disappearing.

Wolfrik knew this was not the last time he would see Puck. He also knew Puck had reinforcements. And Wolfrik knew they were nearby, for Puck was a coward and was never alone for long. Wolfrik considered whether or not he should tell Elkwood that Puck had been watching him. He decided, for now, he would keep a sharp eye on the happenings at the store. He was not afraid of Puck or his vile pack. He would be on guard if and when Puck made his move.

CHAPTER 7

BEARIE THE CUB was a kind bear and a friend to all. He lived in the forest of the Big Sky with his mother and brother. He was a beautiful cub, and his thick fur was bright coppery orange, and he had a big black nose. His eyes were dark brown, and there was not an ounce of malice in them. His paws were huge, with long pale orange claws that aided him in foraging. As was the habit of all bears, Bearie loved honey. His mother brought big jars of honey home for him and his older brother, and they sat on the floor of their den, dipping their enormous paws into the jar and slathering the honey into their mouths. There was nothing better in the whole wide world than a pot of honey. Every bear agreed. Often, after enjoying the sweet, wild nutrient, they trekked to the stream so they could wash the gooey, sticky honey off their faces. Bearie was a good cub, and his mother loved him with all her heart. At his young age, he was not yet educated, but his heart was pure. His brother, on the other hand, was a bit of a rapscallion and was constantly encouraging Bearie to join him in the most questionable adventures.

On one such occasion, Bearie and his brother were out exploring the woods when they heard a very loud buzzing coming from a nearby tree. Bearie and his brother had never foraged for honey before, because that was their mother's job. She had warned them time after time to stay away from anything that buzzed, because she knew of the great danger. As they neared the sound of the buzzing, they saw a huge beehive high up in a tree, with thousands of bees flying all around. The hive was positively dripping with fresh honey, a sight that was irresistible to young cubs, even with no formal beehive training.

"That honey looks yummy," exclaimed Bearie's brother. "I bet you could climb that tree easily, little brother, and snatch that honey before even one bee noticed," his brother taunted.

"Oh no, I can't," pleaded Bearie. "Mother has told us never to bother *da* bees for their honey. She said we could get hurt *real bad*."

His brother cleverly replied, "I am not as big and strong as you, Bearie, and I can't climb as fast. I know how much you love honey, more than any bear in the world, and I would go up there for you, but I'm not nearly as good a climber as you." He looked at Bearie to see if his deceit was having the desired effect. "Oh well, I just thought you would really enjoy some honey." He deceptively put on his best pouting-bear face.

The temptation was just too great for Bearie, and the lure of the dripping honey was irresistible. "Do you really think I can do it?" asked Bearie, with great hesitation in his shaky voice.

"Of course you can, little brother. You are the best climber of all the cubs, and I will be right here if you need me," encouraged his cunning brother.

Bearie was an excellent climber, and that honey would taste awfully yummy. After all, they were just tiny bees. What harm could they do? His mother always came home with honey, and she was never hurt.

"I know you can do it, Bearie. Imagine how proud Mother will be when you bring home the honey. You will be known as the bravest and best honey snatcher in the forest," cajoled his sly brother.

Bearie looked up at the swarm of bees and considered his plan of attack. All he had to do was slowly scale up the tree so as not to disturb the buzzing bees, grab a hunk of honeycomb from the oozing hive, and slide back down the tree as fast as he could.

"You are right, brother, I can do it," he whispered as he approached the tree.

He looked back once for encouragement, and his brother gave him a *paws-up*. He turned, and slowly—ever so slowly—he began to climb the tree. He used his strong hind legs to brace himself and push his body up the tree, hugging the trunk with his huge front paws and digging his claws in for support. He moved closer and closer to the dripping honey and the buzzing bees. Nervous, Bearie looked down and saw his brother looking up at him.

"You can do it, Bearie. You can," he whispered. He didn't want to further disturb the bees, but from his view, it appeared the bees were becoming increasingly agitated. Still, he encouraged his brother to go on, because he selfishly wanted the honey.

Bearie turned away from his brother and looked up at the buzzing bees. "A little further, and I will grab a chunk of honeycomb and slide to safety. Just a little further, and I'll have all *da* honey we can eat."

He mustered up all the courage he had as a young cub and decided now was the time for speed. He lunged upward with one big push and was almost to the hive. The buzzing became deafening, and the bees started to dive at him, buzzing around his ears and his head. There was no time to stop, and with one great boost of his hind legs, he reached the hive. The bees were now blinding him in a thick swarm around his head. He felt stings to his ears and his nose, and even stings on his bum.

"*Get down! Get down!*" screamed his brother, now fearing for Bearie.

Bearie could not hear his brother's cries, because of the deafening buzzing around his head. With great determination, he frantically swiped one large paw and hooked his claws in the hive. With the speed of a runaway train, he slid down the tree and landed with a *thump* on the ground.

The bees were furious with the thief and continued to swarm Bearie, stinging him everywhere. His brother was terrified and began to run away from the bees before they attacked him as well. He turned and saw his brother desperately trying to fight off the bees, and he knew he had to help.

He screamed at Bearie, "Follow me to the river! Hurry, Bearie! *Hurry!*"

Through the haze of buzzing and painful stings, Bearie barely heard his brother's screams, and began to run. He was blinded by the swarm covering his head and followed the screaming voice of his brother.

"This way, Bearie! *This way!*" cried his brother.

With one paw locked on the hive and the other swiping at the bees stinging his face, Bearie saw the river just ahead. He took a great leap and plunged into the water with a giant *splash*. He sank into the deep water, and as he surfaced, the first thing to break through the water was his big paw firmly gripping the honeycomb. His brother ran into the river and grabbed it, then carried it to the shore. Bearie emerged with a grimace of pain on his face. The water had washed away all the bees, but he was swelling up with lumps all over his face from stings. The pain was excruciating, and he wailed in distress. The bees, no longer interested, circled in formation and buzzed back to their hive in the tree. Bearie sat in the cold water and splashed his face for a long time, trying to soothe his stings. His brother stood on the riverbank with a look of guilt on his face.

"You shouldn't have made me do it!" cried Bearie. "I have bee stings all over me!"

"But you captured the honey. You are a hero!" Triumphantly his brother raised the honeycomb with his paws.

Bearie took one look at the oozing honey and dove into the water before he became sick. He surfaced and said, "I hate honey and will never eat another drop for as long as I live."

Stunned, his brother replied, "But you love honey. What do you mean you will never eat it again? So you got a few bee stings. Isn't it worth it for the taste of your delicious honey?"

"No!" cried Bearie. "Never again! I'll never ever, ever, ever eat another bite of honey!"

"More for me," said the selfish older brother under his breath.

Bearie heard what his brother had said but ignored him. He was in too much pain. His brother, unable to resist the temptation, began eating the honey from the comb, smacking his lips in delight. Bearie could take no more and walked down the river, staying in the cold water, until he was out of sight.

It was early evening, and Bearie slowly lumbered home to his den, knowing that a stern lecture from his mother awaited him. As he entered, she took one look at him and put her huge paws around him and gave him a big bear hug.

He cried in her arms and said, "I'm sorry, Mother. You told me not to get honey from *da* bees, and I didn't listen. I thought I could do it, and *da* honey looked so yummy. I thought I could make you proud of me. I'm sorry, Mother. I'm sorry." Bearie burrowed deeper into her soft fur as he continued to cry.

His mother was a wise bear, and when his brother had returned with a large honeycomb and no stings, she knew he had put Bearie up to the task of raiding a hive. She ached for her little cub and hugged him, softly licking the stings on his face. She led him to a chair, sat him down, and began applying a paste of leopard's bane and lavender. Bearie's crying turned to whimpers as the soothing paste began to ease the stings of the bees. His face was covered with swollen lumps, and he shuddered at how he must look.

"Mother, all *da* cubs will make fun of me cuz I look so awful," he whined.

"Oh, Bearie, who cares about those silly cubs? The swelling will be gone in no time, and you will be as handsome as ever," she cooed.

"Mother? I don't want to ever, ever eat honey again. *Da* thought makes me want to be sick all over. And now I am terrified of *da* bees. What will I eat now?" he asked.

She thought for a while and, with a large bowl in her paw, said, "I'll be back shortly. You just rest for a while."

She left the den and saw her other cub sitting on the ground, gorging on the ill-gotten honey. She gave him a little cuff with her paw as she walked by, and he looked up with a guilty grin. Her look was enough, and he slumped in shame as he licked the honey off his paws.

Bearie's mother traveled a short distance into the woods to a large whitebark pine tree. She scraped the ground with her claws and raked up the discarded pine nuts buried in the middens of helpful squirrels. She then put them in her bowl, continuing the process until the bowl was full. She returned to her den to find Bearie fast asleep in his bed.

"My poor little cub," she whispered. She knew his brother's devious ways all too well. There was no doubt he had coerced Bearie into challenging the bees for their honey, with no care for the safety of his brother. He was a selfish cub. But Bearie was sweet and kind, and, oh, how he loved honey. Well, not anymore. Honey would not do to feed her cub.

She set the bowl down and began to crush the nuts with her giant paws until they turned into the bear version of peanut butter. This was a treat few bears had ever eaten, for it was from a recipe that was sacred to her clan, and the whitebark pine nuts were scarce. She hoped Bearie would love the taste, and just to make sure, she decided to make some cookies from the bear peanut butter. She mixed the ingredients in another bowl, added the bear peanut butter, and baked the cookies in her oven.

Bearie awoke to the most delicious aroma he had ever smelled. His mother sat down beside him and said, "I don't blame you for not ever wanting to eat honey again." Bearie coughed in disgust at the word *honey* and wrinkled his nose. "I have made you something few bears have ever tasted, as it is quite rare for a bear to not like honey. But for you, my small cub, I have made the most delicious treat. Our clan made these years ago, when honey could not be found." With great ceremony, she handed him a cookie.

Bearie sniffed the cookie and took a small bite. A huge smile came across his lumpy, bee-stung face. "Yummy, Mother! This is even more delicious than honey!"

She reached over and picked up the bowl of bear peanut butter. "Try this, my little cub. It is the bear peanut butter I used to make the cookies."

Bearie hesitantly dipped his paw into the bowl and licked the thick, sticky mixture off his paws. "This is the best thing I have ever eaten in my whole life, Mother. Thank you," he said with his lips smacking.

He continued to dip his paws into the bowl until his face and paws were covered in bear peanut butter. He had never felt so happy. Bearie loved his mother more than anything in the whole world. He reached up, with his paws sticky with peanut butter, and hugged his mother. He started to fall limp in her arms from exhaustion, so she gently removed the bowl from his lap and laid him down on his bed. With a big sigh of contentment, Bearie, the peanut butter-eating bear, fell fast asleep.

Bearie had lived most of his life alone. Hunters had killed his mother when he was a young cub, and he had had to fend for himself. The death of his precious mother had devastated young Bearie.

She had been out gathering berries, as well as more nuts for his peanut butter, when she was shot and killed by a hunter. The young cub had been nearby when the shots rang out, and his heart had stopped. He ran toward the deafening sound, calling out for her, but there was no answer. Bearie stopped dead in his tracks when he found her lying in the grass, then ran to her side and desperately tried to get her to wake up.

"Wake up, Mother!" he cried, hot tears streaming down his face. "Wake up! Wake up! Please, Mother, wake up!" Bearie nudged his mother with his black nose, trying to urge her to rise. He pushed on her with his big paws. Nothing would stir the mother he loved so much. Tears blinded the young cub as the realization that she was dead struck him full force. Bearie lay down next to her and curled up into a ball. He could still feel the heat from her once life-filled body. Oh, how would he live without her? She had been the kindest and most loving mother bear ever.

Bearie was overcome by grief over his mother's death and did not hear the hunters' approach. Suddenly he felt something hard and cold poke him in the side. He looked up and was terrified to see two very large men standing over him.

The hunter poked him again with his rifle and said, "Run along, little bear. We have some work to do."

Bearie was not going to leave his mother's side. He burrowed closer to her and dug his claws into her thick fur. He would not let her go.

"Get out of here! Go! Run away!" yelled the hunter, impatient to finish his work. He prodded Bearie even harder with the barrel of his rifle. "Go on now, get out of here," he bellowed.

Bearie growled at the hunter, and both men laughed. After all, Bearie was just a cub and they both had guns. Tired of the game the cub was playing, the hunter pointed his rifle in the air and triggered one shot. The sound terrified Bearie, yet he still refused to leave his mother's side.

"Stubborn little guy, aren't you?" said one of the hunters. "Look, we didn't know your mom had a cub. Sorry, little bear, but you have to go now." The hunters grabbed Bearie by his hind legs and dragged him away from his mother.

Bearie cried and growled and clawed at the ground, trying to fight off the their rifles in the air and fired off more shots. Terrified and exhausted from the ordeal, Bearie turned and ran. He ran and ran until his lungs burned and he could run no further. With nothing left, he collapsed on the ground.

Hours later Bearie woke up, and the reality of his mother's death hit him with a powerful force. He lay whimpering and trembling in fear, curled up in a ball, not wanting to move. Deciding all he wanted to do was go home, he slowly stood up and shook the dirt from his coppery-orange fur. He made his way back to his den. It was the place he always loved, because his mother had always been there waiting for him. As he walked into the den, he caught the faintest whiff of his mother's delicious peanut butter cookies. Tears welled up in his big brown eyes. He stood swaying back and forth from the grief of his great loss. Then his brother came running into the den, screaming that he, too, had found their mother dead in the forest. He yelled at Bearie and said he should have stopped the hunters from killing their mother.

Bearie could see the grief on his brother's face, and he tried to comfort him. "I couldn't stop *da* hunters. By *da* time I got to Mother, she was dead. They made me leave her. I didn't want to leave her, but they made me leave." He shuddered as he recalled what had happened.

His brother cried and wept over the loss of their mother.

"It is time for me to leave, brother. I cannot stay in our den. There are too many reminders of Mother," explained Bearie.

Bearie looked around the den where he had been born. It used to be the safest place in the world, but no longer. He needed to move away and forget the horrible pain of losing his mother. He walked over to the table, where she had made nut butter cookies for him. Lying on the table was a piece of parchment with the family recipe. He gently picked up the paper and tucked it into his fur. It was the only thing he wanted to take to remind him of his mother.

"Goodbye, brother. Please take care of yourself," *grrred* Bearie softly.

"You can't leave me!" cried his brother. "How will I fend for myself? I will starve or be killed. We can survive only if we stay together. Oh, please, let me come with you, Bearie!" begged his brother.

Bearie felt sadness and compassion for his brother, but his brother was quite resourceful when he needed to be. He knew he would find his way. He could not stay in a place that had once brought him so much happiness and would now only remind him of his great loss. He knew his brother would never understand. He looked upon his brother with kindness, then turned and left the den.

Weeping, his brother watched as Bearie departed, and mumbled, "Goodbye, Bearie."

Although Bearie was in the forest on his own at a much younger age than was usual for a bear cub, he was determined to make his mother proud. He wandered all over the Big Sky, searching for a home, and eventually found the ideal place for his den, set at the base of a rock ledge. Bearie could not believe his luck. The abandoned cave was just the right size for the growing bear. As he *squeezed* through the opening, an opening he would have to widen as he grew, he detected the scent of bears past. He combed the nearby area, snapping pine tree branches and cutting swaths of moss with his long claws, then dragged the bedding into his new home, creating a soft, cozy place to sleep.

Bearie decided it was best to keep to himself until he was old enough and big enough to truly defend his life. He foraged berries and nuts, just as his mother had taught him. He made peanut butter daily, happily slathering it into his mouth, but it never tasted quite as good as the butter his mother had made for him. However, it was certainly better than honey.

Next to the entrance of his cave den, Bearie fashioned a makeshift oven by stacking rocks in the shape of a dome while cleverly creating a center hole to burn the wood. Over the wood compartment, he laid thin pieces of shale rock, which became hot for baking his peanut butter cookies. On a diet of berries, nuts, peanut butter and cookies, Bearie grew rapidly, becoming rather fat, but he did not really care. He was alone and had no one to impress.

Bearie spent time each day exploring the forest and encountered many other animals. He could not afford school, so all the other animals made fun of him because he was not educated and did not like honey. Other bears would not let their cubs play with him, because they did not want them to develop bad habits. Bearie, sad and alone, wandered the forest, eating peanut butter and cookies. He spent all summer filling up on the treats, getting fatter and fatter. Because he had become so fat, he started to have difficulty navigating the forest. He was not particularly clumsy, just too big to maneuver well. The other animals laughed when he came around, because he was always stumbling and bumbling his way around the forest. He did not have a very exciting life, but he was always kind to others and never said a bad word about any animal. The fact was, he was the kindest of bears and only wanted to be accepted by the forest animals. He just did not understand why the others made fun of him. Thus, he kept to himself.

Elkwood and Theodore closed up shop for the day, tired, but elated because they had sold all the cookies they had baked. They were just closing the door when they heard a crashing sound coming from the forest. They looked up and saw a bright flash of orange. Slowly lumbering through the thicket was a huge and very bright coppery-orange bear. He was the biggest and fattest bear they had ever seen. His long pale orange claws scraped the ground as he slowly lumbered his way into the clearing. Clearly, he was not the most coordinated bear in the forest.

Theodore chirped in laughter and Elkwood rolled his eyes as they watched the bear stumble along. As he clamored toward them, they both detected the distinct smell of peanut butter. *Why would a bear smell like peanut butter?* they both wondered.

He didn't look threatening at all, so Elkwood called out, "Hello there!"

The bear looked up and, not seeing the log in his path, tripped and fell to the ground with a *thump*. Theodore and Elkwood tried to stifle their giggles but could not. Seeing the huge bear fall down was just too funny. The bear looked embarrassed as he picked himself up with great effort and continued toward them.

Elkwood instantly felt compassion for the oversize bear and said, "Please come over and join us. I am Elkwood Elkington the Third, from the forest of England, across the Big Pond, and this is my friend Theodore, the red-headed woodpecker."

"*Yo*," replied the bear. "I am a bit tired. Mind if I *sat* awhile?"

"You mean *sit?*" said Elkwood, and the bear looked at him without understanding. "Yes, please come and sit," said Elkwood.

Theodore flew over and landed next to the bear. "What is your name, please?"

"Bearie," replied the bear. With a big *whoomph*, Bearie sat down on his haunches.

"Are you hungry?" asked Theodore. "We have a few delicious Eat Me cookies left."

"Sure, Teddy, I'll have one... or two."

Theodore looked at Bearie with shock, and Elkwood began to laugh until "Teddy" shot him a cold look. No one had ever called him Teddy, except for his mother. Theodore shook his feathers and flew into the store, then came back with a Big Elk, a Big Trout, and a Big Wolf cookie, and dropped them in front of Bearie. The bear swiped up the cookies in his gigantic paw and stuffed them all into his mouth.

"*Bearie* good," he said as he smacked and slobbered while he ate. "Do you got any bear peanut butter cookies?" he asked.

Elkwood cringed at the grammar used by the obviously illiterate bear. "No, sir, we do not have any peanut butter cookies."

"That's bad," *grrred* Bearie. "*Them's* my favorite."

"Really?" said Elkwood. "I thought all bears liked honey."

"Not *dis* bear. I hate honey," the bear said emphatically, and wrinkled his nose in disgust.

"A bear that hates honey? That is simply not possible," chirped Theodore with great surprise.

"Well, it's a long story, but I'll tell it *short*," sighed the bear. "When I was a cub, against my mother's rules, I tried to get *da* honey from *da* beehive up *da* tree, and *da* bees attacked me and stung me all over my face and body. I ran and jumped in *da* water to get rid of *da* bees. It hurt for days. Now I hate honey and am terrified of bees."

"Oh, that's awful," said Elkwood. "But how did you come to like peanut butter?"

"My mother made it for me cuz I wouldn't eat honey. She said our clan used to eat bear peanut butter years ago, when there was no honey. That's what I eat and why I'm so fat. Don't got any now, cuz my oven broke. I tripped and fell down on it and smashed it up," explained the bear, somewhat embarrassed.

Elkwood cringed again at the bear's awkward language. He had been educated in the finest schools in England and had never heard such an awful use of words. He decided the bear, no doubt, had not been educated and it would be cruel to make fun of him.

"Do you know how to make peanut butter cookies?" inquired Elkwood.

"Sure do, *Elkdude*. Got *da* recipe right here."

Theodore began to laugh, and Elkwood sighed and tolerated the slight. Bearie reached into his fur and pulled out a parchment with scribbles on it, then handed it to Elkwood.

Elkwood studied the recipe, although he could barely make out what was written, and said, "Why don't I make a batch and see if you like them, Bearie?"

Bearie nodded in agreement while scratching his ear. He then lay down and began to roll around in the dirt. He kicked his legs in the air, trying to roll completely over, but he was too fat. Elkwood and Theodore giggled at the expense of the fat bear.

Elkwood looked at Theodore and grinned. "Theodore, let's go make a batch of Bearie's cookies and see how they taste. Bearie, you can wait here while we work."

"Okay, *Elkdude*. Here, you *gonna* need this." He handed Elkwood a pot of bear peanut butter, flopped onto his side, and began to snore.

A short while later, Elkwood and Theodore returned to a snoring Bearie, with huge smiles on their faces. Theodore jumped on Bearie, trying to wake him, then grabbed his ear with his beak and pulled.

"*Wake up!*" he chirped right in his ear.

Bearie raised his head and, with a groggy grin, said, "I smell cookies. Can I have some?"

Elkwood handed him a tray of cookies, and Bearie hungrily ate them, smacking and slobbering. "Yum," he *grrred*. "Very good. Thanks, dudes."

"Bearie, we do not know much about you, but you seem like a very nice bear, and your nut butter cookies are very delicious."

Bearie grinned and put his giant paw over his nose. "Aw, gee," he *grrred*.

"I would like to sell your cookies in my store, and we will call them the Big Bear cookie, after you," exclaimed Elkwood.

"What's *da* name of your store?" *grrred* Bearie.

"It is right there on the sign I made," said Theodore.

"Can't read, Teddy." Bearie put both giant paws over his face in shame.

Elkwood looked at Bearie with compassion and kindness. The big brute of a bear was completely honest and innocent.

Theodore replied, "The Eat Me Cookie Company is the name of the store."

"Eat Me?" asked Bearie with a confused look on his face. "*Yer* not *gonna* eat me, are you?" he asked.

Elkwood and Theodore giggled in delight. "No, my friend," said Elkwood. "*Eat Me*…what else would a cookie say?"

Bearie thought for a second, then began to laugh a big, guffawing bear laugh. "Oh, dude, I get it. Pretty funny." The silly bear rolled around with delight.

Elkwood looked at Theodore, and they both nodded in agreement. "We would like you to join the Eat Me Cookie Company and become part of the Eat Me Animal Herd. We will sell the Big Bear cookies to all the animals in the forest, and you will become very rich indeed."

"You want me to join you dudes and make *da* cookies? *Really? Me?*" *grrred* Bearie.

"Of course, Bearie. You are now part of our herd. We must begin gathering ingredients for your cookies right away. Where do you get the peanut butter?" Elkwood asked.

"From *da* bear peanut butter trees," replied Bearie.

"*Of course!*" exclaimed Elkwood, laughing. Right then and there, Elkwood decided he would take Bearie under his wing and mentor him. He would teach Bearie about words and sentences and grammar so he could become a proud and educated bear of the forest. And he would most certainly put the bear on a diet and exercise regime. But they would talk about that later. They had to go into the forest and gather nuts for "*da*" Big Bear cookies.

Theodore jumped on Elkwood's antler while Bearie struggled to his feet, and they all walked off into the forest in search of nuts. Before they had walked twenty feet, Bearie tripped again on the same log and fell down, legs splayed out every which way.

"*Oh!*" he cried. "That one hurt."

"Come my big, peanut-butter-eating bear," said Elkwood. "And please try and be careful."

Bearie nodded, and they wandered into the woods, with Bearie crashing awkwardly through the brush.

CHAPTER 8

ON THE OTHER SIDE of the Montana forest, Bob "the Pumpkin" Bobcat, known to his friends as simply Bobcat, was out hunting with his best friend, Big Shot Bison. Mice were on today's menu for Bobcat. They were plentiful this time of year, but still, it took a skilled hunter like Bobcat to catch the fleet-footed mice. Big Shot guarded the perimeter of the large field, his keen eyes scanning all sides. He was always on the lookout for any danger that might threaten Bobcat. The grass in the field was growing very tall, and all that could be seen of Bobcat was a bobbed orange-and-black-striped tail pointing straight up in the air, quivering and shaking. Then suddenly a flash of orange would pounce through the air in a perfect arc, and Bobcat would land on his prey.

"Got one!" he would shout each time his pounce was on target. Bobcat pounced all over the field, shouting "Got one!" over and over until he was exhausted and his tummy was full.

Bobcat had met Big Shot Bison years ago, when Big Shot was just barely standing an all four hooves. He had been born into a huge heard of thousands of bison on the great plains of Montana. He was careful to always stay close to his family, and his mother in particular. He never left her side.

On a day that started out the same as all the days since he had been born—surrounded by the herd—he was grazing with his family on an endless

103

plain full of healthy grasses favored by the bison. Clouds were beginning to move in, forecasting a storm, but the day was warm, and Big Shot felt happy to be alive. He began to tease and play with the other baby bison, frolicking among the tall grasses and wildflowers. His mother, who always kept her keen eyes on Big Shot, smiled as the baby bison played. He was a good bison, and she was very proud of her offspring. She took a huge breath as her heart swelled with love. She would protect Big Shot with her life.

The sky began to darken, and she knew a bad storm was coming their way. Suddenly, and without warning, loud cracks like thunder were coming from every side of the great plain. Gigantic bison began to fall to the ground, creating thick clouds of dust in the air as the loud thuds of their bodies mixed with the rumble of the thunder. Big Shot's mother screamed for him, and as he began to run toward her, she crashed to the ground, lifeless. Terrified, Big Shot ran to her and pushed as hard as he could with his nose to get her to move.

"Get up, Mother!" he cried. "Please get up! *Get up!* Help me, Mother! *Help me!*" he screamed.

The herd was in a massive, chaotic panic, running crazily in every direction. Bison after bison fell, and the continual sound of their huge bodies hitting the earth was thunderous. Big Shot grabbed his mother with his teeth and pulled with all his strength, but she would not budge. Bodies were falling all around him, piling up so fast he had no time to escape. The loud cracks kept coming until he could stand it no longer. He lay down along his mother's belly, burrowing as close as possible to her while putting his small hooves over his ears to block out the frightening sounds. He did not move. Big Shot could barely breathe. The horror continued for what seemed like hours, and soon Big Shot was covered by death. He had only the small space created by the body of his mother to keep him from being crushed. He screamed and cried, but there was no one to hear his pain.

Hunters had surrounded his herd and attacked without warning. They had successfully massacred all the bison on the great plain that horrible day. All except Big Shot. He lay half-buried in the bowels of death, encased by the carcasses of his friends and family, cradled by his mother's massive body. He could not stop sobbing and screaming, desperate for his cries to be heard. He was frightened, terrified, beyond help. He would die. It was just a matter of time. He could not move, for bodies were amassed all around him. There was no help. Only death. There was no hope. Big Shot lay still for what seemed like days. Hungry, terrified, and unable to move, he waited...

Bobcat was traveling along the ridge of a mountain, looking for dinner, when he heard the cracks of gunfire and the thunderous noise of falling prey. He recognized the sound. He had heard it before. He ran along the ridge toward the deafening noise. From a high vantage point, Bobcat stopped and looked down across the plain and saw the most horrifying and gruesome scene he had ever witnessed. His keen eyes scanned the valley covered with dead bison. There were piles of bison, bloodied and lifeless, as far as the eye could see. Nothing moving, nothing breathing, nothing alive.

The gruesome sight below devastated Bobcat. There was nothing he could do, and he could not bear to look at the death and destruction another moment. He turned, with tears streaming down his face, and began to slowly backtrack along the ridge.

Without even realizing or knowing he was alive, Big Shot once again began to quietly whimper. Filled with unimaginable fear and surrounded by death, Big Shot's whimper became a long and piercing cry.

Bobcat stopped dead in his tracks. Had he heard something? No, it was not possible for anything to have survived the horrific massacre. Again cries of terror seemed to echo from the plain below. Hesitantly he traversed down the ridge as the guttural cries of an animal in pain became louder, penetrating the atmosphere of death hanging in the still air. He followed the sound until he could go no further. Before him stood the most unspeakable sight. He froze. Mounds of bison lay before him, too high to climb, too high to imagine. Towers of death. The stench of already rotting carcasses rose from the massive piles, assaulting his sensitive nose. He grimaced as the stench burned his nostrils. The whimper rose to a wail…and Bobcat began to dig and pull and claw toward the sound.

Amid the horror, he heard the crying and wailing become a hoarse whimper. Beyond all hope, beyond anything possible, beyond any miracle… before him was life. He had found the source, and pulled with his teeth and all his might to uncover the terrified, blood-soaked baby bison.

There was no time to think. He had to act fast, as he knew the hunters would be back in no time. He picked up the terrified baby bison with his teeth, tears still streaming down his face. The baby bison, not even knowing if he was truly still alive, fought and kicked, terrified he would be killed. Bobcat kept pulling and refused to let go. He held on, dragging the battered and bruised baby bison from the depths of death. He would never let go.

Big Shot continued to struggle as hard as he could to free himself, but Bobcat held on to his terrified charge tightly. Bobcat's cave was on the other side of the ridge, in a dense outcropping of rocks and boulders. It was a long way to carry this unruly bison, but he was determined. He had come too far to give up now.

From sheer exhaustion, the baby bison was losing his will to fight. Bobcat arrived at the entrance to his cave and carried him inside. He carefully laid the baby bison down on a soft bed of moss. He quickly trotted across the cave and returned with a bowl of clean water and a rag. He dipped the rag in the water and gently cleaned the dried blood from the baby bison. The water turned dark red. He then pulled a soft moss blanket over the shivering little body, then set about building a warm, cozy fire. Finally, he hung a pot of mushroom broth over the fire to heat.

Bobcat stared at the small heap of pain and tears under the moss blanket. What a brave little bison he was to have survived such terror and death. He must have lost his entire family, and Bobcat's heart ached for this tiny little bison. The mushroom broth began to steam, and Bobcat ladled a small serving of the delicious broth into a small bowl. He slowly approached the baby bison and sat down next to him.

Big Shot looked up at him with fear and anguish in his eyes. Tears soaked his face, and he was shaking uncontrollably. His mother had taught him to fear the big cats, as they could do serious harm to a young bison. But after all he had been through, he was too tired to fight.

Bobcat scooped a spoonful of broth from the bowl and gently held it up to the bison's mouth. Big Shot cautiously took a sip of the broth. It was warm and tasted more delicious than anything he had ever had in his short life. Bobcat fed spoonful after spoonful of mushroom broth to the hungry bison, and as the warm broth reached his tummy, his shivering began to abate. Slowly Big Shot's head fell to the side, and he drifted into a deep and welcome sleep.

The large cat sat for a while, watching the tiny bison sleep. "What a brave little bison," he murmured. He knew he could never turn his back on the bison he had fought so hard to save. Bobcat observed the bison was quite beautiful. He had soft and somewhat curly fur, and the color reminded him of the mustard he made from seeds found in the forest. Earlier, when the little bison had been crying, he noticed his beautiful dark purple eyes were the color of lupine blossoms in spring. He had yet to grow horns, as he was still rather young, but Bobcat imagined he would be a fine and powerful bison when he grew to become an adult. He wondered if his horns would complement his deep-purple eyes. *Oh my*, he thought. *I am getting quite ahead of myself.*

He was exhausted from carrying the small bison to his cave, so he ladled some broth for himself, lapped it up with his tongue, and curled up across from the bison. He purred as he snuggled into his moss blanket. From that day forward, Bobcat would treat the little bison as if he were his own, and as he fell fast asleep, he vowed to always keep him safe and happy.

Bobcat awoke with a start. The little bison lying under his moss blanket was whimpering, and tears streaked his face. Bobcat sprang to his feet and ran to his side.

"Are you hurt? What's wrong?"

Big Shot looked up at him, trembling. "I've lost my mother…my *family*… I'm alone, and now I'm afraid you'll eat me," he cried.

"*Naw,* I *ain't gonna* eat you. But I'll bet you're pretty hungry. How'd you sleep?" asked Bobcat.

"All right, I guess," whimpered the little bison.

Bobcat scurried to stoke the fire and heat some more mushroom broth for the bison. He handed him the bowl, and the baby bison gratefully accepted, slurping the broth until it was gone.

"Thank you," he said softly.

"Aw, it's nothing. What's your name?" asked Bobcat.

"Big Shot," replied the bison.

"That's a cool name, Big Shot. I like it. It makes you sound important and tough. I'm Bob "the Pumpkin" Bobcat, but you can just call me Bobcat."

Big Shot watched Bobcat as he gathered the breakfast bowls and straightened up his den. He was a very big bobcat and was most handsome. His fur was thick and very orange, like a pumpkin. Blended black spots and stipes covered the fur on his lean body. His big green eyes were rimmed in white, and he had black and white facial markings, almost like those of a tabby cat. Large, pointed ears, long white whiskers, and long tufts of fur on the sides of his face completed his roguishly handsome looks. He wore a black leather vest and leather chaps on his back legs. He had a jaunty walk and an air of confidence, and he *did* seem very nice. After all, Bobcat had rescued him from the throes of death and had taken care of him. He had fed him and kept him safe.

Big Shot missed his mother. How awful it had been to see her die. And the entire herd…it was just too much for him to grasp. He decided he must put the horrible events of yesterday behind him and become a good and honest bison, one that would make his mother proud. He could not believe Bobcat had risked his own life to save him. He pledged to himself that he would always protect and love Bobcat. He would lay down his life for him, without hesitation, as Bobcat had done for him. He was his family now. An unlikely pair, he guessed, but so what? Bobcat was his friend, his only friend, and he would never betray that friendship. He would never let go of his friend. *Never.*

Bobcat was amazed by how quickly Big Shot grew. He was becoming a very strong and powerful bison. His horns began to show and were a beautiful lavender color, and they did indeed complement his dark purple eyes. Bobcat was amazed by Big Shot's gentle nature. He was always kind, and whenever Bobcat was in need, which was often, Big Shot was right there by his side, defending him. Even though Big Shot was not very book smart, he was loyal without fail.

Bobcat was a bit of a prankster and a slickster. He had grown up in what high and mighty cats called "the wrong side of Montana" and had a rough life as a kitten. Having become an orphan quite young, Bobcat had learned to fend for himself. He was an alley cat of sorts and loved to play pranks on other animals. He had learned to survive on his cleverness and his wits. Bobcat had a natural sense of humor, but he would generally take things a little too far, and the outcome often angered the other animals. He thought himself quite amusing, but the animals of the forest felt that sometimes he was just plain mean, because Bobcat's pranks often caused them embarrassment. He was a very good prankster, and the other animals always fell for his tricks.

Big Shot, however, saw the kind and loving side of Bobcat. No matter what kind of trouble he caused, Big Shot had his back. Bobcat had a very funny way of talking in the guttural language of a street cat. He loved to wear leather and never left his den without his black leather vest and chaps. He was a rather handsome bobcat, and although he hid it well, Big Shot knew that deep down inside, Bobcat had a heart of gold.

For some time now, Bobcat had been bilking pine cones from the weaker animals in the forest in exchange for his protection. The rabid pack of coyotes, led by the infamous Puck, were a constant threat. He could beat Puck in a fight, but sometimes it was a little too close for comfort. He believed, since he was risking his life to protect the other animals, they should pay him for the risks he took. As Big Shot grew into a full-size bison, Bobcat thought of a brilliant idea. Big Shot would be his "enforcer." If the animals would not pay for his protection, he would send Big Shot out to collect.

Big Shot really did not like being an enforcer, but out of respect for Bobcat, he went along with the charade. After all, it was a bit of a ruse, because all the animals loved Big Shot. He was kind and gentle, and never threatened them. They happily gave up their fee to Big Shot, in order that the young bison might save face with Bobcat. The animals knew Big Shot felt unconditional love for and loyalty to Bobcat, and for this they had great respect and adoration for the big brute. Bobcat had no idea that the animals did not fear Big Shot, for when he was around, Big Shot would put on his fiercest bison persona.

Big Shot awoke early one morning to find Bobcat outside the cave, gardening. "What are you growing?" he asked.

"Pumpkins," replied Bobcat.

Big Shot examined the garden and saw tiny little orange pumpkins beginning to grow on the vines. "Why do you grow pumpkins?" he asked.

"To make my delicious pumpkin cookies. They're my most favorite food in the world. In a few weeks, they'll be big enough to harvest, and we can make pumpkin cookies."

"Oh," replied Big Shot. "I wondered why you called yourself Bob "the Pumpkin" Bobcat. Now I understand, I guess."

Bobcat laughed. "That's the name I was given by the forest animals because I love pumpkin cookies so much. They think of me as sort of the gangster of the forest, so they nicknamed me the Pumpkin, and it just stuck."

"My mother used to make me the most delicious brownies when I was young, and they were the best brownies in the whole world. I guess I should be called the Brownie," said Big Shot.

Bobcat laughed heartily and smiled at his friend. "I think Big Shot is just fine. Do you know how to make brownies? I have never tasted a brownie."

"I think so. Long ago my mother tucked the recipe in my fur so I would always have it in case something happened to her. Brownies really are my favorite."

"Then we must make you some brownies. I know where we can get the chocolate chips, but we have to be very careful, because it is a very secret spot," said Bobcat.

"Could we go today? I would really like some brownies. It would remind me of home and my family," reminisced the big bison.

"Sure, we can. Let me finish my gardening, and we will go find the chocolate chips and make your brownies."

A short time later, the pair headed through the woods to the Lone Peak. Bobcat was very cautious, making sure they were not followed. He put Big Shot on full alert. They sneaked through the woods and finally Bobcat said, "There's the waterfall. Shh, no one can find us."

"A waterfall?" asked Big Shot.

"The chocolate chip waterfall," whispered Bobcat.

Truthfully, Bobcat had only heard of the legendary chocolate chip waterfall on the Lone Peak, but until now he had not really known if it truly existed. But he had indeed found it, and it was loaded with chocolate chips. Bobcat rushed over to the waterfall and began picking chips off the rocks. He threw a *pawful* into his mouth.

"They're delicious," he exclaimed. He picked another *pawful* and gave them to Big Shot.

Big Shot put all of them in his mouth at once and said, "These are delicious! Oh, the best chocolate chips *ever*! More, please! May I have more?"

Bobcat gathered another *pawful* and gave them to Big Shot. They ate chocolate chips until they were both so full they could barely move and the chocolate smeared all over their faces told the tale of their thievery.

"We must gather as much chocolate as we can before anyone sees us, and then we must leave this place," Bobcat directed.

Just as he was about to put his paw into the waterfall and grab more chips, he heard a low, threatening growl. He whirled around and saw a huge bluish wolf crouching low on his haunches. The wolf's teeth were bared, and he was glaring and snarling at him.

Elkwood stepped out of the forest, looming quite large, and asked, "What is the meaning of this? How dare you steal my chocolate chips?"

Big Shot, sensing a threat to his friend, stood up quickly to display his full stature and began swinging his head back and forth, causing both Elkwood and Wolfrik to inhale sharply in surprise. They had never seen such a big, commanding brute of a bison before. Bison were typically animals of the plains, not generally found this high in the mountains. Wolfrik snarled and took a step back…but only one step. He was ready to pounce on this giant bison should he threaten his friend.

"What do you mean, *your* chips?" asked Bobcat with a low hiss.

"Yes, *my* chips! I found the chocolate chip waterfall long ago and claimed it as mine. You are trespassing," Elkwood said with authority.

"I don't see a sign with your name anywhere. So as far as I can see, the chips are ours for the taking," snapped Bobcat.

Big Shot took a deep breath, a bit afraid of the two despite his own size, and said in a very quiet voice, "We just wanted some chips to make my mother's brownies."

Elkwood and Wolfrik von Spice looked at each other, and a grin came across their faces. "Did you say, your mother's brownies?" asked Elkwood.

Disarmed by the change in attitude, Bobcat hissed at the two. Baring his large fangs, and with his claws extended, he swiped his paw through the air.

"Calm down, Bobcat," said Big Shot in a whisper only Bobcat could hear. "I will tell them."

Big Shot looked at the pair, with his deep-purple eyes, in a manner that suggested he could be trusted. "The hunters killed my herd and my entire family. Only I survived, thanks to my friend Bobcat." He nodded toward his agitated friend. "We were only gathering enough chocolate chips to make the brownies my mother made for me when I was young. We did not mean to upset you."

Wolfrik von Spice scowled and replied, "Seems you filled your bellies as well."

Bobcat and Big Shot, embarrassed and looking very guilty, tried to wipe the chocolate off their faces, only smearing it more. "You are very observant, but we took nothing that was not free for the taking," hissed Bobcat.

Big Shot took a step toward the pair. Although his expression was not threatening, Elkwood and Wolfrik knew that even though the bison looked big and clumsy, in reality bison were fast and powerful, capable of inflicting a lot of damage. They took one step back.

"We don't want to fight you, we just wanted chocolate chips. Isn't there enough for everyone?" suggested Big Shot.

"And what is your name, sir?" asked Elkwood.

"Big Shot, and my friend here is Bob "the Pumpkin" Bobcat. I am his enforcer."

"Interesting," replied Elkwood, not having a clue what he meant by *enforcer*. "I am Elkwood Elkington the Third, from England, and this is Wolfrik von Spice."

No one was ready to shake hooves and paws just yet, but they all gave a nod of acknowledgment.

"Did you say you make brownies?" Elkwood asked Big Shot.

"He said he did, *Elkbutt*," spat Bobcat with a sly grin on his mouth.

"Elkwood. My name is Elkwood," said Elkwood in disgust.

As things were about to get ugly, Big Shot jumped in. "Yes, brownies are my favorite treat in the world. They remind me of my mother." Big Shot looked down as tears welled up in his big purple eyes.

That hit a soft spot in Elkwood's heart, so he tried to ignore the rude bobcat. "Have you ever heard of the Eat Me Cookie Company?" inquired Elkwood.

Both shook their heads.

"We are located through the forest at the base of the Lone Peak, at the two dead trees. We sell the very best cookies in the forest. *My* cookie is the founding recipe, the Big Elk chocolate chip cookie." Big Shot licked his lips. "Wolfrik von Spice makes the Big Wolf spice cookie. Bearie lives on the Big Bear peanut butter cookie. And of course, Twinkle Toes Trout has contributed the Big Trout sugar cookie."

Big Shot *and* Bobcat both licked their lips.

"Perhaps you would like to join the Eat Me Cookie Company, and we can sell your brownies as well?"

"Why do you call it Eat Me?" growled Bobcat. "Are you suggesting something?" The big cat smirked satirically.

"Don't be ridiculous Mr. Bobcat. What else would a cookie say?" asked Elkwood emphatically.

Bobcat and Big Shot looked at each other and nodded in understanding. "You can sell my brownies? Really?" asked Big Shot. "Then, can we share the chocolate chip waterfall?"

"Well, of course. I *do* think there are enough for everyone. We shall call them Big Bison brownies. Why don't you come by the store tomorrow? Bring your recipe, and we can make a batch and see how they taste."

Big Shot looked at Bobcat and asked, "Is that all right, Bobcat?"

Bobcat nodded in approval, still wary.

"My friend Bobcat has a cookie too. He makes pumpkin cookies, but the pumpkins aren't ripe yet."

Bobcat's eyes lit up and his ear pricked forward.

"You make pumpkin cookies?" questioned Elkwood.

"Yep, the best in the forest, *Elkbutt*. My pumpkins will be ripe soon," replied Bobcat.

"If they are truly the best, would you like to share them with us? We could call them Big Bobcat cookies, and you can join the Eat Me Animal Herd, but…my name is Elk*wood*!"

"Yeah, whatever, *Elkbutt*. I'm not much of a joiner, but I'll think on it. The Big Bobcat cookie has a nice ring to my ears." He cocked his ears back and forth, grinning. "It will be the best seller and will outsell the Big *Elkbutt* cookie," teased Bobcat.

Big Shot shrugged his massive shoulders, for he knew how Bobcat loved to tease.

"We shall see, *furball*. We shall see," said Wolfrik with a growl. He did not like this cat's lack of respect for Elkwood.

Bobcat hissed at Wolfrik, "You'll see, Ricky. The pumpkin cookies will be the most popular."

Wolfrik laid back his ears and snarled as he swiped the ground with his huge paw. Wolfrik did not trust Bobcat. He had heard rumors of his pranks against the animals of the forest. It was one thing to be funny, but he knew Bobcat was a bit of a thug. He also knew his arch enemy was the evil Puck, so at least they had something in common. Big Shot, on the other hand, seemed to be a genuinely nice bison with no hidden agenda. He wondered how the two had become friends. Perhaps someday they would share their story. He would wait to pass judgment until Bobcat proved himself to be a loyal member of the Eat Me Animal Herd. Yes, he would watch this one, and wait.

After everyone had gathered mounds of chocolate chips, they bid each other farewell.

"Hey, *Elkbutt*! Where is this cookie company you speak of?" ribbed Bobcat.

"Down the Lone Peak and through the forest, in the clearing with the two big trees," repeated Elkwood, quite annoyed.

"The Lone Peak? Where is that?" asked Bobcat.

"You are standing on it," quipped Elkwood.

"Oh, I never heard that name before," said Bobcat.

"I named it because it is *my* mountain," retorted Elkwood proudly.

"You sure seem to think you own a lot around here, *Elkbutt*," said Bobcat with a subtle snarl.

"Because I do," snapped Elkwood.

Wolfrik looked at Elkwood with disappointment. This elk should be taught some humility. Even though the *furball* was goading Elkwood, he was far too arrogant for his own good. He knew Elkwood would have to learn the hard way, and just might get hurt in the process.

The following day, the Eat Me Cookie Company opened to a huge gathering of animals of all kinds, waiting to buy cookies. They were happily surprised to find there was a new treat on the menu. Elkwood and Theodore had been up all night making Big Shot brownies, along with all their other cookies. The work was getting to be too much for them, and they decided they must get the other animals in the Eat Me Animal Herd to help. As the store opened, Bobcat and Big Shot Bison walked up and greeted Elkwood and Theodore.

"Top of the day, *Elkbutt*," greeted Bobcat with a grin.

Theodore chirped in delight. It seemed this big bobcat was determined to take Elkwood down a notch.

"Get in here, both of you. We need help!" begged Elkwood.

Bobcat and Big Shot nodded and eagerly began helping them make cookies. When Wolfrik arrived, he, too, was enlisted into cookie-making service. They were very busy all day and sold every last cookie, as well as all the Big Bison brownies, except, of course, the ones they saved for a snack after the store closed. Exhausted, Elkwood, Wolfrik, Big Shot, and Bobcat sat in silence as they ate their snacks. They all agreed Elkwood had made the Eat Me Cookie Company a grand success.

CHAPTER 9

UP HIGH ON THE LONE PEAK, Baldoin, meaning "brave friend" in Old French, was preparing for a very difficult climb. Baldoin was far from his home country of France. He had spent his life backpacking and climbing throughout Europe, and due to the difficult terrain he had conquered, he was a legend for his skill and daring. He never went anywhere without his backpack, in which he carried all his climbing gear.

He was a magnificent moose with fur the color of deep cinnamon, with a showy blend of rich, jeweled bluish green. Huge, soulful brown eyes framed by long, dark lashes instantly conveyed his wisdom and friendly demeanor. His long face was smudged with blue-green and defined by paler highlights, topped off with rather large ears. He had massive golden-yellow antlers, and his large hooves were of the same color. He valued the bright color of his hooves and antlers because they glowed in the dark and aided him when navigating difficult terrain at night. His antlers were like a giant headlamp at night, and his hooves, like beacons.

After backpacking all over Europe, he decided to travel to Montana, for he had heard there were gigantic mountains and challenging trails. When he was a young moose, his mother, who was Scandinavian, and his father, who was French, were both killed in a climbing accident. His fondest memory of his mother was when she baked her very special oatmeal cookies, a delicacy in

Scandinavia. Baldoin loved oatmeal cookies, and his favorite was loaded with lots of chocolate chips, plump raisins, and crunchy walnuts. He loved chocolate in his cookies so much his mother had nicknamed him Le Chocolat Moose.

She would say to him, "Baldoin, you are so covered in *le chocolat*, you look like a *chocolat* moose." He would laugh in delight as he licked the chocolate from his hooves.

The Moose Backpackers, as they were called, were the staple of his diet, because they provided all the nutrition he needed for his climbing expeditions. Plus they tasted delicious and reminded him of his mother. Along with his gear, he always carried a supply of Moose Backpacker cookies in his backpack. When his parents fell to their death in the French Alps, he had found the recipe for Moose Backpackers tucked in his mother's backpack. He was grateful for her gift, but it was the saddest day of his life.

Le Chocolat Moose was a flamboyant character and spoke with the eloquence of a well-educated moose. Although he had not attended any formal schools, his travels across Europe, and the animals he had met, had provided him with a rich education. He was a very friendly moose and loved to entertain those he met with his thrilling stories about moose mountaineering. He had quite a flair for the dramatic and mesmerized all those who listened to his stories of death-defying climbs. His stories were all the more fantastic because those who knew him saw him as quite clumsy by nature.

Baldoin was indeed clumsy, but only when he was on flat and easy ground. His comfort zone was when he was most challenged, while moose mountaineering. He had survived many close calls, but due to his excellent climbing skills, he had avoided a deadly fate. One wrong *hoofstep* could result in dire consequences. His close calls made his stories all the more exciting. When he was moose mountaineering, his clumsiness disappeared, and he was as sure-footed as a mountain goat.

Everyone loved and respected Le Chocolat Moose. He was always seeking knowledge and loved to read. When he was not climbing some treacherous mountain, he was reading. He was determined to make his parents proud of him. Plus he needed to learn everything he could about moose mountaineering, so he read every book he could find on the subject. His father had taught him that successful moose mountaineering was based not only upon physical skills but also upon the knowledge in one's head. He read about the latest mountaineering gear, about climbing techniques, and also about the weather and snow. The most dangerous time of year to climb was winter. He learned about ice, snow, and the feared avalanches. Avalanches were the biggest danger of all, for getting caught in an avalanche meant almost certain death. He always carried a shovel inside his backpack so he could test the snow to be certain it was safe. He also carried an ice pick strapped to the side of his backpack and a rope for rappelling down cliffs or crossing crevasses. He was prepared for just about any circumstance or emergency.

When he arrived in Montana, after exploring the territory, he settled in the land of the Big Sky. It had the most beautiful mountains and reminded him of home. His current focus was on the very big mountain that looked like a pyramid and stood out with majesty above all other mountains in the Big Sky. It was summertime, and he wanted to learn everything about this mountain before he attempted to climb it once it was covered with snow. The time was now. Le Chocolat Moose laid out his gear, making sure everything was in place. He then filled his backpack and began the steeper part of his ascent up the south face of the peak.

Elkwood had been exploring the Lone Peak on his daily hikes. He had found the chocolate chip waterfall and wondered what else he might find. Plus it was nice to get away by himself once in a while to think. The Eat Me Cookie Company was running smoothly, and he was very proud of the fine *Elk* he believed he had become. He had done what his parents had wanted. He had journeyed to Montana and had become rich beyond his wildest dreams. He was certain the Big Elk was, and always would be, the most delicious cookie in the forest, no matter what the others in the Eat Me Animal Herd believed. His chocolate chip cookies were the best…and that was that. He was the brilliant founder of the Eat Me Cookie Company and had gener-ously allowed the other animals to become part of his success. Yes, he was rich, successful, handsome, well educated, and had many friends. The other animals were nice and had good cookies, but it was *he* who had given them the opportunity to join the Eat Me Animal Herd. Without him they were nothing. And he was quite sure his Big Elk cookies would have been quite successful on their own. He was very proud of himself for sharing his wealth, thus showing off his very generous nature. Yes, he was all his parents had hoped he would become.

As he was walking and thinking about how wonderful things had turned out, he noticed something on the south face of the Lone Peak. He decided to take a closer look. As he climbed up the lower rock face, he began to feel nervous. He did not like climbing anything too steep or rocky, for it frightened him. He was not used to climbing. He was strong but had led a pampered life and spent most of it on the flatlands of England. He chose his steps carefully.

Baldoin heard rocks clattering below and looked down to see a large elk struggling to climb over the rocky face and slipping on his hooves far too much. He snapped into action, and grabbing his rope, he tied it around a large rock with an expertly tied knot. He quickly put his backpack on his back and looped the rope around his waist, hooking it with a carabiner. As he began to descend, sliding the carabiner down the rope, he called out to the elk, "Stay where you are! I am coming to get you, *oui*?"

Elkwood looked up to see a moose dancing down the rocks with ease, hooves flashing. In seconds Baldoin reached Elkwood and said, "You should not be up here. It is very dangerous, *non*?"

"I know," said Elkwood softly, somewhat embarrassed. "I was curious about what you were doing."

"I was preparing to climb this mountain, *oui*? What is your name?"

"I am Elkwood Elkington the Third, from England, across the Big Pond. Who might you be?" he asked.

"I am Baldoin and I am from France," replied the moose mountaineer with a heavy French accent.

"What an interesting name. What does it mean?"

"It means 'brave friend' in my language," answered the moose. "I would ask you to join me on my climb, but I think you would be safer if you watched from a distance, *non*?"

Elkwood agreed that it would indeed be safer, although he wished he could summit *his* own mountain. He was very impressed by Baldoin and very much wanted to see him climb the Lone Peak.

"Do you need help moving to a safer vantage point, Elkwood?" asked Baldoin.

"Thank you, but I think I can manage. I will settle in and watch as you climb *my* mountain."

"*Your* mountain? *Non!*" exclaimed Baldoin. "How can you claim a mountain you have not climbed?"

"Because I named it the Lone Peak. Thus, it is *my* mountain," stated Elkwood most emphatically.

Baldoin thought this elk was very arrogant to claim a mountain as his own when he had not yet climbed to the top. He had summited many mountains but had never claimed one for his own. That did not seem right, for mountains could not be owned. Nevertheless, he did like the name Elkwood had chosen, and he thought it nice that he wanted to watch him climb.

"I will be back *bientôt*, soon, Elkwood. Please be careful on your way down, *oui*?"

Before Elkwood could say thank you, Baldoin was hoofing up the mountain with ease and grace. Elkwood descended a short distance and sat down to watch Baldoin summit the Lone Peak. The moose mountaineer was magnificent. Elkwood had never seen such agility and skill. He wondered how Baldoin had learned to climb with such ease and expertise. Climbing must be something the French did, he mused.

It was not long before Baldoin was standing atop the Lone Peak. The views were spectacular, and he could see for miles in every direction. It was one of the most incredible panoramas he had ever seen. There were mountains in every direction, and he planned to climb them all. Although he had taken the easier south side for his first attempt, the summit offered him the chance to look at all the other approaches up the Lone Peak. He walked around and surveyed every aspect of the mountain, making mental notes of the terrain for his future ascents. Each side was different and more challenging, and he would be very occupied tackling them all during the summer months. He stood at the highest point for a few moments, thinking of his parents. They would have surely loved climbing this magnificent mountain. He was quite sure they would be proud of his mountaineering skills.

Baldoin took a few more moments to soak in the breathtaking views, then turned to begin his descent. In no time at all, he was at the bottom, walking over to Elkwood. As he approached the flat, smooth area of grass where Elkwood was sitting, he slipped and almost fell down. Elkwood began to laugh, and so did Baldoin.

"For such an expert moose mountaineer, you are certainly quite clumsy, my friend," laughed Elkwood.

"Ooh la la, you are quite correct. My hooves do not like the flat and easy ground, *oui*? It is my curse." The humble moose laughed.

Elkwood liked the easy and fun spirit of Baldoin, and the fact that he could make fun of himself.

"My parents taught me that to take anything for granted is very dangerous, *oui*? When you fall, you must get right back up and try again, *non*? I know I am clumsy by nature, but that is no matter. It is when I am climbing that counts the most, and there I am *sure-hoofed* and skilled, *oui*? It is on a mountain that

I am at my best. On the flat land, not so much, my friend. Learning to laugh at oneself is a good thing, *non?*"

"No. I mean, yes, I suppose it is a good thing. But does it not frustrate you?" asked Elkwood, trying to understand.

"*Oui*, at times, but it is being on the mountain that is most important to me. We all have our strengths, the things we do best, but we all have weaknesses… *non?* Some things just cannot be helped, so we do our best at the things we do best, *oui?*"

Elkwood contemplated what his new friend had said. With all the *non*s and *oui*s, he was very confused. He had always thought he was the best at everything. Maybe there was some wisdom in what Baldoin was trying to tell him. Maybe he was telling him to be satisfied with trying to be the best he could be. Maybe no one could be the best at everything. He was not sure what to think, as this was a very new concept to him.

Baldoin sat down next to Elkwood on the soft green grass and pulled off his backpack. He opened it and reached inside, then pulled out a small sack. He asked Elkwood, "Would you care to try a Moose Backpacker?"

"What is a Moose Backpacker?" inquired Elkwood, very curious.

"The most delicious moose snack in all the world, *oui?*"

Baldoin opened the bag, pulled out a cookie, and handed it to Elkwood. Then he grabbed another and hungrily began to eat. Elkwood took a nibble of the cookie, and a huge grin came across his face.

"This is delicious! Where did you get these cookies?" he asked.

"They are from *ma mère*'s recipe. I always carry some with me because they provide the nutrition I need to climb mountains, plus they are very delicious, *oui?*" replied Baldoin with a grin and chocolate smudged on his face.

"Oh my, Baldoin! You have chocolate all over your face," giggled Elkwood.

"Oh, *oui! J'aime le chocolat*," laughed the moose as he tried to lick the chocolate off his face with his massive tongue.

Elkwood could not stop laughing at the massive moose in front of him, trying to lick his own face.

"I always seem to get *le chocolat* all over my face. It is why *ma mère* called me Le Chocolat Moose." A sad look came across Baldoin's face. "You can call me Le Chocolat Moose if you like, *oui?*" He tried to muster a smile for his new friend.

"Where is your mother? Does she climb with you?" asked Elkwood.

"Both *ma mère* and *mon père* died in a climbing accident when I was young.

I found the recipe in her backpack. It is the only thing I have left of them." Baldoin had a look of great sadness on his face.

"I am sorry for your great loss, my friend."

Baldoin nodded in appreciation.

"I have an idea. I own a cookie company called the Eat Me Cookie Company, and I sell only the very best cookies in the forest. I have several cookies, mine being the Big Elk chocolate chip cookie, which, of course, is the best." The moose grimaced. "The rest, well, you will just have to come and taste them and meet the Eat Me Animal Herd. I believe we have room for one more cookie, and you will become rich beyond your wildest dreams," chattered Elkwood with great enthusiasm.

Baldoin replied, "The Eat Me Cookie Company? Well, *mon ami*, that is a funny name, but what else would a cookie say, *non?*"

"Quite right!" agreed Elkwood, and the new friends laughed.

"I do not care about becoming rich, as I am rich beyond measure in other ways, *oui?* I would like to meet your herd, as I have decided to make Montana my home. It would be nice to be part of something special, *non?*" pondered the moose.

"No. I mean, yes. Why don't you come back to the store and meet the rest of herd? You can tell them about your climb to the top of the Lone Peak. They will be most impressed," exclaimed Elkwood.

"I would like that, *Monsieur* Elkwood. *Merci.* Please lead the way, *oui?*"

The two walked for a long time while Elkwood told Baldoin all about the other animals in the Eat Me Animal Herd. Elkwood was pleased with his new friend because they had so much in common. They were both the best at something. He was not sure he understood Baldoin, but he liked him very much and hoped they would become the best of friends.

The two heard a fluttering in the air nearby and looked up to see Theodore racing toward them. He landed on Elkwood's antlers and Elkwood greeted him. "Hello, Theodore! Meet my new friend—"

Theodore's frantic chirping cut him off. "No time, come quickly. Twinkle Toes is in trouble!"

"What?" cried Elkwood.

"There's no time! Hurry! *Hurry!* Follow me, *please!*" begged the bird. He flew off, and Elkwood and Le Chocolat Moose ran at full speed after him.

CHAPTER 10

IT WAS A GORGEOUS DAY, and Twinkle Toes was lounging on the pond bank, quite immersed in her beautiful vision mirrored in the water. As usual she was splashing herself with her fins as she admired her exquisite reflection.

"*I have never loved another "animal" the way I love myself,*" she hummed softly.

So completely enraptured was she by her own image reflected in the water, she did not see Puck and one of his pack dogs crawling silently on their bellies toward her. They were *slowly* licking their lips in anticipation. The beavers were off gathering willow, so they were not available to sound their alert, warning of looming danger.

Without warning, a paw landed on Twinkle Toes and pinned her to the ground. She squealed and turned her head to see two sets of very large yellow fangs drooling over her.

"You are beautiful, my little carp, but today you will taste far better than you look," growled Puck. "Any last words?" he asked sarcastically.

Twinkle Toes eyed the evil dogs. Their rancid breath made her wrinkle her nose in disgust. She calmly replied, "*When I'm caught between two evils, I generally like to take the one I never tried.*"

She flipped her tail fin with all her strength and slapped Puck hard on the face. The force surprised him, and he lost his grip on the trout. Just as she flipped her tail fin again to leap into the water for safety, Puck recovered and swung his paw at her, hitting her with a *smack* that sent her flying across the clearing.

"Now I have you, little carp," he sneered as he stalked toward her, fangs bared and a hungry look on his face. The other coyotes circled around the far side of Twinkle Toes, and she realized she was trapped. She tried to flip her tail fin and spin her side fins to cross the distance to the pond, but it was no use. She was trapped. Puck slowly edged closer, enjoying the fear he saw on the beautiful trout's face.

"Yes, you will make a delicious meal, and I have waited a long time to eat you," sneered Puck.

With that, he leaped through the air in one last, triumphant pounce. In midair a force broadsided him, knocking him sideways and sending him crashing to the ground. Puck gasped for breath as the force of the impact knocked the wind from his lungs. He scrambled to his paws and turned to see Wolfrik von Spice standing next to his dinner, snarling at him. He had never noticed how truly large and menacing this wolf was, and he knew this could be a battle he may not win on his own. With one high-pitched, rallying howl, the clearing became surrounded by Puck's pack of vile, snarling dogs. Wolfrik wasted no time, for he saw from the corner of his eye that Twinkle Toes was struggling to breathe. He ran toward Puck and tackled him, and the two snarled and tore at each other.

Twinkle Toes, gasping for breath, tried, to no avail, to flip toward the water. She believed in Wolfrik. In fact, she loved him, and she knew he would wipe out Puck and his nasty pack. She lay still, hoping that the other coyotes would not dare eat their leader's meal. The fight was horrible, and the snarls and growls terrified the trout. She lay still, not wanting to draw attention to herself. But she was running out of time…and oxygen.

Elkwood and Baldoin raced to the beaver pond and burst through the woods, right into the middle of a pack of snarling coyotes. They were surrounded by at least a dozen mangy dogs baring their fangs and growling viciously. Wolfrik and Puck were locked in battle, standing on their hind legs with teeth gnashing. Wolfrik clearly outweighed Puck, but Puck was fast and kept breaking free and biting Wolfrik on his hind legs.

Elkwood heard a scream and saw Twinkle Toes flapping on the ground, struggling for oxygen. He jumped toward her to grab her, and Puck's pack charged him. He reared up in the air, and his hooves came down hard on two coyotes, and they yelped in pain. He threw his head side to side, striking coyotes with his powerful antlers. He shouted to Baldoin, "Grab her! Get her back in the water, *now*!"

As Baldoin ran toward the flailing trout, a filthy, crazed coyote jumped on his back. Baldoin reeled quickly to one side and threw the dog in the air, and it landed with a sickening crack of its bones and a cry of pain. Wolfrik and Puck were fighting savagely, and the pack kept coming at Baldoin and Elkwood. Theodore was flying above the battle, back and forth, cawing madly, not knowing what to do. There was no time. He must save Twinkle Toes.

He flew into the fray, dove down, and scooped Twinkle Toes up in his beak. Forgetting the bird was her friend and not her enemy, she screamed and struggled in irrational fear. Theodore veered to the pond and dropped her in the water with a big *splash*. She surfaced, spitting and coughing, and struggling to breathe.

Suddenly there was a loud bellow, and Big Shot came crashing through the trees into the clearing, followed by a caterwauling Bobcat. Big Shot stopped and pawed the ground with his massive hooves, then spotted the nearest coyote. He charged, his massive head down, and scooped the coyote up in the air, tossing him over his head with such force that the coyote smashed against a tree with a *thud* and landed in a heap.

Bobcat took one giant leap and landed beside Wolfrik and hissed, "Now it looks like a fair fight, Puck. Shame on you, picking on a defenseless little trout. Want a piece of me?" he challenged as he charged in and tackled Puck.

They rolled in a ball of teeth and fur while the rest of the Eat Me Animal Herd continued to kick and butt at the vicious pack. The scene was utter chaos, and finally the hideous coyotes, beaten and injured, scattered into the woods, howling and screaming in pain... and defeat. They were finished, and with complete and shameless cowardice, they left their leader to battle alone.

Puck leaped away from Bobcat and crouched low on his belly with his dripping fangs bared. His eyes had the wild and manic look of an animal cornered, and the huge yellow orbs were so bloodshot they looked like they would burst like a volcano of blood. He scanned the clearing and saw no protection. His mangy pack of spineless dogs had deserted him. He growled and cursed his pack under his breath. Before him stood a very large elk, an even bigger moose, a still-bigger bison, and a wildcat that was hissing and spitting at him. And that stupid little trout was back in the water, laughing at him.

"Poor little Puck, looks like you are all alone," she taunted. "And I am safe in my pond. Run away now, you ugly dog, or my Eat Me Animal Herd will eat *you!*"

Puck was furious and let out a low, throaty growl. One leg at a time, he slowly backed closer to the woods. With one powerful leap, Wolfrik von Spice flew through the air and landed so forcefully on Puck it sent the coyote skidding and rolling sideways. Stunned by the unexpected attack, Puck slowly rose to his feet and glared at the herd.

"I hate you all and will never quit until I have that miserable carp for dinner," he growled.

"You have no power here," shouted Elkwood. "The herd will always protect Twinkle Toes, and you shall *never* eat her. Now chase after that miserable pack of yours and go! I cannot stand the sight of you."

"I will beat you, Elkwood. You'll see," growled Puck. "I will beat you all. I am cunning and smarter than each of you."

He stood tall and, filled with hatred, again shouted, "*I will beat you!*" then turned with his tail between his legs and escaped into the forest.

They all looked at each other and began to laugh uncontrollably. Twinkle Toes leaped into the air, and spun and danced through the water with abandon. Bobcat rolled on the ground with laughter, and Theodore was zooming, circling back and forth, chirping madly. Elkwood and Baldoin pranced and danced and gave each other *high hooves* in the air. Big Shot was jumping up and down, bucking, and shaking the ground with his great weight. Wolfrik, always the vision of cool and calm, sat off to the side, licking his paws and grinning.

"What a victory for the Eat Me Animal Herd!" shouted Elkwood. All the animals cheered and howled and laughed.

All of a sudden, they heard something crashing through the forest toward them. They all turned to see Bearie run into the clearing like his fur was on fire. Following close behind was a huge swarm of loudly buzzing bees chasing him. Who knew the clumsy bear could run so fast? The bear looked terrified, and with a few more strides, he leaped into the pond, causing a gigantic splash. As he cannonballed into the water, Twinkle Toes flew up in the air, and down she went, smacking her side as she landed. The swarm of bees came to an abrupt halt, hovered for a moment, then turned in unison and buzzed away.

"Whew," sighed the dripping bear sitting in the pond. "*Dat* was close!"

Twinkle Toes dove under the water, then came up in a great leap and *slapped* the bear on the nose with her tail fin.

"What'd ya do that for?" asked Bearie as he rubbed his nose with his paw.

"That's for almost landing on me and disturbing my pond," scolded Twinkle Toes.

Laughter broke out again among the herd, and Bearie sat in the pond, looking quite disgruntled. He waded to the edge of the pond and heaved himself onto the shore. He was soaked, and his waterlogged coat created a huge pool of water in the clearing.

"*Da* bees, they was trying to get me. I hate bees and I hate honey." And with that, Bearie pulled out his pot of nut butter, opened the lid, scooped up a *pawful*, and slathered it into his mouth with delight.

The animals wailed in laughter at the bear. "Our victory over Puck calls for a celebration," declared Elkwood. "But first I would like you all to welcome the newest member of our herd, Baldoin, which means 'brave friend' in his language. He is a magnificent moose mountaineer from France, and today he climbed to the top of the Lone Peak. And…he loves Moose Backpacker cookies, which have oatmeal, raisins, and nuts, and are loaded with extra chocolate. They are delicious. In fact, he loves chocolate so much his mother nicknamed him Le Chocolat Moose."

They all cheered, except for Twinkle Toes, who lazed on the pond bank, looking quite bored.

Le Chocolat Moose bowed in appreciation. *"Merci. Merci.* Please, call me Le Chocolat Moose, *oui*?" They all laughed with joy at the French-speaking moose.

"But, *suga*, what about the celebration? That *is* a marvelous idea," interrupted Twinkle Toes, ignoring the moose but always ready for a party.

Elkwood turned to stare at Twinkle Toes. "How *could* you?" he scolded. "You put the whole herd at risk because of your vanity. Do you want to end up as Puck's dinner?" The herd went silent. "What if Wolfrik had not come along to save you? Would you have him sacrifice his life to save yours? You are a selfish, stupid trout, and…oh, I am very angry with you," stammered Elkwood.

Twinkle Toes swam to the shore and rested her fins on the pond bank. "I'm sorry, *suga*. Thank you all for saving me," she said quite demurely. Then with a delicious grin on her face, she said, "'*When I'm good, I'm very good, but when I'm bad, I'm better,*'" and she winked at Wolfrik.

Wolfrik gave Twinkle Toes a big, sweeping bow, and she fluttered her fins in delight.

"She will never learn," murmured Elkwood. "*Never.* Her narcissism will be the curse of us all," he said under his breath. But he had suggested a party, and that was what they should do.

"On to the Eat Me Cookie Company for our celebration!" announced Elkwood. All the animals agreed.

Wolfrik pulled up his motorcycle with a loud *vroom*, and Twinkle Toes happily flipped her tail fin and jumped into the water-filled sidecar. With another loud *vroom*, Wolfrik sped off into the forest, followed by the rest of the herd. It was time for a grand celebration.

Puck leered at the herd from his hiding place beyond the clearing. He had almost finally succeeded in making that carp his dinner and had been ousted by those arrogant animals she called the Eat Me Animal Herd. He was so close to eating her that he could taste her meaty flesh in his mouth. His tongue ran slowly over his yellow teeth as he growled in frustration. They may be bigger than he, but he was smarter and very cunning. Someday he would eat that carp, and that would be the day they all learned to respect him and never mess with his dinner again. And now they were going to have a party celebrating his defeat? Puck's anger was eating at him from within… He would have his revenge.

The Eat Me Animal Herd gathered at the clearing in front of the store and built a gigantic bonfire using wood they had dragged from the forest. It was a dark night, and a million stars were twinkling. The bonfire lit up the clearing, with huge orange and gold flames licking into the air. In the chill of the evening, they all gathered around to enjoy the warmth. Wolfrik had parked his motorcycle next to the fire, but not too close, so that Twinkle Toes could join in the fun. She discovered the light from the fire illuminated her sidecar pool, making it possible for her to stare at her beautiful reflection.

Wolfrik shook his head in dismay. He adored Twinkle Toes, but her narcissism was destructive, and he feared it would cause more trouble in the future. He had been relieved when the herd had showed up to help him defeat Puck and his evil pack of dogs. He was a big and powerful wolf, but no animal was safe when confronted by a pack of bloodthirsty, mean coyotes. He knew that their power came from traveling as a pack; they had strength in numbers.

Today had been too close for comfort, and Twinkle Toes had almost paid for her vanity with her life. She had only two methods of alert: the beavers' warning and that of peering at the reflection in the water of her enemies approaching. With the beavers out gathering willow, her incessant adoration of herself blinded her to danger. She was easy prey.

I must uncover a way to keep her safe, thought Wolfrik. *I must either kill Puck and his pack or find another solution.* He thought about Bobcat, who was clever and full of tricks. Perhaps his pranks could be put to good use. He would consort with him later about what to do about Twinkle Toes. He would hate to see her come to a tragic end.

After the fray with the coyotes, the herd was elated by their victory... and hungry. Elkwood and Bobcat came out of the store, carrying large trays filled with every kind of cookie and, of course, brownies for Big Shot. Big Shot was enjoying his trayful of brownies with grunts and smacks as he devoured them all.

Elkwood ran back to the store and came back with a large pot overflowing with bear peanut butter and presented it to Bearie. "For you, my friend. You were running away from those bees so fast you probably burned a lot of calories," he teased.

The herd all giggled in unison. Bearie did not mind the teasing and dug his paws into the peanut butter, then shoved the gooey treat into his mouth. After the feast of cookies, brownies, and peanut butter, the herd danced and pranced around the clearing in the firelight, their shadows making them look as if they were many. Elkwood and Baldoin did a soft-shoe dance, with the moose tripping a little every few steps, but no one cared, as they were filled with joy. Big Shot and Bobcat danced a jig, and the ground rumbled under the weight of the huge bison hopping to the rhythm of the music. Theodore, ever present and supportive of his friends, flittered about, weaving in and out of the dancing herd, chirping with joy over their grand victory. Twinkle Toes danced on her tail fin and spun her side fins in time to the music, never failing to catch numerous glimpses of herself in the firelight-illuminated water.

Surprising everyone, Twinkle Toes announced, "I have a little song I would like to sing to say thanks to all you *sugas* who saved me from that evil coyote Puck. You were all just marvelous." She began to sing a lively tune about Puck's attack and the victorious battle fought by the Eat Me Animal Herd.

She danced in the sidecar and, although limited by space, put on quite a show. The herd, stunned by the trout's gesture, continued to gyrate, raising their hooves and paws in the air, in continued celebration of their victory. They even tried to imitate the fights they had each had with Puck, as Twinkle Toes sang a lively number about each brave battle.

Wolfrik, off to the side as usual, kept a wary eye out for Puck and his pack. He knew Puck and would not be surprised if he tried again. He noticed Bobcat was also putting his nose frequently in the air, sniffing for any unwelcome scent. Perhaps he had judged Bobcat too harshly, as he did seem to have the herd's best interests at heart, although his pranks seemed to prove otherwise. And he clearly loved Big Shot like he was his own, and for that Wolfrik respected him. Maybe they could become friends after all.

Under the dark cover of the forest, Puck was nearby, planning his next attack. No one would expect him to rally after the beating he and his pack had taken earlier that day. He was close enough to hear the herd—the bane of his existence—celebrating his defeat, but not so close that his scent would be detected. The aroma from the cookies was hanging in the still air of the forest, driving him crazy with hunger. Regardless, it served to mask his scent from his unsuspecting enemies. He had left his pack back at their den, knowing he could move faster and would be stealthier on his own. He had been conjuring up an idea for some time, and tonight seemed the perfect time to enact his plan. Those detestable animals were so distracted, dancing and celebrating his failure, that they would never know he was afoot. That Eat Me Animal Herd thought they were so special, and their success made him seethe with anger, jealousy, and hatred.

"What if they could no longer sell their cookies?" he mused. "That would fix them. If I put them out of business, they would not be so high and mighty then, would they?" With delight, Puck continued plotting.

His yellow, bloodshot eyes gleamed at the thought of his brilliant idea, and a wicked smile crossed his lips. He planned to steal all their recipes while they were distracted. Yes, that would show them he was the superior animal. Then he would open his own store and use their recipes and be rich beyond *his* wildest dreams. He chuckled shamelessly as he savored their inevitable defeat. He would name the store the Coyote Cookie Company and call every flavor the Big Puck cookie. He hugged himself with glee as he envisioned his own store and all his success.

Puck sneaked through the forest, low on his belly, barely making a sound. His evil eyes glowed in the dark night as he cut a wide berth around the clearing and came up behind the Eat Me Cookie Company. He began to dig below the tree as fast as he could, clawing and scratching his way into the store. The sound of music and laughter coming from the clearing muted the noise of his digging but served to further fuel his anger. In no time, he had dug a tunnel under the tree and broke through the floor of the store. He clawed the ground to widen the opening and dragged himself through the hole and into the dark space. The aroma inside the store was intoxicating. It made him lick his lips in anticipation as he drooled on the dirt floor. But first he must find the recipes.

He moved slowly around the store, feeling his way in the dark with his paws as his eyes adjusted to the darkness. "Where would that stupid elk hide the recipes?" he muttered as he cursed Elkwood under his breath. He pawed his way along the floor and found a box. He slowly opened the lid, then reached inside and felt the rustling of parchment. He had found the recipes. That stupid, arrogant elk. Hiding the recipes in a box was such an obvious choice and so easy to find. He grabbed the pile of recipes and noticed several small bags marked "secret ingredient." What luck, and what stupidity. Elkwood had put the secret ingredient for the cookies in with the recipes. He knew there was a reason the Eat Me cookies were so delicious, and now *he* held the secret.

He crept across the floor back toward the hole. He stopped and looked around for a sack. There was one on the floor, and he grabbed it and filled it with cookies that were still warm from the oven. He crawled back through the hole and strutted into the forest, grinning a most hideous and malicious grin. "Take *that*, you stupid animals," he hissed. And he swiftly disappeared into the forest.

The Eat Me Animal Herd partied late into the night until they were exhausted. Bearie was fast asleep in front of the bonfire, and no one wanted to disturb him. They said their farewells, each leaving the clearing and heading back to their homes. Wolfrik sped off into the night, with Twinkle Toes waving a final adieu. Bobcat and Big Shot headed for their cave, and Baldoin walked silently into the forest. Elkwood and Theodore sat next to each other by the fire, warming themselves before they headed into the tree house to their beds.

"You saw him, didn't you?" asked Theodore.

"Of course I saw Puck. I knew he would try to steal our recipes to put us out of business. He is in for a big surprise," chuckled Elkwood.

"What? He stole the recipes? Oh dear, what will we do?" sputtered Theodore.

"Nothing. I was prepared for this all along. Without our recipes, we have no cookies. I hid them away where no one will ever find them, not even Puck. But I knew he would try something mean, so just in case, I left out a key ingredient in each recipe and added one *pawful* of the 'secret ingredient.' I put it into bags and left them with the recipes," chuckled Elkwood.

"I don't understand. What secret ingredient?" asked Theodore.

"Peppers, very hot peppers," whispered Elkwood. "I picked wild, hot peppers, dried them, and ground them up. All we have to do is sit back and watch the fun."

"Then you don't care if he broke into our store and stole the Eat Me cookie recipes?"

"Absolutely not. I suspect he will try to start his own cookie company to compete with us. When all the animals discover how awful his cookies taste, and their mouths are burning from the hot peppers, he will be the laughingstock of the forest. Then he will leave us alone, knowing he has been outsmarted."

Theodore thought about Elkwood's brilliant plan but asked, "Won't all the animals who buy Puck's cookies be mad at you?"

"Of course not," laughed Elkwood. "They will blame Puck."

"Won't Wolfrik want to investigate this cookie caper? You know he was a famous operative in Germany, don't you? He could be risking his life if we don't tell him about your cunning plan," worried Theodore.

Elkwood pondered this potential glitch in his plan. "If we tell the herd, our deception might get out and Puck will know the recipes are fake. I want him to go through all the trouble of opening a store, only to be humiliated in the end. He deserves to be taught a lesson. We will have to pretend the real recipes were indeed stolen and play along with the ruse in order to trap Puck."

"But Wolfrik could be in real danger if he tries to steal the recipes back from Puck. Would you put him in danger, Elkwood?" wondered Theodore.

"We are all in danger with Puck in our midst," protested Elkwood. He was beginning to think his plan was not so brilliant after all, but it was too late. Perhaps if he trusted Wolfrik with the truth, Bobcat might jump in and try to solve the cookie caper.

That's it, he thought. "Theodore, I will ask both Wolfrik and Bobcat to solve the cookie caper. Then Wolfrik will not be alone against Puck. Bobcat is very clever and loves to play pranks and would relish the chance to go after Puck. They are bitter enemies."

Theodore kept finding flaws with Elkwood's plan and raised another question. "What if they get the recipes back before Puck has opened his store and sells the awful-tasting cookies? Then the plan is all for nothing. And if they do not get the recipes back in time, then Bobcat and Wolfrik will feel like they have failed the herd. And once they find out you tricked them, they will be furious with you."

"Theodore, you are overthinking this entire caper. Puck is a clever and devious menace, and he will certainly guard the recipes with his life. Although Wolfrik and Bobcat are quite skilled, they will not find the recipes Puck stole until it is too late. Then it will not matter, because Puck will have been humiliated in the eyes of all who live in the forest," stated Elkwood emphatically.

"I hope you are right," Theodore said with great doubt in his voice. "Perhaps you will have unleashed an even more dangerous foe should your plan succeed."

Elkwood looked at his friend with concern on his face, knowing that was certainly a possibility. However, the wheels had been set in motion. "Let's go to bed, and we will see what happens tomorrow."

They both left Bearie snoring loudly by the fire and went into their tree house to sleep.

The following morning, reveling in the memory of all that had transpired, Twinkle Toes was very much enjoying herself on the beaver pond bank, flipping water on herself and admiring her reflection. She felt invigorated by the party at the bonfire the night before. Wolfrik had looked so handsome standing by the fire. Oh, how brave he had been, attacking Puck and saving her life. She stared at her reflection and thought she had never looked more beautiful.

"Love must be making my colors more vibrant today," she mused. "There is a blush to my scales I have never seen before." She continued to lazily splashed herself while staring at her magnificence. "Wolfrik won't stay angry with me, because I am far too beautiful," she fantasized.

She had seen the way Wolfrik had looked at her when Elkwood had scolded her for being careless. But it was the beavers' fault she had been caught by Puck. They should have been watching the pond. She could not bring herself to admit her vanity had caused her to let her guard down, thus putting all her friends in danger. Instead she gazed at her reflection and thought about Wolfrik and how much she adored him.

"'*A "trout" in love can't be reasonable … or she probably wouldn't be in love,*'" cooed Twinkle Toes.

She began to hum, swishing her tail fin rhythmically. Sliding gracefully into the beaver pond, Twinkle Toes began to sing a sultry song about her desire for Wolfrik as she glided and danced around on the water. She had learned nothing. Danger seemed to encourage her vanity. She enjoyed the rush and excitement when confronted with trouble. It never occurred to Twinkle Toes that someday her selfish and narcissistic ways would rain havoc upon those who loved her most.

While Twinkle Toes was basking in the sunshine at the beaver pond, enjoying herself, the forest dwellers were chattering nonstop about the new Coyote Cookie Company, soon to open. Puck had wasted no time in spreading the news about his new venture. He bragged to everyone about how his cookies would be far tastier than the cookies at Elkwood's store.

Without much thought and no time to search, Puck had settled on an old, dilapidated lean-to for his store, which he found, much to his delight, not far from the beaver pond where Twinkle Toes Trout lived. What luck to locate his store so close to a delicious dinner. He began to salivate and drool as he savored the thought of having that annoying carp as the main course for his celebration dinner, once his store was open.

"My cookies will be a huge success on opening day, and that will be the last day for that arrogant carp. She will be at her most beautiful when she is frying in my pan for dinner," quipped Puck in delight.

Puck put the distraction of just how delicious Twinkle Toes would taste aside and put his vile pack to work to get everything ready for the grand opening. The pack complained constantly about the hard work, and Puck growled and hissed at them to get busy and work harder. He wanted the store open the very next day. If any in the pack slacked off, they could be sure Puck would motivate them with a vicious nip at their tails. With each new disastrous adventure, the pack was beginning to secretly loathe Puck. He saw them snarling at him with their heads lowered and their tails between their legs. He did not care. He was bigger, stronger, and fiercer than any of them, and he knew they were terrified of him. They cowered as he berated them nonstop, commanding them to work harder. After hours of agonizing work in the hot sun, Puck was satisfied. The store was completed.

The Coyote Cookie Company was a pathetic pile of old, rotting wood that the pack had tried their best to fashion into a store. A sign hung crookedly over the entrance. Several pieces of wood tied together created a door that had to be pushed aside in order to open the front of the store. A sawhorse table was just inside, where Puck would serve the cookies to all the animals of the forest. The pack had worked tirelessly to clean the cobwebs and filth from inside the shack, but to them, it did not look much better than it had before all their labor.

To Puck, the store was brilliant. He was so crazed with hatred for Elkwood and his ridiculous Eat Me Animal Herd, he was blinded to everything around him. At last, tired and hungry, the pack skulked off into the forest to rest, hoping to at least be rewarded with delicious Big Puck cookies in the morning.

All night Puck worked manically to make the cookie dough from the recipes he had hijacked from Elkwood. He was desperate to prove to everyone that he was the most successful animal in the forest. Each recipe called for a *pawful* of the secret ingredient. "If this made Elkwood's cookies taste so delicious, then two *pawfuls* will be even better," he surmised. Yes, more of the secret ingredient would make the Big Pucks irresistible. He was extremely proud of himself for stealing all he needed to succeed. He baked and baked until he had mounds of cookies ready to sell. It never occurred to him to sample the cookies, because the ones he had eaten the night he had stolen the recipes had been delicious. He knew the Big Pucks would be even better. And he was simply too tired to even think about food.

Puck finished stacking the cookies ready to be baked in the morning. He slid the makeshift door closed, then lay down in a corner of the store on a pile of dried-out, scratchy moss and fell into a deep, satisfied sleep. He dreamed about his success—his imminent defeat of the Eat Me Animal Herd.

CHAPTER 11

THE VERY MORNING PUCK was to open the Coyote Cookie Company, Wolfrik von Spice sped on his motorcycle into the clearing outside the Eat Me Cookie Company. He sprang off the bike, shouting Elkwood's name as he frantically raced inside.

Startled, Elkwood and Theodore simultaneously asked, "What's wrong, Wolfrik?"

"I just heard through *zee forestvine* that Puck is opening a cookie company... *today*! Did you know?" he asked, clearly distraught. "What are we going to do?"

As much as Elkwood wanted vengeance on Puck, he had been worried about deceiving Wolfrik. He knew Wolfrik would do anything to help the herd, even at the cost of his own life. But Elkwood had started this caper and knew he must go along with the charade until the end.

"Puck has stolen our recipes, Wolfrik!" he cried. "There is no time! You must go and recruit Bobcat to help you. You must get the recipes back, or the Eat Me Cookie Company will surely be ruined."

"*Jawohl*," said Wolfrik, and without hesitation, he sped off in search of Bobcat. He would lay down his life for his friends.

Bobcat and Big Shot were in their garden, harvesting their newly ripened pumpkins. They were humming and whistling as they worked, excited to store as many pumpkins as they could. Deep in the far reaches of their cave was a large space that stayed very cold. They carried pumpkin after pumpkin into the natural refrigerator, stacking them as high as they could reach. Bobcat had a bountiful harvest, and he was sure he had enough pumpkins to last a long time. After all, the Big Bobcat cookie was very popular at the store and would be even more popular with the coming of fall.

Bobcat and Big Shot were heading out to gather another load of pumpkins when Wolfrik barreled into the cave, surprising them both.

With a click of his paws he abruptly said, "*Guten Morgen.* Have you heard that *zee* cookie recipes were stolen by Puck during our *Feier*?"

"Our what?" asked Bobcat, still startled by the intrusion.

"Celebration," replied Wolfrik impatiently.

"*No!* He stole the recipes? *Why?*" asked Big Shot.

"Puck is planning to open his own store…*today*," stated Wolfrik. "I passed by many animals who told me they were on their way to *zee* grand opening of the Coyote Cookie Company, near *zee* beaver pond," he explained. "Elkwood is most distraught and asked if we would solve the cookie caper and recover *zee* stolen recipes. Will you help me?" he pleaded.

Bobcat grinned with excitement. "Yep, that coyote has met his match. We will hunt him and stalk him, and trick him into giving us back the recipes. Count me in!"

Bobcat began dancing around the cave like a prizefighter, punching at the air with his front paws, growling and hissing with a mischievous grin on his face.

"Me too," said Big Shot as he pawed the ground and snorted in delight, creating a huge dust cloud.

Blinded by the thick dust cloud, the trio began coughing and laughing as they stumbled outside to breathe in the fresh air. They left the rest of the pumpkins in the patch for later, and with urgency and excitement, they headed out to find Puck and the stolen recipes.

In no time at all, Wolfrik, Bobcat, and Big Shot began seeing animals of the forest, in greater numbers than normal, all traveling in the same direction. They knew they were going to the grand opening of the Coyote Cookie Company, so they stopped to formulate a plan for their cookie caper. They decided they would wait until the throngs of animals were waiting in line to buy cookies, knowing that Puck would be distracted. They planned to split up, Wolfrik on one side of the store, and Bobcat on the other side, both hiding in nearby trees. Big Shot was far too big to hide behind a tree, so he would be positioned at the back of the long line waiting for cookies, ready to charge when the plan went into action.

The trio arrived just as Puck and two of his mangy pack dogs were pushing the rickety door to the side to open the store. Puck stood in front of the store and proudly announced what he thought would be his greatest accomplishment and the best day of his life.

"Animals of the forest in the Big Sky, welcome to the grand opening of *my* Coyote Cookie Company, located at the base of what I have now named Puck's Peak. My cookies, the Big Pucks, are the *best* in all the forest, in fact in all the *world*. Today I triumph and defeat those… *others*. Now step up, and taste the most delicious cookies in all the forest, at the Coyote Cookie Company."

Cheers rang out from the fickle animals waiting in line to buy Puck's cookies. None had eaten breakfast, not wanting to spoil their appetites in anticipation of snacking on a warm, delicious cookie right out of the oven. The air smelled wonderful, and if that was any indication, the Coyote Cookie Company was sure to triumph. Puck's pack, who had slaved so hard the day before to help their leader open the store, were the first in line, and they were ravenous. None had eaten dinner the night before, because they had been so exhausted from their day of hard labor. One by one, the animals stepped up to the dilapidated structure and purchased their cookies. Puck was prepared for a busy morning. All the cookies were stacked and ready to sell. They practically flew out the door. The forest animals found places around the clearing to sit and enjoy their morning treat. Oohs and aahs could be heard all around the clearing. As much as everyone disliked Puck, they could not resist a delicious cookie, and Big Pucks were delicious… or so they thought at first bite.

Duped by the delayed reaction of the "secret ingredient" of hot peppers, suddenly one, then two, then three… then dozens of animals began to violently sneeze, gag, and cough. Puck's pack were the first to become sick, and their reactions were severe, for they had each ravenously devoured several cookies at once. Their faces began to redden and swell, and a few began whimpering. The heat from the "secret ingredient" was taking over, and in a matter of seconds, the entire gathering was in an uproar, not knowing how to soothe their burning mouths and throats. Wolfrik, Bobcat, and Big Shot looked on in utter disbelief. What in the world was happening? Puck was in shock. Everything had been going so well. He had no clue why all the animals were getting sick.

The wails and whimpers from the forest animals had developed into a crescendo of all-out agony. They began running to find water, crashing into each other in desperation. Some were grabbing *pawfuls* of grass and stuffing the cool green turf into their mouths, hoping for relief. Hooved animals were digging up the ground and eating dirt, trying to quell their burning mouths. Smaller animals were rolling back and forth in the dirt, trying anything to stop the painful burning. The disaster unfolding before Puck had him frozen like stone, staring in disbelief at what was now his greatest failure.

Unbeknownst to all, Elkwood, with Theodore perched on his antlers, was some distance away, observing the scene through a pair of binoculars he had found near the river.

"Oh, Theodore, this is better than even I had anticipated! *Look!* Just look at the mayhem. Puck must have put more than one *pawful* of the 'secret ingredient' in the cookies, because this reaction is so much better—*ahem*—worse than I expected. Oh! This is wonderful! He is paying for his evil ways. He wanted to be so much better than the Eat Me Cookie Company, he must have thought that increasing the 'secret ingredient' would make his cookies better. The forest animals will drive Puck away, and we will be rid of him forever."

Elkwood was shaking with laughter and began to prance and dance with glee over the success of his plan. Elkwood put the binoculars in front of the red-headed woodpecker's eyes, and Theodore shuddered when he saw the devastation caused by the wild peppers.

"Oh no!" whispered Theodore. "I fear this is not going to end well. The animals will be furious with you, Elkwood. I was afraid this would be bad, but not *this* bad. Yes, this is very, very bad, Elkwood."

"Oh, you worry too much, little friend. The animals of the forest will hate Puck, not me. I have done everyone a great service by getting rid of him, once and for all."

Theodore shook his head in doubt. He had a very, *very* bad feeling about the entire cookie caper.

During the utter bedlam at the clearing of the Coyote Cookie Company, Wolfrik signaled to Bobcat that it was time to make their move. Big Shot saw the call to act and made his way toward the shabby cookie store. Unbeknownst to Puck, who was still frozen in shock, they were steps away. Wolfrik von Spice leaped through the air, falling squarely on top of Puck. The two went down in a pile of dirt and fur, and being much larger, Wolfrik easily pinned Puck on his back and held him firmly down with his powerful body. Puck was dazed, not quite realizing what had happened.

Bobcat, with a giant grin of triumph on his face, rushed into the cookie store and began to rummage around for the stolen recipes. In no time, he came up with the prize. He had found the recipes. "I found them! I found them! We've solved the cookie caper!" he cried as he discovered the small, empty bags labeled "secret ingredient." He opened a bag, took a big sniff, and promptly sneezed.

Holding up the bags, Bobcat shouted, "Wolfrik! You won't believe what I have found. Bags of very hot ground peppers labeled 'secret ingredient.' Puck was set up. He must have thought this was the ingredient we use to make our Eat Me cookies so delicious."

The revelation jolted Puck from his state of shock. Wolfrik was just beginning to snicker over Puck being bamboozled, when Puck, fueled by a sudden insane anger, furiously wrestled and broke free of Wolfrik, then scrambled to his feet. Catching Wolfrik off guard, Puck took one powerful swipe at him, claws extended, and sliced open Wolfrik's face. Blood spurted from the wound. Big Shot, now outside the cookie shack, guarding against Puck's pack, reacted to the injury of his friend with a fury rarely seen from the large bison. He pawed the dirt with his hooves, took two lunging strides forward, and charged with his massive head lowered, hitting Puck with all his force, and catapulted him through the air.

Puck landed with a bone-cracking thud, but his utter fury numbed the pain, and he immediately sprang to his feet. He found his next mark and charged Bobcat, who was still in the store. He hit Bobcat so hard it threw him against the wall of the makeshift store, collapsing the structure. Bobcat screamed as a large piece of wood crashed onto his bobbed tail. Wolfrik ran to his friend's aid and pulled the rubble from atop Bobcat, freeing him from the prison of broken and splintered wood.

From the corner of his good eye, Wolfrik saw Puck crawling out from beneath the rubble. With one giant leap, he pounced on Puck and, once again, pinned him to the ground. "Never again, Puck. This is *over*," he said, as blood dripped from his wound onto the twisted face of Puck.

The scene was horrifying to witness. Puck was livid. His hate was so intense he could barely think or see straight. All he knew was he wanted to kill everyone in sight.

"If you ever come near any of my friends again, I will kill you," promised Wolfrik. "I have allowed you to live, but this is *zee* end. You stole our secret recipes, or so you thought. You have been tricked and made a fool of to everyone in *zee* forest. It is time for you to leave and never return." Wolfrik loosened his hold on Puck and shoved him away.

Puck staggered to his feet and dropped his head as he growled at Wolfrik. His yellow, bloodshot eyes and the blood and dirt on his face made him look like a rabid demon. In a very quiet and guttural voice, he hissed, "You will never beat me, never," and he turned and ran away.

"How could this have happened? Who would have done this and put us all in danger?" asked Big Shot. "Wolfrik, you are wounded," he said, concerned. "You look just awful!"

Wolfrik reached a paw to his face and scowled when he saw the blood. He had not realized in the frenzy that he had been so badly injured. It brought back a fleeting rush of painful memories, ones he wished never to relive. "Thank you for your help," said Wolfrik. "You are a true friend."

Big Shot pawed at the ground with his head down, a bit embarrassed at Wolfrik's show of fondness toward him. With a grimace on his face, Bobcat walked over, limping from his injured tail. He was in obvious pain.

"And I, uh, appreciate you thrashing that dirty coyote for me, Ricky. Nice to know you got my back, pal," mumbled the wounded cat. "I believe we have *Elkbutt* to blame for this. He must have suspected Puck was going to steal our recipes, and he put all this in motion. What was he thinking?" groused the cat. "Didn't he realize he would put us all in danger when he asked us to retrieve the stolen recipes and go on this cookie caper?" The trio shook their heads in dismay over what Elkwood had done.

"The only good news is that Puck is finished," declared Bobcat. "All the animals in the forest now hate him. Even his pack of filthy dogs were hood-winked by the hot pepper cookie caper. I have to admit, *Elkbutt* sure got one up on Puck," laughed Bobcat, appreciating the clever plan. "But he's selfish and didn't think about what his actions might set in motion. I sure don't like *Elkbutt* very much right now." Bobcat stroked his wounded tail, obviously still in pain.

Wolfrik snorted and shook all the dirt from his glorious fur. Big Shot hung his head in sadness, as he knew it was the end of the Eat Me Animal Herd and their cookie company. How could they ever forgive Elkwood for putting them all in such danger?

Suddenly Wolfrik realized, "Twinkle Toes! Hurry, she is so close and could be in danger!" The trio whirled and ran out of the now empty clearing and headed toward the beaver pond.

The forest animals had left the clearing at the Coyote Cookie Company in a giant, pain-filled exodus. Many ran off screaming into the forest, while others ran toward the beaver pond to try and cool the burning in their mouths and throats. Nearby, Twinkle Toes was enjoying her day as usual, slowly swimming around the pond, scooping up scum into her cup for a delightful drink. Without warning, a desperate migration of animals, including deer, elk, bears, foxes, rabbits and squirrels, to name a few, burst out of the forest screaming as they leapt into the pond. The force of the animals hitting the water created a giant splash and swell which threw Twinkle Toes up into the air, landing her on her side with a painful *splat*. Just as she came up, sputtering, angry and bruised from the force of the impact that would have killed a lesser trout, Wolfrik, Bobcat and Big Shot ran out from the forest to a scene of complete chaos. The trio skidded to a halt when they saw the danger Twinkle Toes was in and they all felt anger that Elkwood's cookie caper was now threatening her as well; the one they all tried so hard to protect.

They raced over to the edge of the pond to see if Twinkle Toes was injured. Animals were pulling themselves out of the pond after having taken long drinks of ice-cold water. Their slurping from the giant trough was so loud it was almost comical, had their leap into the pond not almost been the end of Twinkle Toes. They moved slowly away from the water, leaving puddles all over the clearing.

"Twinkle Toes, are you alright?" asked Wolfrik, with deep concern in his voice.

"Of course, s*uga*. You know how I love danger and excitement. '*If a little is great, and a lot is better, then way too much is just about right!*'"

Wolfrik gazed at her with a slightly condemning look, but he was relieved she was safe and unharmed.

"*You only live once, but if you do it right, once is enough.*'" She slid onto the pond bank and reached up with a fin to gently touch the dried blood on Wolfrik's cheek. "You are injured, my brave and beautiful wolf. Will you allow me to rinse the blood off your cheek?" she cooed as she lovingly stroked his face with her fin.

He stepped back slowly, knowing he was falling into the trance that Twinkle Toes could so easily cast with her charms. Not being a wolf of obvious emotions, but one of chivalry, he bowed down to Twinkle Toes and said in a low voice, "My injury is not severe, my little trout. Never fear for me," although he shot her a stern grin.

Twinkle Toes replied, "'*I like a "wolf" who's good, but not too good, for the good die young, and I hate a dead one.*'" She giggled and flipped her fins, leaped off the bank, and dove deep into the pond. The surface erupted as she broke through and flew into the air in a magnificent leap with three twists. Everyone breathed a sigh of relief that she was not injured. She returned to her position on the bank of the pond, and the herd began to explain to Twinkle Toes all that had happened. She listened intently, then, losing interest, resumed admiring her reflection in the pond.

Bobcat had met a lot of animals, and although she was truly beautiful, he had never met a trout as selfish as Twinkle Toes. "You are selfish and only concerned about your own pleasure," he blurted out. "Don't you realize you could have been killed? And don't you care that Wolfrik was horribly clawed and my tail is now badly bruised? Don't you care that Elkwood caused all of this to happen simply because he wanted to win against Puck? I think you're a silly little trout!"

True to form, Twinkle Toes looked at Bobcat with loving eyes and replied, "'*I'm no model "trout." A model's just an imitation of the real thing.*'" She continued. "Of course, my beautiful Bobcat, I'm very happy you're all safe, and thank you so much for coming to my rescue. But honestly, Puck and his antics are of no surprise to me and shouldn't be to anyone. '*Those who are easily shocked should be shocked more often,*' suga."

Wolfrik grinned at Twinkle Toes, and she winked back, adoring him more with every encounter. She found the entire dangerous cookie caper exhilarating.

Twinkle Toes looked at Bobcat and said, "'*There are no good "trout" gone wrong, just bad "trout" found out,*'" and she winked at him too.

Bobcat hissed at the trout, frustrated that she refused to take responsibility for anything.

Just as everyone was about to disperse, Theodore flew at supersonic speed into the clearing and landed on one of Big Shot's lavender horns. He started sputtering out words, but he was so completely out of breath, no one could understand him. Big Shot tried to comfort him and urged him to catch his breath and start over. After a few deep inhales that puffed out his pure-white chest, Theodore began to speak in a more controlled manner.

"I just heard from a deer family that the entire cookie caper was a disaster and Puck went crazy and Wolfrik was hurt and Bobcat's tail was smashed and Twinkle Toes was almost crushed, and, oh, it is all just so awful. Elkwood said no one would get hurt and that this would finally be the end of that mean Puck. He was so excited about his plan to trick Puck by leaving bags of horrible hot peppers, crushed to look like a secret ingredient. He told me everything would work out just as he planned," he said. Flustered and increasingly distraught, Theodore lost his breath again, not noticing the increasing look of anger on the faces of the herd.

"I told him all the ways the plan could backfire and be dangerous, but he... well, he said it just wasn't so. He said everything would be fine." Theodore looked around as he unraveled the story, and could now see the animals were furious.

Wolfrik calmly said, "Theodore, are you telling us you warned Elkwood this cookie caper could be dangerous? You tried to get him to stop?"

"Well...yes," replied Theodore hesitantly. "Please forgive him. Please! He really was only trying to help the herd and make the forest safer for all the animals. He thought it would be fun to see Puck humiliated when everyone tasted his awful cookies. He had no idea they would be so hot as to make all who ate them sick. Oh dear, please forgive him. The entire caper has just snowballed out of control. Elkwood has no idea what has happened. We were looking on from afar through the binoculars he found at the river, and from that distance, things appeared as he had planned and did not look *that* awful. He never saw anyone get hurt. Please, he did not mean for anyone to suffer."

Wolfrik spoke in a low growl that almost sounded menacing. "Do you mean that Elkwood saw what happened and *still* did nothing to help? He knew all *zee* animals were in terrible pain from *zee* hot peppers? And he did *nichts*?" he demanded, reverting back to his homeland language of German. "Elkwood knew *zee* recipes were fake, yet he asked us to go after Puck and get *zee* secret recipes to save *zee* Eat Me Cookie Company. He has gone too far in his quest to be *zee* best. Elkwood is no longer our friend. He does not know the meaning of *zee* word. He cannot be trusted."

Theodore did not know what to do. He felt responsible because he had known of the plan and known it might end in disaster. He should have tried harder to stop Elkwood, or at least warned the others that it was all a setup. He hung his head in shame.

"I am sorry, Wolfrik, Bobcat, Big Shot, and Twinkle Toes. So very sorry. No harm was meant to happen. I will go tell Elkwood what has occurred and that you no longer consider him your friend. I know he will be heartbroken. Truly heartbroken."

Theodore had barely taken flight when he lightly settled back onto Big Shot's horn, seeing Elkwood enter the clearing. Elkwood was humming and dancing and prancing along, as jovial as could be. After all, he had defeated Puck, and all the animals were saved from the evil coyote. His plan had worked and he was a hero. He had no idea of the utter disaster that had unfolded as a result of his cookie caper.

He froze in his tracks when he saw the blood caked on Wolfrik's face, and he noticed Bobcat licking a very swollen tail. He looked at his friends in disbelief, and all the warnings Theodore had tried to instill came flooding back to him.

"Wolfrik, what happened to you? And, Bobcat, your tail? Who did this to you?" he cried.

They all said nothing and just looked menacingly at Elkwood.

"I do not understand. Puck is ruined. The hot peppers worked and now everyone hates Puck. The Eat Me Cookie Company has been saved, and we will never be bothered by Puck again. I won. I beat him. Surely you all know I was only trying to make the forest safe once again for everyone," he avowed. The herd was silent.

"Oh, please listen to me! Wolfrik, if I had told you of my plan, it would not have worked. You had to believe the real recipes had been stolen by Puck. Please understand why I had to keep the cookie caper a secret. I never meant for you to be hurt. I only wanted to defeat Puck once and for all…for the entire forest. For all of my friends."

Twinkle Toes, perched on the edge of the pond, lazily splashing herself, said, "*'The score never interested me, only the game. To err is "animal," but it feels divine. One and one is two, two and two is four, and five will get you ten if you know how to work it.'*"

Wolfrik gave her a scolding glance, and she shrugged her fins and continued to stare at herself in the pond.

"Please forgive me! You are my friends, my family! I would never hurt you!" begged Elkwood.

One by one, Wolfrik von Spice, Bob "the Pumpkin" Bobcat, and Big Shot Bison turned and, without a word, walked into the forest. Theodore flew off Big Shot's horn and landed next to Twinkle Toes on the pond bank.

Elkwood could not believe what had just happened. He walked over to Twinkle Toes and Theodore, and, with tears welling up in his giant, long-lashed eyes, said, "Oh, why, why did I not listen to you, Theodore? You told me every way my plan could go wrong, but I would not listen. Now I have lost the respect and love of all my friends. What happened? Why did everything turn out so badly?"

Theodore explained how Puck had doubled the "secret ingredient" and how all the animals had been crazy with pain and many of them had run to Twinkle Toes's pond and had almost killed her when they jumped in to cool their burning mouths and throats. He explained how Wolfrik had jumped on Puck and pinned him down while Bobcat had run into the store and found the recipes and the "secret ingredient." He described how Bobcat had laughed when he realized Elkwood must have duped Puck and how that had set the next horrific part of the caper in motion. Theodore's voice was shaking as he described Puck's rage and how it had given him the added strength to free himself from Wolfrik, enabling him to slash his face.

Elkwood kept saying "No, no, no" and shaking his head as giant tears rolled down his face and splattered onto the dirt. He could not believe what a mess the cookie caper had become and the danger and injury his friends had faced, all because of him.

"How can I ever undo what I have done? And how will my friends ever forgive me? Theodore, do you hate me too?"

Twinkle Toes said in a slow, lazy drawl, "'*It takes two to get one in trouble*,'" and with a wink, she gracefully slid into the pond and dove deep, out of sight.

Theodore looked at Elkwood with tears in his eyes. "No, Elkwood, I am not angry with you. I know your heart was in the right place. Be patient; the herd will come around. They will forgive you. I know they will."

Elkwood turned to leave the clearing and looked over his shoulder at Theodore. His antlers felt like a massive weight on his head, and he found it difficult to hold them up. After several blinks sent more massive tears tumbling down his face, he said, "Thank you, Theodore. I am very sorry I dragged you into my cookie caper. I am very grateful you were not hurt. There is no longer a place for me in the Eat Me Animal Herd, and I must leave the Big Sky. I deserve to be exiled, for I do not know how to be a real friend to anyone."

Theodore was so choked up he could barely see as a flood of tears fell from his little eyes. He could not imagine his friend leaving. He could not bear to see Elkwood so sad.

"Elkwood, please give everyone some time. They will come around. I know they will. What will I do without you? What will happen to the Eat Me Cookie Company? Where will you go?" he cried.

"Please tell Wolfrik I am giving him the Eat Me Cookie Company. He is so brave and loyal, and will always protect the herd. And it is time for him to once again be his pack alpha. Ask him to teach Bearie proper grammar and perhaps put him on a diet." He smiled a little as he fondly thought of the huge, nut-butter-eating Bearie.

Then his voice cracked as he spoke of his dear friend Le Chocolat Moose. "Tell Baldoin I am sorry. He will be so disappointed when he learns what I have done. He tried to tell me how valuable a friend can be, and I did not understand. I always wanted to be the best, no matter what. I thought that was the right way to be. I thought I was the most important. Tell Bearie to listen to Wolfrik. Tell Big Shot to always watch out for Bobcat, as he does tend to love trouble. And tell Twinkle Toes I will never forget her."

Twinkle Toes was listening from under the edge of the pond bank. She pushed herself to the edge and said, "'*No one ever does*,'" and she smiled lovingly at Elkwood.

"And you, Theodore, my little friend, thank you for helping me to find the Big Sky and for creating the Eat Me Cookie Company with me. I know now, I never could have done it without you. In fact, I now see it never would have been such a great success without the entire Eat Me Animal Herd. We were stronger as the herd. Two are always better than one. Acting alone only creates pain and chaos."

Elkwood took a few slow steps toward the forest, turned around one last time, and looked at Theodore and the beautiful little trout.

"Theodore, I love you. Please help to watch out for Twinkle Toes."

Elkwood looked at his dear friends for the last time and sadly walked away into the forest.

On his way to pack for his journey to leave the Big Sky, Elkwood made one last visit to the chocolate chip waterfall. He realized he and Theodore had never put up a sign declaring his ownership of the waterfall. "That is a good thing. I do not deserve to own anything," he said, sniffling.

Elkwood sat down next to the waterfall and began to cry giant tears as he scooped up chocolate chips with his hooves and slathered them into his mouth. Elkwood's hot tears of pain and regret melted the chocolate chips, and he was soon covered in chocolate. The more he cried, the bigger the mess he became. His face, antlers, and hooves were covered in gooey melted chocolate. Finally exhausted by his remorse and self-pity, Elkwood decided he should go to the river to wash off the chocolate and his tears. As he neared the river, he marveled at the beauty of this place he had called home. He would miss the Big Sky, but there was nothing he could do to regain the love and respect of his friends.

He walked into the clear, cold water and dove in to rinse off the chocolate. As he surfaced, water and chocolate drained from his face and fur. After submerging himself several more times, he walked to the riverbank and heaved himself out of the water. A tiny shiver followed as his head hung low and his nose grazed the ground. Elkwood felt exhausted from everything that had happened, and his grief over choosing himself over his friends weighed heavily upon him.

The temperature was dropping as the sun set, and a light fog began to roll across the river. Elkwood shivered again. It was time for him to return home and pack his knapsack for his journey. As he raised his head to turn and walk away, he froze. Through the mist, he saw something very large looming on the other side of the river. As the fog thickened, Elkwood squinted, trying to make out the enormous shape. With a gasp, he realized it was the giant *Elk* he had seen so many times in his dreams…or what he had thought were dreams. He had an instant flashback to the night of his graduation party, when the giant *Elk* had introduced his parents onto the stage. Another memory struck him, of when the giant *Elk* had confronted him in the hallway of the ship. Surely this could not be the same *Elk*?

The giant *Elk* walked into the river and began to swim across the swift current toward Elkwood. The sight of his massive, ghostly antlers floating across the dark water in the misty dusk was eerie, and it frightened Elkwood. As the *Elk* neared the shore, Elkwood retreated from the edge, fearful of this massive beast. The giant *Elk* rose from the river, and torrents of water poured in streams from his thick coat as he heaved himself onto the shore. With an immense shake of his entire body, water flew in every direction. Elkwood shuddered again as the droplets hit him, stinging him like a thousand bees. He was so tired and sad, and his defenses were gone. Thus, even a droplet of water was a shock to his body.

The *Elk* was enormous. He seemed even larger than Elkwood recalled. Elkwood took another step back as the giant *Elk* turned in his direction. He looked at Elkwood, and his eyes seemed to bore right through his soul.

"You have not learned, Elkwood," said the *Elk*. "You betrayed your friends and paid no heed to Theodore's wise counsel. You wanted to be the most important. It's always all about you, Elkwood."

Steam puffed out of the giant *Elk*'s great nostrils, and once again Elkwood inhaled the robust loam-and-dirt scent he had smelled when he met the massive *Elk* on the ship.

Fearful, but somewhat determined to defend the indefensible, Elkwood quietly replied, "But I *have* learned. I am sorry, but no one will forgive me." Tears welled up in his giant dark brown eyes.

"Forgiveness has to be earned," bellowed the giant *Elk*.

"How?" replied Elkwood, now terrified of this great beast.

"That is what you have to learn for yourself. Remember, Elkwood, success is determined by the friend you are to others."

"But…but I *have* tried," defended Elkwood. "I love my friends. They mean everything to me." He desperately wanted the giant *Elk* to know his heart was pure and that he really *did* want to be a good friend.

"Friendship is not selfish, Elkwood." A light breeze kicked up, and the fog thickened and swirled around the giant *Elk*. He turned and slowly walked toward the tree line along the river. Just as he was about to disappear into the fog and the forest, he turned and said, "Sacrifice, Elkwood. Let go of your arrogance. But never let go of a friend."

Elkwood blinked back a big tear and looked into the fog, but the *Elk* had disappeared. He shivered again, deep down to his bones. He had let go of the herd, and he believed they would never forgive him. Elkwood knew the only thing he could do was to leave and never return.

Slowly Elkwood made his way through the forest to his home in the big tree. He could not bear to spend one more night in his tree home, for he feared he would not have the strength to leave in the morning. He walked inside and grabbed the knapsack his mother had given him at the start of his journey. He filled it with his few belongings, including a clean ascot, a bag of Big Elk cookies, and the recipe his mother had sent with him as he had embarked upon his journey to Montana.

Just as he was about to leave, he saw some parchment on the table and decided he should write a letter to his friends. He reached into Theodore's nest and found a feather to use as a quill. With the feather in his hoof, he sat for a moment and thought. Again the tears began to flow, dropping into a small cup of cinnamon used to spice the cookies. He dipped the feather into the cinnamon liquid and began to write.

To my friends of the Eat Me Animal Herd,

I am sorry—sorrier than I have ever been—to have put any of you in danger. That was never my intention. I have taken all of you for granted. I thought your friendship to me was more important than my friendship to you. I only wanted to help. I know you will never forgive me, so I am leaving because I do not deserve your love and friendship. Please, someday…forgive me.

Love, Elkwood

P.S. I have copied the Big Elk recipe for you on the back of this note.

Elkwood left the note on the table and walked out the door. As he walked through the clearing, he stopped, turned, and took one last look. So many memories flooded his mind, and tears streamed down his face. His eyes traveled next door, to the store, and rested on the Eat Me Cookie Company sign Theodore had made for him. He loved Theodore and would miss him terribly. He loved them all. But he had to leave. He turned and disappeared into the woods.

Elkwood's first night alone in the woods was restless, and he had no idea where he would go or what kind of life he was to endure.

CHAPTER 12

No animal willingly enters the Scary Forest. And none ever return.
The legend of the Scary Forest is diabolically entwined with
rumor, danger, evil, mystery, fear, and even curiosity.
It is the perfect place to go if you want to disappear...forever.

THE NEXT MORNING, the sun was brilliant, and the birds were chirping in delight. The air was crisp, and Wolfrik could see his breath. As he quietly walked through the forest, Theodore caught up to him, and they both sat and talked for a while. Theodore told Wolfrik what Elkwood had said before they had said goodbye. He told him Elkwood was leaving and would not be return-ing and he had given Wolfrik ownership of the Eat Me Cookie Company. He explained how sorry Elkwood was for the fiasco of the cookie caper. Theodore handed Wolfrik the letter he had found earlier, when he had gone to check on Elkwood. Wolfrik read the letter in silence. Both friends sat in the woods for a long time without speaking.

Elkwood was a fairly large elk, and although he was not as brave as Wolfrik or Baldoin, he was no coward. He knew a life in exile would be difficult every day, but he believed he deserved whatever was to be his fate. He was heading west into wilderness he had never explored. He had no way to know that he was not alone.

Unsure of what lay ahead, Elkwood continued his trek into the unknown. The further he traveled, the fewer animals he encountered. Most merely looked at him and moved on, without showing any interest. He wondered if they had all heard about what he had done, for none were particularly friendly. Maybe he would find a new place and make new friends who would not know about his past. Perhaps he could find a new beginning. He pondered, with every step, what had happened with the cookie caper. Theodore had warned him of myriad ways the plan could be dangerous, but he had refused to listen. He had been determined to rid the forest of Puck, but more importantly, he was now realizing he had wanted to be crowned the hero. He had wanted to be elevated above everyone as the bravest and smartest animal of all. Introspection made Elkwood wonder…perhaps he was no better than Puck after all.

Elkwood certainly was not feeling very smart. He had lost his home, his business, and, most importantly, his friends. He wondered if they were having fun without him. Was Wolfrik opening the store every day? Was Puck still causing trouble? Even after everything Elkwood had done, Puck was still a threat to his friends, and now he was running away. Wolfrik was far more capable of protecting Twinkle Toes and the rest of the herd than he, and Puck would not dare go after Wolfrik. He had been defeated by the powerful wolf too many times. He tried with every mile to convince himself that this narrative was true. The herd was better off and safer without him.

Each day and night he spent alone took him further from the Big Sky and the place he had called home. As he traveled, he thought about the mysterious *Elk* he had spoken to at the river. The giant *Elk*'s words made sense, yet Elkwood could not figure out how to change. He still believed he was a good and trustworthy friend. Perhaps that was the arrogance the giant *Elk* had told him to let go. But someone had to be the best, did they not? Someone had to be the leader of the herd. There had to be a "best" cookie.

Elkwood pondered the idea of leadership. He thought about Le Chocolat Moose and realized that although Baldoin was the best moose mountaineer in the world, he never made anyone else feel awkward. He possessed a great humility about his extraordinary talent. He never bragged. He in fact laughed at his lack of agility on flat land. Although they had never seen him, Elkwood had witnessed Baldoin at Twinkle Toes's pond, taking dancing lessons from her. He would sit in the forest, undetected, and quietly laugh at the sight of Baldoin learning to dance. His friend was nothing if not awkward, but Twinkle Toes patiently coached him into becoming more graceful and less clumsy when not mountaineering. He realized the two were helping each other. Baldoin was learning to be more agile from Twinkle Toes, and she was learning to be less selfish.

He thought about Bearie, and although he was terrified of bees, he knew Bearie would run through a swarm of them to save a friend. He knew Bearie was not educated, but the bear had a great desire to learn. Elkwood had promised Bearie he would teach him to speak more eloquently, but he was so busy with everything in his life, he had never taken the time to honor his promise. He realized that was very selfish of him, yet Bearie was still his friend.

Elkwood smiled when he remembered Bob "the Pumpkin" Bobcat. While he loved to pull pranks and tease, underneath he had a heart of gold. Bobcat was always up for a fight and *always* had everyone's back. Theodore had told him about how Bobcat had thrown himself at Puck to protect Wolfrik during the cookie caper battle. He recalled how Bobcat had saved Big Shot's life when he was young, and how much he loved the massive bison. He wondered if he could ever be that selfless. Elkwood knew Bobcat would protect the herd in his absence.

Big Shot was special. He exhibited the qualities of a great bison. Although his best friend, Bobcat, took money in exchange for his protection of the other forest animals, it really was all in good fun. What Bobcat never knew was that Big Shot Bison secretly returned all the money he collected, using his own profits from the Eat Me Cookie Company. He had no need for money, because Bobcat always took care of him.

Wolfrik von Spice was an enigma. Elkwood had never told the other animals, but he truly loved his spice cookies. Wolfrik didn't know that Twinkle Toes had told Elkwood about what had happened to Wolfrik and his family in Germany and how he had lost his eye. Elkwood was always amazed by Wolfrik's bravery and that he would die fighting for those he loved. He only now was beginning to realize how painful it must have been for him to lose his mate and pups. Then, to fight and kill the brother he had so loved, only to have to ultimately leave his pack, must have been beyond devastating for the wolf. The herd was Wolfrik's pack now, and he would protect them with his life. Elkwood wondered if he could ever be that brave.

Twinkle Toes Trout was, in a word…magnificent. Her dancing and singing talents were unparalleled in the river, and she was envied by all who met her. Although she was truly selfish and narcissistic, she had a good and caring heart. She was smart. She was tough. And she was not afraid. She had braved everything to find the beaver pond and risked her life to be safe and free. Even though she constantly put the herd at risk, her talent, beauty, and wit always made the herd love her. Her protection had simply become a part of the herd's responsibility. Everyone accepted her flaws and loved her in spite of them.

Elkwood stopped at a beautiful creek to rest and eat a Big Elk cookie. Ahead of him, the mountains loomed, big and intimidating. He most certainly did not have the skills of his friend Baldoin. It would be wise for him to rest before he continued. Yet where exactly was he to go?

Suddenly a crow flew in and sat nearby on a rock in the creek. "Hey, elk. Whatever you're eating looks mighty delicious. Feel like sharing with a friend?" the crow cawed.

Elkwood looked intently at the black crow, not trusting him for a minute but feeling like it might be nice to talk to the bird. He broke off a piece of his cookie, and before he could offer it, the crow swooped in and grabbed it from his hoof.

"Delicious!" said the crow as he settled back on his rock. "You wouldn't be Elkwood, owner of the Eat Me Cookie Company, would you?"

Elkwood was startled that the crow had heard of him and that he was that famous…or perhaps infamous. "Yes, Mr. Crow, I am Elkwood Elkington the Third, from the Big Sky, at the base of the Lone Peak."

The crow slyly looked at Elkwood and responded, "What are you doing out here, so far from home yet so close to the Scary Forest? Would you by chance be running away from the mess you caused for all your friends?"

Elkwood was immediately angered but then took a deep breath. The crow was right. It did not matter how he knew about the cookie caper. Obviously, his reputation was known by all. He would never have a friend again. Changing the subject, Elkwood inquired, "Mr. Crow, can you please tell me about the Scary Forest? I would like to go there."

The crow cawed loudly. "No, you wouldn't, Elkwood. The Scary Forest is a bad place from where animals never return. You would do best to go in another direction and find a new home elsewhere."

Elkwood thought about the danger but knew he had nothing left to lose, and if truth be told, he no longer cared what happened to him. "Then please tell me where it is so I am sure to avoid taking that trail."

The crow thought that seemed reasonable and replied, "The trail across the creek heads into the mountains. You will see a sign that says 'The Scary Forest.' If I were you, I would turn back and run." And with that, the black crow flew off his rock perch and disappeared.

Elkwood finished his cookie, had a nice long drink from the creek, picked up his knapsack, and continued on the trail to the Scary Forest. He had no idea what his fate would be, but something at his core told him he had to find the Scary Forest.

As Elkwood climbed the trail, he thought about his wonderful friend Theodore. Would he have ever settled in the Big Sky were it not for his guidance and support? Would he have ever started the Eat Me Cookie Company without the encouragement of Theodore and without his never-ending energy and hard work? Oh, how he truly loved Theodore. That silly red-headed woodpecker was always there for him no matter what. He was the only one who forgave him for the cookie caper fiasco. Yet he had taken Theodore for granted. So many times, he had thought about helping Theodore create his own cookie so he would truly feel a part of the Eat Me Animal Herd. He knew it bothered Theodore that he did not have his own cookie, but Elkwood had been too busy making money and being famous to help his dear friend. Now he would never be able to make that right for Theodore. In spite of his selfishness, Theodore loved him anyway.

As Elkwood climbed higher up the trail, thoughts of his friends and their never-ending devotion and love for him swirled in his head. How he missed them already, but there was no turning back. They would never forgive him… *ever*. All of Montana seemed to know of his deceit and betrayal. He was now truly infamous. Yes, exile was the best thing for everyone. His head drooped in shame as he hiked, weighed down by his massive antlers.

Elkwood looked up suddenly, and before him was a large sign that said "The Scary Forest. Turn back or die!"

Elkwood shivered. He thought of the phantom *Elk* at the river. The clouds began to darken, and a slight breeze kicked up. He heard a *snap* and abruptly turned toward the sound. There was nothing there. Was someone following him? He heard another *snap* and turned to see a large grouse scurry across the ground, then disappear. The crow had filled his head with doom and gloom about the Scary Forest, and it clearly had him on edge. A storm was brewing, but rather than fret, he pushed on, looking for a safe and warm place to spend the night. He *had* to focus on finding shelter.

As he entered the Scary Forest, he noticed all the trees were dead. They were leafless and lifeless, and had been decimated by the harsh environment and winter's subzero temperatures. Fading colors of gray twisted around the trees, induced by the high altitude and never-ending winds. The tall, stark branches looked like arms to Elkwood, reaching out, almost as if for help. Or perhaps to grab him. Elkwood began to see horrible faces in the knotted trunks of the trees. They seemed to be mocking him and soundlessly screaming at him. It was as if he was surrounded by death.

With hesitation, and with a sense of foreboding, Elkwood proceeded into the Scary Forest. The fur on his back was spiked, raised in reaction to the fear he felt inside. He just could not shake the feeling that he was not alone. He stood still for a moment and raised his nose into the air, trying to catch the scent of another animal. Nothing. Feeling rather silly for his fear, he shook a mighty shake and continued on the trail.

"That's better," exclaimed Elkwood. "Perhaps I should hum a little tune, and that will brighten my spirits." Elkwood hummed a lighthearted tune, and his steps became livelier, and he felt a great sense of relief. The Scary Forest was not so bad after all.

As Elkwood traversed deeper and higher into the deadwood forest, the trail became rockier. The wind began to pick up, and the once lifeless limbs of the trees began to shake and creak as if they were groaning and waking up from their eternal death. Again he sensed he was being followed. He stopped humming and stood very still, scanning the forest, trying to hear or see something. The *hoo-hoo* of an owl startled Elkwood and sent shivers down his spine. He looked to the right and saw a cranky-looking owl perched on the dead limb of a giant tree. Except for the blinking of his eyes, the owl did not move. "Oh, you are just a silly owl. I am not afraid of you," taunted Elkwood.

Just as Elkwood turned to continue up the trail, he felt something brush against his left side. He shied to the right and felt something brush his rear, so he spun around. There was nothing there. "What is happening to me?" groaned Elkwood. "Whatever you are, *leave me alone!*"

Suddenly a screech echoed through the forest, and Elkwood was not at all interested in finding out what had made that horrible sound. He began to walk faster and again felt something ruffle his fur. Fear gripped Elkwood. Something had definitely touched him. He was not imagining anything. Something flew right past his nose, so close he felt the swoosh. And again another pass, and again and again. Elkwood began to run. He wanted out of the Scary Forest.

Elkwood tripped and fell and was immediately surrounded by a swarm of vicious black bats. He felt something wrap around his hind legs, and through the dense throng of bats, he saw roots from the dead trees shackling him. Elkwood struggled to get up as the bats nipped at his face and bit his ears. Their fast, fluttering wings felt like tiny leather straps slapping him across his face, head, and body. He rolled onto his back and began to kick in the air to free himself of the roots that bound his legs. How was this possible? The trees had come alive, and their seemingly dead roots were trying to trap him. He had seen bats in the forest many times, but these were no ordinary species of bats. These bats were trying to eat him.

He then felt an ancient root slither around his neck and begin to tighten. With every ounce of strength he could muster, he managed one mighty lunge and rose to his feet, freeing himself from the roots that had seemingly come alive to kill him. The bat attack was relentless, and his face was stinging from tiny bites. All he knew to do was run.

He blindly ran as fast as he could, but the bats followed. Elkwood could barely see where he was running, but he refused to stop. He ran harder and faster until he could run no longer. He collapsed on the hard ground and groaned in pain. Slowly he opened his eyes. The ghastly bats were gone, and he was no longer in the Scary Forest. He breathed a sigh of relief. He was alive. Never in his life had he encountered anything so terrifying. Never.

His face throbbed. He struggled to pull himself up and looked around. There was a beautiful babbling creek speckled with summer flowers a short distance to his right, and he walked into the water and lay down to refresh his tired body. He put his head under the water, hoping to wash away the pain. Elkwood's blood colored the water red, and he watched it fade as the current carried it downstream.

"What a sight I must be," he moaned. He took a long drink, rose from the water, and shook a mighty shake, sending water droplets flying. Miraculously he still had his knapsack, and now another pain, that of hunger, was tugging at him. His face felt swollen from the bites, and he wondered what to do.

"Hey there, Elkwood! You look like you could use some help," whistled a rather large yellow-bellied marmot.

With his nerves still on edge, Elkwood jumped sideways at the sound of a voice. He blinked several times at the chubby marmot before him. "Who are you, and how do you know my name?" asked Elkwood. The marmot looked harmless enough, but at this point, Elkwood trusted no one.

"Everyone has heard of you, Elkwood. Why, you are very famous in the Big Sky and beyond," stated the marmot. Elkwood lowered his head in shame, as the marmot likely knew everything about what he had done to his friends. The marmot was a jolly fellow, and sensing Elkwood's embarrassment, he offered him some help for his many bat bites.

"Hey, that face of yours looks mighty painful. I have just the thing!"

The marmot scurried over to the creek bank and plucked several lavender flowers. He gently removed the flowers from their stems and placed them on a flat rock along the creek. Using a smaller rock, he ground the lavender and, with his paw, scooped up small amounts of water from the creek to create a mush. When he was satisfied with his concoction, he waved for Elkwood to come to him. "Put you head down so I can reach you, Elkwood," instructed the marmot.

Elkwood was hesitant, but the pain was getting worse, and anything was worth relieving his agony. He bent low for the marmot, who proceeded to smear *pawfuls* of his purple concoction all over Elkwood's face. Almost instantly Elkwood could feel a tingling sensation and some pain relief from the wicked bites. He leaned over the marmot and looked into the creek to catch a glimpse of his reflection, a trick he had learned from Twinkle Toes Trout, and began to giggle for the first time in a very long while. Clumps of the purple remedy were smeared all over his face, and he looked quite ridiculous. He did not care. It was working. The marmot chuckled with Elkwood. It felt good to laugh with a friend.

He turned to the marmot and said, "Thank you, my friend. I cannot thank you enough for what you have done for me."

Just then the ominous clouds opened, and a ray of sunlight burned through, making Elkwood shiver. He had not realized how cold and tired he was after his brush with death in the Scary Forest. The warmth from the rays felt good on his body. "Do you know of a safe place for me to rest?" asked Elkwood.

"Sure do. Follow me!" offered the marmot.

The marmot scurried to a nearby rock outcropping, and Elkwood followed. Several of the large boulders formed a small arched open cave, and it looked just big enough for Elkwood. "You will be safe here, Elkwood, and you can even build a small fire. I will get you some kindling and pieces of wood." And off went the marmot.

Elkwood sat down in the cave and thought about all that had happened. Throughout his terrifying experience in the Scary Forest, he had never lost the feeling that someone or something was following him. Not wanting to dwell on such a depressing thought, he chalked it up to the demon bats that had attacked him. He decided they must have been there all along.

From the safety of his cozy hideout, Elkwood looked at the daunting mountains that rose all around him. He was surrounded by the craggiest and meanest-looking mountains he had ever seen. There were very few trees, and the steep cliffs were weathered and rugged. The face of every mountain had sharp rock outcroppings that led to peaks so jagged they looked like they could slice through the sky. There appeared to be no way out, for he was surrounded by a horseshoe-shaped mountain range. Unless he went back through the Scary Forest, which was not an option, he would have to climb over the mountains and hope there was a better place to call home on the other side.

Elkwood was lost in thought when the marmot returned with a small stack of sticks and some kindling. He dropped them in a pile and began rubbing two of the sticks together, quickly generating sparks and a small flame. As the fire began to crackle and pop, Elkwood could feel the warmth penetrate his tired and sore body. Having forgotten how hungry he was, the stabbing pangs returned. He reached into his knapsack and pulled out two very large Big Elk chocolate chip cookies and handed one to the marmot.

"You have been very kind to me, and the only thing I have to give you is one of my Big Elk cookies. Please stay and enjoy the warm fire and a cookie with me."

The marmot was overjoyed, and as he took the cookie from Elkwood, he said, "Is this a famous Eat Me Cookie Company Big Elk cookie? Oh, I have heard about your delicious cookies, and I have wanted for so long to try one but never made it all the way to the Big Sky. Thank you, Elkwood." And he took a giant bite of the cookie. The last rays of sun had warmed the cookies and melted the chocolate. They both smiled as they devoured the snack, and their faces became smeared with gooey chocolate. They laughed in unison as they looked at each other. The marmot could barely contain himself at the sight of the lavender paste all over Elkwood's face, now covered in chocolate.

"I have never tasted anything so delicious in my entire life," exclaimed the marmot. "No wonder the Eat Me Cookie Company is such a great success and you are so very famous."

Elkwood grinned, but behind his grin, he hid the pain and regret for what he had done to his friends. But that was behind him now, and perhaps this marmot was a new friend, and the start of a new life. "Thank you, marmot. You are very kind." The two finished their cookies in silence in front of the crackling fire.

Elkwood was exhausted, but he was afraid to close his eyes and go to sleep. He was still unsettled by the horrifying attack he had suffered in the Scary Forest. The entire ordeal of the past few days had drained him more than he realized. They both gently cleaned the chocolate from their faces and felt sated. The last ray of sunlight disappeared behind the ominous mountains, and the thick clouds again covered the peaks in foreboding grays.

The marmot, thinking it was time to leave, stood up and said, "Thank you for the wonderful cookie and your company, Elkwood, but I should be on my way." As he turned to leave the rock shelter, Elkwood spoke up.

"No, please do not leave just yet," beseeched Elkwood. "I would very much like it if you would keep me company before I continue on my journey tomorrow. It is nice *not* to feel so alone in this very big place. Perhaps you would like another cookie," offered Elkwood.

"Oh, I could not eat another bite," said the chubby marmot with a chuckle. "I do have to watch what I eat." He grabbed his soft and very ample belly and made it jiggle. They both giggled at the self-effacing humor of the marmot. "But I'll stay here with you tonight, Elkwood. It can get very lonely and even frightening up here in the basin. And I *am* a bit tired to be venturing home."

Suddenly Elkwood flinched at what sounded like a branch breaking. "What was that?"

"Probably just a critter running home for the night. Nothing to worry about," reassured the marmot. "You are safe here, Elkwood. There is nothing here that will hurt you."

Elkwood curled up, very much enjoying the warmth of the fire. The marmot added more sticks to the glowing embers, igniting a cheery flame that nullified the chilly night. The marmot sidled closer to Elkwood and leaned back against his soft tan underbelly. While the small fire crackled against the silent night, they both fell fast asleep.

The Eat Me Cookie Company was not the same without Elkwood. Although Theodore knew the recipe for the Big Elk cookies by heart, he could not bring himself to make them any longer. Wolfrik von Spice became the new owner of the company after Theodore told him Elkwood thought he would be the best choice to take over. Wolfrik had not realized how much work it took to run the business. Every day was filled with gathering ingredients, making all the cookies, selling them, and taking care of the store. He realized Elkwood had never once complained about all the work he had done daily, and everyone in the herd had profited handsomely from his efforts. The forest animals continued to stop by every day to buy cookies, but without the Big Elk cookies, business was most definitely slacking. Although Elkwood had left his recipe, Wolfrik did not think it right to sell the Big Elk cookie when the proceeds were not going to Elkwood. The rest of the herd dropped by to help Wolfrik and Theodore, but no one's heart was in their tasks. Theodore decided he had to do something.

The loyal bird woke up very early the next day, then flew to the home of each member of the herd and sounded the alarm that there was a dire emergency and they had to go to the beaver pond. Of course, they all assumed Twinkle Toes Trout was once again in trouble and that Puck was likely responsible. Knowing that Puck was shameless and would stop at nothing to at long last eat Twinkle Toes, they each ran as fast as they could to the pond. Puck had been lying low since the cookie caper embarrassment. No one had seen him, not even his revolting pack. It would be just like Puck to disappear for a while to throw everyone off, then brazenly launch an unexpected attack.

First into the beaver pond clearing was Baldoin. He had been off on a dangerous moose mountaineering expedition when the cookie caper broke loose. Upon his triumphant return from climbing a very challenging mountain, he was dismayed to hear of his dear friend's fall from the herd's grace. Because he had not been involved in the cookie caper, he did not feel as angry as the others toward Elkwood, but he understood their outrage and could not comprehend the lack of judgment exercised by his friend. Wolfrik and Bobcat had been injured, but things could have been much, much worse.

Big Shot Bison thundered into the clearing, followed by Bob "the Pumpkin" Bobcat. The *vroom* of Wolfrik's motorcycle was deafening as he sped into the clearing in a cloud of dust. Even Bearie, the peanut butter bear, blundered into the clearing with a sense of urgency. Twinkle Toes watched in amazement as, one by one, the herd showed up at her pond. They were all slightly out of breath as they looked at each other, wondering what all the fuss was about.

Bobcat was the first to speak and said, "What's going on? Twinkle Toes, we thought you were in trouble. Are you okay?"

Twinkle Toes was rather amused by the interruption and replied, "'*The "trout" that knows the ropes isn't likely to get tied up.*'"

As the morning sun was rising, Twinkle Toes Trout had been lazily enjoying a pond scum drink on the bank of her beaver pond, zealously admiring her reflection in the shimmering water. The morning sun filtering through the trees was particularly flattering to her colorful scales, and it pleased Twinkle Toes immensely.

"You are not in trouble? Puck has not attacked you again?" asked Bobcat.

Twinkle Toes looked at them all with a confused look on her face. "*Suga*, whatever gave you the idea I was in trouble? '*I've been things and seen places*,' but I'm never in trouble."

"You are the most frustrating of trout," scolded Bobcat. "Theodore said you were in trouble, and I guess that is why we are all here."

"'*There are no good "trout" gone wrong…only bad "trout" found out*,'" teased Twinkle Toes.

"Well, I never really said Twinkle Toes was in trouble," corrected Theodore as he flew into the clearing and landed on one of Big Shot's lavender-colored horns. "I just had to get you all to come together so I could explain some things to you."

"If this is about Elkwood, forget it, Theodore. He ruined everything and my tail still hurts." Bobcat stroked his bobbed tail with his front paw very tenderly, as if even the slightest touch would cause him great pain. "Look at Wolfrik's face. It's still swollen, and he will be scarred for life. Nothing you have to say will change anything, little bird. *Elkbutt* is gone, and good riddance. He betrayed us all, even you."

The herd began to leave, and Theodore pleaded with them to hear him out. "Please, everyone, please wait. I have something to tell all of you. *Please!* If you still want to walk away after what I have told you, then go right ahead. But please…*listen* to me!" The herd reluctantly gathered around Big Shot and looked at Theodore sitting on his horn, waiting for him to speak.

"I know what Elkwood did was wrong. He only wanted to rid the forest of Puck, once and for all, so Twinkle Toes would be safe and not live in fear. He had the best of intentions, but he was blind to the many ways his plan could fail. But he never ever, not even once, thought any of you would be injured as a result of his cookie caper. Wolfrik and Bobcat, he has such great respect for you both. He knew you would easily find the recipes. He believed Puck would fail because of the hot pepper 'secret ingredient' and would forever be banished from the forest in humiliation."

"You told him all the ways *zee* cookie caper could fail, Theodore, and he still would not listen to you," said Wolfrik with a stern voice. "Elkwood cannot be trusted, because he always thinks he is right. He is selfish and arrogant, and only has his own best interests at heart."

"You are wrong, Wolfrik," protested Theodore.

Wolfrik looked on in amazement, surprised by the little bird's audacity to challenge the wolf.

"Let me tell you all what Elkwood thought of each of you and how much you all mean to him." Theodore flew off Big Shot's horn and landed right in front of Wolfrik. He wanted his attention. Theodore looked the very large wolf right in the eye, and for emphasis, he put his wing tips on his hips and said, "Wolfrik, Elkwood told me to ask you to take over the Eat Me Cookie Company. You never asked me why he chose you. He said it was because you are brave and loyal, and will always protect the herd. He said it's time for you to be the alpha of your pack. We are your pack, Wolfrik. He admired you more than you will ever know. He cried for you when he found out about your family and how you lost your eye."

Wolfrik shot an angry glance at Twinkle Toes, knowing she had betrayed his confidence. She shrugged her fins, feigning innocence.

Theodore continued. "He hoped you would help Bearie with his grammar. He promised Bearie he would educate him, but he was so busy each day, making cookies and minding the store and doing the work for all of you, that he never found time. He felt bad he had broken his promise to Bearie."

Bearie looked on with a humbling grin and swiped his face with a giant paw. Wolfrik looked down, feeling quite uncomfortable, and pawed nervously at the ground. After only a few days, he understood how much time it took to keep the cookie store running.

"Elkwood also thought it might be a good idea for Bearie to try a new diet."

Wolfrik looked at Bearie and knew he could help the bear. Bearie gave him a grateful smile and was touched that Elkwood was looking out for him.

Theodore again lifted off and landed in front of Le Chocolat Moose.

"And you, Baldoin. Oh, how he looked up to you. He said, 'Tell Baldoin I am sorry. He will be so disappointed when he learns what I have done. He tried to tell me how valuable a friend can be, and I did not understand. I always wanted to be the best, no matter what. I thought that was the right way to be.'"

Baldoin's lips curled up in a slight smile as he thought of his very dear friend Elkwood. He had not been present during the cookie caper, but Wolfrik and Bobcat had been injured, and Twinkle Toes had almost been killed. Yet he knew Elkwood would never purposely hurt his friends. Perhaps they were being too hard on him.

Theodore turned and said, "Don't you all understand? He was trying to learn to be a better *Elk*."

Theodore flitted over to Bearie and sat on the big bear's paw as he lay on the ground. "Bearie, he asked me to tell you to listen to Wolfrik von Spice."

Wolfrik again scratched at the dirt, obviously quite uneasy.

Theodore hopped over and stood in front of Bobcat. "And, Bobcat, he knows how much you love to play pranks, and he never wanted you to get into trouble. He said, 'Tell Big Shot to always look out for Bobcat, as he does love trouble.'" With tears welling up in his eyes, the loyal bird tried to entreat the herd. "He *knew* you all. He understood all of you and how much you could help each other."

"And finally, Elkwood said, 'Tell Twinkle Toes I will never forget her.'" The bird looked deliberately at the trout. "You know this is true, Twinkle Toes. You overheard him say everything." The herd shuffled in place, each feeling like they should say something.

"What about you, Theodore? What'd he say about you?" asked Bearie.

Tears again welled up in Theodore's eyes as he looked at all of his much-loved friends. "He said, 'And, Theodore, dear friend, thank you for helping me to find the Big Sky and for creating the Eat Me Cookie Company with me. I know now, I never could have done it without you. In fact, I now see it never would have been such a great success without the entire Eat Me Animal Herd. We were stronger as a herd. Two are always better than one. Acting alone only creates pain and chaos.'"

With a giant paw, Bearie wiped the tears from his eyes. "I miss *Elkdude*," he mumbled. Even Twinkle Toes seemed to be paying attention and had a rather melancholy look on her face. Big Shot was sniffling, and Wolfrik's head and tail dropped in sadness.

Theodore pulled out a piece of parchment from under his wing. "He asked me to read this to all of you. 'To my friends of the Eat Me Animal Herd, I am sorry—sorrier than I have ever been—to have put any of you in danger. That was never my intention. I have taken all of you for granted. I thought your friendship to me was more important than my friendship to you.

I only wanted to help. I know you will never forgive me, so I am leaving because I do not deserve your love and friendship. Please, someday…forgive me. Love, Elkwood.' The last thing he said to me before he left was 'Theodore, I love you. Please help to watch out for Twinkle Toes.'"

"What do you mean he left?" shouted Bobcat. "Left and went where?"

"I don't know. I haven't seen him since. He has exiled himself from the Big Sky. He could be anywhere." Theodore was now in tears and kept brushing them back with his wings, now soaked from his grief.

Wolfrik stepped forward and took charge, becoming the true alpha he was always meant to be. "Bobcat, Baldoin, prepare to leave immediately. We must depart on a mission to find Elkwood and bring him home."

"*Jawohl!*" called out Bobcat with a teasing grin as he clicked his back paws together. Wolfrik gave him an affectionate cuff across the ears with his giant paw. A satisfied smile drew across Twinkle Toes's beautiful red lips, and the herd cheered in agreement.

"Go now, *jetzt sofort*! Hurry and pack your supplies, and meet me at the store. We will start tracking Elkwood from there, and we *will* find him." Confused by Wolfrik's switch back to his native German language, the animals stood still. "*Jetzt sofort!* Right away!" he ordered.

Bobcat and Baldoin turned to leave just as Big Shot Bison interjected, having been silent through most of the meeting. "But, *Wolfie*, what about Bearie, Theodore, and me? We want to help find Elkwood too."

Wolfrik looked at the herd, and in his haste, he realized he had not considered everyone. He knew this would be a dangerous journey, no matter where Elkwood had gone, and it was his job to protect his pack. "Big Shot, you are strong and you are mighty, but you will not fare well climbing up steep mountains. I am leaving you and Bearie in charge of protecting Twinkle Toes."

Bearie and Big Shot Bison both looked at each other and in unison announced, "We can do that," and everyone agreed and thanked them for bravely staying to protect Twinkle Toes.

"What about me?" asked Theodore in a very quiet voice. "And does this mean you are going to forgive Elkwood?" Wolfrik slowly walked over to Theodore and lowered himself to the ground so he was closer to eye level with the little bird.

"What about you, Theodore? Do you not think you should stay with Bearie and Big Shot and Twinkle Toes? It would be much safer for you. Who will run *zee* Eat Me Cookie Company while we are away finding Elkwood?"

Theodore looked at the impressive wolf and appreciated the eye-level conversation and show of respect. The little bird stood as tall as he could and puffed out his chest in a show of pride and bravery. "Wolfrik, I am not afraid. I can help you find Elkwood. I can fly high above everything and see far and wide. Please allow me to help find my dear friend. I simply cannot bear to be left behind. I helped Elkwood find the Big Sky, and I must help him find his way back home. And the store should be closed until Elkwood returns and reopens the Eat Me Cookie Company with a grand celebration. I think he would like that."

Wolfrik admired Theodore. He was a true friend and had fought to defend Elkwood in the face of the herd's anger and unwillingness to forgive. He had taught everyone a valuable lesson about friendship. Learning to forgive was the hardest thing to do. The cookie caper, and the entire debacle that had followed, had stirred something in Wolfrik von Spice. He had been a loner for so long, yet finding himself so embroiled in the lives of his new friends made him feel needed and worthwhile again. Theodore had put forth a bold effort to defend Elkwood, and he had refused to give up. This silly red-headed woodpecker, through his love and enduring friendship, had turned a very lonely wolf into the alpha he was always meant to be. His bravery in the face of those unwilling to forgive had allowed everyone to learn to forgive. He had longed for a family, a pack, for so long…and now he knew he had found his home.

Wolfrik stood up, towering above Theodore, who tried his best to stretch his neck to appear just a little taller. Wolfrik smiled at the little bird, then looked over his shoulder and nodded at Baldoin.

The moose mountaineer, who understood the meaning of true friendship, called over to Theodore. He bowed his head slightly and said, "Hop on, *mon petit pic à tête rouge!*" Without hesitation, Theodore took off and, in a split second, landed on top of Baldoin's right antler. His face beamed with pride. They would find Elkwood, together, and bring him home.

Wolfrik von Spice, Bob "the Pumpkin" Bobcat, and Le Chocolat Moose met at the Eat Me Cookie Company not long after the pond clearing gathering. Adrenaline over the excitement of a mission was oozing out of their fur. Readying for their rescue, Theodore poked his head out of the store window and called over to the soon-to-be heroes. "Please, come help me. Hurry, we must get on our way!"

The trio trotted over to the store and went inside to find Theodore had stacks of freshly baked Big Elk, Big Wolf, and Big Bobcat cookies, as well as Moose Backpackers. The aroma was intoxicating. "I have made Eat Me cookies for our journey. Here is a backpack for each of you," said Theodore as he handed a small pack to Bobcat and Wolfrik. "Baldoin, you, of course, always carry your moose mountaineering backpack. He who has the most room, please carry Elkwood's cookies as well. When we find him, I have no doubt he will be very hungry."

The trio looked on with pure admiration and love for the red-headed woodpecker. Theodore truly had a heart of gold, and they were happy he would be with them on their mission. They quickly loaded their backpacks and walked out the door.

Wolfrik began to sniff the ground around the store and almost immediately picked up some tracks. "Elkwood's tracks," he called out. "They appear to be a few days old but will be easy to follow. He is heading *nach* west. Onward, my friends."

Baldoin looked concerned, so Theodore asked him what was wrong. "I have studied the mountains all over Montana. There are some very *belles montagnes, oui*, to the west. But getting to them is *très risqué*. I have heard many rumors about the Scary Forest." The others stopped and looked at Baldoin, their excitement turning to concern.

"What do you mean, the Scary Forest?" queried Bobcat.

"I have also heard stories about the Scary Forest," chirped Theodore. "Is there no other way to the west?"

"The path is surrounded by very *grandes montagnes*," Baldoin explained. "*Pour moi*, it is of no concern, but to find Elkwood, we must go through the Scary Forest. If that is the path Elkwood has taken, then we follow. We *must* find him," he said with great urgency. "I only hope he has survived. We should not wait another minute. We will go to the Scary Forest to find Elkwood."

Elkwood's hoofprints did indeed lead right to the Scary Forest. After many miles, they walked up to the gnarly old sign and fell silent. Each wondered what had become of Elkwood and whether they would ever find him alive. Out of nowhere, a large black crow landed on the sign, startling the group.

"Howdy, all," greeted the seedy bird. "I bet you are looking for your pal Elkwood." Undeterred by the trio's silence, he continued. "He came through here a few days ago, and he was mighty skittish. He shared a cookie with me. Any chance any of you have any more of those delicious cookies? I might have just a bit more information to help you in your search." He smiled with a glint of evil in his eyes.

The crow wanted a payoff. Theodore was just about to give him a piece of his mind, while Bobcat was itching to snatch the crow off his perch and have him for dinner. Baldoin stepped forward and offered the crow an entire Moose Backpacker. "Please, Mr. Crow, tell us what you know about our friend Elkwood." He handed the crow the cookie.

The crow snatched the cookie out of his hoof and began devouring the snack. His speech now garbled with a mouthful of cookie, he went on, "Yep, like I said, Elkwood passed through here a few days ago. He seemed pretty sad, and I told him to avoid the Scary Forest. He said he would, but he lied. He went straight into the forest of evil. And that is all I know."

As the crow was about to take off with the delicious cookie, Wolfrik grabbed him around the neck with one giant paw. The crow squawked in fear. "My dear crow, please tell us what else you know," the wolf demanded.

The crow was an opportunist but smart enough to know his luck had run out. He decided it was best to spill all he knew and move on. "Elkwood made it through the Scary Forest, but barely. He is in the mountains now. But he is not alone."

The large wolf growled at the crow, "What do you mean, he is not alone? Did he find a friend?"

The crow, now feeling his wings being crushed in the wolf's steely grasp, decided to end the game. "Mr. Wolf, sir, please, take your paw off me, and I will tell you what I know."

Wolfrik released his hold on the bird but did not move. His breath was so close that with one snap of his jaw, the bird would be gone.

"Unless you call a very ugly and mean-looking coyote a friend, no, he has not met a friend. You four are not the only ones tracking Elkwood."

"Puck!" cried Bobcat. "I knew that rotten coyote would never give up."

The revelation distracted Wolfrik, and the crow abruptly took flight and disappeared with the cookie in his mouth.

"I can't wait to find Puck and finally end him," hissed Bobcat.

A short time later, the four entered the Scary Forest in search of their friend.

CHAPTER 13

ELKWOOD AWOKE to the steady snoring of the yellow-bellied marmot, who was fast asleep and snuggled against him. The campfire that had warmed them throughout the cold night had burned out and was reduced to a pile of smoking ashes. Elkwood looked toward the mountains. They looked just as fearsome as the day before. The clouds, in every hue of gray, hung heavy over the peaks, and the air was still. Elkwood was used to waking in the Big Sky to the many songs of chirping birds, but all he heard was silence. When the birds were in hiding, it usually meant that a big storm was brewing…or that danger was imminent. As much as Elkwood wanted to stay in the cozy natural cave all day, he knew he must be moving on with his journey. He stretched to relieve his tired body, and his movement roused the marmot. "Good morning. How did you sleep, my little friend?"

"Oh, I had a marvelous slumber, Elkwood. Your tummy is very soft and comfortable. And how are you feeling today?" As he looked up at Elkwood, he began to chuckle.

"What is so funny?" asked Elkwood.

"I think we should go over to the creek and wash the lavender salve off your face. It is now dried and crusty and not at all attractive on such a magnificent elk as yourself." The marmot giggled some more.

Elkwood gave the marmot a gentle shove with his leg, and the marmot rolled over in a somersault as Elkwood stood up and shook himself awake. They both sauntered over to the creek, and Elkwood took a long drink and then submerged his head to rinse off the lavender.

"Looks like my remedy did the trick, Elkwood. Your face is completely healed." Elkwood shook the water from his face. It no longer felt swollen, and the stinging pain from the many bat bites was gone.

"Thank you again for all your help. I feel much better today. And now it is time for me to be going, before the coming storm makes the mountains impassable."

The marmot was very sad, for living in the rock outcropping was sometimes very lonely. He had enjoyed spending time with Elkwood and would miss his new friend.

"By the way, you never told me your name," said Elkwood.

"My name is Sam. Pleased to meet you, Elkwood. I wish happy adventures for you always, and you will always have a friend at the base of the mountains, should you come this way again."

Elkwood leaned down and rubbed his soft muzzle against Sam, then reached into his knapsack and grabbed a Big Elk cookie. He handed it to Sam and said, "I will never forget you, Sam. You have taught me so much about friendship. Be forever safe and happy, my friend."

Elkwood felt tears flooding his eyes, and turned to make his way along the creek toward the mountains. He looked back one last time, and Sam had disappeared into the rock outcropping. *How hard it is to leave those you love,* thought Elkwood.

Not long after Elkwood departed, Sam wandered out of the rock outcropping and sat down to eat the Big Elk cookie his friend Elkwood had given him. It had been very difficult for him to watch his new friend leave on his journey into the unknown. Although they had not talked about Elkwood's life in the Big Sky, Sam knew enough to understand why Elkwood had left and how much pain he felt for betraying his friends. Sam knew Elkwood was on a quest to become an *Elk*, and he hoped his travels would bring him back someday. He had high hopes that Elkwood would find his way and learn the true meaning of friendship.

Just as he was taking a bite of his yummy Big Elk, a filthy paw snatched it away from him, knocking him over in the process. He fell backward and rolled onto the dirt. He recovered and stood up, only to be facing the most repulsive and dreadful-looking coyote he had ever seen. The menace crouched low with his fangs bared, saliva drooling from his mouth. His bloodshot eyes had the look of starvation, and Sam knew he was in trouble.

Puck took a giant bite of the Big Elk and, in a raspy voice, said, "I see you have met my friend Elkwood," and he took another bite of the cookie. "*Where is he?*" he growled.

"Nowhere you will ever find him!" And with lightning speed, Sam dove into the rock outcropping and disappeared.

Puck sat up and finished the cookie he had stolen from the fat marmot. The fact that it tasted so incredibly delicious made him seethe with anger because it reminded him of how Elkwood had tricked him. Over and over he replayed what had happened at the opening of the Coyote Cookie Company. How he hated Elkwood. His hatred fully consumed his every waking thought, and his restless and sleepless nights were filled with nightmares of everything that had happened. He had been repeatedly defeated by that stupid Eat Me Animal Herd. Now he was in his element and could move easily in the mountains. Elkwood did not stand a chance against him. Puck sniffed around and picked up the detestable scent of Elkwood. He was not far behind that arrogant beast and looked forward to eating elk for dinner by nightfall. He licked his chops in anticipation.

Elkwood hiked all day, stopping only for a cool drink in the creek or a quick Big Elk snack. It was a gloomy day and it matched Elkwood's mood. He thought about his time with Sam and how the marmot had gone out of his way to help a stranger. And although Elkwood was positive Sam had heard all about his betrayal, he had never questioned him or treated him meanly. Sam was kind and gracious, and had taken care of his wounds. Elkwood doubted he would see Sam again but hoped their paths would cross someday.

By midmorning Elkwood veered away from the creek he had been following and began to climb the mountains. He let his instincts lead him, for one mountain looked as high, steep, and foreboding as the next. It seemed to matter little which one he climbed. After all, he really did not know where he was going or where he would end up. The mountains surrounding the Scary Forest formed a glacial cirque. Elkwood marveled at the many shades of gray patterned in the granite rock, as well as the massive bowl shape of the mountain cirque. He thought it resembled a giant amphitheater. In his mind, he pictured a grand concert for animals from all over, with his parents, Big Duke and Ella, as the headliners on a gigantic stage. He imagined the acoustics would be incredible. He felt tears well up in his eyes as he thought about how much he missed them both.

Elkwood hoped to summit by midafternoon, in time to descend down the other side and find a place to rest for the night. Occasionally he slipped on loose rock, but after watching Baldoin climb many times, he knew he had to take one step at a time and place his hooves carefully. Now was not the time to be reckless, but he *was* going against the ticking time bomb of the storm.

Elkwood was always amazed when he watched Baldoin climb. He had no fear and was so graceful. He made his ascents and descents look effortless, due to his skill and grace. He missed his dear friend.

Suddenly he heard the unmistakable sound of a rockslide careening down the mountain from above. Elkwood darted to the left and barely got out of the way as the slew of rocks avalanched down the mountain. His heart was pounding and he was terrified. He watched as the rockslide tore down the mountain and disappeared from sight. He looked up, wondering what had caused the deadly slide. Nothing was moving, but once again he had the feeling he was not alone. That had been a very close call, and all he wanted to do was get off the mountain.

The skies had been cloudy all day, but they were now darkening to black, and the wind was beginning to howl. A bolt of lightning lit the distant sky, and seconds later it was followed by a loud crack of thunder. Dry thunderstorms were not uncommon in the mountains, but rain would make the climb impossible for a novice like Elkwood. Gathering his courage, Elkwood continued his ascent to the top. The lightning became more intense and the thunder became louder as the storm moved closer. The mountains all around became darker and even more menacing as the storm threatened. Without warning, more rocks catapulted from above, cascading down the scree field, again almost hitting Elkwood. The smaller rocks pinwheeled down the mountain at breakneck speed. Being hit by one could cause severe injury, or even death.

With every step, Elkwood neared the summit of the peak. Even with his great stature, the wind frightened Elkwood. He felt like, at any second, a giant gust would throw him off-balance and he would tumble to his death. Nevertheless, he quickened his pace because he did not want to be caught on the summit with no protection. He only hoped once he reached the top, there would be an easy way down the other side, or at least somewhere he could hunker down for the night while the storm raged. He began to doubt his decision to summit the mountain with a pending storm brewing. What was he thinking? It was almost as if some force, dwelling within him, was driving him forward. Was this his fate?

Finally, with one last effort, Elkwood reached the summit. He was tired but knew there was no time to waste, due to the fast-approaching storm. Lightning was now cracking almost directly overhead, and the loud crashes of thunder made him skittish. The wind was becoming so strong Elkwood had to make sure he planted each hoof soundly so as not to be blown over. He lowered his head and massive antlers as he drove his body forward into the wind, pushing toward the north side of the summit. Step by hard-fought step, Elkwood made his way to the edge, hoping to discover a way down. As he looked over the north face, his heart sank. All he could see was a steep, nearly vertical cliff that appeared to fall forever, with only a few haphazardly scattered rock ledges. He stared in disbelief. There was no way he could go anywhere except back down the way he had climbed, and with the imminent storm, that would be suicide. How could he ever survive a descent in this storm?

Fear gripped Elkwood. The only solution was to find a small space he could cram himself into and hope to ride out the storm.

"I have been waiting for you, Elkwood," growled the evil and relentless Puck as he crawled on his belly from behind a rock and lay crouched directly behind Elkwood.

Elkwood whirled around and was horror-stricken to see Puck glaring at him with fangs bared. It had been Puck who had been following him all along. With a sickening feeling, he realized he was trapped. Puck was blocking him from moving away from the deadly cliff.

"What do you want, Puck? Why have you followed me?" demanded Elkwood.

"You have to ask, you mangy, deceitful elk? You set me up! You tricked me with your fake 'secret ingredient' and humiliated me in front of the entire forest. Even my own pack of worthless dogs hates me now. But you know what, Elkwood? I hate *you* even more. I have always hated you. You think you are so high and mighty and better than everyone. But look at you now. Your herd has turned against you because you betrayed them and lied to them. You have nowhere to run, Elkwood, and this time I am going to kill you!" screamed Puck.

Elkwood knew Puck was crazy, but he had never seen him like this before. He was skin and bones, with bloodshot eyes bulging out of his head, and he had a rabid look of desperation. For the first time ever, Elkwood felt pity for Puck. He had truly been driven insane by his hatred.

"Enough, Puck!" shouted Elkwood. "All this hatred over who has the best cookie? You stole our recipes! You have terrorized Twinkle Toes, relentlessly trying to eat her. You have attacked and injured Wolfrik and Bobcat. Nothing is worth all this hatred. I have lost everything because I tried to stop you, blindly putting all my friends in danger. When does this end?" he screamed above the noise of the raging storm.

"Good question, Elkwood," Puck hissed. "*It ends now!*"

Puck trembled as he readied, and with every ounce of strength left in his decrepit body, he sprang into the air, hurling himself like a missile toward Elkwood. To Elkwood, who prepared himself to die, the action seemed to be in slow motion. Just as Puck was about to strike his fatal blow, Elkwood dodged slightly to the right so Puck's fully extended fangs would miss their mark. But it was not enough. Fueled by a gigantic gust of wind, Puck crashed into Elkwood with such force, it knocked Elkwood off his hooves, and the two plunged over the edge of the cliff. Good and evil tangled together as they fell. With a thud, Elkwood crashed onto a rock ledge and screamed in pain. Puck lay next to him in a heap of unbearable agony, half of his body hanging over the ledge. Puck began to slip off the ledge, and Elkwood instinctively grabbed one paw with both hooves and tried to stop him from falling.

"Grab my antlers, Puck. I will pull you up!" cried Elkwood.

"You want to save *me*?" laughed the coyote. Puck was hanging off the ledge, and Elkwood could see the fear on his face. Maybe it was not too late for Puck.

"*Please*, Puck. I can save you. It does not have to end this way. *You can change!* I do *not* want you to die. Please grab my antlers. Please, Puck. We can all forgive each other and start over. *I know we can forgive!* Please, Puck, grab my antlers," begged Elkwood. "I will *never* let go!"

Puck seethed with rage at the thought that forgiveness was even a consideration. This arrogant, self-serving, and stupid elk was telling him he could change, as if everything was *his* fault? His hatred had truly driven him insane. He would rather die than let this mortal enemy be his salvation. As Elkwood pleaded for a new beginning, Puck relaxed his paw and began to slip from Elkwood's grasp.

Puck gasped his final few breaths and hissed, "I *hate* you, Elkwood. My only regret is that I did not get to *eat* that filthy carp. I would rather die..."

And he slipped away from Elkwood's grasp. With a blood-curdling death howl, Puck fell into the abyss of darkness and disappeared forever.

The release of Puck's weight threw Elkwood backward as he lost his balance and crashed against the rocks. He felt the instant pain of the sharp rock cutting into his back. He was in shock over what had just happened. He had never ever actually seen another animal die. Tears filled his eyes and spilled down his face. Puck was dead. He had tried his best to save him. Elkwood's shoulders heaved as he sobbed great cries of pain and sorrow.

Then he froze. Daylight was gone, the skies were black and thunderous, and he was sitting on a ledge, on a cliff, on a mountain, with thousands of feet to fall and no hope of survival. The night had become so black he could not see a hoof in front of his face. It was as if he was blind, and he began to feel dizzy and disoriented.

Terror gripped Elkwood. No one knew where he was, and he could not possibly climb his way off this ledge, even in daylight. A gigantic bolt of lightning lit up the sky, and all he could see before him was nothingness. A giant black abyss. If he rolled over, he would fall off the ledge.

Panic filled the terror-stricken elk. He curled up into a ball and hugged the rock wall, terrified he would fall to his death, just like Puck. Maybe that was the best solution. Maybe he should just end his agony now and hurl himself off the ledge into the darkness. What was the alternative? To painfully freeze or starve to death, alone on a rock ledge? That could take days, and the waiting would be unbearable. Better to descend into the darkness than fall in daylight. One thing was certain: he was going to die.

Elkwood did not know what to do. He feared if he moved even a little, he would slip and fall off the ledge to his death. The howling of the wind combined with the lightning and thunder gnawed at his already raw nerves. He flinched every time a crack of thunder exploded from the dark heavens. The terror that Elkwood felt became almost physically painful. His entire body was on edge, constricted in a knot of fear. He could not even think, because his situation was so devastatingly impossible. Not one single option existed to save him, and all he could think, as he cowered in the dark, was death would be better than this torture. He was exhausted, cold, and hungry, and none of the pain he felt mattered, because death was inescapable.

After watching Puck fall to his death, it seemed he had reached a turning point in his life. As much as he thought he had hated Puck, he had never wanted him to die. In the end, he realized he truly felt sorry for Puck. Something very horrible must have happened to Puck to have made him so hateful and evil. The entire disaster seemed like a game gone wrong to Elkwood. Somehow they should have been able to work out their differences. Maybe he had not tried hard enough to help a fellow animal who was so clearly distressed and in pain.

Elkwood tried to focus his mind on happier times, when he was in England with his beloved parents. How he missed them both so much. He remembered his journey across the Big Pond and how he had saved the little elk. He thought about the giant *Elk* and still could not wrestle dream from reality when it came to those encounters. He recalled the beautifully dainty elk that had nursed him after the overboard rescue. He could still envision her deep-purple eyes and knew he could lose himself forever in her sweetness. As the time passed—minutes, hours, he was not sure—he recalled every detail of his life since he had arrived in Montana. He was so lost in his dream, he could even smell the delicious aromas of each and every cookie wafting out of the window of the Eat Me Cookie Company. Theodore, dear, wonderful Theodore. How would he have ever survived without Theodore?

Friend by friend, he remembered all the fun and laughter as he had stumbled upon and befriended each member of the Eat Me Animal Herd. He fondly thought of Sam and the profound impact the chubby marmot had had on him in such a short time.

His emotions were exploding in his mind, and forgetting where he was, he stood up and looked toward the black darkness erratically illuminated by strikes of lightning, and he screamed, "*I will not die!* There must be a way off this ledge! *I will never let go of my friends!*"

Spent from the raw emotion, fear, and determination to not give up, Elkwood crumpled into a heap atop the rock ledge and hugged the cliff. Another lightning bolt lit up the sky, and a deafening crack of thunder filled the night. Instead of returning to pitch-black darkness, Elkwood was illuminated in the glow of a golden light.

"Elkwood! *Elkwood!* Are you alive?" called Bobcat. Still in shock, he looked up to see Bobcat, Wolfrik, and Baldoin looking down at him. The beam from Baldoin's golden-yellow hoof beacons illuminated Elkwood, who was precariously positioned on the narrow ledge. Before he could speak, Theodore flew down and landed on his nose.

"Oh, Elkwood, you are alive!" cried Theodore.

The excited bird flung his wings around Elkwood's large nose and hugged him as hard as he could. Theodore held his friend for what seemed like an eternity. Elkwood closed his very long-lashed eyes and did not move. Tears began to flow as his pain, loneliness, and fear of imminent death were replaced by profound relief. Time seemed to stand still in that moment of forgiveness and love between the two.

"My wonderful friend, you will not be able to fly if you get any wetter," said Elkwood softly.

Theodore gathered his wings, then looked at Elkwood and smiled.

"Hey, when you two are finished with your reunion, maybe we should rescue Elkwood from that rock ledge," called Bobcat, with a slight bit of sarcasm yet also lightheartedness in his voice. "This storm is about to hit and blow us all off this mountain."

Elkwood looked up again and blinked several times. He still could not believe Bobcat, Wolfrik, Baldoin, and Theodore had ventured so far, and through so much danger, to rescue him. "Theodore can easily fly up to you, but how will I ever get off this ledge?" yelled Elkwood above the howling winds, fear gripping his entire being.

"Have you forgotten? You are friends with the best moose mountaineer in the world, the strongest wolf that ever lived, and the cleverest cat of all," laughed Bobcat as he called down to Elkwood.

He smiled up at his rescuers, still not convinced they could help him, but willing, without hesitation, to put his life in their very capable paws and hooves.

"This will not be easy, my friend, but we will rescue you, *oui*?" called out Baldoin.

Elkwood nodded in agreement. He was terrified but grateful that at least he was not alone. How could they possibly get him off this ledge? "Theodore, will you please stay by my side?" whispered Elkwood. "It is very frightening being here alone."

"I won't leave you, Elkwood. They will figure out a way to get you off this ledge, I promise," whispered Theodore. Theodore nestled on the mane of Elkwood's massive neck, burrowing into his fur, and Elkwood blocked the wind with his giant nose. He held on tightly to his little friend. The wind was howling, and he intended to protect Theodore at all costs, even if it meant his own life. He had been granted a miracle and a second chance, and he was not about to take it for granted.

Baldoin immediately went to work. He pulled his climbing ropes and his climbing harness from his backpack, along with some other mountaineering devices. He took two pitons, or anchors, and drove them with his hoof into separate crevices in a large boulder to support the climbing ropes. His idea was

to use two belay systems in order to support the weight of Elkwood. To each anchor, he attached a brake device called a Petzl Reverso. He threaded each climbing rope through each Reverso. One end would be attached to each side of Elkwood's harness, and the other end, to the brake rope, and Baldoin would use the system to pull Elkwood up from the ledge. To minimize the amount of physical strength it would take to lift Elkwood, which would be impossible for any of them, Baldoin created a "Z-system" with a friction hitch, called a Prusik in moose mountaineering terms. He tied a loop knot three times around each climbing rope and pushed it down the rope, creating leverage for better pull strength. Then he attached a carabiner to the Prusik. Baldoin then took the brake rope—the end of the rope they would use to pull Elkwood—and clipped it into the carabiner, thus creating a pulley system. Then, using a figure-eight knot, he tied each climbing rope to each side of the harness. Luckily, Elkwood was similar in size, so the harness would be a good fit.

Bobcat and Wolfrik stood dumbfounded as they watched Baldoin quickly and skillfully rig a pulley system to rescue Elkwood. Unlike Elkwood, they had not spent much time with Baldoin, for he was rather solitary and always off climbing new peaks. They had no idea how truly skilled he was as a moose mountaineer.

Baldoin walked over to the edge of the cliff and called to Elkwood as he lowered the harness to the ledge. "Put the harness on, Elkwood, around your back legs and up over your belly," he instructed.

Elkwood was terrified to even move, but he obeyed the instructions. He pulled the harness over his hind legs, then carefully stood up and pulled the large straps around his middle. The climbing ropes tied on both sides of the harness would pull him to safety…he hoped. He was not afraid to admit how frightened he was to be pulled up the cliff wall. What if the rope snapped? What if they could not hold his weight?

Baldoin called down to Elkwood. "Do not worry, my friend. I have everything set up to bring you safely up from the ledge. But you *have* to listen to me. Elkwood! *Écoute moi!*" he hollered over the wind. "When we start to pull and the rope is taught, you must face the rocks. When you start to rise, try and put your hooves on the wall like you are walking up the rocks. We will gently pull you up to the top. Whatever you do, *do not* struggle, Elkwood. Just relax, and we will have you up here *rapidement*," assured Baldoin. "My hooves will be shining on you the entire way, and I will be here to guide you while Wolfrik and Bobcat pull you up, *oui?*"

"Are you ready Elkwood?" asked Theodore.

"Yes, my brave little friend, I am ready." Elkwood trusted his friends completely.

Theodore gave Baldoin a *wings-up*, and Baldoin disappeared for a moment. He trotted over to Wolfrik and Bobcat, and gave them each their brake ropes. "Every time I say '*Tirez la corde*,' give the rope a tug, then another, and another, until we have Elkwood at the top," coached Baldoin.

"What if we slip? Will he fall, Baldoin?" asked Bobcat.

"No, he will not fall. The belay system has a lock at the boulder. There is no way he can fall. Trust me. Are you both ready? *Oui?*" asked Baldoin.

"We're ready. Let's rescue Elkwood," hollered the pull team in unison.

Baldoin walked over to the cliff edge and looked down at Elkwood. "*Tirez la corde!*" he called. The rope tightened and pulled Elkwood to the base of the rock wall. "*Tirez la corde!*" Elkwood's front legs rose into the air. "*Tirez la corde!*"

Elkwood braced his hind hooves against the base of the rock wall. With each pull, he walked a step up the wall, pawing rocks with his front hooves. Suddenly a powerful wind gust hit Elkwood and blew him sideways, and he crashed against the rock wall.

"*Arrêtez! Arrêtez!*" shouted Baldoin. "*Stop!*" he cried. He looked down and could see Elkwood struggling to right himself to continue the ascent. "Elkwood," he shouted. "Listen to me! *Stop* struggling!"

Elkwood looked up at Baldoin, fear gripping his entire being. The wind kept gusting and pounding him against the rocks. Elkwood's hooves were flailing as he tried to get a *hoofhold* on the wall.

"Elkwood, try and brace your left hooves on the wall. With the next pull, use your right hooves to push yourself upright." Baldoin turned to Wolfrik and Bobcat, and said, "One slow, strong pull, then stop. We have to get Elkwood back on his hooves."

Theodore was clutching the fur on Elkwood's neck. "You can do this, Elkwood. Please relax. Do what Baldoin says. Are you ready?"

Elkwood took a deep breath, which was painful from the bruising on his sides, and nodded he was ready. Theodore gave Baldoin the *wings-up* and held on tightly. Elkwood pawed at the rock wall with his front left hoof and finally caught it in a fissure that he could use for support. With that hoof solid, he moved his back leg into place.

Seeing Elkwood was in position, Baldoin shouted, "*Tirez la corde!*" With the slow pull of the rope, Elkwood kept his left hooves planted and pushed as hard as he could with his right legs, and slowly the force of the pull moved him back into position.

"You did it, Elkwood! *Bien joué, mon ami!* Well done, my friend! Again, *tirez la corde!*" Wolfrik and Bobcat rhythmically pulled with each command from the moose mountaineer.

"*Tirez la corde! Tirez la corde! Tirez la corde!*" called out Baldoin. With each command, Elkwood moved up the cliff, hoof by hoof. The wind continued to thrash Elkwood. He mustered every ounce of strength he had and widened his stance to stay balanced, then continued up the wall.

Theodore was holding on tightly to the thick fur around Elkwood's neck, just below his ear.

"You can do this, Elkwood. We are almost to the top of the cliff. One hoof at a time," encouraged Theodore.

Wolfrik and Bobcat established a rhythm with each command from Baldoin. They were amazed at how easy the process was, because the ropes and pulley system bore the weight of their friend.

"*Tirez la corde!*" called out Baldoin. "Just a few more pulls."

Elkwood was almost to the top, and with the next pull, his front hooves touched the top of the cliff. His friends continued to pull in sync, and Elkwood scrambled onto the mountaintop, safe at last.

"Quickly, everyone, we must find shelter. The storm is about to break loose. Hurry! *Dépêchez-vous! Dépêchez-vous*," urged Baldoin. "*Hurry up!*"

The deafening thunder was nonstop, and the lightning zigzagged across the ominous night sky. Large raindrops began to pelt the group. Theodore was still tightly holding on to Elkwood's neck mane. He was a strong bird, but no bird could fly in this violent wind. Led by Baldoin lighting the way, they spotted an opening between two boulders that created a natural cave, and ran inside. There was barely enough room for everyone, but it was the only shelter atop the mountain and would suffice to keep them out of the raging storm. Just as they made it into the cave, the clouds burst open in a torrential downpour, and the violent winds blew the rain laterally.

"That was the best rescue mission ever!" exclaimed Bobcat. "The excitement, the near-death experience of poor Elkwood…it was all just amazing…exhilarating. It was the best caper ever."

The others looked at Bobcat with amusement, knowing they could never tame the cat's desire for wild and dangerous adventures. Elkwood was exhausted. He could never put into words what he had been through since he had left the Big Sky, or how horrific it had been to confront Puck and see him die. He looked at his friends and could not believe they had come to rescue him.

"Why are you all here? How did you get here? Did you travel through the Scary Forest? Did you see Puck? Oh, I cannot believe we are all together again. But I have once again put you each at risk. How can you ever forgive me?"

Wolfrik had been silent for some time and spoke up as the storm raged outside their small refuge. "Elkwood, we have forgiven you. When I took over *zee* store, I had no idea how hard you worked every day, without complaint. The Eat Me Cookie Company was not *zee* same without you. Your energy and devotion are what made us all a success. Then Theodore gathered us together at Twinkle Toes's pond and told us how you had only wanted to rid *zee* forest of Puck and that you never ever thought anyone would be hurt. He also told us your wish for each member of our herd. We realized your heart was always in *zee* right place. We hope you can forgive us for not trusting you more."

Baldoin sensed his friend's grief and knew it was far better for him to let out the pain rather than keep it inside. "Elkwood, tell us what happened on your quest," he said softly.

Elkwood was choked up, remembering the anguish and pain of the last serval days. He revealed how agonizing it had been for him to exile himself, but that he had never thought anyone would forgive him, nor did he feel worthy of forgiveness. He described his meeting with the black crow and his almost deadly run-in with the rabid bats in the Scary Forest. He told them about Sam. He said Sam's generous and kind nature, in the face of all that Elkwood had done to betray the herd, was a giant step toward him becoming an *Elk*. He said Sam had taught him compassion and understanding, because he was finally ready to learn. He told them that throughout his journey he had had a sense he was not alone. He gave the details of his climb up the mountain and how Puck had been following him all along, only revealing himself at the summit, when Elkwood had had nowhere to run. Sobbing, he explained to them about how Puck had told him he hated him and wanted to kill both him and Twinkle Toes. He relived how he had begged Puck to stop and explained that he could be forgiven and that anyone could change...even someone as lost as Puck.

His friends looked on in utter disbelief. They could not believe what Elkwood had been through and how he had bravely continued on in spite of danger at every turn. Then Elkwood told them how Puck had leaped through the air to kill him and they had both plunged off the cliff, landing on the ledge.

"I tried to save Puck. I told him he could change and start over and that we would all forgive him." Everyone was stunned that Elkwood could forgive

Puck. "I told him I would never let go. I begged him to grab my antlers as he slipped off the ledge. Oh, I tried to make him understand, but he was so deranged with hatred for me he just could not hear my words. I told him I would never let go, but he chose to die rather than let me save him." Elkwood was sobbing and shaking his head. Although Puck was his enemy, he explained to his friends what he now knew to be the truth. "Never let go of a friend. *Never.*"

He closed his eyes as he recalled the horrific details of Puck's death. "He looked at me with utter hatred as he released his hold and was gone. It was horrible. Even though Puck was never our friend, maybe he could have learned to become a friend. He deserved a second chance. Watching him die has changed me forever. I now understand the value of friendship and forgiveness. Or at least better than I did before."

Elkwood inhaled a long, cleansing breath and looked at each of his beloved friends. "I am sorry I betrayed you. I wanted to be everyone's hero, and I thought I could defeat Puck by myself. I now realize that you are all my heroes, and I will never lie to you or betray you again. And, oh, how I have missed you all. Please forgive me. I have learned we are stronger as a herd. Two are always better than one. Acting alone only creates pain and chaos."

Recalling Theodore's explanation of why Elkwood had put the cookie caper into motion, Wolfrik put his large paw on Elkwood's shoulder, a rare sign of affection from the big wolf. "Elkwood, we have already forgiven you. Can you forgive us for not seeing more clearly all you have done for *zee* herd? Without you, we would never have met and there would be no Eat Me Cookie Company. Without you, there *is* no herd."

"Speaking of cookies," interrupted Bobcat, "all this mushy storytelling has worked up a fierce growling in my tummy." He reached into his backpack and pulled out a Big Elk, then handed it to Elkwood. "Here you go, *Elkbutt*! I bet you're starving!" laughed Bobcat.

Elkwood gratefully took the cookie, realizing he *was* very hungry. "Thank you, Bobcat. I cannot believe you brought a Big Elk with you."

"Oh, don't thank me. It was all Theodore's idea. When we met at the store to begin the mission to find you, Theodore was waiting with all our cookies ready to go."

Elkwood looked at Theodore, and no words were needed between the two friends. He reached over and moved Theodore next to him, then broke off a small piece of his Big Elk and handed it to Theodore. The others reached into their backpacks and pulled out their own cookies. They sat silently eating while the storm raged on through the night. No more words were needed between the friends. Forgiveness was understood. One by one, they fell asleep, leaning on and holding up each other. They would never let go of a friend.

Theodore was the first to venture out of the shelter the next morning and was very pleased to see the storm had passed and the sun was beginning to rise over the eastern mountains. Everything looked so different in the sunlight.

"Look, everyone! Look! Wake up! Wake Up! I can see home from here! I can see the Lone Peak! Hurry, please! *Wake up!*" hollered the red-headed woodpecker.

One by one, Elkwood, Baldoin, Wolfrik, and Bobcat stretched and emerged from the rock den. Theodore was positively ecstatic, jumping up and down, then taking flight and zooming back and forth across the peak. The wind had died, the clouds had cleared, and it was a beautiful, crisp morning.

"Look! Look! I can see the Lone Peak!" shouted Theodore. "Let's get going! I want to get home! Hurry! *Hurry!*"

The bird was hysterical with joy as he roused his companions. They all stood in amazement and looked to the southeast. On a clear day, the majestic peak could be seen from hundreds of miles away, and there, visible in all its glory, stood the Lone Peak.

"Elkwood, did you know Puck dared to rename your peak Puck's Peak when he opened his sorry excuse for a cookie store?" inquired Bobcat.

Elkwood paused in thought and looked out over the beautiful mountains in the distance. "I did not know he renamed the Lone Peak, Bobcat. A mountain can never belong to anyone. I know that now. The Lone Peak belongs to everyone from now until the end of time. I would like to think that Puck could have changed. Perhaps we should name *this* mountain Puck's Peak in memory of Puck."

"Why would you want to name anything after your enemy, Elkwood, or even remember Puck?" questioned Wolfrik. The conversation brought bitter memories back to Wolfrik. The betrayal by his brother had plagued him for so long and had prevented him from truly trusting anyone.

"Because unless we can all forgive Puck, he will haunt us forever, *oui*, Elkwood? Harboring anger and resentment will only lead to unhappiness," perceived Baldoin. He truly hoped forgiving Puck would be a cathartic release for the herd. "Let Puck's Peak stand as a monument to never letting go of a friend," suggested Baldoin.

"I like that idea, Baldoin. Maybe Puck will find happiness on the other side of the mountain," mused Elkwood. He walked over to the back of Puck's Peak, where he and Puck had tumbled off the cliff. It was a very long drop, and he could not see the bottom. Baldoin walked over and stood beside him.

"I never wanted Puck to die, Baldoin. I did not let go. You believe me, don't you?"

"*Oui*…Puck let go, Elkwood. His hatred consumed him. He hated long before he met you, or Twinkle Toes, or any of us. Puck's death was not your fault. I know you did not let go."

Theodore was proud of Elkwood. He had learned so much from this terrible experience. But he was impatient and wanted to go home. "We must get home and reopen the Eat Me Cookie Company and have a big party to celebrate Elkwood's return to the Big Sky!" chirped Theodore.

Elkwood and Baldoin stood side by side and looked out over the mountains from the back side of the cirque. It was a place that would always represent the end of a lost soul. It was finally over.

"Let's go home, Elkwood," whispered Baldoin.

As the herd climbed down Puck's Peak on their trek home to the Big Sky, Bobcat regaled Elkwood with tales about their journey. He told Elkwood that they had met the devious black crow and that he had directed them to the Scary Forest. Elkwood was stunned they had not encountered the deadly bats.

"How is it possible you were not attacked by the bats, and the roots of the dead trees did not grab you?" asked Elkwood.

"Not sure, *Elkbutt*," teased Bobcat. "Maybe it is because there were three of us instead of just one of you. After all, we are pretty intimidating." He winked at Elkwood.

"Perhaps," pondered Elkwood. "I am just happy I do not have to go through the Scary Forest alone this time." He breathed a sigh of relief.

Bobcat continued, telling Elkwood about meeting Sam the yellow-bellied marmot. "Sam told us that after you left, Puck showed up and stole the Big Elk you gave him, right out of his paws. That was when we realized Puck was tracking you. We did not pick up his vile scent before, because he cleverly followed you adjacent to your trail. He had you in his sights throughout your entire journey. He was always nearby, *Elkbutt*, watching you."

A chill ran through Elkwood's massive body. "Over and over I felt like someone was following me, but I never saw anyone. Rocks came cascading down Puck's Peak, and I thought it was a natural rockslide. Puck was trying to kill me," Elkwood recalled with sadness in his voice.

"It is over now, *Elkbutt*, and Puck lost," declared Bobcat. "In a fair fight, you would have beat him every time. That is why he waited until you climbed to the summit. He knew he could corner you there. He was a coward."

Elkwood shivered again, remembering his horror when he saw Puck crouched behind him with hatred displayed on his twisted face. "What else happened on your mission, Bobcat?" asked Elkwood, wanting to change the subject.

"We were traveling swiftly, so we were not too far behind you and Puck. We arrived at the summit not long after Puck attacked you," recalled Bobcat. Elkwood inhaled sharply and shuddered. He recalled the terror-ridden time he had spent alone on the rock ledge, knowing he would die. They fell silent and continued to make their way down the steep mountain face.

Making good time, the four successfully descended to the bottom of Puck's Peak and came upon the creek that would lead them to Sam's rock outcropping and the entrance to the Scary Forest. They stopped and took a very long drink of the clear, cold mountain water. Refreshed, they continued along the creek toward home.

"Help! Help!" cried Theodore as he flew up and landed on Elkwood's antler. Theodore had flown off to explore and had gone as far as the marmot's rock outcropping, just in time to see a very large cougar chase Sam into the rocks. Not wanting to miss a meal, the cougar was crouched along the rocks, hidden from view, waiting for Sam to reappear. Driven by hunger, the cougar knew the marmot would emerge eventually, thus making him easy prey for dinner.

"Sam is in trouble!" cried Theodore. "Hurry, we must help him. A cougar is trying to eat him." Theodore flapped his wings in a frenzy.

Elkwood immediately started to run in the direction of Sam's rock outcropping, followed by Wolfrik, Bobcat, and Baldoin. Sam's life was at risk, and there was not a minute to spare. Theodore flew on ahead to make sure Sam was still alive.

Sam was hunkered down in the rock outcropping, cautiously poking out his nose every few minutes to see if the cougar was still stalking him. With the cougar crouched low and hiding, Sam was unsure whether it was safe to come out. As he stuck his nose into the air, Theodore flew in fast, calling out in his shrillest voice to alert Sam.

"Stay put, Sam! Help is on the way!" he called.

The foursome skidded into the clearing next to the rock outcropping while Theodore was frantically flying in circles overhead. They instantly heard the growl and hiss of the hiding cougar. With ears back and fangs bared, the cougar snarled and scratched the dirt in disgust, then clawed the air in a rapid staccato rhythm as the rescuers arrived. Realizing he was severely outnumbered, his demeanor instantly changed, as he thought better of his aggressive stance. The cougar sat up and, appearing unconcerned, began to lick his paw.

"Gentlemen," he cooed in a raspy voice. "As you can see, I am planning dinner, so although I would like to chat, perhaps a rain check?" The cougar, with a sly grin, looked up as if it might start raining. "If you please, continue your journey and I will finish my hunt." He faked a friendly smile that hid his cunning nature.

"Fat chance, *Cougarbutt*," responded Bobcat sarcastically. "Sam is our friend, so unless you want to become *our* dinner, I suggest you hightail it *outta* here…*now!*" Bobcat hissed at the intruder, baring his very large fangs. The last thing Bobcat wanted was a face-off with this nasty cougar, but he felt confident. Having a wolf, a very large moose, and a strong elk on his team would make him the victor.

The cougar could see he was going to have to find a different menu item for dinner, rather than risk his life in a battle he knew would end in his death. He was ferocious, but practical. He continued to casually lick his paw, as though he hadn't a care in the world.

"No need to twist your tail in a knot, kitty cat," purred the now docile cougar. "There will be ample time in the future to dine on marmot." He licked his lips with a knowing grin, turned, and slowly sauntered away.

Bobcat growled under his breath, "Did he call me kitty cat?"

The others snickered.

"That was close!" called out Sam as he scrambled from the rock outcropping and scurried to greet his friend. "Elkwood, so good to see you again, and I see your friends found you. And Puck?"

"Oh, Sam, I am so happy to see you too," exclaimed Elkwood as he bent down and rubbed his big, soft nose against the furry marmot. "I know you have already met Wolfrik, Baldoin, Bobcat, and Theodore. They found me at the top of Puck's Peak just as Puck tried to kill me. Puck is dead."

"Dead? *Puck's Peak?* Oh my! It sounds like quite an adventure. Can you stay awhile and tell me everything?" the marmot hoped.

"We still have a long way to go, and there is just enough daylight to get through the Scary Forest before dark and our next camp. We are all eager to return home. I wish we could stay longer, Sam." Elkwood winced seeing the sad face of the marmot. Elkwood looked at his friends, and each gave him an encouraging nod.

"Sam, would you like to come with us to the Big Sky? You seem rather lonely up here in the high mountains, and it certainly does not seem like a safe place for you to live," suggested Elkwood.

Sam's heart skipped a beat. Then common sense set in, and he replied, "Thank you, Elkwood, but this is the proper home for a marmot, and really, I have a wonderful life. I am hoping to start a family someday, and then there will be lots of marmots in my rock outcropping. Perhaps I can come visit all of you one day." He tried his very best not to look dejected.

"And, Theodore, please accept my most profound gratitude for bringing your friends here so quickly to save me from that mean ole cougar," said Sam. Theodore nodded.

Elkwood was not going to take no for an answer, but he did not want to wound Sam's pride. He knew from experience how difficult it was to leave one's home. "Sam, we have lots of rock outcroppings in the Big Sky. In fact, there is one very near the Eat Me Cookie Company and my tree home. I would consider it a favor if you would come with us, Sam. You see, I will never again let go of a friend. Yes, you would be helping me, in a tremendous way, to become a true *Elk*. Won't you come to the Big Sky and make it your home?"

"Really, Elkwood? You have rock outcroppings in the Big Sky? It does sound wonderful, and I could maybe use a change of scenery. And I guess, if you need me…"

Elkwood began to hope. Then Sam asked, "How will I get there, Elkwood? That is far too long a journey for a marmot such as myself to make. As much as I would like to help you, it is better I stay here," said the now disappointed marmot.

"That is easy, *Monsieur* Sam," exclaimed Baldoin. "You can ride on Elkwood's back all the way to the Big Sky."

"If I can help you in your quest to become an *Elk*, I will come with you, Elkwood," agreed Sam.

Wolfrik quietly watched the scene unfold with amusement. He knew Elkwood was cleverly enticing Sam to come with them. He also knew Sam had made a real difference in Elkwood's life. Nevertheless, Wolfrik was acutely aware evening was coming, and it was time for them to leave in order to make it through the Scary Forest before nightfall.

"My dear Sam, we all agree your friendship and caring has taught Elkwood valuable lessons. His quest was not for *nichts*, naught. He has truly become an *Elk*," Wolfrik declared.

One solitary tear fell from each of Elkwood's big brown eyes, and his heart swelled with pride, but not arrogance. Now that he had become an *Elk*, the prideful side of Elkwood was tempered with humility. It was a very good feeling for a new *Elk*.

"Let us go now before darkness falls and danger surrounds us, yet again. We must get home to reopen *zee* Eat Me Cookie Company and celebrate Elkwood's return. And I think…celebrate your new home." Wolfrik bowed to the marmot.

"Wait just a minute. I will be right back." The furry marmot scampered away and disappeared into the rocks.

"Now what?" complained Bobcat. "I have a bad feeling about the Scary Forest. I am not so sure we will get through unscathed this time."

Wolfrik gave him a look of irritation for always saying aloud what he was thinking. It would serve no purpose to frighten everyone, although he, too, was worried about the eerie, eldritch forest.

Sam returned with a small pack containing his personal belongings. "I am ready to leave, Elkwood," he announced. Sam was beside himself with joy and excitement to be welcomed on the journey with these wonderful friends. And he felt great anticipation about finding a new home. He waddled over to Elkwood, who towered above him, looked up, and asked, "How will I get on your back, Elkwood? I cannot jump that high."

Baldoin trotted over and grasped the furry marmot between his teeth, then gently placed him atop Elkwood's back. Elkwood turned to check on his passenger and gave Sam a little nudge with his long nose. "Easy with the claws, my friend," chuckled Elkwood as the group turned and made their way along the trail to the Scary Forest.

The group stood silently at the entrance to the Scary Forest. A posted sign read "You will not survive twice."

Elkwood flashed back to his first terrifying experience in the Scary Forest. He looked at his precious friends, and his fears calmed: strength in numbers. They could survive anything if they stayed together.

Wolfrik organized the group to best protect them in case of an attack. Because he had the most sensitive nose and could intercept any unusual scents, and also because he was the most experienced in battle, Wolfrik led the way. He was followed by Elkwood and Sam. Elkwood would be at the greatest risk because he had to protect Sam. Thus, the others surrounded Elkwood in case of trouble. Bobcat was next in line, positioned to rescue Sam should the unforeseen happen. The last in line was Baldoin. His massive strength and ability to mortally wound a foe from a mere kick with his back hooves made him the perfect choice to bring up the rear of the little army. In single file, they entered the Scary Forest.

Almost as if on cue, the skies began to darken and the wind picked up, signaling an impending storm. Due to the delay caused by the menacing cougar, it was now late evening, and there was little daylight left. Elkwood had his knapsack harnessed across his shoulders, and Sam decided that crawling inside would be the safest place for him. He burrowed inside the knapsack and turned around so only his head was sticking out.

Theodore was tired from so much flying and landed next to Sam's face peering out of the backpack. "May I join you?" asked Theodore.

"Of course," agreed Sam, and Theodore hopped in next to the marmot, poking his beak out next to Sam's nose. Elkwood turned and gave his precious cargo a nod of approval.

The deeper the friends trekked into the foreboding forest, the harder the wind howled. The sea of dead trees creaked and groaned, as if they were awakening. The brittle limbs reached out with skinny branches like long arms with sharp claws, ready to grab an unsuspecting trespasser. Lightning and thunder exploded in the dark sky. Everyone was on edge. Sam and Theodore retreated further into the safety of the knapsack with each loud crack of thunder. Bobcat, always up for excitement and adventure, acted tough, but truth be told, he was not feeling very fearless in the Scary Forest.

Without warning, Wolfrik stopped and froze in his tracks, forcing the others to follow suit. Deep, throaty growls emanated from the forest. The sounds rolled on top of each other, surrounding them, making it impossible to pinpoint the origin. Maybe the trees really were coming to life.

Wolfrik looked all around but saw nothing. Suddenly three pairs of golden orbs appeared, glowing in the dark. One by one, three unusually large wolves emerged from the black forest abyss and blocked their pathway. Wolfrik was large by any wolf standard, but these wolves were freakish in size. Wolfrik assessed the situation quickly, and although the wolves were menacing and appeared dangerous, he had with him one very large elk and one very large moose who could kill a wolf easily with merely one kick. Against the three blocking their way, they had a chance.

"Wolfrik, I think we have company."

He turned to see Bobcat pointing to six more wolves that had appeared like ghostly apparitions at the rear and flank of the group. Each was equally as large as the three monsters in front of Wolfrik. The six wolves began to move in, forcing the friends closer together behind Wolfrik. They were surrounded.

Wolfrik stood his ground. Not being able to tell who the alpha was of this hideous pack, he spoke to them all. "We mean you no harm and request safe passage on our way home." He took two steps forward on the path and was blocked by the wolf that now appeared to be the leader.

Lowering his head, his ears laid back, the monstrous wolf let out a low growl. "You are not going anywhere, Wolfrik."

Wolfrik was stunned this beast of a wolf knew his name. A long rumble of thunder drowned the forest in noise, giving Wolfrik a moment to assess their predicament. Sam and Theodore had both emerged slightly from their pouch to survey the situation, but when they saw the wolves' glowing eyes, they fearfully ducked back inside. Elkwood, Baldoin, and Bobcat held their breath as they awaited the cessation of the rumble. Although Wolfrik would give up his life to protect his friends, he hoped he could maneuver through the crisis and avoid a battle.

Without warning, a single flash of lightning ripped through the sky, striking a gargantuan tree, instantly setting it ablaze. The fiery tower fractured into two and crashed to the ground. One giant half fell directly behind Baldoin with an earth-shaking thud, effectively cutting off the six rear and flanking wolves. The burning tree created a massive wall of flames, terrifying the wolves. The heat forced them to back away from the inferno, leaving the three wolves in front virtually stranded.

"You might want to reconsider," Wolfrik hissed to the three remaining wolves. "Elkwood, Baldoin, Bobcat... *now!*" And in a split second, they attacked the wolves, kicking them and knocking them to the ground.

"*Run!*" commanded Wolfrik.

With a headbutt to a flailing wolf, Bobcat charged into the lead, followed by Elkwood with Sam and Theodore trembling in his knapsack. Baldoin continued to batter the wolves with powerful kicks from his rear hooves, while Wolfrik sank his teeth into the neck of a foe, flinging him off to the side. Yelps of pain from the ravaged wolves rang through the forest, coupled with deafening claps of thunder. The constant flashes of lightning, in the now pitch-black forest, revealed the ghastly scene, flicker by flicker, resembling an old-time movie.

Before the flanking wolves could find their way around the fiery blockade, Wolfrik cried out to Baldoin, *"Folge mir! Folge mir!* Follow me! Hurry, Baldoin!" And the two fled from the fiery scene, deeper into the Scary Forest, leaving the stunned predators behind.

Baldoin took the lead, and guided by the glow from his antler lamp, they ran until their lungs burned and their legs began to give out. They finally stopped, chests heaving, as they tried to catch their breath.

"Psst, over here," hissed Bobcat. Baldoin turned, and his antlers illuminated four sets of gold and green eyes.

"Bobcat, Elkwood, Theodore, Sam, are you there?" whispered Baldoin.

"Yes, over here. Are you and Wolfrik hurt?" asked Bobcat.

"We are fine, but I cannot say as much for those vile wolves," he said with great satisfaction.

Causing everyone to jump, the *hoo-hoo* of an owl rang through the forest. The skittish herd looked up and saw the glowing neon-orange eyes of an owl blinking at them.

"What is that?" screamed Elkwood, and the band turned and saw several sets of red eyes not thirty feet away.

"Let's get out of here!" wailed Bobcat, and together they ran through the woods, with Baldoin lighting the way.

Three harmless small rabbits hopped out of the brush, their red eyes glowing in the dark.

As they ran past the entry sign to the Scary Forest, the friends slowed and breathed sighs of great relief. In the darkness, they could hear the babbling of the nearby creek. Deciding they wanted to put distance between themselves and the terror they had left behind, they followed the creek for a short time, looking for a good spot to bed down for the night. The storm had passed, and the black, moonless sky was peppered with millions of diamond-like stars.

"If no one objects, I think I would prefer to sleep near the creek tonight, out in the open, rather than under a tree," suggested Elkwood. The friends wholeheartedly agreed. No trees.

"This looks like a perfect spot to sleep," announced Bobcat. As he turned to explore the area, he gasped and let out a cry. "Oh no! Look, everyone! The Scary Forest is burning!"

In sync, they turned toward the Scary Forest and inhaled in shock. Off in the distance, where they had fought to survive, vicious tongues of red and orange flames leaped toward the twinkling stars in the raven-black sky. The breathtakingly beautiful sight contrasted ironically with the forest's imminent destruction.

They stood in silence as they watched the fire. What had been started by the lightning strike that had saved them was now ravaging the Scary Forest. The raging flames became an out-of-control firestorm, devouring everything in its path. The haunted forest of lifeless trees provided the perfect fuel for the fire. The illuminated mountain cirque cradled the blaze, forbidding it to spread further, while the cleansing fire destroyed the forest demons. No one dared to speak.

Witnessing the second death of the Scary Forest was cathartic for the weary travelers. It represented not only a time of challenge and terror for Elkwood, Wolfrik, Baldoin, Bobcat, Theodore, and Sam but, conversely, the freeing of a soul, the strengthening of friendship, and the enlightenment of an *Elk*.

Completely spent, the unlikely ensemble of an elk, a moose, a wolf, a bobcat, a woodpecker, and a marmot lay down, nuzzling each other and creating a shelter of protection and friendship. They fell fast asleep, knowing together they could survive anything.

CHAPTER 14

RETURNING TO THE BIG SKY was better than anything Elkwood had ever experienced. Before he ventured off to surprise Twinkle Toes Trout, Big Shot Bison, and Bearie, he stopped by his tree home. When he saw the flowers in their boxes and the Eat Me Cookie Company next door, waiting to be reopened, he began to prance and dance in joyful glee. How could he have ever thought he could leave this wonderful place forever?

The rest of the trip home had thankfully been uneventful. Elkwood had discovered that everything he truly wanted and needed was right here, right under his nose. His home, his friends, his store—*ahem*—the herd's store, and this beautiful place were all he ever really needed. Now that Puck was gone for good, the animals could relax and finally feel safe. Wolfrik would not have to constantly monitor Twinkle Toes, and although Puck's pack was still in the vicinity, they were not as powerful without their leader. They certainly would never dare to antagonize Wolfrik. He suspected most of them would eventually move on to other places in Montana, as coyote packs often did.

Theodore flew into the clearing with a fantastic display of aerobatic prowess. He twirled and soared and performed death-defying dives and loops. It was like watching Twinkle Toes with wings. He was elated to be home. Stopping midair, fluttering like a humming bird, he dove straight at Elkwood, landed on his long nose, and threw his wings around him, giving him a big hug.

197

"I am so happy to be home, Elkwood! I am so happy you are now an *Elk*!" He hugged Elkwood as hard as he could.

"Do you really think I have become an *Elk*, Theodore?" asked Elkwood with great concern.

"I know you have, Elkwood. We never stop learning, but you faced your flaws and you bravely changed. You are my hero, Elkwood." The little bird hugged Elkwood even harder. A tail feather curved into Elkwood's nostril, and the tickle made him sneeze, blowing Theodore right off his nose. Catching himself in the air, Theodore flew back, landing on Elkwood's antler, and they both laughed with a pure joy they had not felt in a long time. All the peril, evil, and pain was over, and they were home.

"We have to gather ingredients. We must go to the chocolate chip water-fall and get the store ready for the grand reopening tomorrow," encouraged Theodore. "I have already spread the word throughout the Big Sky that you are back and the Eat Me Cookie Company will reopen for business, starting tomorrow. C'mon, Elkwood, we have so much to do," chattered the little bird.

"Slow down, Theodore. First we have to go visit Twinkle Toes and Big Shot and Bearie, and thank them for protecting Twinkle Toes while we were away. She is safe, is she not, Theodore?"

"Oh, yes. I flew by on my way here, and she was, as usual, admiring her reflection in the pond, sipping a pond scum drink. There appeared to be an excess of bugs on her stir stick today." They both laughed.

"I am happy she is safe, but we must go say hello. We have plenty of time to get everything ready to reopen the store tomorrow," advised Elkwood.

Theodore jumped on an antler, and the pair headed to the beaver pond. As they stepped into the clearing, they were surprised to see everyone in the herd gathered, chatting with Twinkle Toes. Bobcat was very animated, dra-matically acting out their adventure for Twinkle Toes, Big Shot, and Bearie. They were fixated on every interpretive scene. Baldoin sat nearby, enjoying the coolness of the green grass. Wolfrik was casually stretched out on the ground, alert as always but also surprisingly relaxed. The scene was so peaceful it took Elkwood's breath away. To see his friends so happy and calm, and not in danger, made his heart nearly burst with joy. He caught the attention of the herd, and they turned to welcome him.

"Elkwood, come join us. I was just telling everyone about your quest... and Puck...and the Scary Forest. *Everything!*" shouted Bobcat. Bobcat was clearly enjoying being the grand storyteller of their incredible adventure.

Elkwood trotted over to the pond with Theodore on his antler. He was so very happy to see all his friends together. But someone was missing. "Where is Sam?" inquired Elkwood.

"I am right here, Elkwood." Sam came scurrying into the clearing. "I found the most beautiful rock outcropping with lots of tunnels and caves and even some other marmots. They welcomed me and said I could share their outcropping with them. Elkwood, this place is so wonderful. Thank you for bringing me here," exclaimed the very excited marmot.

Elkwood was happy beyond his wildest dreams. His friends were together and safe, and that was the most important thing in the world, though some things would never change. Even amid all the excitement, Twinkle Toes Trout—having the attention span of a flea—was back to admiring her reflection in the pond.

"Twinkle Toes, do you never tire of admiring yourself?" scolded Elkwood with an air of teasing.

"'*It isn't what I do but how I do it. It isn't what I say but how I say it, and how I look when I do it and say it,*' suga," said Twinkle Toes in her most alluring voice.

The herd burst into uncontrollable laughter. Twinkle Toes was most assuredly an impressive narcissist, but they loved her in spite of this...and she certainly was entertaining.

In a rare show of humility, and not to be outwitted by the herd, Twinkle Toes focused all her attention on Elkwood. "Elkwood, I'm very pleased you are home and safe. I know you never let go, but I'm still glad Puck is gone. Wolfrik, Bobcat, Baldoin, Theodore, and Elkwood, I missed you." She pulled her fin across her face, feigning shyness. "Sam, welcome. Please come visit me... *anytime, suga*." Twinkle Toes flipped her fin, and she jumped into the water and disappeared. All eyes were on the beaver pond, knowing she would never disappoint. With the biggest leap they had ever seen, Twinkle Toes broke through the surface of the pond and flew so high she almost disappeared. She arched and dove cleanly into the pond with hardly a splash. She broke through the surface in another magnificent leap, flipped three times, and again dove deep into the water.

The herd cheered in appreciation. No one could put on a show like Twinkle Toes Trout. She stood on her tail fin, swaying back and forth, bowing in response to the adulation. She was used to praise from her nightly performances at the Nymph Disco, but entertaining her friends meant far more. They were her most adoring fans.

Wolfrik rose to his paws and bowed to Twinkle Toes. "A truly spectacular show, Twinkle Toes. I must say, you are looking more beautiful than ever." The wolf bowed again, with a sparkle in his golden eye.

"Well, *suga*, I always say, '*Look your best. Who said love is blind?*'" She gave Wolfrik her most flirtatious look.

Not wanting to spoil the reunion but knowing there was a lot of work to do in preparation for the grand reopening, Elkwood interrupted the festivities.

"It is so great to see all of you again, and as much fun as we are having, Theodore and I do have to begin gathering ingredients, baking, and getting ready for tomorrow's grand reopening of the Eat Me Cookie Company. I hope you will all stop by to celebrate." Theodore, still sitting on Elkwood's antlers, looked sad to leave the gathering, but there was work to be done.

"We would all like to help you get ready for tomorrow. We can gather our own ingredients and help you make the cookies," offered Baldoin, who had been silently observing the reunion.

"Oh, that would be wonderful," exclaimed Elkwood. "Theodore and I will see you all back at the store." He turned to leave. With a look over his shoulder, he said, "Thank you all."

It was wonderful to be home.

Elkwood and Theodore hiked to the chocolate chip waterfall and filled Elkwood's knapsack with chocolate chips and other ingredients they found along the way. By late afternoon they returned to the store and found Baldoin, Wolfrik, Bearie, Bobcat, and Big Shot inside, making their respective cookie doughs. Even Twinkle Toes was there in her large bowl of water, lending a helping fin. The store was a disastrous mess, but Elkwood did not care. The scene of his friends working so hard to help touched Elkwood to his core.

"What are you all doing?" asked Elkwood.

"You and Theodore have always done everything, and now we want to help. We are *zee* Eat Me Animal Herd, and from now on, we share *zee* work," declared Wolfrik.

Elkwood was delighted and believed he could never be happier than he was at that moment. Seeing his friends work side by side, knowing they appreciated all his hard work, meant everything to the *Elk*. Without delay, Elkwood and Theodore jumped in to help the herd, readying everything for the grand reopening the next day.

When everything was finished, they cleaned up the rather substantial mess, and one by one, his friends departed. Wolfrik, with a *vroom*, sped away with Twinkle Toes in his sidecar. Bearie lumbered back to his den, Bobcat and Big Shot made their way back to their cave, and Baldoin left for his moss bed, deep in the woods. Theodore was exhausted and flew next door to the cozy nest Elkwood had built for him so long ago, and immediately fell fast asleep.

Elkwood had one more thing to do. He left to explore the woods in the waning light. He found acorns and pine seeds, and scraped a good amount of sap oozing from the pine trees. Finally, he hit the jackpot and found a patch of wild blueberries, huckleberries, and raspberries. When he returned to the store, he mushed his ingredients together and formed cookies from the delicious mash.

Exhausted, Elkwood surveyed the store. Everything was ready for tomorrow. As excited as he was to reopen the store, he had a very big day ahead of him, and his moss bed was calling him. He left the store and quietly entered his home next door, to the soft, rhythmic breathing of his dear friend Theodore. He could not wait to see the look on Theodore's face.

🦌 🦌

Bright and early, Elkwood saw a long line had formed, stretching from the store to the forest. Animals from all over the forest were anxiously awaiting the grand reopening of the Eat Me Cookie Company. The tantalizing aromas of Big Elks, Moose Backpackers, Big Trouts, Big Bears, Big Wolfs, Big Bobcats, and Big Bison Brownies wafted through the forest, heightening the anticipation of the forest animals. They had come from miles around to celebrate with Elkwood and welcome him back to the Big Sky. Every member of the Eat Me Animal Herd was on hand to bake and sell their cookies.

Finally the time had come. The door of the store flew open to a great fanfare. Wild cheers came from all the forest animals. Elkwood stepped forward to deliver his welcome address.

"Thank you all for being here today for the grand reopening of the Eat Me Cookie Company." The crowd went wild with jubilation. "Without my dear friends, I would not be here today. They believed in me, they forgave me, and they saved me." Elkwood looked lovingly upon each one of his friends. He looked up at Theodore, who was resting on his antler, and winked.

"Puck is gone and will never return." The throng of animals whistled and cheered. "He taught all of us a valuable lesson. Hatred and anger will destroy everyone and everything it touches. Our forest is now safe again. Harmony will reign instead of hate." The animals roared their approval.

"Without further delay, the Eat Me Cookie Company is now open for business…again." The cheers and whistles of the forest animals were deafening.

The herd worked together all morning, making and selling Eat Me cookies. Theodore could barely keep up as he handed cookies wrapped in leaf bags to each customer. "Elkwood, come quick! *Look!*" he cried.

Next in line was Sam, the yellow-bellied marmot, and behind him were five new marmot friends. "Hi, Theodore! Hi, Elkwood!" he called. "What a day! Congratulations! We will take one of every cookie, please. I could not possibly choose between any of your cookies," he laughed.

"Oh, Sam, hello," exclaimed Elkwood. "I am so very happy to see you and all your new friends. Theodore, please give the marmots extra cookies, on the house." Elkwood walked to the side and motioned for Sam to follow him. Sam waddled over, and Elkwood bent over and whispered in his ear, "Meet me back here when the sun is highest. I have a surprise for everyone." He winked at Sam. Sam nodded and waddled back to his marmot friends.

"See you later, and thank you for the extra cookies. They smell delicious," whistled Sam as he and his new friends scampered into the woods with their treats.

By noon all the animals had bought every last one of the Eat Me cookies. The herd sat down in the clearing to relax and reflect upon the morning. They had worked well as a team, and everyone was very pleased. Sam waddled over, and Elkwood greeted him with a soft rub of his nose.

"What a grand success the Eat Me Cookie Company is once again," said Elkwood. "Now I have a surprise for all of you. I made extra cookies for each of you, as you well deserve, and we are going to have our own splendid celebration in a very special place I have not shared with anyone."

"Really, *Elkbutt?* That sounds terrific. We could all use a party, so let's go," rallied Bobcat.

"Not so fast, Bobcat. First I have to give something to a very special friend. For so long, he has been by my side. He led me to the Big Sky. He helped me start the Eat Me Cookie Company. He never complained, not even once, and he has steadfastly been my devoted friend. When I made bad decisions, he was still my friend. He is my champion for convincing you all to forgive me." By now all eyes were on Theodore, and he was feeling quite embarrassed by the adulation.

"Without my dear friend Theodore, I would not be here today. We have all contributed our mothers' special recipes…our favorites…to make the Eat Me Cookie Company a success. But Theodore has never had a cookie of his own." Elkwood ran into the store and brought out a tray filled with the new Eat Me addition.

"I made these, just for you, Theodore. No words can ever say how much I love you." The emotional Elkwood handed one of the delicious cookies to Theodore. "It has all your favorite things mixed together, Theodore. Pine nuts, acorns, and all the berries I could find, blended together with the sweetest pine sap in the forest. It will be called the Big Teddy cookie. Please, take a bite and tell me what you think." Elkwood placed a cookie down for Theodore to try.

Theodore was overcome with emotion. His very own cookie! He could not believe this was happening. He had wanted his own cookie for so long but thought it would not be possible for a woodpecker. He carefully pecked off a large piece of the Big Teddy, savoring the flavor. He could not believe how delicious it tasted. It was perfect.

"Elkwood, this is the best cookie I have ever tasted. How can I ever thank you for such a wonderful gift, my friend?"

"It is I who must thank *you*, Theodore. You have been the best friend an *Elk* could ever have. I was so wrapped up in my success, I never realized how much it bothered you that you did not have your own cookie. Please forgive my selfishness, Theodore." He leaned over and gave the little bird a giant lick with his big tongue, knocking over the happy bird.

Theodore sputtered and shook his feathers, giggling. He jumped up and flung his wings around Elkwood's nose and gave him a gigantic hug. The herd cheered with approval.

"You are now officially a cookie-carrying member of the Eat Me Cookie Company, Theodore," announced Elkwood with great pride.

"This is just the best day ever," chattered Theodore. "I imagine the Big Teddy is going to become the best cookie in all the world. You should all be so lucky to have such a delicious cookie." The little bird giggled with delight. The herd laughed in unison over the little bird's clever joke.

"I think we shall never be able to decide who has the best cookie," claimed Elkwood. "But I can say with absolute certainty, I am the luckiest *Elk* in the world, and I will never let go of my friends…ever again." Tears welled up in Elkwood's eyes and spilled down his soft face.

"Did someone say we were going to have a party, *suga?*" asked Twinkle Toes with the most innocent look on her face.

"Yes, Twinkle Toes. Your patience is always an inspiration," teased Elkwood. "Everyone, grab your cookies and follow me." And Elkwood led the Eat Me Animal Herd to the most magical place in the Big Sky.

Above the giant waterfall, there was indeed a magical place. The stream dropped in elevation, and the clear, pristine waters ran rapidly down a well-burnished rock slide into a small pond. Instead of large rocks littering the stream bed, there was one giant flat rock spread across and down the stream, creating a makeshift slide. Millions of years of water pouring over the rock had worn it down, forming the smooth surface. Below the slide, on the far side of the pond, rock cliffs climbed straight out of the water. The water rushed along the base of the rocks and circled back into a calm, deep pool. A floating leaf demonstrated the path as it rushed down the rock slide, *roller-coastered* through a narrow, fast riffle, then hurried along the rocks and circled back into the pond. The water had almost no current and provided a perfect swimming, and dancing, hole. Below the pond, the haphazard collection of rocks in the streambed resumed, and the flow of the water quickened as it approached the giant waterfall. Elkwood thought this was a perfect place for a grand celebration.

The herd was stunned by the beauty of the mountain stream Elkwood had chosen. The afternoon was very warm, and the lure of the cold water and a new pond excited Twinkle Toes. With a *vroom* of his motorcycle, Wolfrik pulled up closer to the deep pond, and with a flip of her tail fin, Twinkle Toes flew through the air, landing with a giant *splash*.

"Oh, what a marvelous place for a celebration, *suga*," Twinkle Toes dove under the water to explore. Moments later, with a great swish of her powerful tail fin, she erupted through the surface in a magnificent yet simple leap, so graceful and controlled that she appeared to be suspended in midair.

The herd set their cookies and treats along the logs next to the stream and, without hesitation, jumped into the water to play. Not at all surprising, Bob "the Pumpkin" Bobcat was the first to try the waterslide. He ran to the top of the slide and leaped onto the smooth rocks, landing on all fours, surfing like a pro down the slide as the fast water catapulted him into the pond with a *whoosh*.

"C'mon, Big Shot," he shouted. "Ride the slide!"

Knowing he could never stand up on the slick rocks with his slippery hooves, Big Shot ran up to the top and sat down on his rump. He rolled onto his back and allowed himself to be swept away, hooves kicking crazily in the air. He soared downward and, picking up enormous speed, hit the pond with a giant *splosh*. The herd applauded with delight at the silliness of the massive bison.

One by one, the animals took their turn on the rock slide. Bearie lumbered over to the top and, with a big, goofy grin, lunged face-first into the water, pushing his giant paws out in front of him. As the water rushed over his head, he flew down the slide, landing with a giant *splash* into the pond.

After the first acrobatic performance down the waterslide, Twinkle Toes grew increasingly annoyed at having her pond continually disturbed by splash after giant splash. She flipped onto the pond bank to avoid the now turbulent water. Frustrated, she realized she was no longer able to see her reflection.

Theodore noticed that Twinkle Toes was out of sorts. He grabbed a Big Teddy in his beak and flew to the pond, landing beside her. He had never really had a conversation with the beautiful trout and was not quite sure how to begin.

"Twinkle Toes, would you like to try one of my Big Teddy cookies?" he asked cautiously.

"By all means, *suga*."

He pushed the cookie toward her with his beak. Twinkle Toes nibbled daintily on the Big Teddy, and a smile crept across her bright red lips.

"Delicious, *suga*." And she continued to nibble on the snack.

Theodore, never at a loss for words, was tongue-tied. He had no idea how to engage the beautiful trout, and although she was enjoying his cookie, she seemed disinterested in chatting with him.

Unbeknownst to Theodore, the fact that the turbulent water was preventing her from admiring herself was not the only reason she was distracted. She was pouting because Wolfrik was nowhere to be found. Wolfrik had been sitting quietly near the pond, then had disappeared without a word. Twinkle Toes had hoped to celebrate with the dashing wolf, but instead, he had abandoned her. With nowhere to go, and unable to look at her reflection in the pond, Twinkle Toes felt lost.

Rarely letting down his guard, Wolfrik cooled himself off with a quick swim and was relaxing next to the pond. It had been a long time since he had enjoyed swimming. He and Ada had loved to frolic together in a small, secret pond that was reserved just for the two of them. He always loved the way the cold water felt, coursing through his thick fur. He would emerge from the pond and shake crazily from head to tail with complete abandon, his body spinning maniacally side to side, showering anything within reach, including his mate. Ada would laugh at how silly he looked with his fur in wild disarray. The memory was bittersweet, and for a rare moment, Wolfrik was lost in his dream of what his life had been with his beautiful Ada.

Jarring him out of his brief indulgence, his nose began twitching, and he smelled something foul. Without being obvious, he scanned the area, and this led him to the cliffs above the pond, directly above were Twinkle Toes had been dancing. He could see several pairs of paws and noses barely peeking over the cliff edge. He suspected they belonged to what was left of the feeble pack once led by Puck. Not wanting anything to disrupt the celebration, Wolfrik nonchalantly rose to his paws, stretched, and wandered away from the others without their awareness. He worked his way upstream, out of sight of the herd, then crossed to the other side.

Stealthily he approached the top of the cliffs. As he neared, the stench of the filthy coyotes burned the inside of his nostrils. Hiding in the brush, he counted eight remaining dogs from Puck's former pack. They were very thin, almost to the point of starvation, and their fur was matted and muddy. These dogs were no threat to anyone. They hid quietly at the edge of the cliffs above the pond, watching. Wolfrik had learned how to read animals so he would never again be deceived. He prided himself on his sound judgment when it came to the determination of whether one was a friend or foe, and these dogs were no threat to any animal. They had no strength left to fight. Even though he was severely outnumbered, he was not in the least concerned for his safety. He knew he could batter the pitiful dogs easily.

"May I help you, boys?" Wolfrik inquired as he stepped out of the brush. The wretched dogs turned and saw their worst enemy grinning at them. Not one muscle moved. They were terrified as they looked up at the massive and very powerful wolf. Each one believed their end was at hand.

Wolfrik took pity on the sad and pathetic coyotes that had been so horribly abused by Puck. They had no idea what happiness felt like, and he could see the raw fear on their faces. There was no threat or fight left in the abandoned coyotes. All he saw was beaten-down pups that perhaps might want a second chance in life. They were starving, and they had crawled on their bellies to watch the celebration, longing to join in and be accepted.

No one dared to speak.

"From where I am standing, you have two choices. I will spare your lives if you leave now and never return to *zee* Big Sky. Or you can follow me and take your chances that my word is my life. I will not harm you as long as you do not betray me or hurt my friends ever again."

Wolfrik could see the longing in their eyes. He was presenting them with a choice, one Puck would never have offered…that of being merciful and kind. Unlike Elkwood, Wolfrik did not believe Puck would have changed. The insanity of hatred had eaten into his very soul, and there was nothing anyone could have done to heal him. He knew what pure hatred looked like, and he would never be fooled again. But he thought, just maybe, these outcasts could start over.

"Choose carefully, but choose now." Wolfrik took a step closer to the indigent band of misfits.

Mustering all his bravery, the smallest coyote stood up and answered. "I would like to go with you, Wolfrik."

"So would I," chimed in another.

"Me too," said the next, and one by one, they each stood up and chose to follow.

Without another word, Wolfrik turned and walked through the brush, followed by eight helpless yet trusting coyotes. He moved downstream, away from the party, and snagged several *pawfuls* of lavender. Stopping below the falls, he spotted a calm pool behind a large rock. He looked at the pack of misfits and ordered, "Into *zee* water. I cannot bear *zee* stench of you."

The dogs looked at him in disbelief. None of them had ever been swimming before. That joy had simply never been allowed. They huddled in a group, not knowing what to do next, completely terrified.

"*Now!*" commanded Wolfrik, and the smallest dog took two leaps and landed with a *splat* in the water. He surfaced, sputtering and frightened, and instantly discovered he could swim. A tiny smile spread across his face as he paddled in circles while the water rinsed his filthy coat.

"And *zee* rest of you?" advised Wolfrik, trying to hold back a grin at the ragtag pack standing before him.

Without further hesitation, they each leaped into the water. Wolfrik watched as they paddled in circles and began splashing and playing with each other. A leaf floated by, and the smallest pup snapped at it over and over, trying to catch it in his mouth.

"All of you, over here," Wolfrik ordered.

As the pups swam to the shore, Wolfrik handed each of them a shoot of lavender. "Rub this all over your bodies, and do not miss a spot. Then rinse off and line up on *zee* shore."

Amused by the little army of coyotes obeying his every command, he watched as they frantically rubbed the lavender flower shoots all over themselves. Wolfrik thought of his own pups, who had been so brutally taken from him. He had looked forward to training them to hunt and protect the pack. Perhaps he could do the same for these lost souls. Immersed in thoughts of his past, he snapped back to the present moment when he heard yips and growls. The band of soaked and dripping pups were wrestling and rolling around on the grass—likely for the first time—just playing and having fun.

Wolfrik growled softly. The pups stood up, shaking ferociously in unison, spraying sparkling beads of water everywhere. Wolfrik picked up the scent of lavender and tried to hide a grin. The eight coyotes that stood perfectly at attention before him looked nothing like the rabid pack that had followed Puck. The transformation was remarkable. Their fur was thick and fluffy, and their tails were bushy. Their ears were standing tall instead of flat against their heads in fear. No longer were they cowering with their tails between their legs and fangs bared. Even Wolfrik, the architect of this makeover, was stunned... and he was pleased.

"Follow me," commanded Wolfrik, and the eight clean and wonderfully smelling coyotes fell in line behind the massive wolf.

Wolfrik was truly amazed. All this band had ever needed was an alpha who loved them and chose to protect instead of abuse. And Puck certainly had not provided them with the leadership they so desperately needed. Instead, he had tortured them and beaten them into submission. Wolfrik shook his head to exorcise the demon, deciding he would no longer think of Puck. Some things just *were* and could never be rectified. Learning to avoid the same mistakes was a better path to follow in the forest.

As Wolfrik, and his highly unusual pack, approached the Eat Me Animal Herd celebration, the smallest coyote stopped. "Mr. Wolfrik, sir, are you sure we should continue?" he asked bravely yet fearfully.

Wolfrik's expression softened toward this brave pup, who was clearly hesitant to meet the herd. After all, doing Puck's bidding, they had fought bitter and ferocious battles against the herd. He could understand why this newly minted coyote would feel fear, sure he would never be accepted.

"What is your name, little one?" asked Wolfrik.

The smallest coyote looked straight into Wolfrik's eye and said, "I do not have a name. We were never allowed to have names. It was too personal."

The compassion Wolfrik felt toward this small coyote caught him by surprise. His experiences had taught him to never trust again. Yet he found himself wanting to trust this young pup who had been so horrifically abused. All the pups had been abused, and he wanted to believe in the goodness of an animal. The herd had provided him with a reason to trust again. Perhaps it was time to let go of his pain and learn to relish life once again...to swim a little more...to laugh a little more. The young pup deserved a name. They all deserved names. He could not believe how they had been forced to be unidentifiable, without a persona, devoid of independence and self.

"I will call you Kleiner, which means 'little one' in German," pronounced Wolfrik.

Kleiner stretched his neck to appear as tall as he possibly could and pushed out his small chest with pride. He had a name! In that one fleeting moment, his entire life changed. He had a name.

Wolfrik saw the immediate change in Kleiner, already brimming with confidence and self-worth. "We will name *zee* rest of you later. Shall we continue?" he asked with a lilt of sarcasm in his voice.

Again Kleiner spoke up. "Are you sure we will all be welcome at your celebration, sir?"

"I gave you all a choice. Now you must learn to trust," stated Wolfrik, and he turned and continued toward the celebration. All eight coyotes scampered after him without qualm. He led the pack across the stream, and as they approached the celebration in single file, the herd stopped their revelry and stared in disbelief. Twinkle Toes was especially bewildered to see her magnificent Wolfrik leading the vile coyotes that had once belonged to Puck...the very coyotes that had tried to kill her.

As the band approached, the scent of lavender became a bit overwhelming, and Theodore sneezed. The reaction broke the logjam of shock on the faces of the herd. Wolfrik halted the troop and addressed the herd.

"I would like you to meet our new friends. They have made *zee* choice to be a friend rather than a foe. And as you can see, they have undergone a remarkable transformation. They need a new alpha, and I have chosen Kleiner, which means 'little one' in my native language of German." He nodded to the smallest coyote. "Little does not mean cowardly. Today he has proven to me he has *zee* will to change and *zee* strength and heart to lead." Wolfrik walked over to Kleiner and spoke. "Treat your pack well, Kleiner, and they will always be loyal. And remember, never let go of a friend."

Kleiner beamed with pride. Standing as tall as he could, he threw his shoulders back and pointed his nose into the air, then howled the happiest coyote howl the forest animals had ever heard. Immediately grins appeared on the faces of the other seven very clean coyotes. A pack had been given a second chance.

Elkwood stepped forward, knowing the pups must be starving. The miraculous change in the pups was unbelievable. He knew Wolfrik had found compassion for the discarded pack. What he was witnessing was confirmation of everything he had learned since he first stepped hoof in Montana.

"We seem to have an excess of Eat Me cookies, and we hate to see anything go to waste. Kleiner, do you think you and your pack could help us by eating the rest of the cookies?" Elkwood winked at Wolfrik.

"*Par ici!* Over here!" called Baldoin, and he motioned the pups over to the large log laden with stacks of delicious cookies. The pups practically knocked each other over as they ran to the log. Baldoin handed out cookies as fast as he could. Behind the filth and fear that had masked the coyotes, pups emerged who were much younger than anyone had expected. Famished, they eagerly ate the cookies with lightning speed, much to the delight of everyone at the celebration. Although one soul had been lost, eight had now been saved.

The celebration resumed, and even Wolfrik, in the spirit of change, decided it was time to give the rock slide a try. Noticing that Twinkle Toes had been a bit sulky, he trotted over to her and bowed gallantly, touching his nose to the ground.

"Would you like to try *zee* rock slide with me, my beautiful little trout?" beckoned Wolfrik.

"Of course, I would, *suga*." She gave him her most flirtatious smile. "But how—?" Before she could finish her sentence, Wolfrik gently scooped her up in his mouth and trotted to the top of the slide. He bent low and ever so gently placed her in the still water behind a rock next to the slide. She giggled with delight, and her heart raced at the touch of the magnificent wolf she loved.

"Are you ready, my little trout?"

With her nod, the two jumped to the center of the rock slide. Twinkle Toes flipped herself onto her tail fin, and Wolfrik, always dignified, surfed the slide on all four paws. Side by side, they careened down the rock slide in a display that could only be called *spectacular*, and they both *splashed* into the pond. Twinkle Toes dove deep and, with all her strength, broke through the surface in a leap so high she reached the top of the cliffs. With one graceful flip, she dove nose first into the water. She surfaced and rose onto her tail fin, dancing in front of Wolfrik as he trod water in the pond. All the animals cheered wildly. Certainly, no one had ever expected Wolfrik to allow himself to have fun.

Not wanting to be left out, Elkwood was next up on the slide. "Hop on," he shouted to Theodore. The little bird flew and landed on Elkwood's antlers just as he leaped to the rock slide and began his descent. Elkwood maintained his balance, and the two surfed the entire way down, joining Twinkle Toes and Wolfrik with a graceful *shush* into the pond.

"Baldoin, show them how you can dance, *suga*," encouraged Twinkle Toes as Le Chocolat Moose stepped up to the rock slide. He took off and raised his front hooves in the air, and as he gained speed, he twirled on his rear hooves with perfect balance, much to the amazement of everyone. The herd roared their approval, and Elkwood could not believe his eyes. Twinkle Toes had taught Le Chocolat Moose to dance. He looked at Twinkle Toes and observed she was actually enjoying watching someone other than herself.

Bobcat and Big Shot were next, followed by Sam and several of his new marmot friends. The marmots flew down the slide together on their bellies, spinning and laughing as they *plunged* into the pond. Everyone was laughing and frolicking while Kleiner and his new pack looked on, still stuffing themselves with cookies. After everything Elkwood and the herd had been through, the celebration was liberating to all who had experienced pain, loneliness, mistrust, and even arrogance. It was a new beginning in the Big Sky.

As the animals exited the pond, one by one, they shook their soaked fur, sending droplets of water flying everywhere. It was as if a dozen sprinkler heads fired on all at once. Everyone giggled with delight as they shook and sprayed each other, ridding their drenched fur of water.

Twinkle Toes resumed her position on the pond bank, no longer so terribly bothered that she could not see her reflection. She called Theodore over to join her. After his last attempt to chat with the beautiful trout, he was hesitant.

Still, being a cheery little bird, he hopped over and focused all his attention on Twinkle Toes.

"I thought you might like to relax with me for a while in the sun, *suga*."

Puzzled, Theodore just looked at her, unsure how to respond. She reached near the water and grabbed an object with her fin, then handed him a pair of small red sunglasses. "I found these in the stream and thought they would look just marvelous on you, Theodore. Please put them on and sit with me for a while."

Completely surprised, Theodore took the sunglasses with his wing and flipped them onto his face. Twinkle Toes giggled.

"Perfect, Theodore! You are indeed a very handsome woodpecker. Once the water calms, you can see for yourself, *suga*."

"Thank you, Twinkle Toes. I love them!"

Theodore was beyond tickled to have received such a wonderful gift from Twinkle Toes. He leaned against a small rock, crossed his legs, and basked in the afternoon sun with his friend Twinkle Toes Trout. The sight of a hot-pink-and-lime-green trout wearing black butterfly sunglasses, and a red-headed woodpecker wearing red sunglasses—sunning and chatting on the edge of the pond—was priceless. Elkwood glanced over and could not help but laugh. The two, immersed in conversation, paid him no mind. Elkwood was seeing friendships of all sorts developing that day.

Turning to see what the rest of the animals were doing, Elkwood froze. He could not believe what he was seeing, and he blinked his large, lash-rimmed eyes several times. Thinking his imagination was playing tricks on him, he saw the most beautiful elk he had ever seen walk out of the woods and stand alongside the stream. Out from behind her stepped a much smaller but very handsome young elk. Her eyes gave her away. They were the deepest purple, a color reserved for royalty, and framed by long, black, lacey lashes. These were the same unmistakable eyes he had looked into when he had awoken on the ship after nearly drowning in the ocean so long ago. And these were the magnificently beautiful eyes he had thought about while he was trapped on the rock ledge, fearing death.

She took a step forward with her beautiful long legs and dainty hooves. Looking at Elkwood, she quietly called, "Elkwood...?" and waited.

Elkwood's heart soared. He trotted over to the elk and said, "Yes, I am Elkwood. Surely you cannot be the same elk who tended to me on the ship after the storm." He breathlessly awaited her answer.

"I remembered you were traveling to Montana, and I hoped I would find you. This is my brother, the little elk you saved the night of the storm." The maturing young elk stepped forward and put out his hoof to greet Elkwood. Elkwood was elated but slightly in shock. He could not believe this beautiful elk had traveled so far to find *him*.

"Look, everyone, this is…" He realized he had never known her name.

"Violet. My name is Violet, and my brother is named Oliver. We are also from England, Elkwood. We never thought we would find you," she said excitedly.

"I do not understand. Why have you been looking for me?" questioned Elkwood. "What could possibly have brought you and Oliver all this way?"

"I am not really sure, Elkwood. Some call it fate. I just knew I had to find you." She smiled and fluttered her long lashes.

Elkwood was completely and utterly smitten by the beautiful elk. Life had so completely changed for him recently that he struggled to process the joy and happiness he felt. He had found a new home, started a company, become very successful, but most importantly of all, he had learned the true meaning of what it meant to be a friend. None of the successes he had achieved had any value without his friends.

Twinkle Toes had been waiting for just the right moment to present Elkwood with *her* very special surprise, although, truth be told, she was now somewhat flustered and a bit jealous a female other than herself was receiving any attention. "*Suga*," she called, flirtatiously beckoning Elkwood over with her fin.

Responding to the trout's summons, Elkwood hoofed along the rocky shore and approached Twinkle Toes. She then rose up on her tail fin in the now calm pond and addressed the animals.

"*Sugas*, in honor of Elkwood, for single-handedly destroying the evil Puck forever, I've created a new dance, called *E-dubbing*. I named it after you, *suga*," she said, pointing her fin at Elkwood. "Here's how it goes." And the entertaining trout began to dance.

Balancing on her tail fin, Twinkle Toes began to slowly shimmy from one side fin to the other. She started with a shimmy of her right fin, and then, as she shimmy-rolled to the left, her entire body joined in, ending with a shimmy of her left fin.

As she began to roll her shimmies from side to side, she winked at Elkwood and said, "'*When "trout" go wrong, "elk" go right after them.*'" She then increased her speed until her scales were a shimmering whirl of hot pink and lime green.

The animals were speechless watching Twinkle Toes perform her new *E-dubbing* dance sensation. As she gyrated in the pond, her eyes were fixed on Elkwood, making sure the *Elk* understood *E-dubbing* had been created just for him. Feeling somewhat embarrassed, Elkwood bowed in appreciation to the magnificent trout, bending one knee forward while lowering his massive rack of antlers to the ground.

Lost in the dance, she slowed and said, "C'mon, *suga, E-dub* with me. Oooh...*'Anything worth doing is worth doing slowly.'*"

Not being one to ever spoil a party, and in the spirit of friendship and camaraderie, Elkwood began to *E-dub*. He hesitantly began by lifting his front right leg with a slight shimmy. Then, planting that hoof, he slowly rocked his massive shoulders back and forth, ending with a tremor as he raised his left hoof. As he shimmied back and forth, one by one, the other animals joined in and tried to master Twinkle Toes's new *E-dubbing* dance. In a hilarious display of fun and friendship, the entire Eat Me Animal Herd, along with Sam and the marmots, and even Kleiner and his new pack, were *E-dubbing*.

Delighted by her success in teaching the partygoers her new dance, Twinkle Toes announced in her usual flamboyant mannerism, "*'It's not the "animals" in my life that count...it's the life in the "animals,"'*" and she disappeared into the pond. Seconds later she broke through the surface, leaping straight up into the air. At the pinnacle of her leap, the magnificent trout hung in midair for just a split second...and *E-dubbed*. It was a moment no one would ever forget.

The herd and their new friends celebrated into the dusk hours of evening. As a chill hit the air, Baldoin built a bonfire along the stream bank, and all the animals gathered around the warmth of the crackling flames. Kleiner and his pack sat snuggled together, still feeling a bit shy about branching out among the herd. Big Shot, Bobcat, Baldoin, Bearie, and Sam and his friends all huddled around the fire. Wolfrik had propped his water-filled sidecar between two rocks, and Twinkle Toes swam next to him, glowing with happiness beside her dashing wolf. Elkwood, with Theodore perched on his antlers, sat closely next to Violet and Oliver. It was the perfect finale to the best day of their lives. But Elkwood had one final surprise for his dear friends to conclude the celebration.

"I have a special treat for you all. I found this bag along the river recently." He held up a big bag of marshmallows left by campers along the river. He grabbed a stack of long willow sticks he had specially selected for his surprise and passed them around to everyone. Then he passed around the bag of marshmallows. Following Elkwood's lead, they skewered the soft white balls with the ends of their sticks. Elkwood pointed his willow stick over the fire and roasted the marshmallow to a golden brown. He pulled the roasted marshmallow off the stick, then smashed it between two Big Elk cookies and took a giant bite of the gooey delight. The animals roasted their marshmallows, grinning at the clever idea of the cookie nightcap. Even Twinkle Toes and Theodore had a miniature version, just right for their size. Elkwood looked around at the friends he cherished and chuckled. What a mess they had all made of themselves, with melted marshmallow clinging to their happy faces. Today had been a very grand celebration.

The night would not have been complete without a song from their favorite entertainer. Twinkle Toes was missing her nightly performance at the Nymph Disco, but for once she did not care. This was exactly where she wanted to be.

With perfect timing, the moon rose from behind the rock cliffs and illuminated the pond. Twinkle Toes flipped her tail fin and landed in the sparkling water. She sang and danced like never before. Then, as she hummed the final bars, she spun into a blur of pink and green, and disappeared into the depths of the water, just as the moon sneaked behind a cloud. The pond went dark and her fans applauded wildly. Twinkle Toes Trout was a legend, and no other trout would ever come close to her exquisitely rare beauty and talent.

The celebration had finally come to an end. The animals began to leave, exhausted but happy. They thanked Elkwood, said their goodbyes, and disappeared into the forest to their rocks, caves, dens, and dwellings. With a *vroom*, Wolfrik started his motorcycle, and with a flip of her tail fin, Twinkle Toes landed in the sidecar, and off they sped. Violet and Oliver had not yet found accommodations in the forest. However, Theodore informed them he knew of the perfect place...for now.

"See you tomorrow," called Elkwood, watching Violet and Oliver trot off after Theodore.

"I will catch up with you in a bit, Elkwood," called out Theodore, and the three disappeared.

Elkwood stood alone near the fire, enjoying the heat from the dying embers. He could not believe how much his life had changed. The joy he now felt had not come easily. When his parents had told him they were sending him to Montana to become an *Elk*, he had been devastated. He had felt like they were punishing him, and at the time, he had had no idea why. He knew they were very wise, but he still wondered why he had been challenged to endure so much pain and hardship in order to become an *Elk*. He wondered if a short-cut to finding happiness was possible.

The moon peeked out from behind a cloud and cast a magical glow over the scene of the day's celebration. The soothing babble of the stream, layered over the dead quiet of the night, gave Elkwood a special feeling of peace. He may never know the answers to all his questions about life, but for today he was satisfied. He realized getting what one needs is more important than getting what one wants. And when the two align... *life is perfect*. He had indeed become an *Elk*.

Elkwood was walking along the path heading home when he heard music in the distance. He followed the sound and it led him to the river. He walked up to the riverbank, and in the dark night, colorful lights flashed from an eddy hole near the riverbank. Elkwood craned his neck as far as possible and could not believe his eyes. Down at the bottom of the river, awash in magical lights, was the Nymph Disco he had heard so much about. On the main stage was Twinkle Toes Trout, singing and dancing as the crowd cheered wildly while pumping their fins rhythmically to the beat. Finally he was witnessing Twinkle Toes, in all her glory, performing at the Nymph Disco. She had made an appearance that night after all. He watched for a few minutes, feeling incredibly proud of his friend. Not only did she have a good heart, but her talent was irrefutable. She was mag-nificent—still completely self-centered—but magnificent. Elkwood laughed softly at the conundrum known as Twinkle Toes Trout.

Elkwood was exhausted, but he felt more alive than ever before. As he made his way home, a light fog began to creep through the forest. Elkwood should have known the fog would be the prelude to what would come next.

Without warning, the mysterious giant *Elk* stepped in front of Elkwood, halting him in his path. Now familiar, the rich scent of loam emanated from the giant *Elk*, and Elkwood could see his breath exhale from his nostrils into the chill night. For the first time, he did not fear the giant *Elk*, but he did remain at a respectable distance.

"Elkwood, you have come far and have learned well," began the giant *Elk*. "Your parents are proud of you, Elkwood. You have learned humility, compassion, and love. You have learned to never let go of a friend. You have become an *Elk*."

Elkwood needed to understand and asked the giant *Elk*, "Why did I have to go through so much pain? Why did this quest have to be so difficult?"

The giant *Elk* snorted and pawed aggressively at the ground, causing the fog to eerily swirl around him. Elkwood caught his breath, suddenly fearing the giant *Elk* might charge him.

"Elkwood, nothing in life is given without payment. The payment is what we are willing to suffer and risk in order to receive the reward."

Elkwood listened intently to the giant *Elk*.

"You are a natural leader, Elkwood. The ability was always in you, but you abused the gift. Consider the pain Wolfrik went through…and Twinkle Toes, Bearie, Bobcat, Big Shot, Baldoin…and even the pups of Puck's pack. Theodore just needed to feel part of something. Most came here because they had lost something precious in their lives. All had to suffer and experience trials in order to find their true selves. But they needed a leader. We do not choose, Elkwood; we are chosen." The giant *Elk* snorted into the chilly night air, nodding his antlers up and down.

"A force inside you drove you to the Scary Forest. Just as you needed to be cleansed and healed, so did the evil contained within the Scary Forest. The forest will regrow, Elkwood, with tall, strong pine trees reaching for the sky. The forest will once again provide food and shelter for the animals now that the evil has been banished. You stand like a tree in the forest, Elkwood. Other trees have been planted around you, and as all of you search for the sunlight, your roots are intertwined. You help each other survive. You grow tall together, Elkwood. Two are better than one. Strength lies within the pack…the herd… the flock. *That* is survival. *That* is friendship."

Elkwood stood mesmerized by the giant *Elk*. He walked to the edge of the forest, turned, and faced Elkwood. The giant *Elk* bent low on his knee and bowed. His magnificent antlers touched the ground in a gesture of respect for his fellow *Elk*.

A chill ran through Elkwood just as Theodore flew up and landed on his antler. "Oh, what a celebration, Elkwood. I just cannot believe everything—"

Elkwood cut him off. "Did you see him, Theodore? Tell me, did you see the giant *Elk*?"

"Giant elk? You are here alone, Elkwood. I do not see anyone, my friend."

Elkwood peered through the fog, hoping to catch just one more glimpse of the giant *Elk*. He had a feeling he would not be seeing him again.

Slowly he walked back to their cozy tree house, with Theodore perched on his antler. His life in the Big Sky at the base of the Lone Peak had just gotten better. All their lives were better. Theodore had his own cookie and a place to call home. Wolfrik was learning to trust again and had a pack of young coyotes to teach about friendship and leadership. Twinkle Toes Trout was seeing past her own reflection. Baldoin had learned to dance. Bearie was going to learn from Elkwood, and this time he would not break his promise to the bear. Bobcat had learned to be a little more sensitive to others and had proven he would always have a friend's back. And Big Shot? Well, Big Shot was the least flawed of all the animals in the Eat Me Animal Herd. He was perfect just being Big Shot.

Elkwood had learned the true meaning of friendship and would never let go of a friend. Never.

There is a place where trees grow straight and tall, mountains eclipse the earth, stars majestically twinkle, and the full winter moons cast shadows like daylight. The diversity of wildlife is stunning, primitive, and free.

This is a place where the fast-running rivers are cold and clear, the spaces are vast, the mountains are tall, and the sky is big. This is the *Last Best Place*. The Big Sky at the base of the Lone Peak. The home of the Eat Me Animal Herd. This is *Elkwood's* Montana.

EPILOGUE

THE SUN WAS NOT QUITE OVERHEAD as the girl approached her favorite spot on the river to fish with her two dogs, Balto and Chaser. After a long, cold, and snowy winter, the river was finally clear and calm enough to fish. The dogs were excited to go fishing with the girl and ran into the water to cool off. The river never seemed to change. The beauty was constant. The cliffs were as high as they were the year before, and the water remained streaked with gold and green. As the girl waded into the river, the sound of splashing caught her attention. In the eddy on the other side of the river...a fish was dancing.

Fishing could wait. She turned and walked to the shore and sat down on a log to watch the show. As she watched the fish dance, she began to think it looked very much like the trout she had seen dancing in the same spot the summer before...the trout she had hooked. She recalled it had jumped out of her hand as she had tried to remove the hook, and had become tangled within the legs of her dogs. She remembered how Chaser had licked the trout and how Balto had lunged at it, trying to bite the poor thing, causing it to scream. Her memories of that day made her smile. The beautiful trout had the same colors of hot pink and lime green, but there was something different. She did not recall the trout having bright red lips.

"Surely this could not be the same trout," she wondered.

The girl had no idea what she and her dogs had set in motion the previous summer when she had caught the very same beautiful dancing trout.

The sun was now directly overhead, and even with her sunglasses on, the glare off the water made it difficult to see. The magnificent trout continued its dance on the river, leaping and flipping and twisting and dancing on its tail fin across the smooth water of the eddy. The girl applauded in delight at the amazing performance by the trout. It was as if the trout was performing just for her. As quickly as the trout had appeared to dance, it disappeared back into the river.

Disappointed, the girl looked up to the top of the cliffs, hoping to see an eagle, and instead saw something she could not comprehend. She blinked, over and over, and shaded her eyes with the palm of her hand. She tried taking her sunglasses off, but that did not erase the vision before her.

Standing atop the cliffs was a regal-looking tan-and-purple *Elk*, a beautiful cinnamon-and-deep-blue-green-colored moose, a dashingly handsome pale-blue-and-russet wolf, an orange-and-black-striped bobcat, a mustard-colored bison with lavender horns, and a very large copper-colored bear... and perched on the antlers of the *Elk* was a red-headed woodpecker.

Suddenly the pink-and-green trout with very red lips leaped from the river, soaring high into the air, reaching all the way to the top of the cliff. The girl took off her sunglasses, rubbed her eyes, and looked again. The animals were gone. She must have been daydreaming...

Sitting on a log alongside the riverbank, the girl enjoyed the beauty and peace of the river. She pulled a Big Elk chocolate chip cookie from her pocket and lazily nibbled on her favorite treat. The dogs sat with their eyes glued to the cookie. The girl reached into her pocket again and pulled out two biscuits. The dogs eagerly took them from her hand and carried them off to eat.

After a while, the girl decided she did not feel like fishing today. She had all summer to fish. She called the dogs with a whistle, and as she stood up to return to the path, she saw a giant *Elk* standing across the river on the edge of the forest. She froze, stunned by its massive size. With a bent knee, the *Elk* bowed low, touching his antlers to the ground, as if giving her his approval. Then he turned and disappeared into the forest.

The girl just loved that each time she went fishing at her favorite spot, she was visited by the characters in her book. It always made the girl giggle. Smiling, the girl left the river.

FINI

ABOUT THE AUTHOR

Tracie Elizabeth Pabst is an avid skier, swimmer, cyclist, hiker, and fisherman. Her love of the outdoors led to her life-long dream of living in the mountains. She relocated to Big Sky, Montana in 2004.

Transporting readers to a magical place where her characters have endearing flaws, mountains are big and the landscape is pristine and untamed, has allowed her to share with her readers everything about living in Montana that touches her heart. She firmly believes that dreams can truly become reality.

With a great love for animals, Tracie is rarely without her three Alaskan Huskies, Balto, Chaser and Scooby Dude, and she even has a cat named Moose. She owns and operates a luxury travel and tour company, founded to save lives and preserve the ecology of the precious and delicate environment she gratefully calls her backyard.

For more information about what's next for Elkwood,
please contact the author: Author@ElkwoodsMontana.com